WE'VE ALREADY
GONE THIS FAR

WE'VE ALREADY GONE THIS FAR

~~~~~~~~~

PATRICK DACEY

HENRY HOLT AND COMPANY

NEW YORK

Henry Holt and Company, LLC
Publishers since 1866
175 Fifth Avenue
New York, New York 10010
www.henryholt.com

Henry Holt® and 🅗® are registered trademarks of
Henry Holt and Company, LLC.

Some of these stories have appeared elsewhere in slightly different form:
"Patriots" in *Bomb* magazine, #104, Summer 2008; "The Place You
Are Going To" in *Sou'wester*, Fall 2010; "Lost Dog" in *Zoetrope: All-Story*,
vol. 17, no. 1, Spring 2013; "Never So Sweet" as "Departures" in *Guernica*,
May 2013; "Incoming Mail" in *Lumina*, vol. XIII, 2014; "Downhill"
in *Barrelhouse*, issue 13, Winter 2014; "Ballad" in *Cleaver*, issue 6,
Winter 2014 and in *Mission at Tenth*, vol. 5, Summer 2014; "To Feel Again the
Kind of Love That Hurts Something Terrible" as "Love, Women" in *The Paris
Review* No. 214, Fall 2015.

Library of Congress Cataloging-in-Publication Data

Dacey, Patrick.
    [Short stories. Selections]
    We've already gone this far / Patrick Dacey. — First edition.
        pages cm
    ISBN 978-1-62779-465-7 (hardcover) — ISBN 978-1-62779-466-4 (ebook)
    I. Title.
    PS3604.A215
    [A6 2015]
    813'.6—dc23

                                                                2015003308

Henry Holt books are available for special promotions and premiums.
For details contact: Director, Special Markets.

First Edition 2016

Designed by Meryl Sussman Levavi

Printed in the United States of America

1   3   5   7   9   10   8   6   4   2

For my son, Colin Archer Dacey

The strangeness of life, the more you resisted it, the harder it bore down on you. The more the mind opposed the sense of strangeness, the more distortions it produced. What if, for once, one were to yield to it?

—SAUL BELLOW

CONTENTS

~~~~~

WE'VE ALREADY
GONE THIS FAR

PATRIOTS

~~~

DURING THE WAR, most of us in Wequaquet hung up a flag to support the troops, though it was clear some of us did it because others were doing it. We pulled out our flags from the last war or went to Hal's and bought a new one. Hal sold out pretty fast, and good for Hal, because usually no one goes to Hal's anymore, the way he charges, though he says he has no choice if he wants to compete with MegaWorld.

Donna Baker went the extra mile. I didn't mind the over-size flag snapping in the wind from the holder beside her door so much as I minded having to look across the street at all the little flags stuck in the lawn and in the light holders on the garage and on the antenna of her Subaru.

After a strong wind or rain, I'd see her out there picking up those little flags and then pushing them back in the dirt or snow and packing the dirt or snow around the little sticks. I would watch her do this while I had my breakfast, and, I'll admit, I timed my breakfast for when she did this.

Then one day, when I saw Donna driving off in her stupid Subaru, I went right across the street and took one of the flags out of the ground and buried it in my backyard. I don't know why. I respected her patriotic pride. Really, I did. Her son, Justin, was over there, and that must've been hard, but no harder than your son fixing city bridges or removing asbestos or driving a stock car. Actually, the most dangerous job in the world is cutting timber. I looked it up. And when Donna got back, she was carrying a bag of groceries in her arms, looking over the flags in her yard, counting each and every one of them. She put down her groceries and stood there for a half hour, counting and recounting and scratching her head. She went next door to the Putters' house, but I guess she forgot they both have jobs and no one would be home. He teaches history at the high school and she's a hairstylist—actually a haircutter. She works at Uppercuts, and what they did to my hair once was not styling.

Then Donna Baker walked across the street to my house and knocked on the door. I didn't answer. Then I heard her knocking on my back sliding door. She was standing on my porch and we saw each other and I made like I was cleaning up some mess behind the couch and gave her the "I'll be there in a second" finger. Then I let her in. She said, "You think those hoodlums are back?" and I thought, the last time we had hoodlums was when her son and a couple of his friends ripped out every mailbox on our street and tore down street signs and stole doghouses and dismantled a billboard and spray-painted WELCOME TO FUCK WORLD on it and put it in Barry Park and that Sunday kids were all asking their parents, "What's Fuck World?" and I thought to say we haven't had any criminal activity around here since your son, you know, but I didn't, and I shrugged and said, "Would you like some coffee, Donna?"

We talked for a while. She was upset about the new standardized testing at the schools and I mentioned a movie I wanted to see that she hadn't seen, either, and so we made a casual plan to go see it but never did. And then she said, "You know, if I had to do it all over again, I'd live close to the water," and I agreed. Then she left and drove off in her Subaru and came back later with another little flag and put it right in the same spot where I'd taken her other one.

I KNOW some things about Donna Baker. People talk. For instance, I know that her sister has a drug habit and stole all her jewelry and took off to Utah, and I thought, Utah? I also know that Donna drives down to the new development in Spring Creek just to watch the men work. I know she's put on twenty pounds—anyone can see that, but not anyone can see that she sneaks mini-muffins in her car every morning. I also know that she drives twenty miles out to Wareham and sings karaoke at Tenderhearts, because my cousin is a bartender there. He says Donna Baker's a terrible singer.

I'm sure she knows some things about me, too.

She knows, like everyone knows, that my husband ran out on me less than a year ago after they shot a movie here in town and he got a bit part as a short-order cook at a diner with his line "Flapjacks and bacon," which he practiced day and night in the house. The lead, a detective, asks a waitress at the counter for flapjacks and bacon, then the waitress says, "Flapjacks and bacon," and Paul repeats, "Flapjacks and bacon."

They didn't even use his line in the movie. But Paul was passionate. He said it didn't matter how old he was, he was going out to Hollywood to try his hand at it, and if he didn't try his hand at it, then he'd resent himself for the rest of his life and he'd die an angry man. I'll tell you this. If my husband were shot dead, more people would've come over and said how sorry they were.

WHEN JUSTIN left, Donna Baker stuck a dozen or so yellow-ribbon stickers to the back and sides of her Subaru. We all know the yellow-ribbon sticker is there to support the troops, and who wouldn't? But I'll bet Donna doesn't know that the yellow-ribbon sticker is also a symbol for suicide prevention, bone cancer, and endometriosis. It's true. I looked it up. After Justin died, Donna took down the yellow-ribbon stickers and stuck a white-ribbon sticker to the bumper of her Subaru. It's a symbol of innocence. It represents victims of terrorism. It's also a symbol for retinoblastoma, which makes sense. But it's black from the mud and dirty snow and you can't clean a ribbon sticker, and a black-ribbon sticker is a symbol for gang prevention, which I know Donna Baker supports, too, after all, but I don't think she knows that's what it means now.

JUSTIN'S WELCOME-HOME party was not fun like parties should be, like the party Gail Prager threw for her father-in-law when he turned eighty-two. Being around someone that old made you feel good to be where you were in life; it made you feel like you had time left. There was a cake, but Mr. Prager couldn't eat the cake, because he couldn't open his mouth wide enough to take in food, and when Gail's daughter, Francesca, tried to feed him the cake, she ended up just smearing it over Mr. Prager's lips and cheeks, and we all laughed.

That was a feel-good party. It didn't even matter that they were Jewish.

Hard to feel good when someone comes back from a war.

You see it on television and you figure the one you know is the one hollering and firing his automatic weapon into the dunes, and, really, how do you react to someone like that?

There wasn't any cake. There wasn't even music. What kind of party doesn't have cake and music? Justin brought a woman with him, Kiki-something. Who names their daughter Kiki? I mean, you might as well set up one of those stripper poles in her bedroom, right? She was so tall, almost another body taller than me. She had a big, round chin and wore gaudy makeup and was dressed in this leopard-print sundress, and we all figured she was a whore. She ate more than anyone at the party. Justin was sitting on a beach chair on the back lawn, rolling cigarettes and smoking and sipping a beer, and some people walked around him and others stood near him and a few shook his hand and asked him questions. His super-tall woman sat down on his lap and at one point I saw them necking and it looked like she was eating him. Calvin Baker grilled hamburgers and hot dogs and brats, because that's Justin's favorite, but Justin didn't eat one and the brats were piled up on a serving plate that Donna Baker gave to George Falachi because the Falachis are poor and she felt bad for them, which I'll tell you is in poor and bad taste to do in front of people at a party.

The main reason why it wasn't a good party for me was because later, after a few too many gin and tonics and Jimmy Buffett songs, Donna Baker and I got into an argument about the war. She was saying how we were doing great things over there, building schools, establishing a government, letting the people decide what's best for their country, et cetera. And I interrupted, saying how I thought that was all political propaganda, that we couldn't even get that right in *this* fucking country, how were we going to get it right over there? Right? And she called me a traitor, and I called her a gullible bitch, and she said I was a condescending wacko, and I said she was an unrealistic cunt, and she said that my collection of wind chimes drives her nuts, and I said her collection of flags and ribbons drives *me* nuts, and she said that the brownies I brought over were dry and you could see nobody wanted them, and I said her potato salad tasted like fucking glue. Then she called for Justin, and everyone stopped and stared at him. Donna Baker said, "Tell her, Justin. Go ahead." And Justin said, "Tell her what?" and Donna Baker said, "Tell her what it's like," and Justin said, "It's like nothing." Then we sort of drifted back to our houses, trying not to upset all the little flags in the yard. Two weeks later, Justin went back, and Donna Baker kept up with her flags and ribbon stickers, and we didn't talk for a while.

THE SUMMER passed. I spent most of my time on the back porch. Sometimes I cried about Paul. Sometimes I broke a dish or a glass. One day Donna Baker came by to warn me that the terror level had been raised to red. I didn't know what that meant. She seemed pretty nervous.

"I doubt they'll come after any of us, Donna," I said.

"You can't be too sure. For my sake, keep your eyes peeled."

"Okay, Donna."

She warned everyone in the neighborhood, except for Muslim Joe, who I sometimes think might just be wearing that turban so no one bothers him.

After Labor Day, Nancy Dwyer came over with some gossip. She was all excited, like she gets when bad things happen to one of us, standing in the kitchen with her chest sticking out like two torpedoes that have taken off but won't ever land. She told me she saw Donna's husband, Calvin, out in Falmouth, having coffee with a gorgeous woman at Dunkin' Donuts. I don't know too many gorgeous women that drink coffee at Dunkin' Donuts, and Nancy's a big liar, anyway. (She once told Cindy Putter that the reason I didn't have kids was because I didn't like the way they looked. All kids, mind you. Of course, I don't like how some kids look. Some kids are real ugly. Kids like Cindy Putter's kids. The reason I didn't *have* kids is because I didn't *want* kids.) "They're going to split," she said, and she held her hand to her throat as if something were stuck in it. "Can you believe it?"

I thought, hearing that about Calvin, Donna might stop by to ask me what it was like to lose a husband, because, even though I didn't like a lot of things about her, she was still my neighbor. But she didn't stop by, and so I thought, You're on your own, Donna Baker.

Then I heard that Donna was setting up a committee to send parcels and gift boxes over to the soldiers to let them know that we cared over here. Those I had spoken to said they didn't RSVP because of how things turned out at the party. And even though I wasn't invited, I said I didn't RSVP, either. We all agreed that it was better we didn't have it right in our faces anymore. Most of us didn't keep up with the war, and because it was almost football season, our neighborhood was more concerned with what the Red Raiders were going to look like in the fall, rather than any new developments over there.

IN OCTOBER, Justin was killed by one of his own men. I found out from Nancy, who had read about it at the grocery, and I knew she was telling the truth because she was shivering and crying and she hugged me, and Nancy never hugs. After she told me, I spent the next couple of days looking across the street to see if Donna would come out and then maybe I'd act like I was leaving to get something at the store and could just bump into her and say how sorry I was about her son, because really I was.

But I didn't see her, not until that Saturday, when Calvin Baker showed up. And Donna came out crying and crying, and then Calvin tried to hug her, but Donna stepped away and doubled over, and even though we weren't on speaking terms, I couldn't stand seeing her cry, and I started crying. Then Calvin grabbed her from behind and pulled her into him, and I could see some of my neighbors looking out of their windows, and I figured they were thinking like I was. Thinking what it must've felt like to be Donna Baker just then.

THE FUNERAL was very sad. The biggest, toughest men you've ever seen broke down. Donna Baker took the folded flag and put it on her lap and she let Calvin hold her hand, which was sweet, considering. George Falachi wore sunglasses even though there wasn't any sun that day, and I guessed he was probably stoned. Nancy Dwyer asked me how much I paid for my bouquet at Jane's, and I told her too much. Gail Prager wasn't there and we all noticed that. Cindy Putter and her husband, Leonard, brought their two kids and they ran around the plots, jumping over the buried bones, taking the flags from the ground and playing swords with them.

When the soldiers raised their guns and fired, I flinched.

AFTER THE funeral, I decided to take my wind chimes down. I'm not sure why I started collecting them in the first place. I liked listening to them clatter and ring in uneven tones. It was a nice distraction in the morning and at night. I didn't think; I listened. It's good for me not to be thinking all the time.

As I was taking them down, I heard footsteps behind me and I turned and there was Donna Baker, and she said, "Why don't you leave a few up? I can hear them from across the street. They're pleasant at night."

I said, "Okay, Donna."

Then I felt good. I felt so good that the next day I planned on returning her little flag. I'd put down a bluestone over the hole where I buried the flag, and I'd uncovered the flag and picked up the bluestone to put it in the garage when I saw Donna Baker pushing a cross into her lawn. I thought, This is ridiculous, and really I was going to go over there and pull it right out, but the bluestone fell from my arms and landed on my foot.

WHEN WE got back from the hospital, Donna helped me inside. Then she ran to her house and grabbed an ice pack and set me up on my couch with a pillow underneath my foot and the ice pack wrapped around my toes. She sat down in the chair next to me and we watched the television for a while. She didn't mention the flag.

"How is it?" she said finally. "How's the pain?"

"There's no pain," I said. "It's just numb."

"Oh, look," she said, pointing at the television.

There was Paul, right in front of my eyes like he'd been all those days in the house, except now he was on the screen. Donna turned up the volume. Paul was sitting with two young boys, trying to explain to them the importance of brushing their teeth. Then a big green space alien tore open the roof and came down with a glowing fluorescent tube and a giant toothbrush. He smiled and his teeth blinded Paul and the children with their brightness. Then the kids looked in the mirror and saw that their teeth were as clean and white as the alien's. They cheered and Paul crossed his arms over his chest and shook his head.

"Well, how about that," Donna said. "I can't believe I know someone famous."

"He's not famous," I said. "It's a commercial."

"But, still. Didn't he want to be famous? Isn't that why he left?"

"He left because he didn't want me anymore."

"That's not true."

I sat up on the couch.

"How do you go on like this, Donna? Tell me the secret." My voice was sharp, and Donna pinched her knees together and her shoulders tensed up. "Really, Donna. I'd like to get inside that head of yours and figure you out."

"I don't appreciate the way you're talking to me," she said. "I'm leaving. I hope your foot feels better."

"God damn it," I said.

She stood up and slapped down her skirt, sending out a puff of loose hair and dust.

"I pray to God you don't think it was worth it," I said. "Do you, Donna?"

She turned to me. Her eyes were sharp as cut glass. I thought I saw it in her—she'd been fighting anger for so long. She put her hands out, and her fingertips shook like little Christmas bells. Then her eyes softened, and I could see she was trying to forgive me for what I'd said. I can't say if she did, only that it seemed to me she was trying.

We haven't spoken since then, but I feel closer to Donna Baker than I ever did before. I know she's there, across the street, with her pain and fantasy, and on certain days when I can't find any peace in what I'm doing, I'll pretend to be Donna and imagine what it must be like to live the way she does.

TO FEEL AGAIN THE KIND
OF LOVE THAT HURTS
SOMETHING TERRIBLE

~~~~~~~

KENNY PACED ALONG the driveway, kicking stones, saying to himself, "Finish your milk, finish your homework, finish your prayers."

Huffing, exhausted, he slowly chanted, "Dolphins, dragons, pelicans, trampolines, submarines, jelly beans."

He sat on the lawn with his hands wrapped around his knees and whispered, "Coca-Cola, rock 'n' rolla, supernova . . . shit, shit, shit."

He started over, from the beginning. Because it had to be right, or else everything would go wrong.

Casanova!

He stood up and walked over to the dying maple near the edge of the lawn. Leaves fell in the slight breeze. He plucked a few from the ground, crumpled them in his hand, and shoved the bits into his mouth. The orange ones tasted best. There weren't many orange ones left. It was almost winter.

He turned and shouted toward the house, "Let's get this shucking fo on the road!"

FROM THE bay window, Phil and Mary watched Kenny crush and eat leaves. They used to worry Kenny would get poisoned, but there's only so much you can control.

"Fourteen-year-olds don't eat leaves," Mary said.

"Maybe he's a vegan."

"Tasteless, Phil. Just tasteless."

Going vegan might not be a bad idea for the boy, Phil thought. He was short and chubby, and Mary cut his hair in a way that made his face look like a pale balloon. Some days he was way up. Other days he was way down. One night, a few months back, Mary found a hole in the bathroom wall behind one of her dopey signs about love and light. Phil was in the garage, drinking beer, flipping through an old nudie magazine he'd found behind the seat of his Bobcat. He had had to park the Bobcat after his third DUI. Mary came in from the house and snuck up on Phil sitting in the cage looking at the crumpled spread of a naked woman straddling a fire hydrant.

"When you're done whacking off, I need you to take a look at something," she said, and shut the door.

The hole was the size of a small fist. He reached inside and pulled out a bunch of panties with the tags still on. Some were stuck together.

"He's stealing girls' underwear, and, you know," Mary said.

"I see that."

"Must be in the genes."

Then Kenny punched another boy in the neck. The boy had a condition. He started shaking and foaming at the mouth. Luckily he didn't die.

When Phil asked Kenny why he did it, he said he was trying to save the world from an alien takeover.

"You should be friggin' thanking me," he said.

This was before the meds.

Phil and Mary had taken Kenny out of school and put him in the hospital. Nothing short of a small fortune to watch him solve puzzles and make his bed. But he didn't put any more holes in the walls.

Mary crushed Kenny's pills and sprinkled the dust into his eggs.

"I don't know if this is such a good idea," she said, breathing on Phil's neck as they watched Kenny stomp around in circles outside.

Phil was taking Kenny on his first date. They were going skating at the hockey rink near the bridge.

"Please be good to him," Mary said.

"Why wouldn't I?" he said, pressing a finger against his gums.

"He's very nervous. I can tell."

"He's always nervous. Why'd you let him wear a suit?"

"Look how handsome he is."

"He'll stick out like a—"

Phil's tooth ached so bad he smacked the counter. Mary jumped back, then popped him on the arm.

"You scared me," she said.

"You think *that* was scary?"

In a way he felt nervous for Kenny, felt like he was responsible for making today a day he would remember for the rest of his life. But then, those first few dates with Morgan Price, did he even want to remember them? When they'd gone paddling on boogie boards in the lake behind her house and he kept his shirt on because he was chubby and embarrassed. She had said she liked him because he was different.

"Take your shirt off," she said.

Then the last boy she liked came cruising by on a motor-boat and tipped them over on their boards with the swell and blew an air horn and everyone on the lake looked over at Phil standing in the shallow water, his bathing suit bunched up between his legs, waddling like a penguin back up the beach to Morgan's house, his chin quivering. Later, in the kitchen, they quietly nibbled on tuna fish sandwiches with her mother.

SINCE PHIL'S last DUI, they only had the one car. In order to start it now, he had to blow into the Breathalyzer hooked to the dash and wait for the machine to record his blood alcohol level.

He told Kenny that he and Mom were being paid to have someone monitor what type of radio programming they listened to while driving.

"I'm not stupid," Kenny said.

"No, you're not."

"You have a problem."

"Lots of people have problems."

"I know that, too. I saw a woman on TV with no arms and legs. She was like a ball in a chair and she moved the chair around with her mouth."

"That's one kind of problem, sure."

"My problem is mental."

"What do you mean? Where did you hear that?"

"Mom said it. I heard her on the phone. She was telling someone that I had a mental problem."

"She said that?"

"I think it's better than being a ball in a chair, don't you?"

Phil reached over and gently squeezed the back of Kenny's neck.

"You look good in that suit, pal," he said.

"Thanks, I know."

"Girls like a man who dresses nice. When I met your mother, she thought I was a hippie because of how I dressed. I just thought I was rebellious. Anyway, she changed me good."

"I have no idea what you're talking about, Dad."

"Oh, okay, you want to focus, is that it? I'll let you focus."

Phil turned on the radio. He had to keep the sound low because the machine beeped every fifteen minutes, calling him to blow in the tube. Supposedly the engine shut down if he didn't. He wondered what would happen if he were on the highway and forgot, if the car would just stop and he'd get barreled into by a fleet of cars. He hoped he'd survive, because then he'd sue the state and be rich.

Bored with classic rock, Phil had begun listening to jazz. It all sounded like one long song with different pieces. He imagined that the instruments had beating hearts.

"Why are you taking the long way?" Kenny asked.

"What long way? There's only one way, pal. Point A to point B."

"Don't screw with me, Dad."

"Watch it, Kenny."

But what could he say? The kid was smart. And erratic. And possibly dangerous.

They'd been to the rink once before, when the Olympic speed skaters came to Wequaquet for a public exhibition. After that, he taught Kenny how to skate on the pond near their house. Then Kenny always wanted to skate, even when the ice was too thin. Then Phil had to lie about why they couldn't go out, and it broke him a little each time, because he knew Kenny was smart enough to know.

"You want to be a little late," Phil said. "Keep them waiting."

"What if she leaves?"

"She won't. She'll hang around just to let you hear about it."

"Then what?"

"Then you apologize, and take her hand, and apologize again."

"I've never heard you apologize to Mom."

"That's because I don't have to anymore."

Kenny pulled at his crotch and looked out the window. Phil knew he wasn't just worried about being late. He was worried about the world catching fire. He'd been reading about climate change on the Internet. Mary had to take his laptop and tablet and phone away. One night Kenny ran through the house calling, "Code Nine, Code Nine!" He packed the pantry into a duffel bag and the three of them camped in the basement. Mary and Phil played cards while Kenny hugged his knees and rocked back and forth.

The trick, the doctors said, was to acknowledge Kenny's actions but not to engage.

Phil was trying his best to disengage.

IF FRESCA'S going to be there before me, Kenny thought, then I have to find a way to jerk off. He'd been jerking off since last year, when he saw another boy doing it behind a tree at school. The boy had said it was the only way to get rid of all the stuff inside him. Kenny didn't know what stuff the boy was talking about. Not until he practiced. And when he got rid of his stuff, he felt less anxious and his thoughts slowed down and food tasted better. He jerked off in the bathroom stalls and behind the Dunkin' Donuts after school and once right in class through his shorts.

"I have to poo," Kenny told his father.

"Jesus. I thought you didn't want to be late."

"I don't. But I don't want to poo my pants, either. What's the difference? Make her wait longer, right?"

"Not too long. Then she'll probably leave."

"But you said—"

"What the hell do I know, Kenny?"

His father turned in to an Exxon station.

"Be quick," he said.

In the bathroom stall, Kenny thought about Fresca's dark hair and wide eyebrows and her skin, a butter-cream color like a toffee candy. She called Kenny "Kenbo." He liked that name. It made him sound like he was some kind of karate master. He would sit behind her in class. She wore low-cut jeans, and he could see her thongs. She liked bright colors. It didn't take him long to come after picturing her skating around in her fluorescent-green underwear.

PHIL WATCHED as a car pulled up behind him and out came Coach Linnehan, all bug-eyed and mournful, standing at the pump and studying the screen as though it were an Egyptian hieroglyph.

At least he wasn't that bad off. Not yet, anyway.

When he and Mary had started out, it felt like he'd been drugged with joy. Overwhelmed by the insane happiness of New. Colors seemed brighter, simple objects made him curious, days flew by and exploded into dust like clay pigeons.

He watched Coach Linnehan slide his card in and out of the slot at the pump. Such simple desperation made him feel better.

Kenny hopped back in the car, smelling like gas fumes and cheap soap.

Phil blew into the Breathalyzer tube and started the engine.

"So what's this girl's name?" he asked.

"Francesca," Kenny said.

"That pretty little Jew girl?"

"So what if she's Jewish?"

"Right. Of course."

"She likes to be called Fresca. That's her favorite soda. I hope the machine at the rink has it."

Phil remembered how when Kenny was a baby he'd fall or bang his head on something and get this terrified look in his eyes, and his mouth would open and his face would scrunch up, but he wouldn't cry, he wouldn't make a sound, then, all of a sudden, like an archer stretching a bow to its limit and finally releasing the arrow, he would scream, and the sound would cut through the house with so much velocity it felt as if he'd pierced Phil's breastplate.

It was hard to get anything on girls like Fresca; sometimes what you got was by not trying to get anything at all. She was always surrounded by her two equally beautiful friends, Alex and Sara. But Fresca had green eyes instead of blue and brown, and her hair was long and wavy instead of short and straight, and maybe it wasn't that she was so beautiful after all, maybe it was how when she looked at you it was like she trapped your entire life force in her gaze.

So it was pure luck when a few weeks ago Kenny had been sitting outside against the cafeteria wall trying to make his thumb disappear when he heard this voice like a cat being stretched apart. He went over to the recess in the wall near the dumpsters, and there was Fresca with pink pods in her ears, eyes closed, singing some shitty pop song. Watching her without her knowing, it was like she became real to him, not like the girl who rolled her eyes in math class or flirted with Dean Vechionni, the fat lesbo warlord who nixed wearing baseball hats and hooded sweatshirts at school because they were places kids might hide weapons.

Fresca freaked when she saw Kenny, pulled the pods from her ears, and cornered him against the wall.

"Don't you tell anyone about this," she said.

"It wasn't that bad," he lied.

"Why are you smiling? Don't smile. You're going to tell. I know it. You freak. God."

Her breath smelled like nectarines. He grabbed her hair and kissed her and she pushed him off, hard against the wall, and he fell on his butt and bruised his tailbone. He had to use Mom's heating pad for the next three nights while he thought of a way to get close enough to Fresca to kiss her again.

The next day, when he passed her in the hall, she was the only one of her friends who actually looked at him. He could tell she was nervous, not about how he was walking bent over because of the bruised tailbone, but about her singing and if he had told anyone. Who would I tell? he thought. And why would they believe me? Then he realized it would be pretty easy to trick her into thinking he was going to tell.

After math class he snuck up behind her and said, "You know I recorded your performance on my phone."

She stopped and her friends stopped. They looked at Kenny like he was a puke stain on the wall.

"You're not allowed to have a phone on school grounds," she said.

Another one of Dean Vech's laws.

"What's he talking about, Fres?" her friend Alex said.

So Fresca had a nickname for her nickname. He said it over and over before going to sleep that night.

"Nothing. He's mental," Fresca said.

"You stink like a dead fish," Alex said.

"Ever heard of deodorant?" the other girl, Sara, said.

"Yes, I've heard of—"

But they were already halfway down the hall, arms locked with a couple of no-neck Red Raiders wearing their Friday game shirts.

After school, near the number-five bus, he felt a hard flick against his earlobe.

"Okay, what do you want?" Fresca asked.

"I want to see you outside of school," Kenny said, rubbing his ear.

"Like where? Where can I see you and not be seen by anyone else? And don't say your room. I can't imagine what kind of weirdo stuff you have in there."

"I don't have weirdo stuff. I have normal stuff."

Except for the panties he stole from MegaWorld, which he kept adding to every weekend. That was probably pretty weird.

"How about the skating rink?"

She looked over her shoulder, then stood on her tiptoes and looked over his head.

"Fine. But you have to swear you'll erase that video."

"I swear," he said.

"You have to swear on something."

Kenny raised his right hand.

"I swear on my right hand; may it always stay attached to my arm."

"God, you're such a freak-o," she said, and walked off.

PHIL'S FATHER had been a pilot. His heart stopped while he was flying from Chicago to Anchorage. He had never flown that route before but had agreed to take it on to keep his job.

Phil thought that, seeing the icecaps from fifteen thousand feet that first time, his father's body was unable to sustain the beauty. Lucky for the passengers, the copilot was able to land the plane. Phil imagined that time stopped like that, when you see something so beautiful, something like love. He felt that the first time he saw Mary. Maybe all the years between then and now had been his attempt to get back to that one moment of clarity.

But he didn't know where to begin.

He looked at Kenny.

"Stop biting your nails," he said.

"I wasn't."

"Your thumbnail's hanging by a thread."

Kenny tore it off and sucked on it like he did when he was a baby. Phil hadn't been able to help but feel anything other than joy. His little guy all bundled up with his thumb in his mouth, making those cooing sounds, dreaming of what? What does a baby dream of?

"Let me see," he said.

Kenny showed him his thumb, the blood speckled behind the nail.

"That'll dry up before we get there."

"I hope so."

"You need to start working in the yard. Your hands are too soft. Girls don't like a guy with soft hands. I had to tar foundations when I was a kid. Heat up the tar with kindling and an iron grate, then bring the buckets down the stepladder into the hole, over a hundred degrees down there if not more, sweating, painting on the hot tar, hands blistering up. That was work. And when I was with your mother, she knew I—"

"Dad! Please!"

"What?"

"I so don't want to hear about you and Mom and whatever you two did."

"I'm talking about love, Kenny. Women. How they need to be held and touched and talked to. You need to know these things if you want to have a chance with this girl."

He stopped at a traffic light and looked at Kenny looking out the window at the floating dancers in front of Big Tim's Auto Emporium.

"Kenny?"

"Yeah, Dad."

"Did you hear what I said?"

KENNY PANICKED when the Breathalyzer machine began beeping just as Fresca and her mother pulled into the next space over. His father was literally breathing into a long plastic dick-tube with his cheeks puffed out. Maybe Fresca didn't notice, because in no time she and her mom were at the door to the rink. Fresca held the laces of her skates with the precision of a puppeteer; they already seemed to be spinning on the ice.

"That her?" his father asked, placing the Breathalyzer back in its holster.

"Yep."

"She's pretty. And her mom's not half bad, either."

"Please."

"Oh, shit, Kenny. Just two guys talking. How much does it cost to skate around in circles these days?"

"I don't know."

Kenny took the mangled bills plus some change and pocket debris.

"That should do."

When Kenny went to open the door, his father put his hand on his arm, just holding it there, his fingers pressing lightly into his biceps. He wasn't looking at Kenny. He was looking in the rearview mirror. Kenny turned and saw some garbage heaped up against the cement slabs in front of the parking spaces.

"Dad?" he said.

His father let go of his arm.

"All right, kiddo," he said. "Go get 'em."

Mary was so deep in the past, Phil thought, but also right here, so close he felt like he could grab hold of her waist, and then what?

Hang on for dear life.

Never complain.

Never say a negative thing about her hair or clothing or weight.

Kiss her in the morning and at night and when she least expected to be kissed, when she was just in from the yard or finished washing dishes.

Take Sundays off to drive out somewhere beautiful and remark on how beautiful it was.

Finally go on that picnic. Make the sandwiches, pack the basket, find a soft pad of grass in the shade.

Shower together.

Make love slow and heavy and fall asleep naked with the smell of sex hovering over their spent bodies.

Do it all over again, better and better, like practice for a game that will never be played.

Because now, every day he was going home to her but not her, a version of her he had built out of fears and mistakes. He wanted her to know how much he missed being in love. Could he tell her that? Just that one thing?

Today, he thought. Today my life could change forever.

But the car wouldn't start. He blew into the plastic tube again and the machine beeped and he tried the ignition, but nothing sparked. He picked up the Breathalyzer and broke it against the dashboard. The robotic female voice sighed and died.

His tooth hurt so bad he tried to punch it out of his mouth. The punch numbed the pain.

"When you fall," his father used to say, "get back up again, unless some big black bastard is standing over you. Then you stay down."

His father had a way with words.

Phil wanted to die like he did, staring straight into the beautiful.

ONCE HE saw Fresca on the bench, lacing up her skates, Kenny got a boner. And because he'd grown out of his suit since Grandpa's funeral, you could see the boner sticking straight out like an arrowhead.

Before he had time to cover it, Fresca looked over and said, "Ew, gross."

But she smiled when she said it, and laughed.

He sat down and put on his hockey skates.

"Nice suit," she said.

"Thanks. I know it's weird."

"It's not weird. It just doesn't go with your skates."

"Oh."

"Hey, what about me?"

"What about you?"

"Jesus, you're a nut job."

"How you look, you mean?"

"Duh."

"You always look good. I can't stand it, you look so good."

She glanced at him. Her face candy-pink.

Then she was through the gate and on the ice. Kenny raced past her, forward and backward, and as she spun in a slow circle, he circled her. She reached out and grabbed hold of his arms and they spun together, and she let go and they skated around awhile and met up near the boards on the far side behind the nets. That's where she kissed him, kissed him with her nectarine breath filling his nose, kissed him so soft he slipped and fell on his butt again, but this time it didn't hurt so bad.

PHIL COULDN'T remember the last time he cried. Last time must've been when Mary told him she was pregnant. No, it was when he had found out they were having a boy. He was happiest then. He got that same feeling seeing Kenny and that pretty Jewish girl kissing on the ice.

An hour and three beers later, Francesca's mother returned.

Phil didn't feel like explaining about the situation.

"We'd really appreciate a ride," he said, and looked at Kenny. But Kenny didn't seem embarrassed.

He was flying. He was in love.

Nothing hurt so bad.

On the way home, riding in the back of Francesca's mother's Jeep Liberty, Phil put his hand on Kenny's knee and mussed up his hair.

"My baby boy," he said, softly and without regret.

DOWNHILL

~~~~~~

Every so often my little boy, Jasper, will ask me what the sky looks like. I used to be creative, but after a while you realize that what you're creating is only relative to what you've already created. One cloud looks like a bulldog. Then, what does a bulldog look like? Then, what does Grandpa look like? Lately I've been struggling with similes. We've had nothing but gray sunless days here. The ground is trapped under mounds of snow, and the relentless cold charges every person in town with a certain kind of dread and fear.

Jasper was born blind. He's four years old now and very curious. I make up a lot of things. Like when we listen to music in the car and I tell him there're little men inside the stereo playing tiny instruments just for us.

"What do they eat?" he asks.

"Smaller portions of what we eat."

"How do you feed them?"

"With a tiny fork."

"Do they ever come out?"

"Sure, when they need a break."

"Can I hold one?"

"Be careful."

I shut off the radio and take his hand. It's the tip of my finger forming infinity signs in his palm.

"What happens when he gets older and starts finding out what's true and what's not?" Darlene asked me one night after a gang of thugs threw a rock through our living room window for no apparent reason other than to make us feel what they felt. I told Jasper that the rush of air coming through his play circle was a flock of birds flying above us. He ran around the living room, jumping up and trying to grab at them. It was beautiful.

"Better he imagines the world this way while he can, don't you think?" I said to Darlene.

She knows it is possible Jasper might never see at all. Our medical bills are through the roof. We've maxed out our credit cards and the house is in foreclosure. Life for Darlene and me is a long, frozen march between home and work, the grocery store and the hospital. But not for Jasper. As far as he knows, we go everywhere. In the summer, it's the beaches in Spain (a polluted lake near the highway). In winter, it's the mountains in Switzerland (a hill near my old high school). Go to sleep, I say. When you wake up, the plane will already be on the ground.

The next step is corneal-transplant surgery in both eyes. I don't even want to tell you how much that's going to cost. It's like, I'm reading online about how these kids from New Guinea and Paraguay get this free surgery and they're watching TV and playing with crayons, and I'm thinking, What about Jasper? How broke do I have to be?

On this day, one week before Christmas, I'm lucky to have

just sold a used 2005 Honda Accord to a young couple that seems to have that same spark Darlene and I had when we first got married. So, all things considered, I'm having a pretty decent morning when Big Tim comes into the showroom and says, "Did you hear about those five North Koreans shot to death trying to cross over into China?"

This is the last thing I need to be thinking about right now.

"I didn't hear," I say.

"No? It was all over the news. Seems like every good citizen of the planet should keep up with what's going on in the world, Falachi. It *might* make you a better salesman."

"I just closed a deal before you walked in."

"For that beater?" He looks out the showroom window at the newlyweds, who are staring at the hood of the Honda uncertainly. "Hardly a game changer."

"I need to get my commission check by this afternoon, if that's okay?"

"Hmm," Big Tim says, stroking his chin. He used to have a beard, but then he read somewhere that Americans don't trust men with beards anymore. "I'll see what I can do."

Last Christmas, I wasn't able to get Darlene anything. I made a card and used a coupon for free perennials from Stop & Shop. For Jasper I stole a toy truck from the playroom next to the repair shop. It was all scratched up and a wheel was broken off and the little horn got stuck when he pushed on the steering wheel so this long, intolerable wail sounded and made him cry. I tried to fix it but ended up smacking the thing against the coffee table until it broke. I did my best to paste some of the parts together and make the sounds that a truck would make: a high-pitched *beep* when he backed it up, a *vroom vroom* when he pushed it forward, a rumbling motor when he let it go.

"See," Big Tim says, "the thing about the Koreans is that it turns out one of them wasn't completely dead. They shot him in the stomach so he'd have to suffer. When the human-aid workers found him, he wasn't able to speak and they didn't have the capabilities to save him, so *they* had to kill him. How do you think that makes those people feel, Falachi?"

"It sounds awful," I say, not paying full attention.

"It *is* awful!" he says. "What about the missing girl they found in a dumpster in Albuquerque? She'd been gone a week. The search was called off. Then it turns out these two maniacs who lived in her neighborhood had kidnapped her. She wasn't more than three blocks away. The things they did to her! You know what the girl's father said? 'She's in heaven now.' Exact quote."

Does it make me a bad person if I don't care all that much about the North Koreans or the dead girl in Albuquerque? Or every other bad thing you see and read and hear about? Maybe. But what can I say besides, wow, God, Jesus, damn?

"Don't even get me started on Mexico," he says. "Heads are rolling in the streets of Juárez. Like, *actually rolling down streets*."

"Jesus."

"Have you ever seen a rolling head, Falachi?"

When Big Tim gets worked up like this, crying is inevitable. He lets out a long whine and starts choking up to catch his breath. A string of spit hangs off his bottom lip and this little bubble forms between his lips. Once it pops, that whine starts again.

"It's all right, Tim. You're not responsible."

"Oh, no? You don't think? We're human, Falachi. Human! Those killers and rapists, they're human, too."

"But it's Christmas, and we've got this big promotion going, and I think things are going to get better."

"Have you seen our sales? Do you have any idea how much

money I owe the bank? The government? It can't get any worse, is that what you're saying? Because if that's what you're saying, oh, boy, you better prepare yourself."

Big Tim covers his eyes with the sleeve of his suit jacket and heads to the bathroom so none of the other salesmen can see him. His sobs echo through the showroom. It's a good thing we don't have any customers.

A bum wanders in and pours a cup of coffee, sits in the lounge, and thumbs through a golf magazine. Some high school kids draw penises in the frost on the plate-glass windows. Plows pass by in a row, like military vehicles. The used Honda is the first car I've sold in a month. We've had snow for three weeks straight. My mornings have been spent scraping ice off wind-shields, running the engines, laying down salt. Jeff and Luis haven't sold a car since summer. Their eyelids are yellow and puffy from lack of sleep. Jeff took a second job as a telemar-keter. On Sundays, he plays Santa Claus at the mall. Luis's wife divorced him and he had to move out of the colonial they bought a few years ago to his cousin's place in the Heights, which if you've ever been to the Heights you'd know is a big step down from anyplace else. I'm twenty thousand dollars in debt and Darlene has been threatening to leave and take Jasper to live with her parents in Florida. She has faith in me, but faith only goes so far, especially when the old days keep getting older and your memory of them isn't quite the same anymore.

So the commission check is a pretty big deal.

A few minutes later, Big Tim's looking much better. He's wet and combed his hair, and his face is no longer flushed. He scans the vacant showroom before walking into his office. Swirls of snow sweep across the front lot. Jeff is playing hearts on his computer. Luis is staring at the fish. The aquarium tank was meant as a way to keep kids entertained while we went over the numbers with their parents in one of our cubicles. It's a monster, close to eighty gallons, with dozens of tropical fish: striped tiger barbs, neon tetras, zebra danios, white clouds. Problem is, none of them seem to be moving.

"Are they dead?" I ask Luis.

"They were dead, but if you stare at them long enough, they start moving again. It's like a miracle."

"We need to call someone."

"Yes, a priest."

"Falachi!" Big Tim shouts from his office. "Come here. I want you to see something."

"Really," I say to Luis. "Get on the horn and have this tank taken out of here."

It's hard to get comfortable in Big Tim's office. His old high school trophies and a collection of photographs from his playing days are on display in a glass case against the wall, and over in the corner is a full-size cardboard cutout of him with his arms flexed and two Playmates squeezing his biceps. He used to be the local Bud Man back in the eighties. On his desk are more-recent photographs of him with his ex-wife and their adopted son, Brutus. Looking around the room is like looking at the devolution of Big Tim when you finally let your eyes settle on him in the flesh.

"Watch this," he says.

On his computer screen is a still shot of a large crowd in some market in Asia. Big Tim pushes PLAY and the crowd begins to move. The camerawork is shaky. You can hear sirens and car horns and bells and this eerie crackling sound that must be a hundred or so people and animals and scooters making noise at the same time. Then a man crosses in front of the camera and bursts into flames. There's this massive *pop* like an engine backfiring. The man runs into the market, and people are screaming and trying to get out of his way. He falls to the ground, flailing. Someone tosses a blanket over his body, but the fire eats through the blanket. Finally, a man blasts him with a fire extinguisher. I can't tell if he's dead or alive. The video ends.

Tim plays it back.

"Listen," he says. "Is the cameraman laughing?"

"Maybe he's nervous," I say. "Tim . . . if I can get that check—"

"Look, he doesn't even attempt to save the guy. And see this here on the side? There're all these links to videos of exploding people. If this many people are exploding while someone happens to have a camera going, think about how many are exploding when there's *no* camera."

"Come on, Tim. Let's take a deep breath."

But it's too late. He chucks a stress ball in the shape of a clown's head across the room and begins to whine. I can already see Darlene packing up what little we have left. I shut the blinds around his office and close the door behind me. Everyone can hear him, though. This has been going on for a while now. Part of the reason there's such low energy in the showroom.

"Don't let anyone see him like this," I tell Suzy, his secretary, an old, callous woman whose refusal to pity Tim might be the only thing keeping the place afloat.

She looks up from her computer screen.

"He's already sent these videos of exploding people to everyone in the building," she says.

"Damn."

"You know what I think? Men are bigger babies than actual babies. When a baby falls, it gets up and looks at you with this kind of stunned amazement. Grown men, they just keep falling."

I picture Jasper on the beach in Florida, the water creeping up the shoreline toward his small, ticklish body. Maybe it's the hands of thousands of sea creatures trying to pull him down into their secret world. Maybe the crashing waves are really falling buildings. Maybe when he leaps into my arms, it doesn't have to be him saving me.

"I'm at lunch," I tell Suzy.

I walk through the repair shop, where the mechanics are sitting on tires, playing cards on the flat side of a big wooden spool. There're no cars in the bays. We were given a bad name last spring when Channel 5 sent an investigative reporter into the shop to have his brakes looked at. The mechanics told him he needed to have new brakes put in, and while they were at it, they took a look at the transmission, and that needed to be replaced, too. But there was nothing wrong with the car's brakes, and the transmission was just fine. The piece ran on their weekly report "BUSTED!" Big Tim came off real bad, pushing one of the cameramen into the giant inflatable air dancers we had lined up outside the dealership. "From high school football star to scamming you on your car, Tim Tucker gets *busted!*" the reporter said, just before Tim lowered his shoulder and drove him into the ground.

Outside in the back lot is where we keep the real clunkers. Jeff is getting stoned in the front seat of his used Mercury, which has two broken taillights and a garbage bag ripped and taped over the passenger-side window. Seeing Jeff in his car like this, I can't help but wonder what the hell is going to happen to all of us. He's been wilting like a sun-starved cactus ever since Jamaica Man, the local tanning salon, went under. His skin is a pale, sticky-looking hue now, and he's lost a good twenty pounds, which I think has more to do with his lack of sales.

Big Tim is convinced Jeff is dying. Last month he invited all the boys out to Tally-Hoes on Industrial and we had to pony up twenty bucks apiece for a dark-skinned girl named Chardonnay to straddle Jeff and call him Papa Bear. "When you're dying, nothing's better than a pair of tits in your face," Big Tim said. It did seem to make everything bearable for a few days after.

"How you feeling, Jeff?"

"Better than ever," he says, and passes the pipe out the window toward me.

"No, thanks."

"It's your reality."

"What about putting a good word in for me with the telemarketers?"

"People are actually standing in line to sit there and take a beating all night for less than eight bucks an hour, and you want to be a part of it?"

"I'm in a bind this season."

"There're better ways to make a buck."

"You mean illegal ways."

"Who's really watching us, partner?"

"What's your plan?"

"You're looking at it."

"You want to rob Big Tim?"

"The insurance will cover whatever we take. It's foolproof."

"Then what?"

"Then we live in paradise."

A world Jasper can see. The long strip of white sand stretching the length of the Caribbean, the blue water and tropical fish; maybe the red rocks out west, the smooth canyon walls, the twinkling stars at twilight. I feel colder than ever and fold my arms tightly across my chest.

"Falach? Are you listening? You could be the lookout. Just like a real heist. We could get a truck in here on Christmas Eve, no problemo."

Listening to Jeff, I can understand why Darlene thinks fantasies are dangerous.

"I'm not a criminal," I say.

"Jesus, man, you really have no idea what's going on. Always keeping your head up, but never looking side to side. Just think about it."

I walk toward the high school where I went twenty years ago. Back then I thought I'd make it further than working at the car dealership next door. When Darlene and I got together, we looked at a map of the country and picked out where we wanted to live once we had enough money: somewhere out west, in the mountains, with a city close by. Then things started piling up. When I was making good money, it didn't make sense to leave, and when I started making no money, we couldn't leave. Trapped in this inertia, you look forward to the holidays.

I remember those Christmases when my father would take me to the noontime movie, some shoot-'em-up that was much easier to forget than his tall, lean body standing outside the theater, smoking cigarettes, calling his bookie to get the spreads on the games that afternoon. I don't think he ever watched a movie straight through. When it was finished, I'd find him resting in the car. "Ready to go, chief?" he'd say. "How was it?" As he drove back through the whirls of snow and chimney smoke, I described every detail I could remember, learning to condense information into neat packages, to invent what I'd forgotten. To change just one thing meant I had to change everything. Mom was home cleaning up the pine needles under the tree, folding the clothes given to me by aunts and uncles, checking on the turkey, playing

Christmas carols on the stereo. My father stretched out on the sofa, setting the new watch she had given him.

A young boy in snow pants and an oversize wool cap is half-way up the steep hill near the practice field behind the school, pushing his boots into the hardening snow, dragging a plastic sled. At the crest of the hill is a row of snowy pines where I found a dead cat last fall with the name *Julio* shaved crudely into her fur.

When the boy reaches the top, he sets the sled on the plateau and, before getting in, waves to me, and I wave back. Standing there with my hands in my pockets, watching the boy fly down the hill, I can feel my eyes well up from the rush of air, the free fall. I remember the tiered hillside behind my uncle's house, where we went for Christmas Eve dinner. There was a lake at the end of the hill. My older cousins were all hockey players and set up goals and skated effortlessly while my younger cousin, Randy, and I took turns on the sled, seeing how much speed we could generate by bending our bodies into bullets, how close to the lake we could get. Once, I put my head between my knees and Randy pushed me with all his strength and the metal skis of the sled zipped through the fresh, powdery snow, and at that speed, I thought, there was no way I'd get held up at the bottom. The snow climbed up over me like a wave, and in that last moment, I looked up and realized the sled had veered off course and was headed toward the playground set in the backyard. I tried to pull up on the brake handles at my sides, but it was too late. The braking sent me headlong into the metal pole on the side of the swings. I knocked out one of my teeth and split my bottom lip, which stiffened into an awkward pout as I trudged back up to the house. The adults were concerned at first, but later, at dinner, when they were half-drunk and in good spirits, they laughed at how swollen my lip had gotten. They called me Monkey Lip.

The boy makes a tiny shriek when the sled hits a mogul. The sled bounces and he's able to straighten it and finish the run by spinning ninety degrees, stopping just before he reaches the sidewalk. What unappreciated talents we develop at that age! He's red-faced and wide-eyed, and his hat has gone crooked on his head. I have the impulse to reach out and fix it for him.

"Hey, buddy!" someone shouts from behind me. I turn to see a tall, broad-shouldered guy in a heavy winter coat walking toward me.

"What are you, like, checking out my kid?"

"What's that? No. What do you mean?"

"You're standing here with this goofy grin on your face."

"No, that's not it. That's not it at all."

"What, then? You just come out to watch boys sled down hills?"

He's got a face like an anvil, cigarette smoke on his breath, a blackened front tooth. A real man, it seems, from not so long ago.

"Look, I'm sorry you got that impression. I was just remembering what it was like to be his age, you know? I got excited, that's all."

"I'll fucking bet, pal." He's balled up his fist and my hands are raised slightly, prepared for the blow. "If the boy weren't here, I'd kick your ass," he says.

The logic doesn't make sense, but I'm relieved when he unclenches his fist and grabs his son by the wrist, pulling him off the sled. The boy cries. His father picks him up and puts him over his shoulder.

"It's okay, sweetie," he says.

Snot is coming out of the boy's nose, freezing around the

edges of his nostrils. His father pats him on the back and walks off toward the parking lot.

They forget the sled.

Maybe a kind gesture would keep them from thinking of me as a pedophile for the rest of their lives. But it's almost perfect, with just a few dings and scrapes along the plastic siding.

When I was a boy, my friends and I carried metal trash-can lids to the tops of hills and gave each other a great shove forward. We fell and tumbled and broke bones. We were in it for the gratification we got on crisp winter afternoons, for the hot chocolate in the backseat of mom's car, for the homemade sauce cooking on the stove at home. That was Christmas in America. *That* was paradise.

No matter where it comes from, Jasper deserves the same joy I had.

Sitting on my lap at the top of the hill, he'll feel the wind in his face and my arms tighten around his body. Don't worry, little guy. Nothing bad is going to happen. You're going to feel this rush just before the end, as if we're flying through the sky. It'll be scary the first time, but you'll want to do it all over again once we're at the bottom.

Remember that, I'll tell him, as we drag the sled up the hill. And everything else I've told you, too.

FRIEND OF MINE

~~~~~~

I WAS ON the porch watching these two cute-as-hell bunnies in Coach Linnehan's yard playing this game where they stared each other down until one of them sprinted forward and the other hopped up to avoid the inevitable collision. Then they turned and stared off again and kept at it until the one sprinting caught the other so that it was his turn to be the hopper. I was thinking about how I used to play games like that and couldn't remember when I stopped playing those games and how as kids we must've invented them from watching little animals, and that's all I was when I was young, a little animal, but then I started having all this shit thrown at me about what I was supposed to be and what I needed to do to be it and how I could keep on being it if I did certain things, certain right things, and at one point my head must have basically exploded so I couldn't do anything and I couldn't get back to that time when I was a kid playing those little animal games.

It's rare I get a moment where I can remember what it was like to be who I was then, hopping around, playing games, not thinking about anything. Watching those rabbits, I felt at peace for the first time in a long time. In my heart, I'm saying. I felt calm.

Then Coach Linnehan comes out onto his front steps and shoots both rabbits in the gut with his nine millimeter.

"What the hell, Coach," I shout from the porch. "They were just playing around."

"Damn buggers eat up my gazanias," he says.

"Look at the one on the right. He's all twitching and shit."

Coach sights it with the gun and splatters his head with a bullet.

"Only decent thing I could do," he says.

"You could've not shot them in the first place."

"They ate my gazanias."

"Fuck your gazanias," I say, looking at the bunnies, their insides now soaking his perfectly trimmed lawn. "You totally ruined my morning."

I USED to play ball for Coach Linnehan when I was in high school. I was a guard on the offensive line and I had a quick first step, which was necessary when we ran trap plays and I had to take out the defensive end on the other side of the line. Then I crunched my neck my senior year and missed the last five games of the season. Coach recommended me to some small schools in the area based on my performance during junior year, but my grades were bad and I had to take summer school just to graduate and I honestly didn't have the heart to play anymore. Sometimes I still feel this little twinge in my neck.

After I got out of high school I was hanging around town, living with my parents, working as a landscaper with my buddy Justin, who ended up renting a little place in the Heights, right next to Coach. He let me move in to split rent. Justin had barely graduated, too, and was training for the Army, getting strong and lean, drinking these protein shakes that made his sweat smell like manure. After work we'd sit out on the porch and drink beer and, before Justin enlisted, smoke a little pot and listen to Pearl Jam, and once it got past a certain time Coach would come out standing there in his tight shorts and stained T-shirt with his little bitch tits hanging to the sides, looking like some old-timey asshole, chewing on the end of a cigar, saying we had no taste in music, or culture, and how would we define the word *legacy*, did we even know what a legacy was?

"You two are never going to make it," he'd say.

By that time his authority meant nothing. We laughed like hell and turned the music up louder and kept going till daylight, when it was time to gas up the mowers and mix the oil for the Weedwackers, toss the rakes and leaf blowers and pitchforks in the back of the truck, and drive to a job site. Then we'd smash a few energy drinks and drop some Visine in our eyes, slap each other in the face, and work like dogs, digging up roots, transplanting rhododendrons, mowing lawns as short and perfect as a country-club fairway. When we finished, we went to the packy, stocked up, dumped the beer in a cooler, drove down to the lake, and watched the fifteen-year-old girls swim in circles while we got buzzed, then hit a bar or two looking for chicks our own age. We usually ended up back on the porch, in that cool summer night breeze, talking shit about what I can't remember, but sincere enough that once in a while

Justin or I would break down and we'd hug it out and say thanks for listening to all that. Then we'd blast the music and call out plays until Coach slammed his window shut.

But during that summer, I always had it in the back of my mind what Coach said about making it. What did he mean by making it? I felt pretty good about the way my life was going: I had cash in my wallet, and the weather was perfect, and sometimes I got laid, and other times I was so tired I went right to sleep without thinking about anything. I guess I had dreamed of playing professional ball at one point, but what the hell for, when all these guys are drooling from their mouths at age forty, asking their wives where they are, not remembering fuck all from the past.

When I was even younger, I wanted to be a fireman, because the local fire chief came to our class to teach us CPR and told us a story about how he saved this little girl from a burning apartment complex. There was so much smoke and he was so full of fear, but he didn't care, because that was his job and his responsibility and he was prepared to give his life up for this girl, and once he had her in his arms and brought her out of the smoke, he asked her, "Where's your mother?" but she was coughing and couldn't speak and pointed to the apartment, and so he went back into the fire and found the girl's mother pinned against the wall of her bedroom by a piece of fallen ceiling. He pushed the piece of ceiling out of the way, picked the woman up, and put her over his shoulder, even grabbed a half-burned stuffed animal lying in the hallway, and got her out before the floor fell through. It was such a powerful fucking story, and the guy had the stuffed animal, this floppy-eared dog with a stitch in its eye and a toasted paw, which was his endgame, I guess, because all of us were pretty much stunned, little shits that we were, and a few of the girls had tears in their eyes. The fire chief passed around the stuffed dog as evidence that this happened. While we touched its burned, prickly head, he stroked his big gray mustache and said if we were interested in one day becoming firemen or firewomen, this was the kind of reward we'd get. We'd get to save lives.

I don't know when I stopped wanting to be a fireman. It's not like I couldn't go up to the community college and learn to be one if I wanted. It's just that I don't care so much anymore about saving lives, considering there're so many pieces of shit in this world and you might save some life that doesn't deserve to be saved, and this someone goes on to do something completely fucked up, and you have to live with the guilt that you were the one who kept him in the world when it was all set for him to burn.

But I still wanted to know what making it was, how I could make it, why Coach Linnehan believed he had made it and was in a position to be critical of those he felt weren't making it. He coached the Wequaquet Red Raiders to three championship seasons during his fifteen-year tenure and finally retired after his second consecutive losing season, when people around town were saying he didn't have it anymore, had lost his focus when his daughter died and his wife left him not long after. He was usually alone, except for when he went out on Thursday nights and brought home some divorcée that clearly couldn't stand straight, and who knows what kind of lovemaking they did in there, because Justin and I could only hear this horrible, ear-splitting jazz coming from his bedroom. Other nights he would smoke his cigar on his porch and read these giant biographies of ex-presidents like Jefferson and Nixon, and occasionally he'd drop in some quote when criticizing us. He told us Nixon had said, "There's always the day before the day everything changes." Justin nodded and stroked his chin and said, "I'll eat your face off, Linnehan."

In a way I felt sorry for Coach, even if he was a complete douchebag, and I guess that maybe making it meant just making it for a while so that you had some idea what it was.

TOWARD THE end of summer, Justin stopped staying up late with me, quit drinking beer and smoking weed, ran ten miles every morning before we even got in the truck, all so he could fly through basic training and get his ass blown up in Iraq. At least, that's what I told him, because I didn't want him to leave and I didn't like the way he was changing, and it hit me that maybe what Coach had said about the day before the day everything changed had got to him, even when he brushed it off the way he did, because it was around that time we sort of drifted apart.

The week before Justin was deployed, Coach left a copy of *The Art of War* on our front stoop, a book that he had read from as part of his pre-game pep talks. We would smash our fists against our helmets, Coach holding the book high like some kind of preacher, all of us growling and barking, and Coach howling a prophetic affirmation, something like, Invincibility lies in the defense; the possibility of victory in the attack! By the time he opened up the big metal door to the locker room and we saw the lights on the field, we were ready to tear apart the other team and anyone associated with them.

EVER SINCE that summer Justin left, I've been waiting for the day when everything will change, thinking yesterday was the day before this day, which is the day I've been waiting for. But nothing has really changed, except for what's gone on in the world, which I don't have any control over and is just a bunch of fucked-up shit I don't want to think about anyway.

Then today I see the two bunnies playing their bunny game and I'm like, That's it! That's the thing! But Coach comes out and smokes both of them without giving two damns how it might affect him or me or anyone else who might've seen it (some neighbors are outside looking around after hearing the shots) and how it obviously affected the bunnies. He's standing there with the gun in his hand, lowered to his side, his pudgy belly quivering, and with his free hand he catches the step and sits down, places the gun at his side, and puts his head in his hands and starts sobbing like some kid with no friends, which I'm thinking is a good reason to cry, because ever since Justin left I've been feeling real lonely, sometimes talking to him even though he's not here.

"Coach?" I finally say.

He doesn't move. It's not like I'm going to go over there and hold the guy, but I don't go back inside, either. I turn on some music and drink my coffee and watch him until he eventually collects himself and goes around back and returns with a shovel, scoops up the bunnies, and puts them in a black garbage bag.

"I probably didn't have to shoot them," he says, loud enough for me to hear.

"You did what you had to, I guess," I say.

Then he looks at me as if he's never seen me before, and I'm thinking maybe there's something wrong upstairs, something he can't control. Half the neighbors are on the street, staring at him holding the bag with the dead bunnies in it, his eyes red and puffy and the brilliant sunburst of his gazania plot intact. I'm thinking he just needed to let off some steam, which is something I can understand, because sometimes I'll go down to the basement and punch Justin's old heavy bag until my hands are sore and I'm tired and hungry and don't feel so much rage over what I can't control.

But Coach is still standing there like a statue. I turn off the music and walk across the lawn, carefully stepping over his gazanias. First I put the gun in the back of my jeans. Then I take the bag from his hand.

I say, "Let's go inside, Coach."

"All right, Mac," he says, half here, half out there. "Let's go inside."

SOME FUNKY brown streaks on the walls from all his cigar smoking, clothes thrown over the stair handrail, dirty plates on the coffee table: all the signs of a man alone. I'd never been inside, but I recognize the trophies on his mantel from our championship run, polished to a fine metallic glow. There's a row of framed photographs of his daughter as a baby, a girl, and a teenager, the last one in black and white, an action photo of her in mid-stride, legs stretched like wings, forever suspended above the glow of the studio floor. We used to joke about her—you know, kid stuff, how her flexibility was something to admire. Then there're some taken by his ex-wife, I'm guessing, of the two of them together, one of them at Wequaquet Beach behind some shitty, misshapen sand castles, and another of them trying to catch up to the pack during a three-legged race. Who knew the fat bastard ever smiled?

"I need a maid," he says.

I put down the bag of bunnies, then I pull the gun out of my jeans and empty the clip—something Justin taught me when we went shooting at the reservation last summer—put the clip in my pocket, and place the gun on the end table next to the couch.

Coach carries the bag of bunnies into the kitchen. I wonder why I was so frightened of him when I was in high school. Why just his voice made my nerves coil, or even his slow walk out to the center of the field at the end of practice, twirling and untwirling his whistle around his forefinger, shouting for us to gather around in a circle. "The bullring," he called it. Short but strong, he never blinked, and we waited for him to call a name and then another, and once the match was set, we gathered around the two, pounded our thigh pads twice, and clapped our hands together, slowly at first, then faster, until the sound echoed off the brick walls of the school and Coach blew his whistle and the two in the middle got down in their stances, and Coach blew the whistle again, and like pit bulls they went after each other, trying to stand the other up, to get underneath his pads, raise him off his feet, and drive him into the dirt. Then Coach selected another challenger to take on the winner, and we began to pound our pads again, and sometimes the winner took on four or five of us until he was too tired to win again, unable to survive the entire team's attack, and we said, "Hoo-ah!" for his effort, but he received nothing but a drink of water from the rusted buckets on the sideline, not even Justin, who took on twenty-three of us at the end of one practice, me included, but lost his footing when the rain started and rolled into a chunky second-string tackle, spraining the kid's knee, causing Coach to issue a penalty for chop blocking, saying, "You just cost us fifteen yards, Baker!" I can still see Justin standing there, covered in mud, a divot of dirt and grass stuck in his face mask, as clearly as I can Coach, whistle between his teeth and the rain streaming down his Red Raiders windbreaker, the rest of the team silent, waiting for instruction on what to do next.

The last game of that year we played against the Serpents. They had this beast of a running back with offers from about every Division I school in the country. Despite his scoring three touchdowns in the first half, we were able to keep the score close. Our defense strengthened over the course of the game, and with a minute left, we were down by three on the Serpents' five-yard line, drawing out the clock for one final play. Then Coach, a stalwart traditionalist, surprised us all by calling a trick play, a fumblerooski, a play we had practiced maybe twice since I'd been on varsity. It was fourth down, and we were on the left hash. The obvious play was a pass out to the flat or a pitch to our running back with Justin and me blocking out front. But this was a chance to make history, go undefeated, and take down the mighty Serpents, who were ranked number one in the state. Jamie, our QB, nervously called the play in the huddle. His voice cracked at the *rooski*. It was all up to me: my hands and legs and heart. Jamie snapped the ball and put it on the ground. The running back darted toward the right hash, followed by our offensive line and most of the Serpents, in their sleek black-and-green uniforms. I pulled the other way, picked up the ball, and started toward the end zone. The Serpents' middle linebacker, a mean-looking, spit-spewing fuck, raced after me and threw a forearm up under my chin, knocking me out of bounds right before the goal line. The Serpents ran out on the field pumping their fists in the sky. Mothers threw cardboard hot dog tubs onto the field, and little kids reenacted the now-infamous last play, embellishing how I went down. "A fucking fumblerooski?" one of the fathers shouted as we were walking back to the locker room. I remember Coach in his office while we cleaned out our lockers, sitting there with this kind of grin on his face, like he enjoyed the fact that we lost. But now I think he enjoyed making the call, taking a chance, and even though it didn't work out, he still did it, called a fumblerooski, gave me the opportunity to be a hero, or something like one.

A PHONE rings from somewhere in the living room. I look around but don't see a landline. The ringtone is playing the Velvet Underground's "Sweet Jane." I walk toward the sound and see a corner of the phone underneath one of the couch cushions.

Coach is standing next to me.

"Aren't you going to answer it?" I ask.

"It's not my phone."

"Whose phone is it?"

"My daughter's," he says.

I pick it up and look at the caller ID, a number with an out-of-state area code.

"Leave it," Coach says.

The ringtone stops and I place the phone on the couch, thinking it's time to leave.

Shit's about to get deep.

"They're all wrong numbers," Coach says. "Did you know Toni?"

"She was a few years behind me, wasn't she?"

"I guess that's right. You kids all seemed to be the same age back then."

He picks up the phone, puts it in his pocket, then sits on the couch.

"She was a dancer," he says. "She couldn't stay here and be a dancer, so she went off to New York. I didn't agree with her plans. She was too young, too frivolous. Her mother and I went to visit and she's sitting there on this futon with her leg hanging over the thigh of another girl and they're laughing and kissing each other on the lips, right in front of us. We couldn't understand it. We thought, sure, plenty of queers in those musicals, but our daughter? We refused to see her perform, and once we got back home, I said I couldn't speak to her for a while. Though by now she was an adult and could make her own decisions, I just wasn't going to have a bunch of queers sitting around the tree at Christmas. We went to see Father Macaby about it, but he didn't have any quality advice. He said that God loves all creatures. I guess I felt like Macaby was giving me the runaround about my daughter and what I should do. Then Toni's mother gave in, went to New York, and stayed a week, said it was the best time she'd had in twenty years. All of a sudden she was this different person, younger looking, full of spunk, wanting to go out dancing. She got a tattoo of a hummingbird on the inside of her thigh. I said, 'What the heck is wrong with you? We can't support this kind of thing. She's our daughter. We had plans for her.' 'What plans?' she says. 'You can't predict the future. If you could, you'd be a much more interesting person.' See, I had always imagined I would retire and have Toni nearby, married to a man who treated her right and gave me a couple of grandkids, and Toni's mother and I would sit out on the porch and watch them run around on the lawn, and if they were boys—in my mind they were boys— I'd teach them how to play ball, and those days would be the best days I'd ever see. I couldn't get over it the way her mother could. Later that summer, Toni traveled through Europe in a dance troupe. She sent us letters, in her beautiful handwriting, with these little drawings of sculptures and cathedrals and street scenes. I didn't look at any of them until after she was gone. She was riding one of those motor scooters just outside of Florence, and I can still see her, gliding along the highway, hair whipping around her face, that coy little smile, like she knew something you would never know. A truck carrying a bunch of chickens clipped her wheel and sent her flying down a hillside."

Coach looks at me as if I'm capable of understanding his pain.

What can I do?

So I ask him if he wants a beer or something.

"A beer sounds good," he says.

SOME DAYS are like that.

I'm sitting on the porch with Coach, drinking beer at ten o'clock in the morning. I got this list of clients waiting for their spring cleanups, but the worry of getting to them passes.

We don't talk much at first. We're like two acquaintances that haven't seen each other in a long time. What've you been up to? How's work? How's the house holding up? Have you seen the new cans on that Dwyer girl's mother? It's been hot but not too humid; they say it's going to rain all next week.

One beer after another and I got a nice buzz going. Coach is laughing at his own thoughts, or maybe it's the three kids kicking a can down the street.

"I used to skip school once in a while," Coach says. "I should've skipped more. Those were great days."

"Once in a while, Justin and I would drive to Wareham and get a jug of this misty-looking booze and sit out on the harbor with our heads spinning, coming up with all kinds of plans."

"Boys don't really change that much. But girls do. It blows my mind what they wear around here. I can pretty much see their ass cheeks in those short-shorts; you can't help but notice."

"I hear you, Coach. I mean, I don't have a daughter, but I

can see how it would probably wreck me if I did have a daughter and she was dressed in next to nothing, going out to the Pines with a bunch of gorillas like we used to be."

"You don't have any control over it. If you do end up getting married and having a family, you have to let go of any notion of control."

"I don't feel like I got any control now."

"Somehow it changes. You don't care about what's going on in the world. You don't have time. One day you have long hair and you're listening to Led Zeppelin and talking about revolution and you feel so strong you could eat a box of nails, then the next you're at the barbershop every two weeks and watching what you eat and suddenly you got all these *things* you have to take care of, so you're checking your bank statements every other day, putting money up against your own life in case something happens to you, which you never even thought about when you were young and didn't have all this stuff. I used to feel so light then. Now it's like I got these weights around my ankles."

"You don't look bad for an old guy," I say, trying to bring us up again, "maybe just a little pale. You should get out of the house more."

"You're right. I should get out of the house more. But I get so exhausted."

We went on, sitting there drinking, going back and forth about what it was like when he was a kid and what it was like when I was a kid. And I'll admit that I started to enjoy Coach's company. I had forgotten about the bunnies, or forgiven him, and even smoked one of his cigars, which made me cough and turn green and Coach sat there laughing at me, then smacked my back so hard I felt my spine crack, and I put him in a headlock but he managed to get my free arm and twist it back till it felt like my forearm was about to snap. I was impressed with how strong he was. He could kill me if he wanted.

I'M NOT sure which of us came up with the idea to go for a drive, but somehow it's already dark and we're in my truck, singing "American Girl" at the top of our lungs, Coach beating the top of the cab with his fist. "I love this song," he says. "Wait, pull over here."

"Mrs. Little's house?"

"She used to call me Bug Eyes in school. She'd walk up behind me with her friends and say, 'Stop staring at me, Bug Eyes.'"

Coach stumbles out of the truck and up to the front step, unzips his pants, and takes a piss right there in the open. Once he's finished, he rambles back to the truck and shouts for me to go.

We bull-rush at least a dozen mailboxes along Hingham Street. I hit one post made of marble and mess my shoulder up. One of the mailboxes is in the shape of a sheepdog's head, and Coach is opening and closing the lid, barking for me to take him to Lakeshore. He holds the sheepdog mailbox in his lap. I can barely see the road now that it's dark, and with one headlight out I'm worrying I might get pulled over.

"Don't sweat it," Coach says. "I know all the cops in town."

AT LAKESHORE, you can't see the lake, because the houses are built up so high.

"There was nothing here when I was a kid," Coach says, "just trampled grass and beach. We used to skinny-dip every Friday night."

He tells me to pull up near one of the houses on the lake. I see a FOR SALE sign just left of the pebbled driveway. I can make out a red front door and columns on the porch and windows in the moonlight beneath the gabled roof.

"What are we doing here, Coach?"

"Can't you read the name on the mailbox?" he says. "This is my house."

He says his wife is gone for the week, and the way he's walking now, sure, confident, I can tell this is something he does on a regular basis when she's out of town.

"She's got someone new living here. I don't know who, but there're some men's toiletries in the bathroom and a gym bag full of extra-large clothes and a couple suits hanging in the closet I know for a fact aren't mine. I stole a pair of his shoes last time I was up here. He's got big, specific-sized feet. Size thirteen and a half, wide. Now when I'm out, I'm looking down at men's feet. She's free to do what she wants. It's just the idea of her with another man. You know too much about someone you've been with for so long, and then you're thinking, wait, is she making that little move with her tongue on him?"

"So you want her to be alone?"

"I don't know, Mac. It's complicated. Everything I don't want to know, I want to know. It's like when you see that booth for the smallest woman in the world at the state fair. You don't really want to see her, but something makes you give the guy at the tent a dollar and all of a sudden you're in there looking down at this poor little creature and it makes you sick to your stomach and you're better off not having gone inside at all because now you have this image of her in your head forever, grim, with big silver teeth, lying in a bed of hay, and you keep asking yourself, What the hell possessed me to go in there? Why couldn't I just walk past the tent?"

"I sometimes do stuff like that because I don't feel good about my own situation. I'll be at the McDonald's and I'm done eating, but I'll sit there and watch that real fat guy with all the pockmarks on his face shuffling around behind the counter, calling out orders in his high-pitched voice, and then I get depressed."

Coach bats off the mailbox at the foot of the drive and sticks the sheepdog's head on the post, but it slumps to the side and is barely hanging on. He walks up the drive and turns over a few big rocks, scratches his head, looks up at the sky, at the silver clouds in the dark, asks me if I know how to pick a lock.

I point to a window on the side left open an inch or so, and Coach pushes it up.

"Go on, get up there," he says.

Coach holds out his cupped hands and I step up and he pushes from underneath and I grab hold of the window ledge, pull myself up, and worm forward in the dark, feeling a soft carpet beneath me. Then Coach gives my feet a shove and I tumble into the room. My knee cracks against something hard.

"Open the front door, Mac," he says.

I get up and find a light switch and look back at the carefully made bed and the throw pillows on top and the framed painting of an empty beach chair and a few floating seagulls against the pink sky of dusk. It smells like lavender, a healthy, middle-aged scent I once smelled on a woman's neck when we were drunk and in my truck and she kept saying she was old enough to be my mother.

My hand runs along the wall of the hallway, toward the dim light left on in the living room, shining a foot ahead of the front door, where through the side windows I see Coach's bug eyes and grape head peering in impatiently.

"Home sweet home," he says when I open the door.

Coach goes through the refrigerator and pulls out bags of deli meat and mustard and nods toward a cabinet, where there's a loaf of bread.

"She's not starving, that's for sure," he says.

I'm thinking, "How did I end up here?" I remember the bunnies and Coach on the doorstep with the gun in his hand and his sad, dirty living room. Now everything's reversed—everything's clean and neat and orderly. There's no water mark in the sink, I notice, and then I puke in it after eating half the sandwich Coach made for me.

I wash my hands and face and slurp a handful of water, gargle and spit. Coach is upstairs. I can hear his heavy footsteps above me. Out the window above the sink, the lake looks like a dark-purple sky. On the inside ledge is a tiny framed poem that reads:

> Mommy and Daddy are in the trees
> Making sounds like little bees
> When they fall down I won't frown
> I'll put Band-Aids on their knees

Coach is standing in the hallway with no shirt on, in a pair of tight swimming trunks, the veins on his legs coiled and popping out of his skin.

"Toni wrote that in the second grade," he says. "Let's take a dip."

"I don't know, Coach," I say.

"Don't be such a pussy. It's refreshing."

Near sober from puking my guts out, I'm back to feeling bad about Coach, wanting him to feel good, so I strip down to my boxers and we walk out on the dock and he dives into the lake, hollers out that it's cold, man, it's cold, and I jump in after him and we swim out toward the circle of light shining like a spotlight on just this one place in all the world.

Coach goes underwater, comes up spitting like a seal, his thin hair matted down on the sides of his head. I can see the boyish face he grew up with, his big eyes and tiny ears and plump lips, bobbing in the water like a buoy that's been out here forever.

My body warms up and I'm floating on my back, kicking my feet beneath the surface of the lake, feeling a sense of freedom, of safety, of calm. I turn over and slither below and come up with my ears plugged, squeezing my nose and blowing hard until they pop. I look around for Coach, but he's gone.

I call out, "Coach, Coach," turning around in the water, paddling my hands and feet, until I see his arms flailing, splashing. I swim out and take his heavy body on my shoulder and wade toward the dock. Now it's a matter of lifting him up onto the wooden planks. I ease up onto the dock and dig my hand into the slab of skin on the back of his neck. I've got so much adrenaline that Coach feels almost weightless. I pull him out of the water as easy as a panfish and roll him over onto his back. His eyes are closed and his cheeks puffed out. I can't tell if he's breathing. I tilt his head up and move close to his pudgy lips, pry them open with my fingers, and blow hard into his mouth until he spurts up water and I'm able to ease him over on his side.

He's squirming and coughing, shaking his head like an old dog gone deaf.

Eventually he gets up and stands there on the dock, his belly hanging out over his trunks and this empty look on his face.

"I've been swimming this lake all my life," he says.

I put a towel around his shoulders, but he doesn't move, just stands there shivering, water dripping down his legs.

I help him across the dock to the lawn, where we sit in a couple of Adirondack chairs, where his ex-wife and her XL lover must sit. We're quiet, Coach looking out at the lake that's always been there, before the houses, before us, the wind cool on my skin and the light of dawn slowly blending into the sky.

IN THE deep humid morning, I pull up to the small house in the Heights, and Coach holds out his hand for me to shake it.

"You're all right, Mac," he says.

His not thanking me is a sign of respect, a pact between men. But I know he knows things are different now.

Next day I don't get up till noon. I make a pot of coffee and sit out on the porch, listening to music as I go over the schedule. I got a hell of a lot of jobs to get to, a hell of a lot of angry voice mails.

Another day, and who knows what to expect?

Coach is outside filling the bird feeders. He salutes me. Then he gets out the hose and waters his gazanias. Those beautiful gazanias blazing, unharmed.

NEVER SO SWEET

~~~

MY UNCLE NEVER did a bad thing to anybody, but one day while he was on his front porch eating an ice-cream cone, two men pushed him inside, tied his hands and feet, robbed his house, and shot him in the head. He was in a coma for a week. I was nine years old, and my father took me to see him that first Saturday he was in the hospital. I remember his forehead was wrapped up and someone had placed a straw hat on his head. On the television mounted to the far wall, a hefty Italian woman stirred a pot of tomato sauce.

"How can he watch television when he's asleep?" I asked my father.

We heard the toilet flush and out walked Tutti, my uncle's girlfriend.

"How's he look?" she said, gesturing to the hat.

"Like a dead farmer," my father said.

"Whoa, I just had déjà vu," Tutti said, her hand at her chest.

"Any news?" my father asked.

"Nothing. Absolutely nothing." She could tell my father was unhappy about the hat. "This is only to keep me entertained. I've been here for hours. I didn't mean anything by it." She took the hat off his head and put it on. She looked pretty.

"What are you two doing this afternoon?" she asked.

"We didn't have anything planned other than to visit the hospital. Maybe we'll go down to the beach for a little while. Right, bud?"

My father patted me on the back.

"I would just love it if I could come with you."

"What if he wakes up?" I said.

"He won't wake up while we're at the beach," Tutti said.

Tutti was from Ottawa. She didn't live with my uncle. At that time, she had a condo in Naples, Florida, provided for her by another lover, a wealthy man who sold Mercedes-Benzes and turned over foreclosed houses. She was in her mid-forties and married to her high school boyfriend, Thomas, who managed a Tim Hortons donut shop. She flew to Canada in the summers and stayed with him for a month or two and then flew to Boston to be with my uncle in his little cottage near the beach in Wequaquet. Her lover in Florida unknowingly paid for everything. With him, Tutti pretended to be one of the top interior decorators in the world. She had phony business cards and a clientele of rich-sounding names like Thurston Bell and Conner Macintosh. I thought she was beautiful, but I didn't really know what beauty was. My mother died when I was three; she was an artist, and her paintings hung in our house. There is one of a cathedral in Mexico that I particularly like and that I have with me still. The cathedral is off to the side of a dirt road. The viewer stands on the road, considering whether or not to enter the cathedral. She died from a brain embolism. My father and I were asleep when it happened. "She died dreaming," my father used to say. In photographs she was still and easy to forget. But Tutti moved. Her breasts bounced. Her skin changed colors. Her hair glowed in sunlight.

On the way to the beach, my father stopped for coffee and bought me an orange juice and a sugared jelly donut. Tutti sat in the backseat, smoking. I had offered her the front seat, but she said she wanted to stretch her legs.

"You're lucky you weren't here when it happened," my father said to her.

"I know it. And the funny part is—well, not funny really but fortunate, for me—is that I had planned on being here last week but your brother called and said he wasn't feeling well and I should wait a few days before I came down. Maybe he knew something was going to happen."

"He ate a bad clam," my father said. "Where are you staying?"

"I'd planned on the cottage, but I guess the cops are still investigating."

"You can stay with us," I said, and glanced at my father.

"That would be perfect. All the motels in this town smell like seafood."

I laughed at this, but I don't know why. Tutti was odd, and back then I laughed at anything that seemed odd. It was a problem. My father had been depressed ever since my mother died, and maybe before. But I was always laughing.

At the beach, Tutti went into the women's restroom carrying an oversize leopard-print bag. My father and I changed into our bathing suits. We waited for Tutti. The sand was hot under my feet. I dug them in where it was cooler. Tutti was wearing a green polka-dot bikini. There were puffs of hair under her arms, a curled line below her navel, and coils around her calves. Her pubic hair webbed out from beneath her bottoms. She caught me staring and winked.

My father seemed impressed. He had always believed in keeping everything natural. As an architect, he melded the tough peninsular landscape with each house he drew up in his specs. We lived in a classic Greek colonial with cherrywood finish and a mahogany deck. In the winter, we heated the house with a wood-burning stove and fireplace. We bathed three times a week to conserve water. When we went to the beach, he never brought towels or chairs or something to read. He swam for about twenty minutes, then lay down so the sand spackled his entire body. I didn't like the feeling and would run along the shore until I was dry, then sit cross-legged watching the seagulls hover above families with picnic lunches.

"You want to play shark, bud?" my father asked me.

"What's shark?" Tutti said.

"Just a game."

"I want to play, too."

We jogged down to the shore. I stopped at the water's edge, choosing to ease myself in. My father dove straight ahead, the oncoming wave a portal from one world to the next. Tutti knelt down and put her palms on top of the water. Then she stood and faced me, lowered her arms behind her head, arched her torso, and sprung into the water. I was last in and farthest away from my father. I swam out to where I couldn't put my feet down and moved my arms as hard as I could, pretending I was a bigger shark or some sea monster sharks feared. My father went under again and breached the surface with his palms pressed together, his fingers forming the frightening fin. In the North Atlantic, human bodies are invisible underwater. I sensed movement, and that's what made the game fun. When my father caught me, he picked me up on his shoulders and flung me back into the water. I crashed awkwardly, never fully prepared, swallowing and spitting seawater. Tutti burst out laughing. My father came for her next. But he treated her capture differently. He picked her up and carried her to the shore, as though he wasn't sure what he had found.

Tutti lay on her stomach and undid the knot on her bikini top. A faint white line ran across her back. Her hair was darker from the water and speckled with sand. She brought it around her shoulder, squeezed it like a wet rag, and flung it back. She put her hands on her upper arms and rested her chin just inside her left shoulder. She looked at us.

"This is all I've ever wanted from life," she said.

My father gave me a dollar to buy some candy at the snack bar. Full of sugar, I went off to play Wiffle ball with a group of boys near the volleyball nets. The sky was clear. There was a slight breeze. I could see everything.

Later, we lingered at the edge of the shore, silent, listening. There is a time when everyone begins to depart from the beach, as though the beach itself urges them to go, casts them out gently in the falling light, so it can be alone. Then the beach becomes a different place altogether. You can hear the water as well as the internal rhythms of the body. The sun moves downward on an arc. The moon, a phantom, appears.

We drove back to the hospital. This time, Tutti sat up front. I rolled down the window and put my hand out, let the wind push it back. The inside of the car smelled like the sea.

The sheets under my uncle's body were whiter than before. Tutti kissed his cheek.

"They'll trim his beard for him, won't they?" she asked my father.

"I'm sure."

"To be alive and not know it," she said.

We sat in the room until visiting hours were over. Tutti ripped a page out of a magazine and showed me how to make a swan. My father sat near the window with one leg crossed over the other.

The rain started that night and carried into the next day. Tutti and my father stayed up late and played cards and smoked pot. Later, she read his palms.

"All the pain in your life has passed," she said. "See where these lines cross at the bottom? They never cross again."

"Maybe it's the other way around," my father said.

"No. We don't care so much about pain when we're old."

"Do me," I said.

She held my hand in hers and turned it slowly. I felt it was something separate from my body. She had long fingernails, pointed at the tips. She traced the lines in my palm with the end of her ring finger.

"Yours is different than your father's," she said. She seemed concerned. I started to take my hand away. "No, it's okay. Your lines branch out into these three paths. I think it means there will be three distinct periods in your life. Now you are young and learning. Later you will be successful and have a lovely wife and healthy children. Then you will live comfortably, even if the world is falling apart all around you in your old age."

"Sounds horrifying," my father said.

"Oh, don't," Tutti said.

"I mean, we all need to suffer a little. You don't want to fill his head with this idea that there won't be any pain in his life." He turned to me. "Bad things will happen. They have to. They're good for you, anyway."

Then he told me to get some sleep. My father let Tutti have his bed. He said he would sleep on the couch.

In the summer, there was no limit on how much time I could spend awake. I tried to fold a piece of paper into a swan like Tutti had showed me. I arranged my music cassettes in alphabetical order. I went under the bed and imagined what it would be like to be buried alive. I entertained the Wimbles and the Wobbles, two factions of planetary warriors, who, in their battle for universal domination, found themselves floating aimlessly in the ether, waiting for me to decide their fates.

Then I heard the bed in my father's room creaking. My father had fits of restlessness and bad dreams. His doctor had given him pills to help him sleep, and it'd been a while since I'd heard any noise from his room during the night. I went out to the living room and saw that the blanket was spread open on the couch and my father was not there. I heard Tutti moan and the bed creak. Then I heard my father get up and use the bathroom.

THE NEXT day, my uncle died. It happened early that morning. A series of muffled cries from the living room reached me in my sleep and, like a remnant from a dream, a sort of soft rain, I woke and went downstairs to find Tutti with her head on my father's knee. She seemed smaller than before, like a sister only a few years older than me. My father stared straight ahead, an arm across her shoulders, as though he were driving somewhere.

Later that afternoon, I heard Tutti on the phone in the kitchen. She was whispering, but her voice was so high-pitched that even a whisper was sharp and clear.

"You didn't have anything to do with this, did you?" she said.

"He was harmless. It was all me. I don't know why I do these things."

I could hear her whimpering now. I peeked out and saw her sitting on a stool at the kitchen counter, her shoulders slumped forward, her face cocked to the side with her left hand hovering over the receiver.

"I do love you. . . . No I don't think you're a fool. . . . Oh, God."

My legs were trembling; whatever was in my gut had poured down into them.

My father entered the kitchen from the sunroom, where he often read in the late afternoon.

Quickly, Tutti's voice changed. "Oh, yes, yes, it's been beautiful here, Mother."

I watched my father give Tutti a kiss on the forehead. She covered the receiver.

"I'll only be another minute."

"Don't be a snoop," my father said, and pinched my nose as he passed by on his way into the living room.

I KEPT quiet about what I'd heard. I felt sick, the kind of sick you feel right before you're about to puke. I went with my father to the funeral home and to the places he had in mind to spread his brother's ashes. They had a sister living in Amsterdam, who my father kept trying to reach. He hadn't spoken to her in ten years.

I didn't know my uncle very well. I really didn't know anyone at that age, and only now when I look back have I come to the conclusion that the entire history of my family is a sort of fiction, misunderstood by me alone. According to my father, my uncle was a spiritual man. Whether people thought he was a peacenik or hippie didn't matter. He'd been touched, as they say, by some kind of light. That's what I remember about him. His eyes glowed in the same way a woman's does the moment before they begin to well up.

"I missed the lottery, but your uncle didn't," my father said.

We were driving to collect my uncle's ashes. Tutti was with us. I tried not to look at her, but it was impossible; I kept seeing her even when I closed my eyes.

"Lucky for him," my father went on, "he was a terrible shot. He was sent to Germany, where he worked as a transition agent for soldiers heading back to the world, as they called it then. No one liked him very much until he started dealing hash. He used to hollow out Roman candles and stuff it in the center so the dogs couldn't smell it. But one night he got busted crossing the French border. 'Too many candles for a grown man,' the officer said. He was discharged.

"When he returned, he had all these ideas about the cosmos. He said that this life he'd been living was just one of many lives and that he no longer feared death, because this was only one part of him, and there were other parts out in the universe that he had yet to experience. Maybe I'm not explaining it well. What I remember is that he was sincere about these other lives he was living. Mirror lives, he called them."

"So like different versions of ourselves?" I asked.

"That's exactly right," Tutti said, her voice a pinprick in my ear.

"When I think about it," my father said, "he never worried about anything. Sometimes that infuriated me and sometimes it made me envious."

We were heading out to Chatham, on Cape Cod, a town that looks the same now as it did then and as it did when my father was a boy: cottages scattered along the coast, an old-style pump-handle gas station, seafood shacks, and cluttered used-book stores.

"I think he would've liked to have his ashes spread out here. This way, the ocean can take him in all different directions."

Tutti put her head in her hands and began to cry. My father looked at me somberly. I didn't feel scared. It was something else, something I recognized a few years later. That was the first and only time I ever pitied him.

THE MEN who shot my uncle came from Fall River. They were brothers in their mid-thirties, failed fishermen who, like many in those decaying towns along the Eastern Seaboard, had been relegated to car-repair work or boat cleaning but, shunning that sort of labor, took to robbing houses in the alcoves where a handful of wealthy holdovers from a once-prosperous time still lived. Their name was Bodfish. They'd both spent time in prison but not for the same crimes. Carey, the older brother, did five years in Walpole for auto theft, and Stephen did fifteen months in Dedham for unarmed robbery. It wasn't clear when the two decided to become killers. It was Carey Bodfish who'd fired the gun.

Either way, they weren't very good at killing, or stealing. They left their fingerprints all over the cottage, and one of the brothers had used the toilet, forgetting to flush. With their profiles already on record, police raided their vacated apartment, discovering some of the stolen goods my father had reported missing: a twelve-speed mountain bike, my grandfather's stamp collection, a bronzed statue of Miles Davis, a Les Paul electric guitar, and a worthless reproduction of a Mayan mask that, nevertheless, meant a great deal to my uncle because he'd watched a man in Morelia create it from a block of wood. Except for the stamps, which my father kept in a safe-deposit box in case we ever needed to sell them, the rest of my uncle's things were stored in the garage, still sealed as evidence. Years later, when I graduated from college, he asked if I wanted anything from the house for my apartment in Boston, and I took the mask and the statue of Miles Davis and the electric guitar, though I never learned to play.

The Bodfish brothers were mean-looking black-eyed Irishmen. All through the investigation, trial, and sentencing, they didn't mention any names. They were given life in prison without parole. In the papers they were known as *The Statue Brothers*, because their faces never changed in the courtroom. If you still read the paper closely, which I tend to do, you might've seen a brief blurb in the Metro section of the *Globe* about Carey Bodfish dying of lymphoma. He was fifty-seven years old, the same age my father was when he passed away three months ago.

"I WANT you to know everything," Tutti said on the night of my father's wake, twenty years after my uncle died, in the unusual dark of a June evening. "I mean, none of it really makes sense. You start trying to tell your life story and you realize how random it all is. That's why I don't like novels or movies. Everything's so neatly condensed. But, still, I think it's important you know the truth."

Those next few weeks after we spread my uncle's ashes, Tutti stayed with us. She went shopping and made big, hearty meals of meat and potato stew, steak tips, and baked cod. She claimed her cooking acumen from growing up as the child of a single father. Her mother had been a professor of Eastern religions and fell in love with a graduate student from Ghana.

The two ran off together and left Tutti and her father alone. Soon they moved out to the countryside, to a decaying farmhouse where her father's grandparents had once lived. Her father got the farm running again and bought two cows and a dozen hens. Tutti learned to cook. She enjoyed watching her father eat.

I SPENT the rest of that summer out of the house. Sometimes I'd hook up with Ryan or Sean and we'd talk about stealing candy from the store on Southbay or make like we were trying to break the windows of the old Tradewinds Hotel. One day I threw a rock as hard as I could, which was a no-no because we had an unspoken agreement that we weren't actually going to commit crimes, only talk about committing them, and Ryan and Sean took off, and an alarm sounded, and I ran in the other direction. Ryan and Sean didn't come to the meeting spot anymore, and I was alone.

Sometimes I'd cruise on my bike along the coastal trails that wound past Wequaquet Harbor into the port and up the cliffside properties where rich folks posted No TRESPASSING signs along the street, and reflected in whose wide, floor-length windows I could see what they saw as they drank their morning coffee: the fog low and thick above the ocean, the fishing boats easing through the gray. I climbed the hill to the country club, where I collected golf balls in the gullies and marshes and resold them outside the club's entrance for a quarter apiece. Later, I swam in the ocean and sat under the Wequaquet Bridge with a chicken salad sandwich, watching the silver-bellied fish shoot up from the river. I rode to the gas station and put air in my tires. In the insect hum of noon, I playacted tragic death scenes in the swampland behind the Taylors' burned-out house.

Covered in filth, eaten by mosquitoes, tired and wet and hungry, I returned home, washed in the tub, and ate at the table with my father and Tutti, who by then had begun to love and care for each other. In the soft laughter that followed an unintentional burp, the playful smack on the hand when my father attempted to serve himself, the way they spoke each other's names like cherished objects, I became invisible and so further penetrated the fantastical and unexplainable worlds that hung in my brain.

A month or so after my uncle's murder, during a night when I had been so lost in a struggle between the Wimbles and the Wobbles, I was struck by the greatest fear I'd ever known, the fear that there is nothing beyond the universe. That we were contained by an infinite darkness was inconceivable to me, and this single, piercing thought caused me to break out in a fit of screams.

Though I remember screaming, I don't remember how long I went on for, as is the case when, on occasion, I find myself in the kitchen or living room, suddenly overwhelmed by a flash of white, a thought, a memory of a voice or smell I realize I have missed for so long. Only now it is my wife who comes to me and holds me and kisses my neck and cheek and takes my hand in hers and sits by my side until I'm spent, relieved of whatever force has overtaken me. If ever I was scared when I was a boy, my father would turn on a light and sit beside me reading a book until I fell back asleep. That night, though, it was Tutti who came to my room.

I was sitting up in bed with my head between my knees. She switched on the bedside lamp and sat down. She was a little drunk, I could tell, smiling at me, at my eyes peeking out at her.

"It's just me," she said, and laughed brightly, her eyes sparkling in the soft lamplight.

I was nervous with her so close, as if I knew what she was really capable of. But I was also tired and afraid of something bigger than the two of us, and I acquiesced to her easy voice and gentle smile.

She took my head in her hands and brought it out of the small hole I had created between my knees, as an archaeologist might lift a petrified skull from the earth, guiding me toward the pillow, not wanting to shake up any more of the thoughts in my head.

Tutti lay down beside me and turned her head. Her breath smelled of wine and cigarettes and cake, a silent midnight snack saved from that night when she and my father had gone to Alberto's to give her a break from cooking. I felt the warmth of her palm hovering an inch above my chest. Her fingers drifted back and forth like wheatgrass.

"I want you to say these things with me," she said, her voice unchanging. "First, I'll go. Then you repeat what I've said. Okay?"

I nodded. Sweat gathered in a shallow pool at the base of my neck.

"I am not a boy," she said.

I was silent. I didn't understand.

"Say it, sweetie. You'll feel better. Think of this as a departure from yourself." She repeated, "I am not a boy."

"I am not a boy," I said quietly, somewhat embarrassed.

"I am not a son."

"I am not a son."

"Good," she said, continuing to draw her fingers in a gentle swoosh down the middle of my chest. "Relax, now. Listen to your voice.

"I live nowhere."

"I live nowhere."

"I want nothing."

"I want nothing."

"I need nothing."

"I need nothing."

"I am never awake or asleep."

"I am never awake or asleep."

"I have no eyes, no ears, no mouth, no body."

"I have no eyes, no ears, no mouth, no body."

"I am nothing I know."

"I am nothing I know."

"I am an unchanging, eternal being."

"I am an unchanging, eternal being."

"I was never born, and I will never die."

"I was never born, and I will never die."

It seemed like listening and repeating what I had heard did more to soothe me than what was actually said.

MY FATHER did seem happier, though I believe it had more to do with not being alone than with Tutti's mantras and meditations. He would jog in the mornings, stretching beforehand in the kitchen, a sweatband tight around his head guarding the thin black curls of his hair. He exhaled in quick bursts just before darting out the door. I remember the smell of new sweat, the stain on his shirtfront like some kind of godhead, and the veins along his arms uprooted as he drank a large glass of water.

That fall, I began middle school. I would leave the house early and ride my bike past the river and up a long, winding hill that opened onto a pleasant street with small cottages guarded by looming maple trees, then through the cemetery where my mother was buried, wondering, How is it where you are? Past Big Tim's Auto Emporium and down Isaac Road, where children in buses screamed to me from the windows en route to that hideous, flat Y-shaped building that was Wequaquet Middle. With the exception of my desire to see the young teaching assistant in my social sciences class, Ms. Cone, naked, nothing from the time spent there has stayed with me.

But at home I was beginning to learn how love can be born from violence and misery and odd circumstances. Tutti had left for a weekend. As my father and I played cribbage in the kitchen, a sudden uproar of chirping birds caused his hand to tremble over the board. I can believe now that Tutti possessed a certain power over men, as the greatest women often do, that when that power takes hold we are no longer controlled by our pasts, the places in which we live, the people we know or have known, or the public spectacle of sport and politics, which at that time consisted mainly of disarming and killing a mustachioed man in a beret, from a country whose name sounded like a deathly cough. Tutti consumed my father. I understood that a woman could do this to a man, could strip away all misfortune and pain, leaving us even more naked and vulnerable.

When she returned, Tutti brought with her two large suitcases full of clothes, a dozen books on New Age spirituality, certain childhood possessions she felt she could not live without, and word that she had finally divorced Thomas, who, in a vain attempt to rekindle their marriage, had brought Tutti to a ski resort outside Montreal.

The Wimbles and Wobbles had signed a ceasefire and I was bored. I sat at the top of the stairs and listened to Tutti explain herself.

"I let him make love to me," I heard her say. "But then, halfway through it, he stopped and said, 'It's over, isn't it?' He could tell by the way my body felt. Then he cried. All night he cried. I went out and hiked up to the empty ski lifts and sat in one of the chairs for so long I fell asleep. A woman from the hotel woke me and said it was going to get cold and they didn't want to be liable if I were to get sick. When I went back to the room, Thomas was gone. He'd packed and left and put some money on the dresser as though I were a prostitute. I guess I deserved to feel that way, but I only felt sad for him. I want good things for Thomas. He loved me."

The three of us had slowly acclimated to the unusual trajectories that had brought us together. My uncle's death seemed so long ago. We believed we were a family, that whatever was past was past, and moving forward through each small yet significant change to the house's interior—the kitchen painted red, the living room rearranged, the dusty trinkets my mother had collected boxed away and replaced with thick, clean-smelling candles—we became comfortable with the rituals of life that included Tutti. She made lunch for me on weekday mornings, set a wonderful spread for Thanksgiving and Christmas, and, because I grew three inches that year, took me to the Atrium in Braintree and bought me new clothes.

We weren't without our struggles, though. This was during the last housing crunch, and my father's company hadn't sold a new home since the summer. Local businesses were yielding to corporate buyouts, and Wequaquet began to resemble the thousands of towns and suburbs across the country unable to hold out through the crisis. Electronics stores and clothing outlets and fast-food joints I had only seen in the city were popping up all over our small town.

Seagulls perch on the gabled entrances, swooping down to peck at the strewn garbage in the sandy parking lots. But this is the present, on a sad, beguiling drive through my old town, kids dicking around in their W-printed letter jackets, with no sense of the future, as we pass MegaWorld on our way toward the beachfront, unchanged and drenched in sunlight; my wife in her retro green one-piece bathing suit; we, like any other tourists, down for Labor Day weekend, lying on the same beach under the same sky listening to the same waves my father and mother and childhood self once did. I can see them in the pockets of unclaimed sand.

THROUGH THE spring and into the following summer, my father was out of work. He picked up odd jobs. He mowed lawns, built decks, and repainted some of the houses he had designed. When I was off from school, I worked with him. I cannot remember a time when I felt as comfortable with my father: his big, callused hands holding me up from the ladder so that I could sweep out the gutters; stripping and priming and painting the long wooden fence along Farm Acres Road; spreading the thick, sour-smelling mulch around the shrubs and flower beds of those large houses on the water; and in the cool summer afternoon, listening to sports radio, packing up our tools, and coiling the extension cords, the sweat dried into our shirts, stinking and spent but alive, sensing the tightening of the muscles in my forearms and chest, and the windows rolled down on the ride home, listening to the air rush by, the sun an orange disc descending over the town, light moving through us, giving way to night.

I recall feeling present, without worry, free. But I'm not sure that was the case. Or maybe it's that I've lived awhile now and have never been able to get back to that feeling. Or it could be that my memory has tricked me into believing that at one time I lived between the drastic highs and lows that come with each passing day. Sometimes I feel so overjoyed I could break down in tears, so enraged I could smash my fist through a window.

My tendons and muscles and nerves stretch tight as newly strung guitar strings, until somebody, dead or alive, plucks an off chord, sending a shiver throughout my body.

Last February, I lost a tooth in a fistfight outside a bar. I wasn't very drunk. There was just something about the place, the music, the people—this sense of dread and fatigue, a general apathy to the living world—and without provocation I decked a sorry-looking man who was sitting by himself in the barroom corner. We were thrown out onto the street and a crowd gathered. The man was a quick and thoughtful fighter. I must have swung low and mistakenly brought my body forward, exposing the right side of my face, which he struck with the hammer-like bone of his elbow, sending an expensively crowned molar flying into the snow. How pathetic it was to be searching out there in the unplowed street for my tooth. Though, as I dug my hands into the soft, cold powder, I felt something close to that sense of freedom I knew when I was a boy.

MAYBE IT'S because that time in my life was so short and strange that I think about it often. I dress Tutti in short-shorts and a tight-fitting top and my father in worn khakis and a polo shirt. We eat fried seafood out on the boat at Baxter's Landing, throw French fries to the seagulls, and watch the schooners and sailboats drift in the harbor. My father has his arm around Tutti's waist, her head on his shoulder, and we stand by as the old Chevrolets file down Main Street, drivers honking their horns, repositioning the small, newly washed mirrors as their passengers wave to us.

When we returned home from one of these late-summer afternoons, there was a cream-colored Mercedes parked in the driveway. Tutti grabbed hold of my father's arm and steered the car away from the house. "Keep driving! Keep driving!" she shouted. "Please!" My father braked and the engine stuttered; then, with a shot of gas, the car burst ahead.

When you're a kid, a year can feel as long as a decade, and I had mostly forgotten about the man from Florida, what I imagined to be his role in my uncle's death, even the guilt I had felt so strongly after hearing Tutti speak to him on the phone. But it all came rushing back to me then.

What my father said then was, "Oh, fuck this," but what he was really saying was something along the lines of, I knew nothing could be so good. And even before we went back to the house, he had given up on Tutti.

"What are you doing?" Tutti shouted. "Are you crazy or something?"

"That's my house. If someone's in there, then I'm going to throw him out."

"He has guns," Tutti said, her voice lowering, but not enough to keep me from hearing.

"Well if he wanted to kill you, he would've done it a long time ago. Now, if he's come for me, at least there'll be witnesses."

It was instantly clear what was going on.

My father's view of his own mortality put me over the edge. I felt as though I were calling out to him from the bottom of a well. "Please, Dad, listen to her."

"Don't worry, bud," he said with certainty. "We'll be fine."

I heard everything as my father approached the front door. Summer afternoons have an eerie music about them, of swarming insects, water seeping from the bottoms of exposed air conditioners, the buzz of charging electricity through hanging telephone wires. He guarded himself by pulling his left arm across his chest and lowering his shoulder, as though he were drawing a cape over his body, as though he were the assailant, set to unmask himself to an unassuming victim. And although I was afraid, what good did meditation do any of us at that moment? We could not detach from our bodies.

Tutti ran after my father. I jumped out of the car and cowered near the front tire. When my father entered the house, my legs went numb and my face burned hot. I crept up to the door and swiftly moved inside, looking left and right; nothing had been damaged. The house was filled with the foreign scent of strong cologne.

My father was standing by the bathroom door in the hallway. Tutti, opposite him, saw me and put her finger to her lips. The toilet flushed and the man inside the bathroom coughed wickedly, cropping up a wad of phlegm from his throat.

"By God," the man said, and opened the door.

My father struck him in the side of the head and the man stumbled sideways into Tutti's arms. Tutti tried to hold him up, but his weight was in his belly and he slipped from her arms. My father had split some kind of polyp on the man's earlobe, and the blood was streaming down his neck. His eyes were closed and his left arm was stretched out, flailing like a fish on a dock.

"He's an old man," Tutti said. "You didn't have to hit him like that."

"He'll be fine," my father said. "Don't you think he'll be fine?" He bent down and looked at the man, turned and stared at me with eyes still wide, buzzing from the thrill of sudden violence.

"Oh, poor Rudy," Tutti said.

"Poor Rudy?" my father cried. "The man broke into my house. And Rudy? Rudy and Tutti? What a pair!"

Stroking Rudy's face, Tutti asked me to go to the kitchen and pour him a glass of water. I could hear her and my father arguing: She wanted to get Rudy to a hospital, and my father refused, saying he was going to call the police. I hoped for Rudy to wake up. Adults in vulnerable positions made me nervous. This is why children cannot stand to see their parents asleep.

I returned with the water and handed it to Tutti. She had Rudy propped up in her lap now. His eyelids rose slightly and Tutti put the glass to his lips.

"Drink this," she said.

As he drank, he began to cough, and the water shot from his mouth and dribbled down his chin.

"Ah!" he cried.

"Help him up," Tutti said to my father.

"Christ almighty," my father said, and put his arms up under Rudy's shoulders and pulled him to his feet. He slung Rudy's arm over his neck and brought him to the couch. Tutti fluffed up a pillow, and together they laid Rudy down.

Except for the bloodied ear, he was a good-looking older man. He had straight, strawberry-blond hair combed neatly away from his brow and stuck in this position by some kind of mousse—none of it moved from the punch or the fall. He was wearing blue khaki shorts and an expensive-looking yellow shirt. His limbs were weirdly thin in comparison to his hard, curved belly. There was a scar along his left knee, and his legs were strikingly hairless. His belt had tiny sailboats printed on it.

Tutti sat beside him with a towel and a bowl of water. She dampened the towel and cleaned the dried blood away from his ear and neck.

My father stood above us all, looking down as though assessing a sorry litter of dogs he very well knew no one was going to want.

"Okay, then. What's this all about?" he said.

Tutti put the end of the towel in the bowl. The water turned a cloudy red.

"I was sitting out there for a while, hoping to see Tutti, and then I just figured I'd try the door because I drove all the way here and it seemed childish to wait in the car. The door was open. How wonderfully secure you all feel in these old New England towns. This is quite a place. I can see Tutti's influence."

"Right. Right. We live together. How's that affect you?"

"I love her. I've loved her for a long time now, and I don't think it's a mystery that I need someone to take care of me."

"Is that what love is?" my father said, pacing. "Caretaking? Is that what you want, Tutti? You want to make his meals and take him for walks and wipe his ass?"

"Not in front of him," Tutti said, nodding toward me. Her voice was steady and confident. She lived to make momentous choices.

"Listen, baby," Rudy said. "I'm not doing too well. I've got a tumor in my noggin. They say it could be anywhere from three months to a year, but that's with treatment. I don't want to spend the rest of my life in a hospital bed. I'm going out on the boat. I'm sailing to Cape Town. People have always told me it's the most beautiful place on earth, and if I make it there, well, what better place to die in than the most beautiful one? So, what I'm asking is, will you come with me?"

My father and I waited for Tutti to answer, mystified by this man's brashness.

Tutti looked at my father, who stood now with his arms across his chest, then back to Rudy. We were all boys, all the same to her, all wanting and waiting. My father and Rudy were as silent as closed doors, which, if opened, would unveil to her an entirely new life.

"Can't we talk about this in the morning?" she said. "I need some time to think."

"And what do we do with him?" my father said.

"We can't just kick him out now."

My father ran his hand through his hair. His eye twitched. You could tell he didn't want to be so decent.

THAT NIGHT, no one but Rudy slept. Tutti stayed in the bedroom, while my father read in the kitchen. I sat in my room with the lights on and finally went downstairs when I sensed the uneasiness throughout the house.

I took the cribbage board out and asked my father if he wanted to play.

"Not tonight, bud," he said, and went back to looking at the real estate section of the paper. His eyes weren't moving.

Later that night, the Wimbles broke the ceasefire and advanced fearlessly toward the barricade set up by the Wobbles, blasting away the walls with advanced weaponry. During their last intergalactic battle, the Great Leaders of both factions met face-to-face on a distant planet, where they could see the fighting millions of light-years away. First they dined and reflected on what had brought them to this point. Then, understanding that any sort of peace was futile, they had their servants dress them in the dated garb of earthly soldiers, drew their swords, and, with a fateful nod, positioned themselves for a final battle. As they approached each other, I heard Tutti sobbing in the bedroom.

"Oh, I have to," she cried.

And my father's voice: "No, you don't. Don't you see that you have a good thing here? You're going to throw it all away if you leave."

"But imagine if—"

"No," my father shouted. "Don't bring my wife into this."

"But just imagine."

I went downstairs and into the living room. Rudy was still asleep on the couch. I touched his face lightly, feeling the sharp edges of his unshaved chin. His eyes opened and he grabbed my wrist.

"Who are you?" he said.

I whacked him in the mouth with my free hand. He moaned and sneezed and, sitting up, called for Tutti through his hands with a muffled cry.

"I knew it was a bad idea to have him here," my father said, coming up behind me.

"What did you do, sweetie?" Tutti said to me. I realized that I was standing there with my hand still bunched up in a fist.

Tutti inspected his lip and cradled the old man's head in her arms.

"We have to go," she said, and helped Rudy to his feet.

For the first time she looked like an ugly woman to me.

My father had a faint smile on his face. I had imparted a kind of justice for him, yet I didn't feel good about what I had done. I felt that I had to do something more. I had to tell my father what I knew, that Rudy was responsible for sending those men to my uncle's house and that Tutti knew all about it. But I couldn't spit it out. Rudy looked so harmless, so bewildered and broken, that to turn him in seemed like it would only make everything worse.

MY FATHER never saw Tutti again. Until he got sick, he refused to speak about her or to even have her name mentioned in the house. He dated a few women here and there and, just before I left for college, asked one of them, a customs agent at Logan, who was older than him by ten years and carried a gun, if she'd like to move in. He called her his companion. I doubt he loved her, but she cared for him during the remainder of his life, and as my own life began to take shape, I was comforted knowing he was not alone.

When I stayed with him this summer, playing cribbage on the sun porch in the late-evening light, he recounted everything he could remember, leaping from one point in time to the next, from one life to another. He was lucid and free of anger, and he told me about my uncle and about Tutti and the man from Florida, and he also described my mother, how beautiful she was, how much he missed her. What made him so depressed during that time before Tutti was how angry he felt at her dying.

"But it wasn't her fault," he said. "It was just some freak thing that happened."

He wanted me to know he thought most of life was like this: that there are no coincidences, that our lives are strange and never work out the way we think they should.

"And it's all right," he said. "It's better this way."

But then he said, "I can't believe I'm dying. I really can't believe it."

I was with him that night in the hospital. He began gasping for air, and with each attempt at breathing, his body expanded and crumpled. His eyes were so big and his left eye was looking right at me, while his other was rolled back, as though warning me that he was up ahead, close to the other side, and he couldn't see anything yet.

TUTTI SHOWED up at my father's wake alone. She'd cut her hair short and put on ten pounds or so. She had dark circles under her eyes from crying, but she held herself together and gave me a hug and kneeled at my father's casket, making whatever amends she needed to make.

Later, my wife and I were standing outside, waiting for the remaining mourners to leave.

"This is such a stupid ritual," my wife said.

"I guess it's the same as when you're born. Everyone wants to have a look at you and they have no idea what your life is going to be like, so they just look, and when you're dead, they look at you the same way."

A string of fireworks was set off across the road. It was the week before the Fourth of July, and people were already celebrating.

"You were good to have stayed with him all that time," my wife said. She stroked my neck with her long, thin fingers and went back into the funeral home.

I went to the car to get the air conditioner running. Parked beside me was the old cream-colored Mercedes I remembered from so many years ago. New Mexico plates were fixed to the rusted-out bumper. A thin line of smoke escaped from the lowered driver's-side window. I went around to the passenger-side door and looked in. The backseat was piled high with clothes and shoes and bags and one of the flower arrangements from the wake. I tapped my knuckle on the window. Startled, Tutti dropped her cigarette between her boots and hurried to pick it up and stamp it out in the ashtray. She motioned for me to get in the car.

"Oh, my God," she said. "You're so grown up now. It's unbelievable. And I know what they were telling you in there, but you look nothing like your father. I don't even see a resemblance. Well, maybe your nose."

"You're living in New Mexico now?"

"I did for a little while. Santa Fe. It's a wonderful city. Clean. And everyone has so much energy. But I missed the water."

"So, are you in Florida?"

"No. That's a state I'd be happy never to see again."

"My wife and I were down in Miami for a week last year. I thought I saw you in Lincoln Square, but it was someone else."

I had followed the woman, whoever she was, to this little dress shop on a corner. I saw her through the glass window: a plain-looking woman shuffling through short tropical dresses on a rack, the same age Tutti was back when I knew her.

"It's all so phony. And you have to be rich. I guess you can tell that I'm not rich, and hopefully you don't think I'm phony."

"I never did."

"What, then? I mean, what *did* you think?"

"I thought you loved my father. But I also thought that you couldn't change who you were. I know he loved you, and I know that when you left, he wasn't ever as happy again."

"Me, neither," Tutti said. She lit another cigarette and blew the smoke out in patchy clouds, coughing a bit, waving a mosquito from her face. "But I wasn't used to being so comfortable. It scared me, you know? There wasn't anything to be afraid of, but that's what was so frightening. I did try to come back after Rudy died. I called your father and I even flew up here to see him, but he wouldn't talk to me. He was a hard man. Forgiveness is for suckers, anyway. I wouldn't forgive me. That made things easier. Has made things easier. Because now I'm thinking, What would it have been like if I'd stayed? Would I be any different? You know, inside? Probably not. But everything else would be. The outside, I mean."

We were silent for a while. Tutti put out her cigarette, smiled at me, and lowered her head. The last of the people who'd come to see my father started up their cars and drove off. My wife was standing by the door, talking to my father's companion and Mr. Simmons, the funeral director. The light in the parking lot went out. We were two dark figures in a car.

"A whole bunch of other stuff has happened to you, right?" Tutti said then. "It's not just this? I mean, your father and me, we're not everything. We're just a part of the thing. You have a beautiful wife and I'm sure you'll have lovely children, and whatever else is going to happen won't have much to do with the past, I don't think."

How easily I asked her then, thinking that I might never get another chance, if it was true that Rudy had my uncle murdered.

I don't believe she intended to laugh, but that's what she did. I was exhausted in my grief and maybe accepted her apology too easily.

"No," she said. "Two maniacs zonked out of their minds killed your uncle. But when I told Rudy, he had me believe he was responsible, that he had that kind of power. He knew he was losing me; he could hear it in my voice. He must've thought that if I feared him enough, I'd come back, which, as you know, I did. But not because of your uncle."

Tutti raised her head and sneezed three times, a high-pitched, awful-sounding sneeze.

"Bless you," I said.

"Thanks, sweetie," she said, and blew her nose into a napkin. "You don't think I'm a bad person, do you?"

"No," I said. "I don't think that."

*　*　*

I COULDN'T sleep that night. My wife stayed up with me, and we watched television and ate grilled cheese and talked about what I don't remember. It felt like one of those nights in college when she and I lay in bed and told each other about everything we knew, all those stories, so we could stay awake and not be away from each other.

At dawn, we showered together. My wife looked beautiful in the pink light. Her skin was slightly tanned, with tiny freckles on her shoulders. She felt soft against my body. Her hair smelled like something tropical. We made love and lay in bed with the ceiling fan whirring above us.

She'd heard most of what there was to tell about Tutti and my father and my uncle's murder. What I never told her before was that small detail I began this story with, that my uncle was eating an ice-cream cone when the Bodfish brothers attacked him. That, before the lights went dark, the last thing he tasted was something sweet.

She responded in her yawning, half-asleep voice, "How would you know that?"

It was a good question.

How did I know?

BALLAD

~~~~~~

Okay she's gone let's get set up amp cord guitar now this is romantic this is a gift D C G yep way out of tune needs a good tuning can't remember how to tune just listen listen it all makes sense if you just listen that's what Miles Davis once said I think maybe it was Mingus turn the keys thumb the E and A and okay we're in tune music first then lyrics a mix of dark and light of high and low nothing too dark nothing too light it's her birthday she doesn't want a slit-your-wrists song and she doesn't want some loopy gumball sing-along a ballad of course ballad in D too light ballad in E minor too dark ballad in C C to F to D C to F to G something's missing C to F to A minor to G that's it that makes sense there's a balance there okay C to F to A minor to G for a while and squawking squawking why are you upset buddy why are you hiccuping now and that cute-as-hell laugh can't miss that laugh got to take a picture if I time it right though you never do it when I got the phone pointed at you guitar rest camera phone on hiccup and you're looking at me like I'm some creature from Mars wide-eyed scared shitless considering the size of your world for the past ten minutes little stuffed monkeys and parrots and lizards and then this giant indigenous freak from across the river comes stomping through the bush into your perfectly unreal world wanting to strip it bare take you away turn it into a resort which think about it little buddy think about living your first couple years in a beautiful resort no bugs or scary animals just people like your mother all there to serve you while you relax under an umbrella with the sun on your little toes doesn't that sound nice sound like something you could appreciate later on in life if say you were to make a bunch of money and then lose a bunch of money at the point your future wife is five months pregnant surprise and already has you in a convertible crib on credit without considering the possibility that maybe we won't have the money that we'll never have the kind of money we had then and we moved all the studio equipment into the garage where Mommy says it should be anyway considering I haven't recorded a thing since we moved back to her hometown from L.A. fifteen years ago and what was that just a little number called "I Do and I Don't" just a song that put her in the cream-colored Mercedes she rides into Boston to have lunch with Karen and Odessa and Hilary like they're the goddamn New England version of *Sex and the City* like they're impressed by my fifteen-year-old Benz she says I have to take the train in from Haverhill for Christ's sake well at least you have a car and you're not some poor Mexican walking to work along Route 1 okay okay no sad-time Daddy talk I get it come here get rid of those hiccups okay I didn't mean to bring you down let's go out to the living room and you can help with Mommy's birthday present there you go buckle you into your little rocking chair and here's your giraffe Sophie and your winkle and let's clean the drool off your lip okay ready no don't squeeze Sophie Sophie doesn't have the right voice for this kind of song she's more a mezzo-soprano not what we're looking for here okay squeeze Sophie we'll work around her not like I haven't had to deal with my share of overenthusiastic background vocalists maybe I can cut her out of the master tape and that cough and that sneeze and don't cry pal nothing to cry about I'm sure Sophie's a good vocalist or maybe you're just not interested in writing a song but if I could afford a present for Mommy I'd get one though it wouldn't even be a present more like a debt and she'd see it in the checking account probably return it claim it's too extravagant just some earrings or a bracelet I don't know something to make her feel pretty but what's more important she'd say me looking pretty or some diapers for the boy yeah no brainer diapers but every once in a while something nice maybe and for the life of me I can't imagine what we'd do if I didn't lift your vitamins and formula and those stupid plastic toys well not lift as much as use the sweet Korean girl who runs the self-check line at Stop & Shop claim confusion with the machine tell her I like her green eyes and her hemp necklace but forty bucks for formula organic formula 'cause it has to be organic or else what you might end up like okay let's sort of cradle you take off the guitar strap okay get this underneath your butt and put your arms up here on the side and rest your chin there in the curve how's that better feel better feel sleepy all right sleepy is good this is going to be sort of a sleepy song anyway now what was that chord progression G to no C to F to A minor right then G okay C C C C C fucking A buddy you almost fell out of the strap don't make that face I know that face all right okay look at me look at Daddy it's smiley-time right isn't it smiley-time do you even know what the hell smiley-time means it doesn't mean anything that's right that's right keep smiling for smiley-time because smiley-time is a world that only exists in my mind and you won't ever remember that you used to love smiley-time until you have a baby and then you'll probably call it something different some inane phrase that gets stuck in your head and you're walking around thinking about a world where people have smiley-time at some point during the day standing still wherever we are smiling at each other and not with some condescending coffee-house how-you-doing smile but a real genuine smile that can crush your heart the way it does when you see true happiness on a person's face like when they're on a roller coaster or sledding down a hill whatever it is that makes them forget about themselves for a few minutes maybe not a good idea to have you resting your head on the wood so back in the rocker okay now let's get to work take Mommy into the past 'cause that's what a good song does takes you back in time sets you down next to old friends and lovers well hopefully not her old lovers especially not that Australian dude the two of them out in the wild looking at kangaroos taking peyote can hear that stupid accent in my head picture Greg Norman with Mommy's face in his lap while he says 'oy 'oy 'oy but what're you going to do that's the risk you take with a good song a good song brings you back in time a great song brings you to a place you've never been and you feel good being there Jesus you little bugger you were so relaxed there during smiley-time you went ahead and dropped a load right as I was about to say how it has something to do with our past and present and future and how they can work so perfectly together if you never think about time at all if you erase the concept of time from your being and just be okay that's ripe here we go put the guitar down gently diaper wipes a bunch of wipes and all right it's up your back Jesus how long has it been since you took a dump your mother never keeps me in the loop on your dump cycle we need a dump calendar or an eraser board guess we'll have to get you in the tub I've gotten a lot of thinking done in the tub over the years of course a lot of that thinking got lost once I got out of the tub because I never remembered to bring a pen and pad into the bathroom with me so let's clean you up and get a pen and pad and run the water and start thinking of lyrics for Mommy's song all right listen to the sound of the water listen to everything around you that's music everything's music have to make sure it's not too hot too hot and you'll get that pumpkin head screaming like a cat caught on fire all right me first got you up Jesus I hate the tub I look like a washed-up seal what a body no wonder Mommy turns off the lights and my nuts cauterized forty-two years old don't want to risk another well not a mistake no you're not a mistake but well we weren't planning on doesn't matter you're here you're beautiful you ready for the tub ready for the water okay here we go legs first yeah feels good doesn't it now your back and your arms don't worry I got your head I won't let you go under we'll just float you around okay it's warm isn't it you're gonna love the ocean maybe you'll be a surfer or maybe you'll build sailboats or maybe you'll be one of those guys who fishes in the summer and smokes dope in the winter and never really minds what happens around him because he's generally satisfied with his life and doesn't expect too much and never gets his hopes up and hasn't a clue why everyone's always arguing about what's fair and what isn't come on pal not in the tub well at least it's clear means you're healthy and you're smiling because you think you got away with something well okay we should get out of the tub

not much thinking done after all but it'll come to us I mean
you can't stop yourself from thinking it's impossible even
wrapping you up in the towel and the tag says MADE IN CHINA
and where in China it's so damn big though you have to think
some factory where they're pumping out towel after towel
all day it's towels or it's clocks or it's Elvis Presley key chains
whole factories producing Elvis crap and not one of those kids
probably knows who Elvis is or was or how if he didn't stop in
at that little recording studio in Memphis or if he didn't shake
his hips on *The Ed Sullivan Show* or die on the toilet or have this
myth about him still being alive and all these wackos visiting
Graceland like it's some kind of church then none of the Chinese kids would even be working the Elvis factory and it might
be the only factory in their town so without Elvis they might've
lived a happier life working a farm or fishing doing something
outdoors where the air is clean and no one's breathing down
your neck about printing a thousand of those "Jailhouse Rock"
T-shirts by noon your skin's soft too soft maybe hasn't had to
take a blow yet except that time you tumbled out of your little
rocker but you knew to keep rolling and finally pressed up
against the TV stand what's this spot on your belly spider bite
do we have spiders fuck I hope not does it hurt when I press no
good that's good probably bitten a few days ago spiders crawl-
ing all over the house can't see 'em maybe they hide until
night come out in packs crawl into our bed down our throats
that's why Mommy's coughing at night coughing on spider legs
and what if they're pregnant what if they're delivering baby
spiders inside us oh god okay let's zap those spiders out of our
minds okay zap no more spiders get the diaper on your One-
sie your little sweats and how about one of these sweatshirts
a little chilly in here right can't turn the heat up past sixty-four
heat's expensive if we hugged each other all day we wouldn't

need heat at all zip you up looks like you're ready to get back to work are you ready to get back to work good little smile stick your tongue out make that fart sound all right buddy ballad in C for your mother haven't written a song a real song since I don't know when tried to get the band back together but Tamrod runs some consulting firm and Fido works a farm in Montana and Caesar's been cleaning toilets at Logan guessing drugs brought him there or maybe he's off the drugs and that's why he's cleaning toilets maybe he'll be ready to join up again in a year you only really need two founding members who am I kidding you won't ever know your father the rock star you'll probably see me as some old know-nothing like I saw my father until I got older and got interested in what his life was like before he started wheezing and coughing all the time and we needed to hook him up to an oxygen tank 'cause all I knew of him was that he was a finish carpenter he'd talk about staircases and mantels and window trim whatever but later he told me how he dropped out of high school and flew to Madrid and from there trekked through western and eastern Europe and to Egypt and down to South Africa and over to Chile up through South America Panama Guatemala Mexico basically traveled the world except Asia said he wished he could get to Asia and I asked him why there were no photographs from his travels and he said because it's all in my mind it's for me not for anyone else and I came to respect my father more than I ever had before and then well he died died before he got a chance to see you or even know you were coming said how he wished he had a grandchild all the men in our family since the dawn of time failing like it's a birthright to dream big and touch greatness and then crash hard I'm not sure your grandfather ever even went to the places he claimed to visit maybe he was dreaming up a more adventurous past for himself maybe I should too who am I who was I who should I have been for you going to that dark place again try to stay away from the dark if we can so what was the point of right well you'll see videos of me when I had long hair and purple suits and you'll think where's that guy he was famous he was weird he was cool but things change buddy people change and you're my world now and maybe I dream of getting the band back dream of me and Caesar at the Paradise but I know that's not going to happen too many mistakes band's got a bad name I got a bad name put down the booze and coke put up all that dough in a vegetarian restaurant called ROOTS which your mother said was a terrible name and I went with it despite her thinking if it stuck with me then it'd stick with others but it wasn't the name no one was willing to pay fourteen ninety-five for a plate of raw vegetables and even after selling the house and most of my old guitars and becoming sort of not sort of but becoming an actual laughingstock on the local news during a where-are-they-now segment claiming to have a connection with the spiritual world which I don't but I thought it might drum up some interest in my music again and maybe kids'll look up your last name find out who your father was make fun of how I used to look the music I played but you take out the synthesizers and you have some pretty lovely anyway it won't matter shouldn't matter 'cause unlike their fathers and very much like my own father I went for it and I did it and no one can take that away from me just like they can't take it away from you and I know sometimes I talk down about your mother but she's been with me through it all rich and poor and she deserves some slack deserves a break and she's a good mother to you and good woman and she's still the only girl I know knows how to give a decent foot massage and maybe that sounds like it's not a lot but trust me it's hard to meet a woman you can love all your life and when you arrived it seemed to make us love each other even more and I guess that's the point why it's so hard to write a song I don't have any songs left maybe you were my last song and maybe all your mother wants is a deep kiss and a warm bath and to be here with us a family our own little world just beginning.

THE PLACE YOU ARE GOING TO

~~~~~

WALLACE PRAGER LEFT Wequaquet early Sunday morning and drove three days straight, making good time to Buffalo Gap and Rapid City before heading south toward Casper, Wyoming. He stopped at a one-pump gas station and bought a postcard of a cat dressed up like a cowboy straddling a dog. The cat had a rope lassoed out toward a band of mice. The postcard read: *Wyoming.* He drove out to a state park and walked a trail to a set of boulders rounded and fallen in the shape of a sitting bear and tucked himself in the shade of the bear's foot. He wrote to his daughter, Francesca:

> Thought you'd think this was funny. You and I share the same kind of humor. Always have. I miss you and love you and I hope you're doing well. Make sure you're reading your books and don't give your mother a hard time. Now I feel bad for the mice.
>
> Love, Dad

He drove the hard, dry country until night and stopped at a Super 8 in Laramie. He bought a half chicken and vegetables from a diner and ate while watching a movie he thought he might've seen but couldn't be sure. He slept well and in the morning delivered his postcard to a mailbox standing like some lone impenetrable stronghold in the wake of the apocalypse.

He stopped in front of a van with a sign that read BEST HAMBURGERS IN THE WORLD and sat on a stool and ordered the only thing on the menu. The cook had pasted photographs of famous boxers to the inside of the van, and they were signed with notes Wallace couldn't quite read.

"All these fighters ate here?" he asked.

"Every one of them," the cook said. "Every one of them a champion at some point in his career. Except for Tyson. Tyson never ate here. Foreman ate twelve burgers in a sitting."

"Ali?"

"He didn't eat, but he let me take a picture. That's the only one not hanging out here. It'll probably be worth a good cent when he's gone. Not that I like to think about that sort of thing. But you got to be rational, even with someone who changed the world. I mean, look how much money Jesus takes in a year."

Wallace ate his burger and ordered another. They weren't the best he'd ever had, but they were pretty damn good. He drank a big cup of water and set a ten-dollar bill on the counter and as he was leaving he looked at the photograph of Larry Holmes and the note below his signature:

Dead meat, Red meat.

MOTEL SIGNS morphed the sky into a dull electric blue beneath the darkness of night. He took a room and washed his face and wet his hair. His stomach was upset from the grease in the burgers, and he lay in bed thinking of his wife, Gail. They had pushed and borrowed and stolen, and now broke was broke, and Wallace was searching.

In the morning, he showered and watched television as he dressed. A dog was stuck in a tree. It was a puggle, a mix between a beagle and a pug. A woman was crying, and she couldn't say all she wanted to say in the allotted news segment.

HE DROVE through the Rocky Mountains. People snapped pictures and saved them into digital memory. Nothing was forgotten anymore. He didn't want to stop. He didn't want to remember.

He ate a midnight breakfast and, with his bill change, bought a postcard of a sun dog over the mountains. Underneath, the postcard read: *Come to Colorado.*

> I thought the photograph was amazing, but don't try walking to Colorado, because you'll hurt your feet on the rocks. If that's not enough of a warning, I told a falcon all about you and how pretty you are. I said, "If you see this girl, pick her up with your talons and bring her home." So, you see, it's unwise to come to Colorado. Maybe one day we'll drive through all these places together.
>
> Love, Dad

He parked his truck at a clearing and sprayed down with mosquito repellent and bunched up clothing for a pillow and lay in the truck bed. He worried for Francesca. He thought about the way she ran, with her arms swinging wildly.

* * *

AT THE cross into Nevada, he stopped at a gas station and bought another postcard. It wasn't long until Vegas, but he wanted to get the postcard in the mail.

This postcard had a glowing alien head on its cover, and in neon-green lettering the alien said, *"Where am I?"* and, below, *Nevada*.

> I saw this alien today. He was very nice. We had coffee and talked about his planet. It's called Narafulaco-hardeeplin. I think I spelled it right. Anyway, I told him about the city we built and he said he'd been look-ing for a place to settle down and asked if I could give him directions, but I said I'd only do that if he checked in on my daughter. So he's going to visit you and then tell me you were doing your homework and chores and then I guess I'll have a friend there in the city. Who knows? Keep an eye out for this guy and be good.
>
> Love, Dad

Francesca and Wallace had created a city on the edge of an undiscovered ocean.

"This is so new," he'd said. "All we know is that the people who live there will be very happy."

"I never said that."

"Do you think they will be?"

"Not yet."

"Why?"

"Because no one knows it exists, so there aren't any people."

"First things first, right?"

Together they worked on the city. They built houses along the ocean's edge, but not so high that the people who couldn't afford to live in them would have their views of the ocean blocked. They were whitewashed buildings and the sun shone on their fronts and at certain times of the day people were blinded by all that light and when they could see again were stunned by the city's beauty, as though they were seeing it all for the first time. There were cobbled streets and fountains where water arced from the mouths of sea creatures and men and women cooked on the street and the smell of burning wood chips filled the air. There were no roads leading in and no roads leading out. The people who lived there arrived by chance, and by chance more people arrived after being sent a letter from a place and person they did not know.

"Why else would we build the city if it isn't the place you are going to?" Francesca had said.

"What makes you think I'm leaving?"

"I heard you. You told Mom and she told me when you were away this morning. I asked her where you were going and she said you said you didn't know."

"And now I know?"

"Yes."

During his last nights, they'd bought him a house on a hill on the outskirts of the city, overlooking the shoreline and eye level with the horizon. At times the water would turn gold. He slept on a balcony and woke up with salt on his lips and he could see the people that populated his dreams diminishing in the sky.

Wallace had gone to his bedroom and lain down next to Gail. She put her arm around him and fell asleep that way. It was a soundless horror, a body next to his, a mind unable to know any of his thoughts, unable to articulate a single truth about his life. He waited until her breath was steady and even, then lifted her arm and placed it by her side and went into Francesca's room with a pillow and blanket and slept on the floor beside her bed.

He did this for three straight nights. Francesca never woke when he came into the room. He would watch her then in what little light there was through the window blinds—a portion of her face shadowed, an arm, a piece of her leg, or maybe it was a scrap of paper, the outline of the city. He knew he would have to put her together each time much the same way when he was gone, though she would grow and he would not know that person.

On the final morning, he'd said goodbye and Francesca shook his hand as if they had made a deal, agreed on a contract, and he told her to be good. She asked him to send her a post-card from all the places he went, and when the postcards stopped she would know he'd arrived in the city.

"I'll send you a postcard from there, too," he said.

"Impossible," she said. "No cameras allowed."

"No cameras?"

"I made the rule last night when I saw you sleeping. I thought, What if there were no pictures? Then we would have to dream everything we had ever seen and everything we wanted to see, and no one could tell the difference unless they saw it with their own eyes."

WALLACE STOPPED at a large supermarket and bought a baguette and a block of white cheese. He ordered a cup of coffee from a stand to the left of the registers and sat and ate and read the *Las Vegas Sun*. He could hear video-poker cards flipping on screens in a bank against the far wall. Some workers were eating tacos. They chewed slowly, looking out of the dirty windows. When he was finished, he spun a rack of postcards next to a magazine stand and plucked one out that had a photograph of the Sphinx in front of the Luxor hotel. He put it back in the metal holster and spun the rack again and left it spinning.

He drove the long avenues that crossed the city. The lights changed from pink to yellow to blue, and he wished for twilight and solace and no pain.

He headed south toward Arizona. He passed a graveyard full of flowers and thought of the dead building cities from the roots of the earth. Maybe that was why everything was dying up above.

He drove until the desert spread out like a beach, its shore on the horizon, the sky an ocean. He tried to hold the image in his mind so that he could describe it to Francesca as the city they had built.

He had never been to this part of the world.

MUTATIS MUTANDIS

~~~

THE REASON WHY I went on *The Dr. Jack Show* in the first place? I wanted happiness. I thought maybe happiness had something to do with how I felt on the inside and how I felt on the inside had something to do with how I looked on the outside. I let myself go after Ron died, and then when Caroline left for school I pretty much gave up altogether. But I wasn't clueless; I could see my options like a cold sore on my lip: scrapbooking, movie night, yoga for beginners. I wanted a man to hold me and kiss me and screw my brains out. I wasn't going to become like these other women in town. So I took a shot. In my letter to the show, I said I'd put myself in their hands. Face, neck, breasts, stomach, butt, thighs, and calves: They're all yours.

A month later I'm sitting on a super-comfortable orange sofa in what they call "the quiet room," being instructed by Dr. Jack's bubbly blond producer, Melanie, on how to react to the crowd. She says they'll try to change my mind but reminds me that I've already signed a contract.

"Dr. Jack will also try to change your mind, which might confuse you at first, but don't worry, he doesn't really want you to change your mind. It's all part of the show. In six months you'll return a different woman, a stunning, magnificent beauty. Don't be afraid. Dr. Jack's hands are like the hands of Michelangelo."

All I can think is: What happened? I used to be rich. I drove a Mercedes and had a mink coat. My ring was heavy on my finger. We lived up in the Applewood Estates in a community of successful people whose children all played an instrument of some sort and put on concerts in the central gazebo on Sunday afternoons in the spring.

Melanie explains that Dr. Jack probably won't get into the children and the gazebo and all that, but he'll certainly bring up my husband's foolish death and my subsequent financial instability, because, naturally, a crowd would riot if a rich woman were being provided with free cosmetic surgery.

"You may want to consider crying, if possible," she says. "Think of something horrific. Think of a little girl with burn scars on her face or a puppy hit by a car lying in the street twitching. Those are just a couple of ideas. If you need more, we'll pipe them in through your earpiece; just blink three times real hard. Believe me when I tell you, crying is the only way to get the audience off your back. It's especially helpful in grabbing the attention of the audience at home, which we know to be comprised mainly of housewives and stoners. They stop what they're doing and wonder, Why are all these people crying? They tune in, turn up the volume, and then they tune in tomorrow."

Dr. Jack's show opens with the Fleetwood Mac song "Don't Stop." I'm introduced through a series of demeaning photographs: eating chocolate-covered strawberries while positioned sideways on a small chair; dancing at a bar, my hands up and belly exposed; caught sneaking a donut in the kitchen, Bavarian cream on the corner of my lips. There're not the ones I remember sending in. I try to imagine who was photographing me in such private moments.

Dr. Jack calls my name and Melanie gives me a little shove. "Don't stop," she says.

The crowd applauds. For what? Dr. Jack hugs me and holds my wrists; his hands are as soft as French milled soap. He leads me to a lime-green chair that's raised a half foot higher than your average chair, with a deep back, so that my stomach involuntarily folds to fit my posture. I lean forward and pinch my knees together. Wardrobe put me in a tight floral shift dress. They want me to spill out in front of the cameras. I spill.

I told myself I wouldn't cry, but, just after the weigh-in, here I am, crying. No need to think of anything horrific; the numbers on the board above the scale are terrifying enough. They brought out a silver square that looked like it was made to weigh cattle and, instinctively, I asked to take off my shoes. Dr. Jack said it's a myth that shoes add a significant amount of weight. My eyes were wet as the technicians slowed the numbers to create tension. They finally stopped at 208. The audience gasped.

There're definitely a few women out there who weigh more than I do but, at this point, I'm too deprived of energy to care. I feel like I'm standing in a swamp, sweating, unable to move through the muck.

Dr. Jack takes my hand and guides me back to the couch. Here is a photograph of what I looked like at eighteen. Prom night and I'm wearing a blue scalloped dress. My hair is swept over my upper arm. You can see the slim bones of my neck. My arms are tanned and toned. I'm smiling shyly, though I remember thinking then that I was too good for that school, for that prom, for those cameras. My date is Calvin Baker, the star quarterback for the Wequaquet Red Raiders. Besides some gray hairs, he looks exactly the same today. You broke my heart, he told me a few years back. But I'm glad you did. He was nice enough not to say why.

"Wouldn't you like to look like that again?" Dr. Jack asks me.

I nod, unable to speak as I stare at the girl I was.

"Wasn't she beautiful?" Dr. Jack asks the crowd.

Sounds that all suggest YES!

I can feel the spotlight on me now, the hard light picking up every imperfection. When I was twenty years old and a sophomore at the University of Arizona, I got a tattoo of a Yaqui Indian on the back of my shoulder. He's supposed to be performing a deer dance in which his arms are raised and one leg is in the air. Now he looks more like a crouching Sasquatch.

Dr. Jack is concerned with my flabby neck, my descended breasts, my popover belly, and my crimped thighs. He points to each part with a thin silver wand.

"BLAST AWAY!" he shouts. And the crowd joins him, "BLAST AWAY! BLAST AWAY! BLAST AWAY!"

Then it's a commercial break and the stage lights darken. Dr. Jack has makeup touch up his cheeks and fluff his hair. I look back at the photograph of Calvin and me, run through the life I might have had, the grieving mother of a boy blown away, how horrible, God, I sometimes wish I were her.

Lights up.

"We're back with Nancy Dwyer, who before the break weighed in at a staggering two hundred and eight pounds. Nancy's made the choice to change her life, and what a smart choice you've made, dear."

How could I turn back?

"I couldn't help but notice that over the break you were looking at your former self," Dr. Jack says. "You were her, weren't you? She is you, isn't she? You can be her again, but older, smarter, sexier. No more shyness; only confidence. Head up, body erect, stopping traffic on the street, causing an accident or two." The audience laughs. "Well, hopefully not. We don't want anyone to get hurt.

"And to prove to you, to the audience, to all the people at home, my skill with a knife, here are some before-and-after photos of other women I've worked on. This is Tricia with her crooked nose. This is Bonnie with her hopelessly flat chest. This is Sandra's—how do I put it nicely?—plump tush."

SUCCESS flashes across the screen—the audience is urged to shout the word along with Dr. Jack, throwing their hands in the air like a bunch of Baptists.

"SUCCESS in shaving down Tricia's crooked nose to a charming button; SUCCESS in building Bonnie two perfectly shaped breasts; SUCCESS in getting Sandra back into her favorite jeans by removing fifty pounds of unnecessary fat from her rear end."

Surprise! Here they are now. Who knows what these women are like? They could very well be psychotics. Yet the audience cheers. And who doesn't want to be cheered for? They wave to the crowd. They hug Dr. Jack and gather around me on the couch, legs crossed, high heels glittering. Their faces are caked with makeup. Sandra puts a hand on my knee. She seems to be itching it with her long nail, a nervous tic, I gather, a compulsion that hasn't healed with her receded waistline.

How have their lives changed? Tricia is married to a very successful lawyer in Manhattan. Bonnie owns a chain of lingerie stores in the Midwest that cater to big-breasted women. Sandra no longer feels uncomfortable flying or going to the movies and recently got engaged to Butch, a muscled trash collector, who's sitting in the front row of the audience, pumping his fist.

"All three of them were on the fence," Dr. Jack says. "Luckily, the mean dog of their past pushed them over."

Audience laughs.

Commercial. Tricia, Bonnie, and Sandra take out their cell phones. Dr. Jack does some light stretching. Music plays, camera's on. Dr. Jack kisses each one of us on the cheek, then high-fives everyone in the front row and runs past me and offstage. Show's over. The crowd is ushered out through a door in the back of the theater. A woman shouts, "Go get 'em, girl!" The lights dim. I struggle to breathe. It's a while before Melanie remembers I'm still out there. Like a little girl lost, I'm taken down a hallway and guided toward a town car, which will bring me back to my hotel.

"We'll call you in the morning," Melanie says. "Make sure you don't eat for twenty-four hours. It's imperative."

I've already got well over a thousand friend requests on Facebook, and most of them want to wish me good luck or tell me how brave I am, while a few of the slimy ones, especially Wendy Bishop from Seattle, who works as a pharmaceutical technician, have posted on my wall a series of brutal-looking photos of botched boob jobs and tummy tucks.

Later, I order a blueberry sundae and watch TV in my bra and panties.

Last days of yum, yum, yum.

MY SURGEON isn't Dr. Jack. It's Dr. Stevens. Dr. Jack isn't board certified—a bit of a shaky past.

"Someone that amped up doesn't have the patience for

cosmetic surgery," Dr. Stevens says. "Look at me. This is not a face you want to see on your television every day, is it?"

Without the mole on his chin or the pockmarked cheeks, Dr. Stevens could be quite handsome, and, so it's a mystery why he doesn't get work done himself. I don't pry.

First thing he does is draw lines on my body, a map of removal.

"Nothing is going to hurt until later," he says.

The anesthesiologist is young and pretty, with shimmering blue eyes and long, elegant fingers. She reminds me of my daughter, Caroline. I try to tell her about Caroline, but I'm already going away.

Strange dream of driving a convertible down Fifth Avenue in Manhattan, then up Lord & Taylor, the car leaping from building top to building top, until there are no building tops, and I sink underwater, picking up all kinds of sea creatures who speak to me in Spanish, and I can speak Spanish, too, and we discuss why it's best to live a spiritual life rather than a materialistic one. "Look at us," the bluefish says. "All we want is to live in the ocean and be happy." They swim out of the car and up toward the light shining on the ocean's surface. I leave the car and follow them. I'm awake in my new body. My new body won't let me move.

"How do I look?" I say.

"Relax, Ms. Dwyer," says a nurse. "If you move, you might just fall apart."

RESULT: FIFTY pounds of me sucked out and burned in an incinerator. Neck tightened, face lifted, brows pushed back, breasts pumped up, Yaqui Indian tattoo removed. Four months later I can pretty much walk upright.

What do I think?

Game changer.

Already I recognize men in cars at stoplights reluctant to go when the light turns green or how George Falachi dropped a gallon of milk on his son's foot when he saw me in the grocery store. Is it too much? Perhaps. But go big or go home, right? Do I care if Deborah Sanders snubs me at the dry cleaner's? Or that Gail Prager hasn't invited me to her father's birthday party? Not a chance. No time left to waste on what I can't control. I did this for a reason. Now it's like, where to go? The new me doesn't shop at MegaWorld anymore, not that their deals are anything to sneer at, it's just this body deserves high-ticket items, and depending on the salesperson—ring, no ring, bald, round, lesbo—it should be able to get me a pretty decent discount.

So I indulge, drive north to the Atrium in Braintree. What am I, a star? Well, sort of. Maybe it's just the breasts or the way my lips shine, or it's that people recognize me from *The Dr. Jack Show* or from the short money ad I did for Big Tim's Auto Emporium, but the lights are on me in every store. Maybe they don't know how I used to look. Now I'm having second thoughts about returning to the show, but roof over head wins out; plus, it was part of the contract—half now, half when you return, like some kind of drug run.

Outside at the Atrium fountain, while I'm eating my spring salad, a security guard comes up, and I'm thinking, Give him the "Can't you see I'm eating?" just for fun.

"Ma'am," he says. "I think a pigeon did some business on your shirt."

"Oh, God! My Marc Jacobs!"

I take a sanitary wipe from my purse and dab at the greenish-white stain. A group of women are snickering near the Chinese dumpling stand. I quick wrap my Versace scarf around my neck and get up to leave.

"Relax, ma'am," the security guard says. "Getting hit with doo-doo is good luck."

"Yeah? Are those poopers going to pay my dry cleaning?" I say.

"I've worked here almost seventeen years and never been pooped on once."

"Am I supposed to feel sorry for you?"

Then *splat,* right on my scarf.

"Twice!" the security guard says, and smacks himself upside the head. "Hot damn!"

TURNS OUT I've extended my credit as far as it can extend. The new me hasn't improved her financial status by much. Luckily, Caroline won the university writing contest for her story "Blacker Nights," which she wouldn't let me read but I guess has something to do with her and that basketball player, Rufus, and how he dumped her when they were playing exhibition games in Rome over spring break. Either way, she's a thousand bucks richer and kind enough to take us to the Asian spa. Hot stones, mud bath, facial: the works. The women can't stop looking. I go naked even when it's unnecessary, like through the lobby after the stones and before the bath.

"Mom," Caroline says. "Overboard, geez."

"Oh, psshh," I say.

One of those tiny Asians goes a little too rough on the gams and glutes during the deep-tissue massage. I see swelling in the mirror in the relaxation room. Nothing a little skin toner won't fix. As I'm applying, I notice Caroline's looking a little lumpy around the middle. I suggest a tummy tuck. She turns away from me. Her middle jiggles a bit.

"It's worth it," I say.

"To whom is it worth it?"

"To whom? Oh, God, you sound like Uncle Max."

"Is that a bad thing? Isn't he, like, an actual rocket scientist?"

"Yeah, and he spent half his life getting kicked in the groin."

"Can't say I see your point, Mom."

"Point is, sure, if you can break down algorithms when you're six years old you'll have a way out, but if you can't, then you'd better learn some way to take advantage of this world."

"See, that's exactly what I was talking about."

"You were talking about what?"

"Nothing."

Guess I said the wrong thing, but when I am feeling good, like after a few glasses of wine, I tend to talk over my head. I take it back, of course, because who else is there in my life besides Caroline?

On the way home, I remind her about the show next week.

"Can you believe it's been six months already?"

"You really do look a hundred times different, Mom."

"In a good way, right?"

"Sure."

"That wasn't a really convincing *sure*."

"Well, maybe; your waist is so small and, you know, the rest of you . . ."

She holds her hands out in front of her chest like she's carrying two big water containers.

"That's the point, dear. This is who I am."

"I get it," Caroline says.

But I'm not certain she does.

★ ★ ★

IT DOESN'T seem like women in L.A. take any shit. None of them get shit on. There're birds everywhere.

A black town car picks me up at my hotel, drives me to the back of the studio. Melanie greets me at the door and directs me to a private dressing room, where it's hair, makeup, and wardrobe. I'm wondering if this is how those other girls were treated. During the pre-screen interview, she hands me a piece of paper with five questions on the front, two possible answers.

"How would you describe yourself?" she asks. "Look into the camera when you answer."

Choices are: *A) I'm gorgeous. B) I'm atrocious.*

"Do people check you out on the street?"

A) People are always checking me out on the street. B) People run away from me.

"Two plus two equals four."

A) That's right. B) That's not right.

"If someone offered you a free vacation in the French Riviera, what would you say?"

A) You can't turn this down. B) I can't stand the French.

"What would you say to someone who wanted to physically abuse you?"

A) Don't mess with me. B) Go ahead, I deserve it.

After the question/answer, she tells me to flip the paper over.

"What's this?"

"Think of it as a play," she says. "You and Dr. Jack are the leads."

"But . . . huh, why would I harass a woman in row three?"

"Good question, and look, right there, where it says, *Harass woman in Row Three,* we've planted another actress who will be working alongside the two of you, in a supporting role, of course."

"But I don't want people to get mad at me."

"Yes! Yes! That's exactly what you want. What better way to show the world the new Nancy Dwyer than by drawing envy and jealousy and general hatred from those who cannot be you?"

"And this, in italics, *Wag your finger*—what's that supposed to mean?"

"You know, like—" Melanie puts a hand on her hip and stares out over my head, raises her index finger and wags it, and says, "Nancy don't take no lip. Or, you know, whatever. Improvise. Have fun. Listen, we've decided to go with a different format. It's not your fault. Dr. Jack doesn't know as much as people think, and it's hard trying to find people with debilitating illnesses or psychological problems who are both nonthreatening and willing to come on the show. My advice is to just go with it. Rock their socks off! You're on in ten."

A goldfish floats around on the monitor in the quiet room until the screen flickers and I hear "Don't Stop" and see Dr. Jack running up and down the aisles high-fiving the audience. He says, "We've got a special show for you today. Do you all remember the sweet-natured homely woman from Wequaquet, Massachusetts?" Yes, they claim to remember me. "Well, she's back, and you won't believe how much she's changed! Take a look."

Now it's a montage of quick edits and close-ups of me from earlier, with this spastic hip-hop music playing, and me saying, "I'm gorgeous," and "People are always checking me out on the street," and "You can't turn this down," and "Don't mess with me."

The audience is booing before I'm even out onstage, then

they're standing and pointing and pumping their index fingers down as if to suggest to Dr. Jack, with his despotic power, he feed me to a rabid beast.

Cue cards read:

WAVE TO AUDIENCE

STOP IN FRONT OF DR. JACK

TURN 90 DEGREES TO LEFT AND BACK

TURN 90 DEGREES TO RIGHT AND BACK

SIT DOWN

PRETEND AS IF SWATTING FLY AWAY FROM FACE

More boos, until Dr. Jack holds up his arms and, as booing dies down, brings his hands together and bows slightly.

Stunned. So much so that I can't hear Dr. Jack's first question, and not until Woman in Row 3 shouts, "Answer the man, bitch," do I finally snap out of it, feel full of anger at being called a bitch on television, want to show the world I'm not the bitch, she's the bitch, and she's got a big gap between her teeth and purple eyeliner, and the cue card reads:

WHAT CORNER DID YOU JUST STEP OFF OF, HO?

Then, well, when you see it—except for the curses, which I'm sure will be bleeped—you'll witness her running down the aisle and Dr. Jack's meager attempt to get in our way, and the sudden muscle deficiencies in the burly bodyguards as they lazily pick Woman in Row 3 up under the arms and let her kick wildly, catching my right eye with the toe of her heel, until the other bodyguard grabs her legs and turns them over and together they fold her up like a lawn chair and take her offstage.

Dr. Jack asks, "Tough being beautiful, isn't it?"

Given this recent experience, I can only say, "Yes. Yes, it is."

"Was it worth it?"

Silence. Blank cue card. Empty seat in row 3.

I think, Might as well go all the way.

"Damn right it was worth it."

MY MAILBOX is full of letters. Who writes letters anymore? Turns out the people who write letters are daytime-television watchers with a lot of anger inside.

"Hate mail is better than no mail," Melanie tells me over the phone.

"Well, can you stop sending it to my house? This one guy told me he was going to cut out my . . . you know . . . thing."

"How medieval," Melanie says. "According to our research, only point zero zero zero three percent of all threats are actually acted upon."

"That doesn't make me feel better."

On the table is a drawing in green crayon by a little girl named Amber, who lives in Wheeling, West Virginia. The two pictures are supposed to be me before and me after. The one on the left is a far-from-perfect circle, and the one on the right looks like a hot dog with eyes. Next to the circle she's written: *FAT BITCH*. And beside the hot dog: *SKINNY BITCH*.

"Listen," Melanie says. "We understand that our audience can be somewhat frightening, but if you were out of work and eating cheap caramel clusters in the middle of the day and your kids were screaming and the house looked like a demolition zone, wouldn't you find yourself overly invested in shows like ours? Try meditating. Dr. Jack, he squats against the wall in his dressing room with his hands covering his eyes for two hours before every show. Then he does one thousand sit-ups. Then he has one of his security guards punch him in the stomach until his hands hurt. His hate mail could fill a cathedral."

I thank Melanie for her advice, end the call, and trash the mail.

BUT FOR weeks the mail keeps coming. Everett stacks it in boxes outside the door and rings the bell. He's back in his postal van and waving through the window by the time I get outside. He's always been a quick, porky guy. Even in grade school, when he used to hand out the little blue notebooks to the class before each test.

I leave the boxes. Next day, Everett rings the bell and stays at the door.

"You have to take your mail, Nancy," he says.

"Who says I have to?"

"The United States Postal Service, that's who."

"Can you help me carry it in? I really don't have the strength."

Everett tries to carry too many boxes at once and the letters spill out on the floor. There's a card in one of the boxes from Donna Baker. It's a get-well-soon card. There's a child watering a dying plant on the front. Inside, the plant has grown tall and green, with lavender-colored flowers blooming from its leaves. She signed the card, *With Love*. No hard feelings, I guess. I'm the one who broke the news about Calvin and that chick he was seeing. Why none of us single women in town have gotten together, I don't know. Maybe I'll arrange a weekly wine-and-cheese night.

Everett puts the mail back into the boxes. His shirt has come untucked and there's sweat on his brow. I ask him if he'd like a drink.

"Got any beer?"

"Sure, I think there's a beer or two."

There's a six-pack, actually. I bought it for a guy I met online.

He said he liked this particular kind of beer and dried apricots and that he was looking to settle down because his life had been hectic and unforgiving. When the night came for us to meet up, he didn't show. I knew it meant he probably searched me on Google and saw a YouTube video of me on *The Dr. Jack Show*. But then, days later, the news had a story about a man—with the same name and photo as on his profile—spontaneously combusting like a bomb outside a CVS. He was married, had three little girls, and worked in a power plant.

"Here," I say to Everett, who cracks open the beer and slurps up the foam with his chubby lips.

"That's refreshing," he says. "So, I heard something about you being on TV."

"That's right," I say.

"I don't own a TV. But you look like you could be on TV. I mean, you look like a star."

Even though it's coming from Everett, I feel my face blush, the first pleasant feeling I've had in months. It almost makes me want to cry.

"Did I say something wrong?"

"No. It's just that . . . you're a good guy, Everett. People don't know it, but you are."

"I appreciate you saying so, Nancy."

He finishes his beer, stands, and tips his postal cap. I realize I'm nearly a half foot taller than him as we head to the front door. He turns back and blinks his eyes a few times.

"Remember when they used to call you Fancy Nancy because you wore those pearl clip-on earrings every day?"

I do remember. And I also remember how they used to call Everett *Tick* because he'd always be clinging to one group or another until someone shoved him away. I remember once at recess I pushed him and said, "Get away from us, Tick," and all the girls laughed and Everett smiled in this way where he was trying to keep from crying.

I lean down and put my hands on his bristly cheeks and give him a peck on the lips. I can feel his body freeze up, and then he nearly falls down the steps when I let go of his face.

"I'm sorry," I say.

"That's okay, Nancy," he says, stumbling backward. "I'll see you tomorrow, all right?"

WINTER COMES early. Snow covers the car and roof and lawn. The heat fogs up the windows. I put on Linda Ronstadt and play Treasure Hunt online. Later, I make myself a turkey sandwich. I consider my dresses and shoes. Last week I took all my old things to Goodwill, and just yesterday I saw a homeless woman outside Hal's, asking for change, in my plus-size silk chiffon cocktail dress. My scars are healed but still visible. Dr. Stevens prescribed me a cream, but it doesn't seem to be working. I put on a black evening gown, with white gloves and a fake diamond necklace. I bend forward, push my breasts together with my elbows, and blow a little kiss to myself in the mirror. My lips are too big. My face seems frightened by them. Oh, hell. I snap off the gloves and sit with my back turned to the mirror. I pick up a novel I bought one day when I was in the bookstore at the mall trying to get men to notice me. I'm not even sure what it's about. Lots of rave reviews on the back, though. The first line reads: *Maybe I was a dog in another life.* Inside, there's a photograph of a tired old woman with wavy gray hair, holding a pair of reading glasses up to her face. "You're a stupid cunt," I tell her. I change into my Juicy Couture shorts and bra top. After a good ten minutes of Pilates, I go out to the street and look down the block to see if anyone's coming.

* * *

CAROLINE CALLS me on my cell and asks how I'm doing. She hides her frustration well. Even at her age, she's aware that bright people can make mistakes. The smartest people in the world have committed the worst crimes in history, she says.

"I didn't commit a crime," I tell her.

"I know, Mom. I'm not saying you did."

"Good."

Beautiful is the pain on your face.

That's one of the lines I remember from a poem she wrote in the ninth grade. I must've done something right with her. Even when she was little I knew she was capable of sympathy. It's what makes her such a good person, why boys fall in love with her, and why she's able to write so well.

She says she's almost done with her novel, some interest from publishers. I ask her again what it's about, but she won't say.

"It's about me, isn't it?"

"No, Mom. For the hundredth time."

Then the doorbell rings. I wipe down the glass and see Everett standing to the side with the American flag stitched into his shirtsleeve.

A sense of excitement flows through me. I can feel it in my sewn-up belly.

"I got to go, honey," I tell Caroline. "Be good."

I open the door and Everett hands me another stack of letters, though it's a bit lighter than usual.

"I didn't expect you today."

"Neither snow nor rain nor heat nor gloom of night stays these couriers from the swift completion of their appointed rounds."

"Oh."

"It's the postal service's unofficial motto."

"I see. Well, come in. I'll make coffee."

He stamps his feet on the steps, unties his boots. The big toe on his right foot is sticking out of his sock.

"You have a hole," I say. "Take them off. Let me get you a fresh pair."

"You don't have to do that," he says.

"There's a box of Ron's underthings in the garage."

"No, I wouldn't—"

"Please, Everett. We've known each other how long? Now, have a seat and take off those wet, nasty things."

I put the coffee on. It's been a while since I had a man in the house. I'm noticing how plain everything looks, how I haven't thought about the rooms for months—cracks in the ceiling, dust on the shelves, vents clotted up with hair and dirt and balls of gray fluff.

"How do you take your coffee, hon?"

It comes naturally, calling Everett *hon*.

"Just cream," he says.

I nearly drop the mugs when I see Everett's feet up on the ottoman. I pinch my eyes shut, then look again. He has only four toes on each foot.

"Freaky, isn't it?" he says, wiggling them.

Makes sense now how he managed to get out of P.E.

I put the mugs on the coffee table.

"They work just the same, only no rock climbing for me. Don't look so shocked. I thought, you know, considering."

"Sorry, I just need a moment to adjust. I've never seen anyone with four toes before."

"And I've never seen anyone with such an impressive figure."

"Please."

"I'm serious. You've got to be the most gorgeous woman in town."

"You don't mean it."

"Do I look like I'm in a position not to mean it?"

"Drink your coffee, you fool. I'll get you those socks."

In the garage is more than just a box of Ron's underthings. There's his desk and file cabinets and the stupid wooden bust of Sitting Bull from when he went on a spiritual retreat to South Dakota and came back wearing a poncho and holding the bust in the crook of his arm. He said he had a vision during the sweat-lodge ceremony. He said he saw faces on his hands and legs, and in the dirt, too. He said everything is made of faces. For the next week he ate with his hands and took baths in a big metal bucket in the backyard. I thought I had lost him until later that week, when he was back to day-trading, screaming at his monitor, slamming drawers. He said something like, "Sitting Bull never lost a thousand pork-belly futures in five minutes," and that was the end of his spiritual awakening. Then July 4, 2006, and, as always, he had to put on the biggest spectacle in the neighborhood, drove all the way to the New Hampshire border to load up on fireworks, and, who knows, maybe those visions came back to him and that's why he stood over the lit fuse so long. Either way, I've seen horrific things before, so Everett's toes are no big whoop. They're actually kind of cute.

"It's funny," Everett says, pulling up the socks. "I've never been invited into anyone's house before."

"I should've; I mean . . . I don't think I was ever a nice person."

"My whole adult life I've delivered mail, never missed a day of work."

"I probably wasn't happy. I could never keep a secret. Now

it's like I'm the secret people are keeping from me. I don't know how to get outside myself, you know? I don't know how to get free."

"Even during that hurricane we had a couple years back, I remember the wind was coming from all sides, sort of holding me in place like a giant hand, and I had on my rain slicker, and my hat went flying off my head, and people had their generators running, and not one of them asked if I felt like holing up inside for a while. I ended up sneaking into the Putters' shed, and then the roof got peeled right off like the lid of a tuna can. Finally I made it back to my truck, and the rain came down so hard I could see paint fleck up off the hood. Next day, post office gets a dozen calls about missing mail, and I get chewed out for trying to save my own life."

"My mother used to dress me up and put makeup on me when I was little. Sometimes she'd make me sing for my father and my older brothers. Other times I'd dance with her and she'd lead. She was teaching me how to be pretty and subservient and stupid. She was a stupid woman. She made my father proud, and my brothers are both successful and have pretty blond stay-at-home wives. She showed them how to break a woman down."

"Every day, just before I head out on my route, I check my own mail first. It's almost always junk mail. I even deliver it, like it's any other person's house."

"Oh, Everett."

He takes my hand in his and holds it there by his knee for a while. I rest my head on his leg. He pets my hair and hums.

He keeps the socks on in bed. He traces my scars with his bitten fingernails. He kisses my neck, belly, and toes. His body hair is knotted. There's a pink birthmark on his side in the shape of California. He struggles to find me. I guide him with my hand. He's slow and gentle and loving.

He says, "Jesus," and "Oh, God," and "Yessah!"

He makes me feel full again.

And it's got to be the best feeling in the world.

ACTS OF LOVE

~~~~~

TARA WAS IN the kitchen slicing vegetables for a soup. I snuck up behind her and put my hands around her stomach. I pulled her into me. She pushed back. I tried to kiss her neck. She turned away.

"What is it? What's the problem?"

"I don't know. I'm trying. I've been trying."

"You have to try?"

"I don't like how it feels when you touch me. Please don't make me explain."

"Is it the baby?"

"Probably."

I went out on the back porch. That morning's snow glittered in the moonlight. I could hear Cal Baker's dogs barking to be let out. They went chasing after a squirrel, then stood around the tree like patient hunters until Cal whistled for them to come back inside. I waved to Cal and he waved back.

Everything was as it should be, except that Tara no longer loved me. Her not loving me made me feel boyishly afraid. Each room of our house seemed new and frightening. The same for the street we lived on, the town, and the office where I worked. I didn't know how to perform simple tasks. I panicked in the break room, grabbed at my chest, stumbled, and fell over the table of donuts. I was rushed to the hospital. The doctor said my heart was fine. He asked if I was under any acute stresses. He wrote me a prescription for alprazolam and referred me to a psychiatrist. The psychiatrist wrote me two more prescriptions. The pills made me feel heavy, and I sank into bed. I slept for three days as though sick from the flu.

Finally, Tara asked me to leave. She said we'd find a way to work things out with Colin.

"You named him?"

"Do you like it?"

"I want to be a part of his life."

"First take care of yourself."

"Please don't."

Her face was motionless.

WE WERE two men alone, standing outside our doors at the Affordable Corporate Suites near the battleship in Fall River, smoking, shivering in the cold, abandoned dogs too old to pity.

We wore knit caps and loose-fitting jackets and sweatpants and running shoes. Occasionally we glanced at each other, shoulders hunched, faces blurred by the yellow light flickering inside the plastic globes fixed above our doors.

We should have never known each other—not like this. We were lucky. We were men. White, privileged men. We could afford to take things for granted. Our dreams were attainable. Other successful white men mussed our hair and gripped the muscle between our shoulders and neck and called us good boys. We were good. Even when we were bad.

DURING THE second week I was there, the other man's car wouldn't start. I was going for my morning walk as if I had someplace to go. He asked me if I had jumper cables. He was driving a maroon Pontiac Sunbird, something out of the late seventies, worn and wheezing when it ran. I had heard him leave early some mornings. The passenger-side door was scratched and dented. He had New Hampshire license plates (LIVE FREE OR DIE), and the upholstery hung from the car's ceiling. In the backseat was a dog leash, a couple of water-fattened Robert Ludlum paperbacks, crumpled fast-food bags, and empty Styrofoam cups.

He had to pry the hood open with a crowbar. I watched him. He was a big, heavyset guy, with a hint of handsomeness he'd carried with him from boyhood. He lowered the hood onto the standing crowbar and attached the cables to the battery.

"That should do it," he said.

"I'll give it some gas."

The battery sparked when he turned the key. After a couple of tries, the motor turned over.

He thanked me and said, "You're in the corner room, right? Do you have a good view?"

"Of what?"

"Right," he said, and took a cigarette from his pack.

I understood he might want to talk and so I joined him. But we didn't talk. We listened to the motor rumble like a handful of change spinning in a laundry dryer.

I was hungry and the snow had started coming down. I went back to my room and made eggs and toast and sat on the bed in front of the TV.

The car ran for a half hour, until I heard the door slam and the tires spin out when he turned out of the parking lot onto the main road into town.

THE WEATHER had gotten warmer, though at night it was still cold. You could hear the residents of the Affordable Corporate Suites banging the electric heaters in their rooms. But the sky was clear and I could see the tall glimmering stars out the lone window of my corner suite. I watched them with the same blind awe with which I watched the television.

I had trouble sleeping. I took a blue pill, a yellow pill, a green pill, each developed to numb me into a state of irrevocable emptiness, where my thoughts and dreams and pain are flushed out into the space beyond space.

Sometimes I closed my eyes at four and woke up at seven. This happened both in the morning and evening. I tried masturbating. It was boring, or hopeless. My attention drifted toward the window, the frosted rooftops, the pink light that bloomed out of the sky at sundown and sunset.

TWO IN the morning, yesterday, or the day before yesterday, Pontiac Sunbird man was outside his door, reading the newspaper under his yellow light, his hands shaking, not from cold but from something else, nervousness maybe, or too much coffee. The skin around his eyes was red and puffed. He looked like a large child who, after threatening his parents for so many weeks that he was going to run away, had finally done so but now had gone too far and was looking for a way back home.

Maybe he doesn't remember me, I thought. People come and go from this place every day. We are interchangeable. To recognize each other is to recognize our own helplessness.

But enough, we are breathing, so let me tell you what happened the next day, today, when finally that Pontiac's engine wouldn't turn over and I got a knock on my door, my neighbor standing there in his coat, wearing a pair of jeans, washed and shaved, chewing a piece of gum.

He says, "This is such a morbid place. Let's get out of here for a while."

He holds out his hand, says his name, Doug. Doug Asplund, from Moultonborough, New Hampshire.

He's been doing survey work for the past two months. I don't know what that means, but it sounds just as boring as my job was, so I don't ask. This is the first day he's taken off work since he left New Hampshire. He's divorced and has two little girls who won't speak to him.

"Work keeps my mind from going dark," he says.

"That's natural," I say.

He looks at his broken-down Pontiac and says, "Let's grab a bite. I could use the company, and you probably could, too. I can hear you in the next room, through the bathroom wall. I don't know what person thought to build a place like this. I know your story, or parts of it, anyway."

Then he must have heard me sobbing the other night after I spoke with Colin on the phone. Though not really speaking with him but to him, saying, Hey, buddy, hey, little guy, what are you doing, you being good for Mama, are you having fun, do you miss your dada . . . and hearing his coo like a dove, his playful scream, his impatient sigh at not being able to reach through the phone and touch my eyes and nose and mouth. I couldn't take it. I had to hang up.

Doug heard how I had ended up here at the Affordable Corporate Suites. The guise that he was an indifferent guy smoking outside next door had been lifted. We could be friends. Or we could be enemies.

"Did you get your Applebee's coupon at the front desk?"

"What do you mean?"

"When you check in, they give you a twenty-five-dollar coupon for Applebee's. I thought we could head over there and have dinner."

I walk into the office but no one's at the desk. I wait. There were times before, when I needed more toilet paper, and eventually someone—a girl or the manager's sister—came out to meet me, having heard the buzzer when I entered. I don't know who the girl belongs to, the sister or the manager. She doesn't look like either. But all three of them seem generally content.

Doug is standing by the door, rubbing his hands.

"I could eat a horse," he says.

"No one's in there."

"That's fine. I'll cover the extra cost if necessary."

"I have money."

"No problem. I was just making a gesture."

"I am hungry, though."

"Good. Let's head out."

ONCE WHEN Tara and I passed by an Outback Steakhouse, she said that if you can't afford an extra ten bucks to support your local cuisine, then you shouldn't be eating out at all.

So we never went out. We didn't have any money.

But sometimes I'd sneak a quick bite at the Chili's down the street when they had specials or at the Cracker Barrel for their weekly fish fry. Something about the uniformity of those places is comforting. My waiter is always friendly and sincere; the food is hot and mediocre; drinks are strong and cheap.

At Chili's one night, I drank too many margaritas and fell asleep with the side of my face pressed against a plate of cold nachos. When I woke up, they didn't treat me like some skid-row drunk. We laughed. The bartender tossed me a washcloth. They had a picture of me on the wall the next time I went in, asleep on the nachos. I said it was fine if they wanted to leave it up, but if they wouldn't mind could they black out my face with a marker.

"My wife," I said. "Just in case."

But it wasn't my sneaking out for dinner or my coming home plastered or the moods of dreaminess I dropped into, a fishing bobber floating on the surface of what was real. I wanted to be a musician, an actor, a boat captain, a pilot, a seeker of precious metals. Time had run out. I was too old to start over. We had benefits, health and dental, and a 401(k). Tara instructed me to get on top when we made love. She said it was the best way to get her pregnant. I barely knew her. How could I know her? She was born with different parts. At my desk one morning, I flipped out and smashed my keyboard and flung my papers out into the hall. I drove the car up onto the lawn and spun the wheels until the sod and mud peppered the house. Tara screamed from the front step. I was blasting "Willie and the Hand Jive." Her face was freckled with dirt. I'd gotten to the bottom of the earth. There was nowhere else to go but away.

After two weeks inside Reflections, a rehab up in Duxbury, my insurance stopped paying, and I was back at my desk. There was nothing on it except the PC. I waited all day for a new password, but whoever gave out new passwords found a Band-Aid in his microwave chili cup and went to the hospital. The next day I got the password. The day after that it was like I never left. Months like days, then Tara standing in the kitchen; how beautiful she looked with Colin growing inside her, and how I wanted her more than ever. But by then it was over.

You can never go back to how it was. The time we went clamming on the shore and steamed them in the kitchen and then made love; or when we went up to Maine and stayed at the Fly by Night motel, where I sipped tequila from her belly button; or down in Florida, when she convinced the car-rental guy to upgrade us to a Corvette convertible; dressed like movie stars, we passed by the lines at the clubs into the VIP sections, living like there was no such thing as a past or a future, just living.

What could ever be better than that?

At Applebee's, Doug and I take a table in the bar area. We look at menus. Turns out we can get two meals for twenty bucks and a free appetizer if we combine options from box 1 with options from box 2, but not box 3, unless we want to pay five bucks extra.

Doug wants a burger—"They butter the buns here," he says, "just like my mother used to when I was a kid"—and a Bud. I'm considering one of the healthy options from box 4, maybe the honey-glazed chicken breast sandwich. It couldn't hurt.

We order. We stare at the basketball players on the televisions over our opposite shoulders. The boys fly across the court like electric charges.

Neither of us has a stake in either team, and during halftime Doug sifts around in his coat pocket and pulls out a tiny cylindrical piece of red birchwood, one of those old birdcalls my grandpa used to have.

"This little thing is a lifesaver," he says, winding up the instrument.

We listen to it call out of context. Heads turn. The sound is as unpleasant as it is unwelcome in a place like Applebee's.

"My father gave me one of these when I was a kid," Doug says. "I could never attract a bird with it. I thought there was something wrong with me. Dad said to keep trying. Then one day, you know, when I was least expecting it, a rose-breasted grosbeak perched on my shoulder. I hadn't even twisted the caller. And that magnificent bird rested on my shoulder for no more than a few seconds, but I swear to you, I can still feel it there, the light grip of its feet, just the slightest pressure."

Can I tell you I'm on the verge of breaking down right here and now?

Because I am.

Even as he complains to the waitress that our Southwestern egg rolls are cold after he's eaten half the plate, or when he lets out an openmouthed belch after sucking down his first beer, or how he indiscriminately challenges the couple's conversation at the table beside us. Even now I want to just let it all go.

And you might think I'm crazy, because your Doug Asplund is so different from my Doug Asplund. But neither is really Doug Asplund, can never be Doug Asplund. You'd have to shrink down to the size of a gnat, crawl up inside his brain, and buzz around awhile to understand Doug Asplund.

What I'm saying, I'm saying, you would have to not be you.

By the end of the night, we are good and wet, stumbling back to the Affordable Corporate Suites like rovers in a new land. We shake hands, friends.

"Until tomorrow, good sir," Doug says.

"Until tomorrow," I say.

* * *

Next day I get a call from my cousin in Tucson. He heard I'd fallen on hard times. He says he's been running a fairly successful contracting business and is more than willing to hire me as an adviser. Basically, I'd make sure his books were in line. "I'm no good with numbers," he says. He also says, "This is no charity gig."

But I know it is, and I couldn't care less.

For the first time in weeks, I welcome sleep.

Then there's a knock on my door. I open my eyes and stare up at the water stain on the ceiling. I hear the knock again, get up, and look through the peephole to see Doug standing there with his big arms across his chest.

"My heater broke," he says. "Is yours working?"

"I was asleep."

"Feels like yours isn't working, either."

"I didn't notice."

He walks past me through the kitchen and sits on the couch, rubbing his thighs.

"I used to be able to handle the cold. I used to be able to handle a lot of things."

"I can make some coffee."

"Sure. Coffee would help."

I dump out the old grounds and start a new pot. I can feel the cold now rising through the bottoms of my feet. While the coffee brews, I wrap myself up in the fleece blanket they give us when we check in. I can tell Doug wants to talk, but I'm too tired to hear new stories. When the coffee is ready, I pour him a cup and lie back in bed.

"This is good," he says. "Strong."

"I can't drink it any other way."

"I miss good coffee. Moultonborough has a little place that imports beans from around the world. I can still remember the smell of that place. I'd buy a pound and order a small espresso and sit outside when the weather was nice and watch the pigeons in the park across the way."

Maybe he's still talking, but I'm halfway to Arizona, visualizing heat as I shiver beneath the covers.

Then I feel the bed tilt and sink away from me. I can hear Doug's heavy breathing as he fixes himself onto his side. I don't move. Not even when he slings his arm across my body and slides up against me.

I begin to warm up. I close my eyes and slide into sleep.

Arizona is here.

So is Tara, and our past and future, the beasts of mind's creation, audacious acrobats flying from star to star. And Doug Asplund. Big, fat, handsome Doug Asplund, sitting alone on a bench at the edge of the universe, twisting his red birchwood birdcall, letting it unwind and twitter, until that rose-breasted grosbeak finally returns.

INCOMING MAIL

~~~~~

April 15

Hi, honey!

I probably shouldn't call you that anymore, especially if one of your bunkmates gets ahold of your letters. Do you have bunkmates? I know you said you sleep in trailers, so I guess they don't stack the beds in trailers, but maybe you still refer to each other as bunkmates, like in camp. You never did like camp, did you? I still have your letters from back then. I remember you saying the counselors picked favorites and that you were a better athlete than the other boys. You said no one liked you. Daddy and I told you to stick with it. We didn't want to get involved. Maybe if we were more a part of what was going on there, they wouldn't have made such a big stink about the fire. Anyway, Daddy refers to you as Private Baker when our friends ask about you.

How is he? Better! No more panic attacks. At least, I don't think so. We still can't go to the Steak and Sirloin for a while, because of his whoopsy, but I think that's more about them than it is about him. I'm sure there've been plenty of "accidents" in there considering how heavy the food is. He's taking medicine. He spends a lot of time in the basement, listening to old records.

Outside of that, there's nothing much to report. It's very warm here, so I can only imagine how warm it must be over there. I hope you're drinking lots of water and that they give you sunscreen. I'd send you some, but I think the air pressure causes the tube to explode. I'll have Daddy pick up those magazines for you, even though you know I don't like that kind of stuff. I probably shouldn't be writing this, but you're old enough now, and I think it's normal. When Daddy used to travel, he'd call me and ask me to talk dirty to him, and that was how he got over being lonely. So the magazines are fine and I bet they'll make you a hit with your bunkmates.

Which reminds me. I saw Caroline Dwyer last week on her spring break. I know you've always had a crush on her, and, MY DOG, she looks amazing. She's the captain of the women's lacrosse team at Cornell and, obviously, a brilliant student. I'm sure Kiki has potential, but maybe not the same potential as Caroline? Anyway, just throwing that out there. You know me, just throwing things out there, hoping they might stick. Remember when you were little and you'd try to catch my words with your little hands and put them in your mouth and swallow them, and then you'd burp and repeat the words back to me in a burpy voice? Daddy didn't like that, but I thought it was so cute I couldn't tell you to stop. I wonder if you remember being that young at all. I hope so. You used to make Aunt Becky and me laugh so hard we'd nearly pee our pants. That was the best time I ever had in my life.

Not that there aren't good times ahead for all of us.

Tough to imagine good times, though, especially when I go into Starbucks and right there next to the half-and-half I see the front page of *The New York Times* and there's always some photo of some Muslim's bloody or charred corpse and U.S. soldiers standing off in the distance. They never show the soldiers doing good things, like you say you do. Bunch of liberal know-nothings. It's like they're saying it's your fault because you're there. Well, weren't there bloody corpses before? See, you're right. I get worked up about it, and then I think, Look at all of us standing in line for our $4 mocha lattes and $3 lemon pound cakes (my little treat), and everyone looks bleary-eyed and, well, stoned, and I want to scream, WAKE UP! WAKE UP, PEOPLE! because they should really appreciate what you're doing more. That's what I think. I think they don't appreciate you like I do. This whole thing has really made me love you more, which I didn't even think was possible, didn't even think there was space in my heart to love you more than I did when you were born and when you lost your first tooth and when you broke your leg that time trying to jump the backyard fence and you squeezed my hand and didn't even shed a tear or yell or anything while we waited for the ambulance and the bone was sticking out of your leg and you looked right at it and said, "Cool." I knew you were a big, strong boy, but I didn't know you were that strong. Daddy says I shouldn't write you as much as I do, but I have so much time on my hands, and it seems like whenever I stop and think I get very anxious. This is about the only thing that relaxes me. I hope you don't mind.

Love, Mom

May 3

Dear Justin,

I've never known you to be so critical before. Sure, I've put on weight, and I guess I'm not the prettiest woman in the world, but at least I've got BRAINS. The last thing I want to do is have an argument six thousand miles apart from each other, especially in a letter . . . and, yes, I know I can e-mail you, but what's the fun in that? You just click a button and see words on a screen. There's something to be said about an old-fashioned letter with the person's handwriting on it so you know it's from them and you know they took the time and effort to make it readable for you. How do you know that if I send you an e-mail it isn't some Joe Schmo pretending to be me? Then he could make me say whatever he wanted and you'd think I was a crazy person.

Well, I guess you think I'm crazy, anyway.

All I was suggesting about Kiki was that maybe she isn't the right one for you. I think you have so much to offer a young woman, and to see you two together last time you were home, it just didn't make much sense. I mean, what she was wearing, it was like, "Hey, everybody, look at me!" and they were only really looking at her because you were with her. If she'd been on the street like that, they probably would've thought she was some kind of carnival sideshow act or one of those street women. I guess that's what girls from Falmouth are like. Trust me, Aunt Becky didn't look too good when I last saw her, and you know she's had her struggles with addiction. So let's call it even. You probably have so much going on that you don't even remember what you wrote in your letter. I'm not trying to criticize you. You're wonderful. Do I wish you'd come back and go to college and meet a young woman who didn't look so strung out? Of course. I'm going to be honest. That's what people appreciate most. That's what Daddy and I taught you. But it doesn't mean I don't respect your choices and YOUR honesty. Gosh, maybe I'm not even making sense. Maybe that's a good thing. Maybe I NEED to stop making sense. Daddy and I used to listen to that Talking Heads album when you were little. Daddy could dance! Did you know that? Can you imagine? Anyway, that was what the album was called: *Stop Making Sense*. Which I guess meant that you had to be fine with the world going crazy, and we were all a little crazy back then, but back then we were INSIDE being crazy. Now it's like I'm OUTSIDE, watching other people being crazy.

If you enjoy Kiki's company and she makes you feel good and says nice things to you, then I won't say another word about it, except, sorry, but Caroline Dwyer is not a stuck-up B. She's about the smartest, most forthright young woman I've ever met. She visited her mother after we had lunch and asked about you and how you were doing. Of course, I didn't tell her what you said, but the fact that she asked, and, according to Nancy, has asked multiple times when you're coming home, makes me think she's worth pursuing, if you want. Did you know she's writing a book? She's only nineteen years old and already she's going to be a published author and I'll be able to buy her novel at the bookstore! I'll admit I don't really know what she has to write about. I mean, she doesn't strike me as someone with a troubled life, but maybe she's writing about vampires or zombies or werewolves. I don't know why people are so obsessed with the living dead. Maybe they need diversions. Fantasies aren't all bad, but to me it seems like people actually believe they can live in a fantasy if they avoid reality long enough. When I was a girl, we used to watch the news every night. Now it's almost like some people just think it's a movie or something, or they'd rather watch a bunch of cartoons farting around.

WrestleMania was on last night. Your father mentioned it in passing. He didn't order it—he doesn't really watch TV anymore. I think it makes him anxious. We were watching *House* the other night and all of a sudden he grabbed his chest and went into the kitchen and put his hands on his head and walked around in circles, breathing through his nose. I thought it was just *House*, but then we tried to watch *Law & Order: SVU*, and he went out in the backyard and lay down on his stomach on the grass with his arms stretched out. He actually fell asleep out there. When he came in the next morning, the side of his face had all these blades of grass stuck to it.

I remember you guys playacting wrestling moves in the living room and once when you pinned him down and he cried uncle and how that was the last time you two fooled around like that. You were too strong for him. I think that got him sad. He keeps saying how old he is, but I don't really notice him getting older. He still looks like he did when we first met— handsome, handsome, handsome.

Love, Mom

P.S. I started taking hot-yoga classes. Not hot in the way you guys say a girl is hot but in the literal way, because the instructor turns the heat up to 104 degrees so that we're sweating our beans off in there. I've lost five pounds already! Don't think I don't listen to you.

May 26

Hi, honey.

I've decided that I can't let my mind focus on the ugly. Like I told you, if you focus on the ugly, you never see the beautiful. Didn't I tell you that? I meant to, anyway. I need to practice what I preach, because lately it's all been negative. Hot yoga helps me sleep better, but in the morning I can't stop my mind from racing. You probably can't tell me, but I wonder if it ever comes up about where bin Laden is? They say this Obama is a Muslim. I hope not. I wonder what you think. Not just about the upcoming election, which, actually, Obama is claiming he'll get the troops home sooner, or at least have a deadline of some sort, but about what you really think on a day-to-day basis. What thoughts go through your mind? Do you see Daddy and me? Do you see your house and the neighborhood and your school and the places we used to go to when you were a kid? I guess if I'm being honest about all this, then it wouldn't surprise me that sometimes you have dark thoughts like I do, that sometimes you think what it would be like to wake up and know you're dead or that everyone else is dead and you're the only one left and how are you going to survive? Or maybe you try not to think at all, which is probably the best thing you can do, because if you think about the past or future too much then you're not focused on what's in front of you in the present moment. That's what I think of most of all. I think about what's in front of you, what you're seeing.

I was reading in *Time* about this soldier's wife who just found out she was going to have twins, when her husband was killed by a roadside bomb. I wonder if you knew him. He wasn't in your platoon, but maybe you crossed paths. His name was Roger something. Anyway, she found out the good news and the bad news on the same day. That's what made it a newsworthy story. Soldiers are dying every day, and they group the numbers together and say them on television or just show them with some sad music playing (then it's *Get Verizon* or *Buy a Toyota* or *Eat at Applebee's*), but they never do a whole thing about it, and even this wasn't really a whole thing about this Roger but about his wife and how, intuitively, she knew something bad was going to happen after she found out about her babies. If you ask me, that's just pessimistic thinking, waiting for the other shoe to drop. But I felt sorry for her, I truly did, and her babies, too, and how I'll never even know what happened to them unless *Time* decides to do a follow-up in twenty years, if there's even a *Time* magazine or any magazine for that matter in twenty years. Either way, I canceled my subscription.

Daddy says hi, by the way. He means to write, but when he starts he just ends up staring at the page and then crumples it up. He is doing better, though, I think. He's gone bowling with his buddies a couple times this month. He gave me a big kiss on the lips the other night (not that that interests you). It felt good. I can't remember the last time he kissed me like that.

Guess what else? I've started singing again. Granted, it's just karaoke, but trust me, honey, they take it pretty seriously. I have to drive all the way to Wareham to this bar called Tenderhearts, and it's mainly just older women like your mother, but there are some super-polished performers there. At first, I could barely get through a song I was so nervous. But all the women are really supportive and they urged me to just let go. Last night I got a standing ovation. I sang Melissa Etheridge's "I'm the Only One." You know the song I used to sing in the kitchen? You don't like that type of music. I never understood why you listen to rap music. I just don't get what they're trying to say. Money, cars, girls. It's like they're making you think you're supposed to care about these things even when you can't get them. Not that you can't get money and cars and girls if you want, just not as much as they seem to have, which is funny, because if you realized that, then you probably wouldn't want to listen to them, but because you listen to them, then they can get those things.

I don't know. I guess when I was your age I thought the same thing about my parents, how they didn't understand me and never would.

There's a big annual competition at Tenderhearts this weekend, and I think I'm going to sing a Patsy Cline song. I've been told that if you want to win, you have to sing something that's not too fast and not too easy, because the judges are all past winners or local musicians and they have very refined tastes. I've been practicing a few songs in the shower so that Daddy doesn't get suspicious and just thinks I'm singing to sing. Our wedding song was "You Belong to Me." Did you know that? You probably didn't. Anyway, wish me luck. The prize is a week's vacation to a resort in Mazatlan, Mexico. I think if I win, that'll be a real treat for Daddy. He needs a vacation.

Enclosed is a picture of him asleep on the sofa. I thought it was funny because he looks just like Andy Capp.

Also enclosed is a comic strip of Andy Capp, in case you don't get the reference. A big box of goodies should be arriving soon. Make sure you share.

Love, Mom

June 19

Happy birthday, my little angel!

You only have to wait one more year until you can have a drink—ha-ha. I'm not THAT naïve. I still can't believe it. That picture of you and your bunkmates, oh, you all look so impressive. When did you get such big arms? Honestly, I shouldn't be surprised, it's just nature, but how you've grown! You used to be the size of one of your biceps. You barely made it, after all. You only weighed three pounds and five ounces, and they had you on a breathing tube and a PICC line, and Daddy and I were by your incubator every day, watching the monitors and waiting for those few moments when you'd wake up and look around with those dynamite black eyes, and how tough you were, not even crying when they had to take your blood or replace your tube. And now you're so big and strong and powerful, it's really a miracle.

Daddy wants me to remind you that you and Moe from the Three Stooges share the same birthday. I never liked it when he called you Little Moe, but I guess it was funny to him, especially when he'd pretend to knock your head with his high school ring and make that cluck sound and you'd laugh and try to poke him in the eyes. He says happy birthday, too.

I'm glad you all enjoyed my cowboy cookies! It's a special recipe, as you know, passed down from your grandmother. I'll tell you the secret ingredient, because, really, who cares if it's a secret? It's just a cookie. Brown sugar, that's it. Not much of a secret, right? Not that you guys are out there baking cookies or anything, but in case you want to impress a nice girl when you get back.

I'm sorry to hear about you and Kiki. Truly, I am. I know I

said some nasty things about her, but it still hurts me when something hurts you. Sometimes, at night, I feel this pang in my chest, and I think, Has something happened to Justin? It's such a terrible thing to have to go through, because there's no way to know. That's when I tend to overeat. Hot yoga was becoming a little too aggressive for me. I kept trying to get into these postures and my back was killing me and all the other women in class were bending this way and that, and I just thought, I'm never going to be able to do this. Needless to say, I've put back on some weight.

Oh, and this just in! Your mother won the karaoke contest at Tenderhearts. That's right—WON! I mean, only four or five people showed up and they had already bought the prize, so it wasn't any big deal, but it sure feels like a big deal. Daddy and I are going to Mazatlan at the end of the month! I'll make sure to send you pictures. He doesn't seem too thrilled, but I think once we get there he'll snap out of this little funk of his. Now I'm practicing my Spanish. *Me gusta.* That means *I like.* Hopefully I like everything. *Me gusta* everything. I'm a little worried about all the violence there, but the travel agent says there's no violence at the resorts. Of course, she's a Hispanic, so maybe she wants us to think that. I guess if you can risk your life, I can risk mine, right? I bought a new bathing suit. It's sort of a classic one-piece. I'm a bit chunky in the middle still, but maybe by the time we leave I can lose some of my muffin top and impress Daddy. We've been married almost twenty-two years. Can you believe it?! When I met him he was in a band called the Fatheads. They were so terrible that it became kind of an event to see them play. He really was a great guitar player, but the lead singer couldn't sing and the drummer couldn't drum and the bass player just thumped the same note over and over.

It was hilarious. Daddy used to play for you when you were a baby. Sometimes I would sing. He liked my voice. He said it sounded husky. I hate that word. *Husky*.

I miss that time in my life, when you were small and Daddy and I spent every day together. I miss a lot of things. Thinking about you makes me happy, though. I know you'll get over Kiki soon. I'm glad you're not mad at me. And don't forget, Daddy's birthday is next week. I remember he said you were the best gift he'd ever been given. You can't imagine how many times I've cried remembering him saying that.

Love, Mom

July 4

My not-so-little patriot,

I'm actually writing this letter two weeks before the 4th so that it'll be a kind of treat to hear from someone back home on this very special day. I wonder how you'll celebrate over there. Of course, ever since Nancy Dwyer's husband died in that unfortunate fireworks accident, we don't get to enjoy the holiday the same way as when I grew up. Sort of strange how people clap over something that blows up. I mean, isn't the point that we stop blowing things up?

Your father's doing better. The other night he told me he loved me. He hasn't told me that in a long time. He's been getting out of the house more, too. There's some color in his face. Hopefully he stays like this. It's hard being alone when you're not really alone.

Please write, dear. Maybe you have and the letters aren't getting to me. Who can trust the postal service nowadays? Everyone who works there looks like they're on dope.

Well, have to start packing for our big trip. Can you believe it? Your father and me in Mexico? Hope I don't get Montezuma's revenge. Guess that's not an image you want in your head. Think of the time we saw all those purple martins when Daddy took us on that Civil War trip way back when. I know you remember, because you wiped tears from my eyes with your little fingers.

Love, Mom

August 10

My sweet boy,

I haven't written because there've been some things happening back home that I'm not too proud to share with you and it's gotten me so down I've lost sight of my main priority, which is you. I'll thank you for the card you sent to Daddy, because he's not able. What's a Haji? Is that what they're teaching you over there, vocab? They should be teaching you how to protect yourself from those crazy Arabs. I mean, they're the ones trying to kill you.

Anyway, about Daddy—

Well, first things first, Mazatlan didn't go too well. I had rented a boat in advance (paid in advance, too), so that we could go scuba diving and see all the wild fish down there and maybe even a shark! That was my birthday present to Daddy. It was such a horrendous flight, so bumpy the oxygen masks came down. The stewardess said they weren't necessary, but because of the turbulence, they stayed hanging there in front of us, swinging back and forth like a constant reminder that any minute could be the last. We landed with a *thud* and the captain said something in Spanish and so I was like, go figure. Then we had to take a bus with about forty Asians, who kept shouting and snapping photos, as if the photos would come out through the bus windows. Daddy spent most of the plane ride and bus ride in the lavatory, doing God knows what. When we finally got to the resort, we were put in this room on the first floor right next to the laundry room so that all you could hear was this whirring sound day and night, because I guess they do laundry every hour of the day, which makes sense, seeing that they have almost four hundred rooms. I went to the front desk and asked if they could put us in a better room, but the place was booked solid for the whole week (some kind of Asian corporate getaway). The toilet wouldn't flush and the air conditioner was broken. I guess they only had one maintenance guy for the whole place, because he said he had to get a part for both things and getting a part meant driving into the city. But he didn't come back until nearly seven at night, and he stunk like alcohol and tried to fix the toilet but ended up breaking a different part and he'd forgotten whatever part he needed for the air conditioner and started banging the sides with his hands. Daddy finally got fed up and went out to the pool and fell asleep in a cabana (which they later charged us a hundred dollars for, because that's how much it costs to rent a cabana by the pool!). This very nice woman said she could put us up in the manager's office on cots if we wanted, because the maintenance man had to get this different part in the morning and the prospect of a working air conditioner that night was slim to none (*manly nun*, she said!). She assured us that everything would be in working order by noon, and, because I couldn't find your father, I followed her to the manager's office and took my shoes off and lay down on the cot. Well, I've never slept on a cot before and never knew I was such a restless sleeper, but something about the travel and the problem with the room and Daddy's strange behavior made it so I flipped over in the middle of the night and sprained my wrist. I thought for sure it was broken. Oh, you never want to spend a night in a Mexican hospital, honey, trust me. But that's what I did. That nice lady came with me—Luisa, I think her name was. And you know what? When I was crying from hurting my wrist, she sang to me, and she had the sweetest, softest voice, and I told her she should become a professional singer, and she said sometimes they let her perform in the restaurant but that she isn't pretty enough to be a professional. I thought that was kind of too bad and I could see she was upset about it, so I began singing, and all the way to the hospital we traded songs, and she sang in Spanish and I sang in English, and it was really beautiful. When we got to the hospital she started flirting with one of the doctors. There was a man with a gunshot in the arm sitting across from me, staring up at the television with his hand pressed against the wound. He kept making these hellish grunting noises. I got him a cup of water.

Next day I found Daddy spread out soaking wet in his pants and collared shirt on a chaise lounge chair near the outdoor bar. Some unruly children whose parents had rented the cabana for that day began swatting him with these swim noodles, and he literally got up and walked right into the pool. You can imagine the eyes on us as I took him to our room. At least the shower worked, but your father had forgotten about the toilet, so . . . DISASTER!!!

Finally, we get on the boat and he doesn't want to go under. I've never seen him so terrified. I mean, he's been on boats before. You and he used to go fishing, if you remember, and I didn't think the ocean would be that different, but he turned white as a cloud and kept shaking his head, and even after the so-called captain gave him a nip of tequila, he wouldn't do it. So, after taking some of those Mexican painkillers (really just

Tylenol!), it was me with the fishes (no sharks, thank God!), and what an amazing experience. What forces created such colors? There was a point where I actually felt like a fish. I wished Daddy was with me. By the time I came back up, he was drunk as a skunk and was talking like a pirate and then went to the bathroom off the side of the boat, which the captain considered the last straw. I felt obliged to tip him forty dollars I was so embarrassed.

Some trip, right?

I guess an Asian couple got lost or sick or who knows, because a room opened up on the fifth floor overlooking the water, and so for the next three nights we had a great view and a working toilet and a cool, comfortable room. But Daddy didn't seem to care. He drank and slept and didn't set foot on the sand once.

I'll tell you another secret. I snuck out one night and went down to the beach, where they were roasting a pig, and ended up smoking pot for the first time since I can't remember when. I was so high, MY LORD! I even danced with these young boys who had tribal tattoos on their arms and legs. They both kissed me on the cheek, and one slapped my rear end. I shouldn't be telling you all this, but what the heck, you're old enough to know some things about your mother.

Daddy's in such a state I don't know what to do. My feeling is that he never really dealt with his mother's death, your grandmother. You were too young to remember her, and just between you and me and a hole in the wall, I didn't really think much of the woman. She was abusive toward your father. Not physically (though he used to make offhanded comments about a paddle that hung in the pantry) but verbally, calling him stupid and a waste of space, those kinds of things. I think he was glad when she died. Maybe that's what he can't get over. The guilt.

When we got back home, he went down in the basement with a package of crackers and a block of cheese and didn't come up until two days later. It gets to me, us being unable to talk like we used to, and I can't really talk to you, because writing and reading letters isn't the same, and so it's like I'm living on these images of the past, but I'm not sure that what I'm remembering is what actually happened or if I'm re-creating what happened to get me through the day. I remember during my one year in college, I took this philosophy course taught by some young guy who everyone knew slept with his students, though that's besides the point, and I remember him saying that none of us are really real, as in, none of us are really what we are; only a trillionth of a trillionth of a part of what we are is what we think we are. It actually kept me up some nights. I'd look at myself in the mirror and wonder where the rest of me was.

When Daddy came upstairs, I asked him if the cheese was a birthday present for his stomach, and he sort of smiled. I ate most of the cake I made for him and gave the rest to Nancy Dwyer, though I'm pretty sure she's off sweets, or can't eat them, considering all the plastic surgery (story for another time!).

Oh, well, that's that. They tell us in the support group to be honest with you, and so I'm being honest. Really, though, I'd like to hear more about what's going on over there. Your letters are so short. Maybe it's just always the same, but that's hard to believe. Hard to believe there could be more going on in Wequaquet than all of the Middle East! I'm at a point where I think I can handle knowing the truth. So, let me hear it.

Love, Mom

September 17

Hi, honey.

Writing this while looking over the photographs you sent me, and WOW! That's a picture of a spider? Well, geez, I'm glad you killed it. Who would think you'd have to shoot a spider?! It's like something out of a science-fiction movie. I have to say, it's strange that the first time I hear from you in almost two months is when you send me this awful photo. But I'm glad I'm hearing from you. And, yes, we heard the phone ring that night, and I actually knew it was you. I could sense it. But the phone is next to your father, and he just picked it up and put it down on the receiver without even thinking. Then I smacked him on the head and he woke up and looked around and went back to sleep. Seriously, sometimes I feel like I'm living with another person altogether. Your father is gone almost every night, and when he gets back he smells like he's been washing with a different soap and I say, did you take a shower somewhere, and he says he went swimming. That's what he does now, I guess, he goes swimming (and after all that happened in Mexico!). It's some kind of group. They call themselves the Late Night Lake Effect. They go swimming at night when it's cold. It gives them a rush. Of course, it's not something I'd like to do because I can't stand the cold, and your father knows that and it's probably why he's picked the most obscure group to join in all of Wequaquet. Afterward, they go to the Y and then have coffee and talk about God knows what.

Luckily your aunt Becky is moving back to town. I know you two didn't get along after you claimed she threw you into the deep end of the community pool that summer, but she's supposedly clean and sober and doing great! I'm looking forward to seeing her. I think it'll help take the edge off.

Please call again soon. I'm sleeping on the other side of the bed now.

Love, Mom

September 30

Dear Justin,

So I guess no one is speaking to me now. Between you and your father, it's as if I don't exist. And Aunt Becky, oh, I'll be surprised if they ever let me into Tenderhearts again. Despite the name, it's not some honky-tonk, and you don't take your top off and get up on the bar no matter how many guys are hooting and hollering and waving dollar bills.

I might as well inform you that your father and I have decided to take a little "break" from each other. Actually, I decided. Whatever he told you (and I know you've been chatting, because the last time we spoke, he said that you were upset about how worried I was and that you needed to be focused on yourself, not on me, which makes sense, but even if I was in the Congo I'd still be thinking about you and Daddy), he probably didn't tell you all of it. I won't go into the dirty details, but you deserve to know. Let's just say your father has found a new person to spend his time with. I guess I could see it coming. He's been out every night with the Late Night Lake Effect and there are men and women in the group, and you know how it is when you have something in common with someone. According to the rumors, your father has been spotted getting very close with a woman at a Dunkin' Donuts in Falmouth. Go figure! So, what did I do? Well, I let it go for a while, until a few nights ago when the phone rang and I thought it might be you calling, and I reached over and picked it up and said, "Hello?" and

I could hear someone breathing on the other end and they hung up. Then I realized your father wasn't in bed. So I dialed *69 and a woman answered and said, "Hey, sexy pants," whatever the hell that means, and I said, "This is NOT sexy pants!" And she said, "How did you get this number?" And I said, "It was pretty simple, stupid." And she said, "I know all about YOU, missy." And I said, "Oh, then you know that if I ever find out who you are, I'll cut your nipples off." Can you believe that?! I literally have no idea where that came from, but I said it, and she hung up, and I sat there in bed with the phone in my shaking hand, and I could feel this violence flow through me, and I threw the phone through the window, which wasn't very smart because it's freezing out, in September!—so much for global warming—and so I had to get some extra blankets from the closet and that's where I saw your father's wet suit, hidden underneath the summer linens, and I knew he wasn't going out with the Late Night Lake Effect anymore; he was seeing this woman! And so what happened that night when she called was that he was on his way to her place (dressed in his SEXY PANTS, I assume) and stopped to help this guy who was standing in the middle of Isaac Road, waving his hands. I guess he was part of a carnival or something, because he was hauling the fattest man in the world in this trailer, but the trailer had come unhitched and he didn't have the strength to pick it up and the fat man was in the trailer crying and the whole thing was like an awakening for your father because, and this is him talking now, he could see how hiding this giant secret was eventually going to cause him to break down. What a freaking metaphor! He ended up dislocating his shoulder getting the trailer up on the hitch, and the carnival guy had to drive him to the hospital, so that's why this woman was looking for him. I didn't know anything about it until he came home around four the next morning with his arm in a sling and I was up, sitting at the kitchen table, having had so much coffee my temples were pounding, and you know what the first thing your mother did was? The first thing I did was console the man. I actually pretended like that woman never called and like I didn't see the wet suit in the closet, and even when he asked why it was so drafty in the house, I pretended like there wasn't a broken window in the bedroom, and I put my arms around him and he said, careful, and I held him, and he said he thought he might be too old to go swimming at night, and I said maybe that's true. Can you believe that? I accepted the lie before he even told it. And I know why. It's because I'm scared to be without him. I can't remember the last time I thought about what to do with a day that didn't include you or your father. Then I thought, Can I change? I mean, look at Justin, he's strong and brave and doing what I could never imagine doing, and now look at Daddy, he's fought through depression and having his son gone and was able to find a new woman at his age. I actually envied him. I thought: Why can't I go out there and do something different, too? So, you know what I did? I got in the car and drove to New York City. Just on a whim! I didn't even know how to get to Manhattan, and I pulled into a gas station and this nice (what do you call them? Hajis?), this nice Haji told me I was in the Bronx and gave me directions on how to get to Midtown and then I saw all the lights in Times Square and I nearly crashed because everything was so overwhelming. I asked someone who looked like he lived in Manhattan which was the fanciest hotel in the city, and he said it depended on what my idea of fancy was, and I said I was looking for a place with big crystal chandeliers, which to him, I guess, meant an old kind of fancy, and so he told me the Pierre, and I knew I'd heard of the Pierre or seen it in a movie, and so I just left the car parked there in Times Square and took a cab to the Pierre and asked the hotel clerk if they had any suites. I didn't even care about the price. They must've thought I was some kind of big deal, because all of a sudden there were two bellhops at my side, asking me if I needed help with my luggage, and I said I didn't have any luggage—I was planning on going shopping the next day—and they nodded and led me to my room and showed me how everything worked and even unwrapped a giant basket of fruit and cheese that was on the oak table in the dining area of the suite. Then you know what one of these men said to me? He said, "It gets lonely in a city this big," and gave me this look like he could help relieve me of this loneliness if I just gave him the okay, but that's not what I was looking for. I didn't want another man. I wanted to be alone, and I told him so and tipped him and the other bellhop and ordered them to have a dish of chocolate-covered strawberries brought up right away. Can you imagine? Your mother in a suite in New York City, ordering grown men to bring her chocolate-covered strawberries! I'll tell you I had the best sleep in my entire life in that bed, and when I woke up, I was looking right over Central Park, over the whole city, like some kind of queen, and all the people below were so small and they all looked the same, and it came to me that it didn't matter what any of us did, because, look at all these people, they don't know me and I don't know them, but we're all moving through the world doing whatever it is that we do and we don't really know what that is and we don't have time enough to find out and so better to do what you really want to do with the time you have. That's what I figured out in New York City. And when I got home, I told your father I knew what he was doing and I wasn't mad and I understood but that we couldn't live together anymore.

And now, for the first time in my life, I feel truly free. I don't have to worry anymore. I don't have to concern myself with other people. Their life is not my life.

I hope you don't think your mother's nuts. I don't think I am. Lately I feel like there's this voice that flows through me, something beyond the world, and it tells me to relax and be calm, everything's going to be all right. And for the first time in my life I believe that's true.

I know this might not make much sense, honey. But how can I possibly explain to you what it's like to be me?

Love you with all my heart and soul.

Mom

OKAY SEE YOU SOON
THANKS FOR COMING

~~~

DAD PULLS UP in his Lincoln Navigator with his new girl-friend, Roxy. She has spiky black-and-blond hair and makeup to match her hair and a loose blouse, so loose that when she breaks her heel in the pothole in the driveway, one of her big fake boobs pops out. Makes me laugh so hard I can barely breathe. Kit gets the bag and I take big breaths into the bag, looking out the window as Dad helps Roxy up to the steps and rubs her toes.

"Feel better?" Kit asks.

"I swallowed a boog."

"I can't stand how sexy you are when you can't control yourself."

"Baby," I say.

I crumple up the bag and toss it behind the couch, meet Dad at the front door, and say, "Let me smell your hands."

"Let's not," he says.

"The baby," I say.

He lets me smell them.

"Yep, need to get you in the decontamination chamber."

"What's that?" Roxy says.

Dad gives her a look like, Didn't we talk about this on the ride up?

At least Roxy speaks English. Dad's last girlfriend was some Puerto Rican named Lupe, who was five years younger than me. Kit and I went down for Christmas, and his house was all done up with depressing scenes of Jesus dying on the cross, votive candles, dead flowers. Dad was watching basketball on TV and Kit gave me a look like, Possible bonding moment? And even though it smelled like Lupe was cooking a pot of trash, Kit went into the kitchen to help out. So I asked Dad what the score was, even though it was clear what the score was, because I could see it on the banner at the bottom of the screen.

Dad said, "You need glasses or something?"

Then he changed the channel to CNN, a special about heroes, and this hero being a guy who built an irrigation system in some dried-out village in India.

"That's impressive," I said.

And Dad said, "What's impressive is putting a roof over your family's head. That's a hero."

He was talking about himself, of course. He did put a roof over my head, for a while. But all these muddy Indians slurping up water and smiling and high-fiving the guy/hero and his team—

"How long have you and Lupe been together?"

"Since last month."

"Moved right in, huh?"

"It's like living with a maid. I might marry this one."

And I guess she was a good woman to have around. She sure was sexy, but, problem was, no one could understand what she was talking about. Unless of course you remembered to bring your Spanish phrase book. Lots of nodding during dinner. Lots of passing around whatever that dish with the bone sticking out of it was.

When we left, Lupe gave me a big kiss and said, *"Feliz Navidad!"*

Kit spent all night in the bathroom and came out the next morning with her head shaved, which was pretty cool actually.

Middle of January, Dad said he was cleaning out the stable again, meaning no more Lupe.

At the sink next to the stacked washer-dryer, Roxy seems confused about what she's supposed to be doing here.

In my mind I'm like, Hey, Roxy, haven't you ever seen an industrial-size tub of orange crystals and a horse brush?

Then she goes, "But, Poopy, my nails."

"She calls you Poopy?"

"It's just a nickname," Dad says.

"So you don't mind if I call you Poopy, too?"

"Don't get cute. Where are the towels?"

I grab some towels.

"You need to scrub your arms, hands, and fingers for exactly two minutes. Remember to get between your fingers. I'll start the timer once the water heats up."

I stand outside the door with the egg timer. I hear Roxy say she can't feel her hands, it's like she has no hands. Good. That means all the critters in her skin are dying. Somber joy at seeing the old man in an apron. Somber because V3's a preemie and his body is still slightly curved like an *S* and there's a bruise on top of his head from where he got stuck in Kit's uterus and because we don't know how he'll turn out developmentally; Dr. Duncan says it's out of our control, a wait-and-see. Dr. Duncan doesn't believe in the nurture theory. Of course, we'll still love him even if he isn't mentally all there, because, really, who is?

"Okay," Dad says.

I check their hands and fingers for any possible debris.

"We're clean. Where is it?"

"It?" I say.

"The baby. The boy, I mean. Where's my grandson?"

A big thump in my chest at hearing him say *grandson* for the first time.

I LIMIT Roxy's interaction to approximately twenty seconds. At sixteen seconds, Vincent Three gets squirmy and she says, "He's like a wet noodle," which, do you have any idea how offensive? I cradle him in my arms and carry him to Dad, who has been carefully avoiding V3 since we walked into the nursery, instead studying the framed paintings of anime stills, which Kit and I collect and trade, flipping open the baby book to the first pages of V3 with his head bloodied and wing split, covered in plastic wrap, purple and blue, scale reading two pounds, ten ounces. He claps the book shut.

Roxy is making faces at V3, and at last he's overwhelmed and his face goes pumpkin orange and he starts wailing like a red-tailed hawk.

Dad turns and looks at V3.

"Boy has some pipes on him, doesn't he?"

"You want to hold him?" I say.

"Maybe when he's calmed down," he says, and takes Roxy's hand.

I hold V3 under the arms. He likes hanging there. He stops screaming and stares at me like I'm a Martian.

"Goo," he says, with those wide black endless universes.

AFTER BABY-VIEWING is over, Dad asks if there's coffee and I say sure and we go into the kitchen and I put the coffee on.

Dad says, "You look good, Vincent."

Whoa, compliment! But pretty sure he's just saying it to say it, because I look exactly the same as I did at Christmas, when he told me I could stand to lose a few. All my life I've been chubby, but Kit loves me chubby. She lays her head on my belly and falls asleep. She says I'm like a big, soft pillow. What's more comfortable than a big, soft pillow? And so there's no reason not to be chubby if Kit loves me, because she's all I really care about, she and Vincent Three, and right now V3 loves everything and everybody, even Grandpa, Dad.

We watch the coffee percolate. Kit comes in and twirls her finger next to her head, her way of saying, Chick is whacked.

Roxy isn't far behind.

"I was just telling your son's wife about my book," Roxy says.

Dad looks at me like, Please don't.

"What about your book?" I ask.

"It's a children's story, but it's based on my life growing up, which wasn't all that pleasant. My father had a lot of people after him about money, and one night he tried to rob a check-cash place with a water pistol and the guy behind the counter shot him in the chest. My sister and I were orphaned. My mother had left before I could know what she looked like. I'm gonna call it *Toy Guns and Broken Hearts*."

"Pretty catchy title, don't you think?" Kit says, grinning.

"I'm writing it because I think there're a lot of kids who don't have nice homes and can relate, you know?"

"Don't kids read books to escape their crappy home life?" I say, and glance at my father.

"See, my thinking is that this idea of escape is what's making kids so crazy. If they had a little bit more reality in their lives, then they wouldn't be shooting up schools."

"Not too big a leap, Kermit," Kit says.

"What did she call me?"

I give Kit a look like, Maybe take it down a notch, because I know she's being smart and at this point Roxy is making me anxious and a little depressed.

"Almost time for dinner?" I ask Kit.

"Sure," she says. "I get it."

FIRST THING Dad and Roxy notice is no chairs, just cushions around the coffee table.

"We're going tribal," I tell Dad.

Kit loves curries. She's got a blog called *Curry Whore,* where she posts about this or that curry. I'm a dumpling guy myself. But I can go for just about anything. Tonight, though, we're having roasted lamb chunks and asparagus and a batch of injera Kit has made from scratch.

When I was a kid, I used to scoop the center out of my dinner roll and stuff as much food as I could inside. Then Dad would take my plate and dump it on the floor of the mudroom, where we kept our shoes and jackets and sports equipment. "Eat," he'd say. "Just like a pig." Now, tables turned. No utensils in this house. And what are you going to wipe your hands with? Your tongue, dummy!

"This is how the Ethiopians do it," I say.

"Not all Ethiopians," Roxy says.

Hmm. Sensing Roxy has some sort of secret involving a man of Ethiopian descent.

Looks like Dad's decided not to eat, and after one bite Roxy's thinking maybe this might do a number on her insides, but Kit and I eat like it's our last meal. We don't care about the grease or gas or especially the mess. Sometimes we have naked day and just do what we'd normally do but in the buff. We're natural sorts. We do what we want. That's why we love each other so much. She gets me and I get her. You can't love someone unless you get them. All of a sudden it just happens, and you're both like, all right, power on.

"Where did you two meet?" I ask.

"You want to tell him?" Roxy says.

"You go ahead," Dad says.

"Well, it all sort of started back when my ex-husband and I were looking for a house on the Outer Banks, and so someone recommended your father, and he was so charismatic, and . . ."

As Roxy drones on, I look at Kit and imagine her with seven heads and how much fun that'd be to get one talking about one thing and another about another thing, and maybe the third one could sing and the fourth could give me kisses, and the fifth could start arguing with the first and second about how they don't know what they're talking about concerning the things they're talking about, and the sixth and seventh would keep watch for photographers who might have heard the rumors about a woman with seven heads.

Roxy says, "Are they even listening?"

I look at Kit on her phone, probably playing Zombie Tsunami, which, go ahead, try to beat my score, babe.

"Honey," Dad says. "That's just their way."

"Yeah," Kit says, looking up from her phone. "It's our way."

"We appreciate you having us over, son, but maybe it's time we get going."

"Wait," I say.

On the mantel are an assortment of misshapen bowls, ashtrays, and mugs from when Kit's stepdad took pottery during his two years on unemployment. They basically stand for, Look, here's a guy who was really bad off and he still tried to do something worthwhile, even though he failed. So some significance attached.

I take down a bowl that's sort of oval shaped, with a kind of mossy-green color to it and the initials R.I.P. in red at the bottom, which, those are his initials—Richard Ivan Pearly—and, sure, why not have a little fun if, say, someone decides to fill the bowl with a bag of mini-donuts or M&M's or nacho cheese, then you'd be like, you know, this bowl is telling me something.

"For you," I say, and hand the bowl to Roxy.

Her eyes brighten.

THE RAIN turns to snow and starts sticking to the mulch and grass and pavement. Soon the cars are covered. Then some tree branches snap, and Kit and I run to the living room to make sure we message the rest of our team that a possible power outage could prevent us from taking Germany.

I hear Roxy in the dining room saying something like, "This entire generation sees the world through screens. It's ludicrous."

I say to Kit, "Someone's taking twenty-first-century philosophy at the Community U."

Kit snorts.

Team says they'll make camp, but how long they can make camp they're uncertain, plus all the artillery Kit and I have collected over the past few months and my skills as a first-class sniper, they'd hate to lose us, but if the Germans discover the camp—

"Fucking hypothetical, Jarvis!" Kit yells.

I love it when she gets mad. Her whole forehead wrinkles up, and these little bubbles of spit pop at the corners of her lips.

"You and Dave take some bong hits and eat some Doritos. We have company."

But Kit knows this isn't a viable excuse. Neither is the baby. At least with the baby I can put him in the Björn and keep playing. I wonder what it would be like if I put Dad in the Björn and carried him around the house.

"What's so funny?" Kit asks.

"I'll tell you later," I say. "You'd fart if I told you now."

Which is true, because that's what Kit does when something's crazy hysterical.

DAD AND Roxy are discussing dining options given the inclement weather. Dad grips the back of my neck, says, "You're doing good with that boy, you know."

I almost want to cry, that's how overwhelming it can get when Dad is kind.

Roxy sniffs her nails.

"I'd like to see that little guy one last time, but I don't want to have to use that stuff," she says.

"You're not really leaving so soon?" I say.

"Looks like a nasty storm coming, bud, and Roxy's starving."

"So?" Roxy says.

"I guess," I say, because maybe she's the best Dad can do.

Vincent Three is wrapped snugly, sleeping peacefully, his head like a large grape sticking out from his swaddling blanket.

"Oh, dear," Roxy says, grinning so hard I can picture her face breaking apart.

I hear one of the Xbox controllers crack against the wall in the other room. Clearly the camp didn't hold and our unit moved on without us. Kit's devoted to our fantastical cause, the same as she's devoted to me and to Vincent Three and our life together, our family.

"Shit-suck-fucker," she shouts from the other room.

V3 spits up on Roxy's blouse.

"Christ," she says. "Do you know how much?"

Dad takes V3 and cradles him while Roxy runs to the sink, her boobs bopping up and down.

I feel bad for Dad, bad and sad, the way he probably felt for me the time he took me to meet a girl at the Putt-Putt and she didn't show and I played all eighteen holes alone, and when I was at the eighteenth hole I saw Dad sitting in the car, waiting, and I knew he hadn't left, but I also knew he believed I should feel hurt—his reasoning being that he had been hurt before, has been hurt since, and unless you know that hurt, you can't know love.

When Roxy snaps her fingers, Dad hinges his neck away from Vincent Three, then hands me my boy. With a look of joy-lessness and sorrow, he takes hold of my shoulders and gives me a kiss on the forehead.

"Thanks for having us," he says.

"No problemo," I say.

And with that he nods, as if confirming something we both know but can't say.

FRIEDA, YEARS LATER

~~~

THIS MORNING LEONARD Putter's kids are poking their bellies, asking if something is wrong with their stomach hole.

"It burns," they say, scratching.

"You have to wash better," he tells them.

"You and Mommy didn't teach us that," they claim.

Surely we did, Leonard thinks. Surely we showed them how to wash and they watched us wash and watched us wash them.

But maybe they're right. Of all the things he can remember, Leonard can't remember teaching them how to clean their navels. Or brush their teeth. Or clip their nails. In fact, both Lucy and Teddy are nail-biters. Cindy's always smacking their hands away from their mouths.

"Go on and play," Cindy says. "Mommy and Daddy are talking."

She sips her coffee, looks at Leonard despairingly.

"Don't pity me," Leonard says.

Last night he'd begun fondling her. Then she said, "To the left," in a harsh, sexless voice. He rubbed her clitoris as though it were a spot on the counter that wouldn't come off. "That's too hard," she said. "Just go ahead and put it in me." But there was nothing doing down there. He stroked himself. "Do that in the bathroom," Cindy said. "I can hear it slapping around. It's disgusting." When he got up, she grabbed the sheets and pulled them over her. He ran the water until the bath was full and eased himself into the tub. He couldn't remember the last time he took a bath. It was so relaxing he woke up a few hours later, shivering, barely able to make it to the bed.

"This sort of thing happens to older men," Cindy says, looking down at her magazine. "It has to do with stress and failure and a lack of reckoning with your past. Here, it's all right here."

She hands Leonard a folded-over magazine and points at an article with a photograph of a man looking lost and confused, sitting on a pointy rock, staring at the sparkling blue ocean.

TROUBLE IN BED = TROUBLE IN HEAD

BY FRIEDA CALLOWAY

. . . As we know, men are easily embarrassed by sex. It's something that stems from childhood, giggling at boobs and butts while covering their stiffening crotches. But with age and experience, especially in this country, comes a period of malaise that can lead to impotence.

Tell me if you've heard these excuses before:

"I've had a long day."

"I must've eaten something funky at lunch."

"My back is stiff."

"You don't seem into it."

Women remember the bra-snapping, dress-lifting, fellatio-mimicking boy in the back of the classroom. We didn't like him then, but we wonder, Where is he now? That horniness comes in handy when you yourself have had a long day.

At first we feel anger, then a period of inadequacy, followed by apathy. You've considered an affair with your kids' soccer coach, but, believe me, he's no different. The real issue isn't . . .

Wait, Frieda the Virginity Collector? He turns the page. At the bottom is a photograph of her in a tree pose on the beach. It *is* Frieda. She had been a senior at Wequaquet High when Leonard was a freshman. She was known for taking boys' virginities. It was like a hobby for her. A year before he started going with Cindy, Leonard lay stiff as a mummy on Frieda's bed as she rolled her hips over him until he burst. Afterward she thanked him and kissed his cheek.

According to the magazine, she's a *freelance writer, life coach, and certified yoga instructor, currently living in Boynton Beach, Florida.*

Leonard pretends to keep reading, looking at her photograph, thinking maybe this is a sign.

LEONARD TEACHES American history at Wequaquet High. Most of what he teaches is washed away in the sludge of microwavable foods, pink music, and reality-television shows. You can't scream in the sludge, he tells his students, they won't hear you. But still they bark in the hallways, shouting, "Imf imf imf!"

It's difficult to get time alone. Sometimes he hides in the janitor's closet to catch his breath. If he's in there too long, he gets high on the ammonia and stumbles out dizzy. This makes for an interesting lecture on the American Revolution.

Home is no solace. Not a room in the house he can call his own; each one a box of toys, foul smells, and bad drawings.

At night, Cindy holds her tablet on her knees, the screen so bright it swells out into his field of vision, making it difficult to read from *Confederate Love Songs,* the book she had given to their children to give to Leonard for his birthday:

> "I have f h in what we're doing, but can I re y on faith
> a ne?"

Cindy taps the screen, it goes dark; taps again, and it shines like a spotlight. Finally she pulls the cover over the screen, shuffles to the bathroom, pees with the door open, flicks shreds of dinner out of her teeth with floss, gargles like a woman drowning, shakes her contacts clean, gets back into bed, and stretches her arms above her head and draws her knees up as if falling from a cliff into a deep blue lake. She says good night in a tone suited for a doorman and, minutes later, asks Leonard to shut the light off or read downstairs. She's got a busy day tomorrow. The tablet will remind them what's next, with a five-second symphony of electronic noise. The past is reduced to useful mistakes: overpriced restaurants, distrustful mechanics, people they shouldn't invite to the kids' next birthday parties, because they didn't bring a gift and ate more than anyone else.

The couch, the quiet, the place that is not this place is instead more horrific. Appreciate what you have, Leonard. Don't be so morose.

> . . . My dear Mary-Alice, I saw a man take a ball to the
> leg during our last battle. They poured whiskey on the

wound and whiskey down his throat. He was given a
rotted tree branch to bite down on while they sawed the
leg off at the knee. His teeth broke through the branch,
broke through his tongue. There's no indication he's to
be sent home. He is valuable in that he is a broad man
with a wide back and we can stack many supplies on
top of him . . .

Leonard tries to relax. He meditates, medicates, and mastur-
bates. Some nights he doesn't sleep. Some nights he thinks
about his mother. He wonders if she's looking down at him, at
the awkward man she produced, gripping his penis and making uncomfortable-looking faces as he comes. His mother had
been a hopeless woman. She always talked about death—death
of her parents, of people in town she knew, of people she had
read about in the paper, and, most of all, her own death.

She had said, "I'm going to die, Leonard. Me."

TWO DAYS later, Leonard decides to take a week off from
school. He tells Cindy that he's flying to Virginia for the annual
National Council of History Education conference. Cindy says
time away will be good for the both of them. She cares, but
maybe she cares too much. As a part-time hairstylist at Uppercuts, she's always trying to make the customers feel better. She
tells balding men they're sexy, overweight women that the hair
is what men really care about, kids with impossible cowlicks
to feel fortunate they're not bald or fat.

"I'll miss you," Leonard says.

Cindy touches her nose. Her sign for *ditto*.

★   ★   ★

AT THE West Palm Beach airport, Leonard rents a car and drives along the coastline to the Marriott. He walks confidently through the doors with his carry-on and greets the girl at the front desk, who's standing in front of a giant aquarium filled with fluorescent fish. He asks her if she's in school. She's not. She says she's as smart as she needs to be. She asks where he's from.

"Imagine the complete opposite of here," he says.

Showered, unwound, dressed in jeans and a green V-neck T-shirt, hair combed and messed like in a casual-it-just-happened-while-I-was-out kind of way, he turns side to side in the mirror. Only problem is his whiteness, too white for Florida.

Every block has a strip mall with a tanning salon, a yoga studio, and a smoothie place. And everyone looks fit, as though they've never had to start from scratch. To be like them, Romanesque, resurrected beings of a past civilization that had no cars, no soft drinks, no Taco Bells. In the Valhalla Palms strip mall, where Frieda's studio is, Leonard decides to stop into a place called Tan-Talizing. He pays for a half-hour cyber-dome special, steps up into the pod and lies flat, with the blue light descending on his nearly naked body. Hypnotic music plays.

What to say? Frieda, is that you? . . . Frieda? I can't believe this. I was in Florida for a conference and saw your card at the tanning . . . Frieda? It's Leonard. Do you remember me? I guess you could say I've changed over the years. Who hasn't? Right, who hasn't?

Pod door rises. The hairs on his body tingle.

"Three more sessions and you should be brown as caramel," the overly peppy woman behind the counter says.

Two doors down is the Healing Zone. Leonard enters the lobby and stands at the glacier-glass door into the main room, rolling his neck. He pulls the door handle, then pushes, and then pulls again. There's a note on the bulletin board to his right: *If you happen to be late, take a seat and meditate.* Lucky for him, unlucky for the plus-size woman covering her bottom with crossed hands, the door opens and he inches his way into the foul-smelling, dimly lit studio.

There's Frieda up front, her back arched, the same plump breasts and flat stomach and strong legs. He remembers how her body was smooth and shaved. He could've spent hours down there. He should've spent hours down there, listening to her moan.

"Now exhale," she says, and lowers down. "Feel the air leaving your stomach, rising up through your chest, emptying from your mouth; feel the pressure release from your fingertips, your hands, your arms, your neck. Lie still as a corpse; relieve yourself of all thoughts; there is no past and no future, there is no you or I or we, there is only the eternal being, the ever-present spirit—"

An old man in a purple sweatsuit sits up and shouts, "Miss! How'm I supposed to relax with you talking all this nonsense the whole time?"

"Most people find it relaxing to listen," Frieda says in an even, deferential tone.

"I'm not so sure about that, miss. I think we need to take a vote. We still live in a democracy, don't we, despite all the evidence?"

A woman, presumably the man's wife, smacks his hand and says, "Harold, let her do her business."

"We've already had one woman do her business in here tonight," Harold mutters.

"Now, breathe in," Frieda continues. "Feel the air enter and fill your body, feel your body expand, listen to your heart pumping, feel the blood run through your veins, hold the air inside you, and then exhale slowly . . . slowly . . . releasing . . ."

Harold is shaking his head, or maybe it's a tremor.

"When do we get to the sexy stuff?" he shouts.

"Harold!"

"We have to loosen everything up first, Mr. Hart," Frieda says, "or else we might displace something very important to us."

As the class continues to breathe, Frieda stands up and follows a path of bare floor between colored mats and sagging, wheezing bodies.

"Is that Leonard Putter?" she says, smiling, those plump lips and the curved tip of her nose and that thick blond hair bouncing about her neck.

"I'm in town for a . . . thing. . . . Stopped to get some lunch . . . Saw your name on the—"

"You've been reading me, haven't you?" she says confidently, hands at her hips, tight black form-fitting yoga pants showcasing her firm thighs.

"My wife showed me an article, but that's not—"

"How is Cindy?"

"She's good. She's sort of okay."

"Oh."

"The thing is . . ."

"This is a purposeful visit, isn't it? This is supposed to change your life."

"I'm not predicting anything."

"I thought I'd see you again. I just didn't know in what form."

"Form?"

"I'm joking. Don't think I'm a wack job just because I'm into spiritual fitness."

"Right. Sorry. I'm nervous. You don't look much older than you did in high school."

"Bull crap. But thank you."

"I mean, I'm having problems back home."

"Leonard." She begins fixing his hair, fanning it across his forehead, a moment of intimacy between old lovers, perhaps. "You're welcome to sit in," she says, and heads back to her mat. "Now it's time to practice our Kegel exercises," she says to the class. "Don't clench, pull. We're getting closer to that sexy stuff, Mr. Hart."

Leonard tries to follow along with the class, clenching his member.

After a short break, Frieda calls him to join her on the mat. She wraps her legs around his waist and instructs the women in the class to do the same.

"Now pull yourself up onto your partner's lap," she says. "You can use your hands if you have to."

Frieda has spider-like legs; her breasts push up against Leonard's chin.

"Just like old times," she whispers. Then to the class, "You should feel your partner growing warm beneath you. Take in this energy, hold it inside you, let it fill you up, let it nourish you; stretch your arms into the air, breathe; you are a tree, growing from that pulsing warmth beneath you; grow, grow, grow."

At this point Leonard's hard as a rock, but Frieda doesn't seem to notice or doesn't care. She's growing. Her breasts hang in front of his face. He remembers those brown-button nipples brushing across his lips.

From the back of the room, Harold Hart shouts, "That's the ticket!"

AFTER CLASS, they sit on stools at the juice bar and catch up.

"What do you do for work these days?" she asks.

"I teach history at Wequaquet High."

"Oh, right, I think I remember hearing that. I must've forgotten because it's so depressing to think of someone you love living in such a helpless environment."

"Did you say you love me?"

"Of course. I love everyone who's been inside my body. How could I not?"

"I never looked at it that way. Does it work the other way, too?"

"It should," Frieda says, and takes a sip of her kale juice.

"I'll be honest. I've been having trouble in bed. I can't make it work. I don't know if it's Cindy or me or what, but being here and seeing you and thinking about us on your parents' couch while they were passed out drunk, fiddling around inside each other's jeans, it's getting me hard."

"See? What irony. It's your own history you've forgotten, and you teach history, for crying out loud! I remember you had such a hard, handsome dick. Not too big, not too small."

"Why do you think it won't respond anymore?"

"Maybe it's bored. Sometimes couples get into this routine where they have sex in the same place, in the same position, with the same beginning and ending, and their privates just get tired of it. They go to sleep and dream of new adventures. You have to remember that pricks and pussies have fantasies, too."

"Like separate beings?"

"I think so. And trust me when I tell you, you're not the only one who has had issues down there. Hitler once had a woman shot when he couldn't get it up. He was a syphilitic bisexual who had to find other ways to get off, so he ordered young girls to squat over him and urinate or defecate on his chest, whichever came first, preferably both."

"I knew I had something in common with Hitler."

Frieda finishes her smoothie and lets out an emphatic "Ah!"

"Have you ever made love during a tropical storm?" she asks.

"No. This is my first time in Florida. Well, except when my parents took me to Disney World for my sixth birthday and it rained the whole time we were there, and at breakfast one morning Goofy pinched my ear so hard it turned red and my father ended up spending half our vacation trying to find the specific Disney authority that handled the firing of Goofy, which there was obviously more than one, and you couldn't really do a lineup, and he kept asking me, after finally tracking down the right official and filing his complaint, 'Do you remember what color pants the Goofy that hurt you was wearing?' That's the only way they can tell the difference. Each one wears different-color pants. And I couldn't remember, so then my father was angrier with my lack of being able to remember than with the Goofy that hurt me, and eventually we left a day earlier than planned."

"Forget your Disney vacation. When the wind and rain start beating against the windowpanes, you can feel the vibration all through your body. It's like some force enters you, and it takes sex to a whole other level."

Leonard wishes the wind would pick up and the ocean would swell and the rain would start pouring down.

"I want to stay faithful to Cindy."

"You're a prideful man," Frieda says. "Even when you were fifteen, you were full of pride. I guess the question you need to ask yourself now is how far has that pride taken you in life?"

★   ★   ★

BACK IN his room at the Marriott, exhausted, lonely, weak, Leonard orders a cheeseburger from room service. Big table, white linen, small ketchup bottle, a haphazard *voilà* given by the Cuban waiter, a burger the size of his palm, a bun twice the size of the burger, French fries undercooked, the cap on his ginger ale impossible to pop off.

The bill is twenty-two dollars, including gratuity.

An hour later, the burger isn't sitting well. There's a rumbling in his stomach. He makes tea and lies down with *Confederate Love Songs*:

> We are in camp, not far from Chattanooga. I am tired and my clothes are streaked with blood. I saw a man this morning on my walk to get firewood. He had been slaughtered two maybe three days ago, it seemed. There were maggots crawling from his nostrils. But that did not trouble me, as I have seen it in this war, for there are so many bodies it is impossible to dispose of all of them in a timely fashion. No. What I saw is unspeakable, almost too difficult to write. But I am alone and I trust you will understand that I cannot sit with these images and still fight this war with a competent state of mind. The body was stripped, everything but the man's socks, which were full of holes, and at the groin there was only a stump, and I thought it good that he was dead. Sylvia, I know you will be troubled by this, but who else can I confide in besides you after God knows now what I have seen? It might not matter, as I cannot be sure the man I will give this letter to will follow through with his promise, which he has given to many men since his discharge. It is very possible he

will be slain, his horse, too, and the letters will be burnt
with the man and horse.

THE PHONE rings.

Frieda says, "I've been thinking . . . the Marriott is overpriced, and I've heard they got bugs. So you'll stay the night at
my place."

"That's kind of you, but I don't—"

"Oh, please. I'm in the lobby. I've already checked you out."

THEY WALK up a rise and over wooden planks to a little yellow
bungalow with a Mayan sundial hanging beside the sliding
door. On the lounge chair is a naked man tapping a pencil
against his head. His body is shaved—pink and venous, like the
underside of a tongue. His penis is a small bulb of light. He's
reading *Your Five-Year Plan,* making notes in the margins. Frieda
doesn't make a proper introduction. She says, "That's Brian. He
rents a room. Despite the nudity, he's a perfect tenant." They
sit on the steps of the deck and listen to the ocean dispense its
collections.

"So," Frieda says plainly, "big picture."

Leonard tells her he's concerned about his marriage. He
can't remember what it was like to love Cindy, to be in love.

"It's still inside you," she says, rubbing his back. "You have
to pull it out, fight against forgetting, or you'll end up lonely
and freakish."

Brian gets up and strolls past them, his penis hanging like a
chili pepper. He stops and scratches the back of his head.

"Frieda," he says. "Year three is impossible to figure out.
After all, what will I do with that money? I've never wanted

anything, but the money will make me start wanting things. Or do I give it to a charity? And then, I think, will I even be here? Maybe I'll go back home and take care of my folks. Maybe I'll move to Barcelona. So many people say Barcelona is the most beautiful city on earth. How would I know? Maybe it's not. Maybe it's Saskatoon." He looks down at his book. "I'm going to make stuffed peppers," he says. "I'll make extra for you and your friend."

On the beach, they are like kids again, jumping, running, diving, splashing, and howling. The waves bound under the glowing face of the moon. They share a bottle of wine. The wind dries them off. They walk into the house, past Brian, who is staring at a recipe book, still naked, very close to the lit stovetop. Frieda hands Leonard a towel. They sit on the edge of her bed. She strokes the inside of his leg, then puts her hand under his shirt and curls his chest hair in her fingers. She kisses his neck and the spot just behind his earlobe.

"Fuck me," she whispers.

"What?"

"Jesus, how long has it been?"

"Sorry, oh . . . you want me to fuck you?"

"I doubt you remember the little mole near my vagina, or the scar along my rib cage from when I tried to sneak back into my house through the doggy door."

"No. Yes. You were in the hospital. My mother brought me to see you. I gave you a chocolate orange."

"Uh-huh. And do you remember where I was most ticklish?"

"Your armpits?"

"Now that's where I like to be kissed and licked. What about Cindy—where is she most ticklish?"

"Her feet."

"Have you ever sucked on her toes or licked the bottoms of her feet?"

"No."

"These places where we laugh when touched, we moan when kissed."

Frieda stretches her arms over her head, creates a bow—unshaven, smell of salt and some animal scent Leonard can't quite identify. He needles his tongue through the soft hairs. She shivers. Her moans are like gasps. Each time she rocks forward, she checks his temple with her elbow. Finally, she lowers her arms and puts her hands on his shoulders.

"Should we turn the lights off?" he asks her.

"Darkness poisons a good fuck," she says.

That kind of language, Leonard thinks. I miss saying it out loud.

"Lights on, then?" he says.

She leans back and spreads her legs wide.

"Look at my vagina," she says. "Tell me what you see."

He's on his stomach, examining the opening.

"I don't know what to say."

"Your view is different than mine. It will always be different. I have one hundred and thirty-six versions of my pussy. Don't you understand?"

"Well, it's . . . it's sort of like a little house, I guess you could say, with a cupola on the roof here."

"Oh, mmm . . . keep your finger . . . yes, rub that, what did you call it? A cupola?"

"If you hadn't put me on the spot—oh, there's the mole. I remember now."

"I spy. That's what you used to say. Now put your cock in me and hold still."

Slowly, she pulls him farther inside her, as though ingesting this part of him that now seems separate from his body, without defense against the jungle: its reptiles, insects, and animals, and the sweet, beautiful flowers they hide behind. The farther he's drawn in, the firmer he gets. She arches her back, squeezes him at the base until he can no longer feel himself. He watches her as a boy watches an old mystic woman at the far end of a carnival, her hair wild, eyes rolling back, veins stretching in her neck, until finally he's released, dripping at the head. She falls back onto the sheets, her body shuddering in little spasmodic bursts.

"Is there some way I can . . . repay you?" Leonard asks.

Frieda laughs.

"I'm not a hooker," she says.

"Right, sorry. I think I need some air."

"Bring me back a stuffed pepper," she says. "I'm starving."

BRIAN IS outside on the porch, drinking a beer. Leonard sits down beside him. In the dark, he can see Brian's protruding shoulder blades, like wings trying to emerge from his skin.

"It's peaceful here," Leonard says.

"Too peaceful," Brian says. "Set for a riot if you ask me. Did you try the peppers?"

"Not yet."

"You know what the most popular food in prison is?"

"What's that?"

"Honey buns."

"Really?"

"Really. Do you know how many calories are in one honey bun?"

"How many?"

"Four hundred and forty calories. Two hundred and twenty-five of those are from fat, mainly saturated fat. But do you know why they're so popular?"

"Because they're cheap?"

"No, no, no. The reason they're so popular"—Brian finishes the bottle, jabs his chest with his fist—"the reason they're so popular is because they remind the inmates of home. That's how powerful something like a honey bun can be. It can bring back memories. This fat hunk of sugared dough has the capacity to resurrect a place and time. You've never seen so many full-grown men with glazed lips, laughing, telling stories, acknowledging you as a brother in their honey-bun community. It's a really beautiful thing."

LEONARD PLACES two stuffed peppers on a napkin and brings them to Frieda in the bedroom.

"Your friend is a little strange," he says, handing them to her.

"He's had a rough go of it. I swear he could get caught stealing a pack of chewing gum."

"Is he . . . you know . . . on the run?"

"He's a friend of a friend. I don't know his story, haven't asked. He's a magician in the kitchen and pays his rent on time."

"And his being naked doesn't bother you?"

"I understand it. If you've always been one way and it's never worked out for you, then it makes sense to try the opposite."

They eat the stuffed peppers, silent, munching.

"These are delicious," Leonard says.

Frieda sits back against the headboard. Her hair is sprung from her head, face flushed from the heat of the pepper.

"Sometimes I think about home," she says. "But I think about it the way it was when I was young, when everything was big and it took a lot of work to get from one place to the next. Last time I was back there, everything seemed so small, as though the houses had all shrunk. I'd heard about Donna's kid being killed, and I drove by her old house, but it was the house she grew up in and there were other people living there, and I was thinking about how Donna and I used to sneak out together and smoke cigarettes near the lake and talk for hours about what we were going to do with our lives, how we were going to travel and meet interesting men and be rich—you know, stupid dreams. At home, I could barely move around in my old room. My mother called me to dinner and I felt this incredible stabbing in my chest. I actually had to go to the hospital. They said I had generalized anxiety disorder. GAD, they called it. 'She's GAD,' I heard the doctor tell the nurse. I kept repeating it in my head. I'm GAD or I'm a GAD. Anyway, they gave me some pills. I threw them out. I don't think I'll be going back home anytime soon."

"Maybe I should think about moving here."

"Oh, Leonard, this is not the place for you."

"Why not?"

"It's just that . . . you're attracted to what's new, but what seems strange at first becomes normal, becomes reality, and then what will you have? You'll get lost. You won't *mean* anything."

The idea of meaning something takes a second to sink in. What do I mean to my students, Leonard thinks, to my friends, my kids, Cindy? They depend on me, don't they? They need me, don't they?

"Time for bed," Frieda says, sinking beneath the covers. "Could you get the lights, please?"

* * *

LEONARD CAN'T sleep. Frieda lies beside him, snoring. The kitchen is a mess: empty wine bottles, dirty dishes, black smudges dried on the baking sheet, now sticking out of the sink like a boat going down. He misses Cindy. He misses their house and how it smells. He misses her soft touch on the back of his neck as he does the dishes after dinner, her asking if he'll read to the kids, if he can remember to pick up this or that tomorrow, if he'll move some savings into the checking account so she can repaint the bedroom. Simple things, a life, mysterious and strange when your son says he saw a bear roaming in the backyard and your daughter tosses everything from the fridge into a giant bowl and mixes it with a wooden spoon and serves it for dessert. Yes, he already misses that.

He drives to the airport, checks in.

"Your plane doesn't leave for another five hours," the lady at the counter says.

"I have a book."

Leonard takes a seat on a cracked leather chair looking out at the tarmac and opens *Confederate Love Songs*:

> Dear Eleanor, I can say now for certain I will be coming home. By what means and course, I do not know. I am not sure where we are, though a fellow soldier has said we are not far from Virginia. He can tell by the air and the shape of the sky and the foul smell of dogwood trees. I do not know if you are alive or if the children are safe or what has happened since I left Franklin. It is green here, very green, and there are lightning bugs. The other night I caught one and felt it fluttering in my cupped hands, and I thought of you and Maggie and William and little Jacob. I wept, and while I wept I prayed and forgot about the bug, until I finished pray-

ing and saw that it was crushed into the lifeline of my
palm. . . .

The book slips from his hands. Of course, he thinks, dozing off,
what does Rome know of rat and lizard? The rats and the lizards, what do they know of each other?

He feels a tap on his shoulder and looks up at a cute, petite
flight attendant.

"Sir, is this your plane?"

Leonard nods.

"We're leaving now," she says. "Everyone's waiting for you."

LOST DOG

~~~~~~~~

THERE ARE TIMES when absolutely nothing is happening. That's when you know something's about to happen. You hear F-17s flying overhead, the sound like tearing paper. Then the missiles and the crushing force of wind and all of us grabbing our gear and jumping into the Humvees, barreling toward the smoke in the distance. No one looks scared. Sure, guys are puking out the windows, but that's on account of the heat. Some of it splashes on the windshield. Our squad leader issues the coordinates. Everything looks the same. We pass the same palm tree over and over, as if we're going through a time warp that takes us five minutes back every five minutes. Then we're in a village—what used to be a village. You've never heard women cry like these women here. It comes gushing out of their bodies. We have to keep them at a distance even though they look like they want to be held. I've seen them explode.

"I miss my kid," Owen says. "She lost her first tooth a few

days ago. It came loose when she was eating pizza and she didn't realize it and ended up swallowing it. There was nothing to put under her pillow, but Julie gave her a five-dollar bill, anyway. Now she knows for sure there isn't a tooth fairy, because the tooth fairy doesn't pay for nothing."

The air is full of dust. We're not destroyers; we go through what's been destroyed. I see a Haji's arm stuck like a small flag in the sand, the first three fingers blown off. There's an infantry watch around his wrist, still ticking. "This wouldn't be such a bad advertisement for the manufacturer," Owen says. He picks up the arm and it flies out of his hand. "Fuck, it's burning." We look at it, up ahead in a divot in the sand. Maybe it'll move again. I once saw a movie about a killer hand. It could be they got the idea from something like this. Then a Humvee rolls over the arm and it sticks in the treads, waving back at us for a brief moment before the wheel cuts a furrow through the wreckage.

OWEN SAYS he hasn't taken a shit in three weeks. It's the camel spiders, he says. "I'm afraid they're going to bite my nuts." I tell him to get a bucket. He says it doesn't matter. At mess, we eat chicken livers and onions, mashed potatoes and broccoli. Someone feeling sorry for us sent over three giant boxes crammed with supermarket cupcakes. They're dry as hell, and most of us just eat the frosting.

SOME NIGHTS I lie awake and listen to them talk in their sleep. Owen has sex dreams. He raises his arms and grabs at the air and says, "Let me touch those big round titties." Tate always shouts the same thing: "It was me! I'm the one who did it!" The other night, Miller gave a fairly coherent sermon on right and wrong. The story had something to do with a boy whose friend had stolen some candy, and if the boy told, he'd lose the friend, but if he didn't, he'd go to hell. When Miller was through, he began to snore. I looked over and saw that a few of the other guys had been listening, too. So as Miller slept on, we shaved his legs. Next morning we whistled at him in the shower.

NO ONE touches us. You realize this about three months in, during a moment of quiet. You realize that all your life you've been touched by people: parents, grandparents, brothers, sisters, girlfriends, wives. You knock elbows with a stranger in a movie theater, shake hands with a friend of a friend, dance in a bar with a woman you just met.

A group of cheerleaders flew over here a couple of months back, and some of the guys got to hug them and get their pictures taken with the girls on their laps. The cheerleaders smiled and giggled and waved and cheered. I only got close enough to smell them. They smelled like peppermints.

When they left, the guys were sad as hell. They burned the photographs. One guy named Silver went out and shot three cats and brought them back and buried them. He was analyzed and discharged. While he packed his stuff, a bunch of us gave him a hard time. He didn't say anything. Right before he left, he pulled me aside and told me to take care of those cats.

"They don't have anyone to look after them," he said. "And you can't trust these jerk-offs to look after themselves, let alone a harmless animal."

I doubt he remembers any of this. I hear they put so much stuff in you.

SOMETIMES IT'S boring out here. You never know when you're about to be sent into the night, so you never really sleep. Owen knows a guy who sells opium in small black pads the size of a thumbprint. He's real polite, Owen says. He knows how capitalism works. He knows we're not over here promoting American democracy but American business. He's willing to learn, get ahead of the game.

We break up the opium and roll it with tobacco. We get high but stay alert. It's a mysterious drug. I can see why people fall in love. When we're high, the desert is a peaceful place. We hang out and shoot the shit and it's like any other place that's ever been.

Later we go over to the trailer and watch Ultimate Fighting.

"This is what I'm going to do when I get back," Tate says.

He's got a book on judo and another on Brazilian jujitsu. They're both old and water-stained. Certain sentences are underlined in blue ink. One reads: *A wise opponent will transition to a choking technique.*

"What the hell are you guys on?" Tate says.

Owen is sitting in front of the television screen, softly whispering, "Boom, pow, zap." I'm holding the jujitsu book upside down and craning my neck to read it.

Tate flicks Owen's ear. Owen lunges dazedly for Tate but misses and crashes through the coffee table. Tate pins Owen's arms back and presses his neck forward. Owen's face is blue. This is a wise time to transition to a choking technique.

★　★　★

SOME OF the guys are glad to be here. Usually it's a girl back home. Things weren't working out. Or it's no money and two kids, or a wife with fat ankles and a fat ass. "I'd rather be killed," Miller says. We tell our pasts like horror stories.

SO IT gets depressing and we let go, turn to our guns and ammo, clean, check, and recheck. We play cards, wait, watch DVDs that constantly skip, rip them out and fling them across the room, wait, jerk off, sleep ten, twenty minutes at a time.

When we're out on patrol, I think about my girlfriend, Kiki. She's blond and big—five feet ten inches, not a scratch on her. I think about her legs; I wrap them around my waist, squeeze them tight, bury my face between them.

"You got a good one, Baker," Owen says.

"Me, I fit all the old ones together and make something perfect," Miller says.

"I haven't been able to jerk off in this place," Tate says.

"Camel spiders?" Owen says.

"What?" Tate scratches under his helmet, pulls off the strap, keeps scratching until there's blood in his fingernails.

"Think about how in, like, fifty years scientists will be able to design a woman to look just the way you want her to," Miller says.

"What good'll that do you when your nut bag's hanging around your ankles?" Tate says.

"Maybe they'll fix that, too."

FOLLOWING WEEK, Miller steps on an IED and his right leg's blown off at the thigh. He's knocked out, but there must be a pulse, because Owen's giving him CPR. Problem is, blood's shooting out the opening with each pump to his chest. Finally, Tate smacks the back of Owen's head, stuffs the leg with Quik-Clot, and ties a bandage above the wound. Medics arrive. A chopper. So mouths are moving but no one can hear what anyone's saying. I'm saying, "We need to get the fuck out of here."

That night, Tate and Owen play horseshoes until dawn. I try to sleep, but I keep seeing particles of Miller's leg floating around me like dust. As they stumble into bed, Owen lets an iron fly right past Tate's face. Tate gets up and punches him in the neck. Owen staggers back and gasps for breath.

"Don't fight it," Tate says.

Owen collapses onto his bed, still gasping.

Anytime I got hurt when I was a kid, my mother would sing to me. She had a terrible voice. I never told her that, because it made her feel better to think she was making me feel better.

What I think I mean is that as long as we're not alone, it's not so bad.

THE WAR has to end at some point. At least that's the thought. Or maybe thinking that makes it easier to be so out of line.

Just before night patrol, Tate fills a cup with arrack and pours water in it so that it looks like milk. "Nightcap," he says, and he takes a gulp and bats the sides of his head with his fists. He passes it to Owen, then to me. I don't drink the stuff, because it makes my stomach burn, and because someone's got to drive.

We're trailing three HVs; radios murmur; Tate lets out a sickly belch.

No fire yet. Nothing yet. So it's waiting for us. You can only refer to it as *it*, the thing that tries to kill you.

A while passes, you get into this daze; this daze gets you into trouble. I haven't noticed that our BFTs are down and the HVs ahead are out of sight. What I see up ahead is a dog. Black ears, black snout, big paws, ribs shoving through a narrow torso, sloped head, eyes stretched back almost to the sides of his face.

"What kind of dog is that?" I ask.

"Fucking beast," Tate says.

"He looks scared."

"That's how he pulls you in."

Owen steps out, flashes a light on the ground. He's worried about the spiders. The dog doesn't bark, doesn't whine. As Owen approaches, the dog lies down and rolls onto his back. Owen rubs the dog's stomach, and his legs wave in the air. Tate and I get out and move toward them. So much shit attached to us it's difficult to squat down. But there's nothing moving out here except the wind and the sand. I take off my pack and my rifle, unhook my vest, open an MRE, let the dog eat.

"I wish I were a dog," Owen says. "Short life, no responsibilities, always getting petted."

"Shut the fuck up," Tate says.

But then the dog is licking Tate's palm. "Oh, Jesus," he says, and he rolls over and the dog puts his paws on Tate's chest and licks his face and ears and Tate laughs and says, "No, stop it, no," but in a way that makes it clear he doesn't really want it to stop, he wants it to go on forever.

Then Tate's gun fires and the dog darts into the night.

"You fucking idiot," Owen says. "Now they'll know we're here."

"The fucking spiders?" Tate turns his light on the empty desert, on a whirl of dust rushing nowhere. "We've got to find him," he says.

"Find who?" Owen says.

"That dog. He's all alone."

"You're out of your mind."

"What's that?" Tate levels the gun at Owen.

"You don't scare me, pal."

"Let's vote on it, then," Tate says democratically, and he flicks his eyes to me.

Crazy has my support, 100 percent. "I think the dog deserves better," I say.

"That liquor's got you high," Owen says.

"I didn't drink any of it."

"Maybe you should have; maybe you'd see things more clearly."

"The longer we stand around here arguing," Tate says, "the farther away he gets."

THE HUMVEE'S motor echoes like we're driving in a cave. Owen keeps smacking the BFT panel. We see palm tree, palm tree, three-foot stone wall (check for Haji; knock it down), palm tree. Then an abandoned car with no windshield. We stop the Humvee and walk toward it slowly. The paint is peeled off, console torn out, dog feces in the backseat.

"This must be where he sleeps," Tate says.

He checks underneath the car, turning the light back and forth, and finds a score of camel spiders.

Owen freaks, jumps to the hood and then the roof, leaving a dent that pops up with a bang. Tate whips out his gun and fires into the dark.

"What the hell's the matter with you?" I say.

Tate snaps the dust off his uniform. "Let's clear out."

"I'm not going anywhere," Owen says. "I counted thirty-three of those big bastards."

"Don't be such a fucking baby. We can't stay here. We can't

let that dog just wander around with these spiders everywhere."

"They're everywhere?" Owen says. "I counted thirty-three."

"Can you make it back to the Humvee?" I ask Owen.

"We're not taking the Humvee," Tate says. "We're not going to find the dog in the Humvee."

"So what are we going to do?" I nod my head at Owen, speak quietly: "I think he's not well."

"Then it's you and me, Baker. We're pretty well fucked either way."

Tate turns and walks into the night.

I follow. When I look back for Owen, I can only make out his light, scanning the ground.

Tate shouts, "Those spiders won't stay grounded for long."

WE WALK for what feels like miles.

The dark sky opens up with a thick burst of ash. "I smell fresh piss," Tate says.

"The sun'll be up in an hour or so. Then what?"

"Then we'll be able to see better."

"I'm worried about Owen."

"Owen's fine. I don't even remember if I saw any spiders or not."

"I saw them."

"Maybe you did, maybe you didn't. It's all in the past now."

SOME SORT of village, I guess you'd call it. Square mud huts form an L, and a rusted old truck with slats of wood fencing framing the bed sits in the center like a piece of modern art. A few kids are kicking a soccer ball back and forth, and when they see us, they stop and stare. One of them picks his nose and puts his finger in his mouth. Behind the truck is a group of Hajis, some squatting, some standing, one squeezing the back of a dog's neck. Our dog.

I know *hi* and *bye*, *yes* and *no*, but that's about it. There's no time to study. So I let Tate take over, and he screams something that means nothing to them at first but over time comes to mean lying facedown in the dirt with a gun pointed at them. And then it can never mean anything else.

Only the guy with the dog doesn't seem to understand, and Tate walks toward him, keeping the gun aimed at his head until the only thing separating them is the gun. The man whimpers; tears push out from his eyes. Finally, his knees buckle and he's on the ground, prostrate, his hands clasped behind his bowed head.

The other men haven't moved. They're like dummies in a shop window.

The dog looks up at Tate, and Tate smiles and lowers his hand, and the dog turns suddenly and scampers into one of the huts.

"Okay, okay," Tate says, and I can tell something terrible is about to happen, like an instinct; some terrible thing has been traveling through all of time to find its place, right here.

The dog barks. Mournfully, Tate looks for him. The men laugh. I scan the huts. The dog is now at the entrance to one, beside a large, cloaked woman. She bends down and pets the dog. Then she slices his throat.

"Oh, Jesus," I shout.

Tate lets out a sound of pure anguish and grabs the man by the collar, lifting him right off his feet. The other men are up and yelling now.

"Shut up!" I cry. "Please, just shut the hell up!"

But they don't understand. I have to fire my rifle in the air.

Still, they keep going. I have to fire at their feet. Finally they scatter.

"I've lost them," I say. "We need to get out of here."

There's no response. I glance around. There's no sign of Tate.

I walk slowly toward the hut, past the dog, blood still draining from his neck, mouth open, teeth chipped. He lets out a cough, just a reflex. When I was a kid we had to put down our Boston terrier, Pickles. After the shot, his body quaked and all that energy left him in a gasp.

The man and his wife are on the floor with their hands behind their heads, mouthing voiceless prayers. Tate's in a fighting position, his right leg slightly behind his left, arms up, aiming his rifle. But he's aiming it above them, at the wall behind. I look in his eyes, and he doesn't seem wholly here.

"Tate?" I say.

He doesn't react.

"Is the rifle necessary?"

"They killed that poor dog," he says.

What to say in a moment like this? Tate's mouth hanging open; the husband and wife on their knees, praying.

I tell him I think the dog's going to make it.

"You lying son of a bitch," he says.

"There'll be other dogs," I say.

"But not that one," he says, pushing the muzzle of the gun against the woman's head. "That dog was perfect."

Quietly, I remove my pistol and train it on Tate. I haven't fired it since basic. It feels light in my hand.

"Put the gun down, Tate."

"It's not right," he says. "Someone's got to make it right." His fingers tighten on the forestock.

I aim the pistol at his calf, but when I fire, it jumps and I hit him in the flank. He's pushed forward by the force of the bullet and he falls on top of the woman, dropping his rifle. The man shoves him off, and the couple scrambles to their feet. They press their hands together and bow as they hurry outside. I pick up Tate's rifle.

He's moaning and cursing, kicking his legs.

"I'm sorry, man. I didn't have a choice."

"You didn't have to put a fucking bullet in me."

I take off his jacket and realize he's not wearing a vest. I apply pressure to the wound. The blood is gushing out between my fingers.

"How'm I gonna get out of here?"

"I'll carry you."

I drape his arm over my shoulder and help him to his feet.

The men from before are gathered around the truck, laughing. The kids, too. One of them mimics being shot and hops around with his hands pressed to his side.

In the shade of the truck, the dog lies in a crumpled heap, bleeding out.

I tell Tate not to pay attention to them, not to even look in their direction. They're harmless.

WHEN WE'RE out a little ways, I give Tate a morphine shot and tell him to keep his hand over the hole. It's hard work carrying both packs, the two rifles, and Tate, who can barely shuffle his feet, but I have to keep moving, I have to get him back. He says he's had a couple of toes blown off and his neck grazed, but never has he been plugged with a bullet.

I can't apologize enough.

"Does it hurt?"

"No, I don't feel anything, unless numb is a feeling. Is numb a feeling?"

"Can I tell you something?"

"Go on."

"You won't get mad?"

"What can I do?"

"I'm not sure where we're headed. I mean, I know we walked fairly straight from that car, but I can't be sure."

"You weren't paying attention?"

"I was following you. You were following the dog. Did we head east, maybe? Is it possible we headed east?"

Tate groans.

I tell him I'm sorry. I'm real sorry.

THE SUN never seems to move during the day. It stays right above wherever you are, cut flat, sucking all the energy from your body. I hold Tate on his feet and give him some water. He chokes it back. The wind picks up, and we're shrouded in dust. To our right is a set of tire tracks.

I ask Tate if he thinks Owen's all right.

"It's hard to give a simple answer to that question, knowing all the intricate actions that take place over a specific period of time."

"He could've been captured? Is that what you're saying?"

"Could've been. Or maybe the spiders got to him. Or maybe he ran back to the Humvee and got the BFT working, radioed for help. Or maybe he's asleep in that car. Maybe he was asleep in that car and the car exploded and he's alive but only for a little while longer. See what I mean?"

We follow the tracks until the wind picks up again and covers them over. I'm hungry and tired and carrying Tate's entire weight. I tell him I have to take a break.

"Didn't we pass a tree?" he says.

"I'm not sure."

"Is there even a tree out here, just one shitty, dying tree with a few shitty, dying palms for some shade? When you don't need a tree, you see a tree. But when you need one—"

"We still have your MRE, right?"

"Why? What happened to yours?"

I dig Tate's MRE from his pack and split it between us.

"Oh, right," he says sadly. "Poor thing. His last meal was some shitty beef stew."

"I think he enjoyed it."

"Look at us, Baker. We think we're enjoying this, too, but it's just because we're hungry. And then we get these melted Tootsie Rolls, impossible to eat, rip your teeth right out."

I tell him we should save some, just in case.

"One tree," he says. "Is that too much to ask?"

HOURS LATER, and still no tree. A few sips of water left. Except for a pack of Skittles, the MRE is long gone. It's getting cold. Night again, then day. No one knows our coordinates. Poor Owen is trapped by the spiders. We've walked close to twenty miles, maybe more. My watch broke. It feels like we're in a pit of sludge. What's the point of having a girl like Kiki if she can't have me? And my poor dad, sometimes he gets so lonely, and right now I understand how that feels, but there's no way to tell him. Does he know how special he is?

Then it rains. Not typical rain but a heavy onslaught that comes in waves, rolling through the sky. Tate sucks water from the folds in my jacket, then slips to the ground.

I touch his forehead.

"I love pizza," he says. "I love ice cream and football and horses and motorcycles and comic books and swimming pools and carnivals and big tits and Christmas and the moon . . . Oh, God . . . Oh, God, what else?"

Soon, Tate falls asleep.

The rain dies, and the dust hangs in the air like fog, and out of the dust runs a dog. He looks no different from the other one, maybe a little thinner.

I tap Tate on the head and say, "The dog's back, Tate. Look. He's back. He wasn't killed after all."

Tate's not waking up.

I check his pulse.

Tate's got no pulse.

The dog starts licking Tate's face. I smack him on the rear and he turns and growls at me.

"Go ahead, then," I say. "Lick his stupid face."

In the morning, it's me and the dog and Tate. My knees are swollen and I can't feel my arms. The abandoned car is full of spiders. Some are as big as my head. A few have been shot and their guts are splattered all over the upholstery. The dog won't go near the car. He's barking like mad. There's no sign of Owen, but I see boot prints on the ground. I follow them this way and that. There's no sign of the Humvee, either.

I drop Tate where we started.

The dog keeps trotting ahead and looking back, his tongue wagging.

"Don't worry," I say. "I'm right behind you."

ACKNOWLEDGMENTS

For their insight and inspiration: Aaron Fagan, George Saunders, Mary Gaitskill, Richard Ford, Neil Young, Mary Karr, Michael Burkard, Arthur Flowers, Lee K. Abbott, Christopher Kennedy, Russell Banks, and Denis Johnson;

For their hard work and dedication: Claire Anderson-Wheeler, Sarah Bowlin, Courtney Reed, Meakin Armstrong, Paul Morris, and Michael Ray;

For their love and support: Kevin, Max, Diane, Frank, Tara, Matt, Dad, Sylvia, and H.P.;

Lastly, to my mother for her creative spirit, which lives in all of my work,

Thank You.

ABOUT THE AUTHOR

Patrick Dacey holds an MFA from Syracuse University. He has taught English at several universities in the United States and Mexico and has worked as a reporter, a landscaper, a door-to-door salesman, and most recently on the overnight staff at a homeless shelter and detox center. His stories have been featured in *Zoetrope: All-Story*, *Guernica*, *Bomb* magazine, and *Salt Hill*, among other publications. Originally from Cape Cod, Massachusetts, he currently lives in Virginia.

To:

_____

From:

_____

Date:

_____

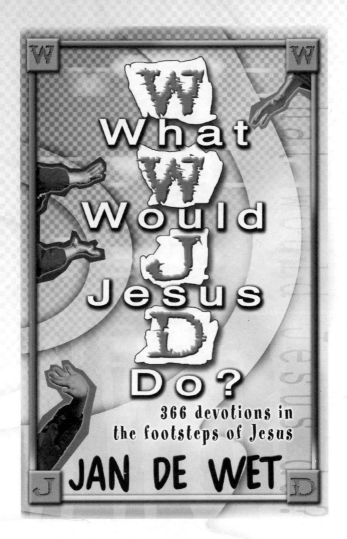

What Would Jesus Do?

366 devotions in the footsteps of Jesus

JAN DE WET

CHRISTIAN ART PUBLISHERS

Originally published by Christian Publishing Company
under the title *Wat sal Jesus doen?*

© 1998

English edition © 1998
CHRISTIAN ART PUBLISHERS
PO Box 1599, Vereeniging, 1930

First edition 1998
Second edition 2002
Third edition 2005

Translated by San-Mari Mills

Cover designed by Christian Art Publishers

Scripture taken from the Holy Bible, New International Version ©
1973, 1978, 1984 by International Bible Society used by
permission of Zondervan Publishing House. All rights reserved.

Set in 12 on 14 pt Palatino by Christian Art Publishers

Printed in China

ISBN 1-86920-579-0

05 06 07 08 09 10 11 12 13 14 – 10 9 8 7 6 5 4 3 2 1

FOLLOWING IN
HIS FOOTSTEPS ...

A certain man lost his job as a laborer at a printing house. Six months later his wife died in wretched circumstances in New York. His daughter had nowhere to go, no one to turn to. For days on end he tried, without success, to find a job in Richmond, Virginia.

One Sunday morning Henry Maxwell preached to a packed congregation from 1 Peter 2:21, *"To this you were called, because Christ suffered for you, leaving you an example, that you should follow in his steps."*

Follow in the steps of Jesus in obedience, faith, and love was Maxwell's urgent plea. Then a man went forward, a man who had been a hobo in Richmond, Virginia, for the past ten months ...

What does it mean, he asked, to follow in Jesus' footsteps? Indeed. What would Jesus do if he should come across someone like this hobo?

Does this story sound familiar? We live in different places, but we encounter the same circumstances. Charles Sheldon's well-known book, *In His Steps*, was written at a time when a group of people undertook to ask what Jesus would do if he were in their place. They would do this before every decision they took for one year.

What would Jesus do? This is the question that Jan de Wet wants to answer in this devotional. He wants to help you, as a young person, to get into the habit of following in the footsteps of Jesus in every aspect of your life so that it becomes a way of life for you.

– The Publisher –

The New Year!

This is the day the LORD has made; let us rejoice and be glad in it. (Psalm 118:24)

At the beginning of this new year my wish for you is that it will be a wonderful year, and that you will be very happy.

It always feels good to start something new. It feels good to wear new shoes. It feels good to ride a new bicycle. You are most probably in a new grade this year with new challenges waiting for you.

If you put your hand in the hand of Jesus, then I know that he will lead you safely this new year, every step of the way. He says in his Word that every day is the day of the Lord and that it is a gift in your hand.

Come, let's be joyful and happy about every new day, and also about this new year that the Lord has given us. Join me now, and let's ask the Lord to bless us and to help us do only what is important to him. With him to lead us this will be a wonderful year.

On this day Jesus would pray,
"Your will be done."

 Not everyone who says to me, 'Lord, Lord,' will enter the kingdom of heaven, but only he who does the will of my Father. (Matthew 7:21)

Winners

But thanks be to God, who always leads us in triumphal procession in Christ. (2 Corinthians 2:14)

It is always nice to be on the winning side. It is great to win a game. When your school's team wins a football game, a baseball game, or a track meet, you are very proud because it feels good to be on the winning side.

Just as there are winners on the sports fields, there are also winners in life. Paul writes that we are running the race of life. This means how we live will determine whether we win or lose. The Bible tells us that if we live with Christ, that is, give our lives to him and belong to him, then we are in the winning team with him. We know Jesus is the great winner. He paid for our sins on the cross and rose from the dead: He overcame death and the devil!

Decide to put your hand in the hand of the great winner, Jesus Christ, right now. Take on the rest of this day as a winner with Jesus. And if something should happen today that is hurtful to you or becomes a problem, leave it in the hands of your great winner, Jesus Christ.

Jesus would not give up,
and he will win.

"Father, into your hands I commit my spirit." (Luke 23:46)

January 2

Is God Dead?

The fool says in his heart, "There is no God." (Psalm 14:1)

Many people say that God is dead. Some think he doesn't exist, some say he has retired, others that he is asleep or is not interested in people. Maybe they say that because they cannot see him or touch him.

The Bible says that someone who thinks this is a fool. That is certainly not a compliment, is it? As we know, fools say and do foolish things.

The Bible says that those who say God does not exist are really stupid. They are making a big mistake. One day a man came up to a pastor and told him that God does not exist. The pastor responded, "But that's impossible; just this morning I spoke to him and he to me!"

Yes, if you really believe in God, you somehow just know, deep down, that the Lord truly lives. He talks to you through his Word, and you can talk to him in prayer. Then you cannot doubt that he exists, and you just know that he lives in your heart.

Does God live in your heart?

Jesus lived so that everybody
could see that his Father lives.

Jesus Christ ... who is at the Father's side, has made him known. (John 1:17, 18)

January 3

STARTING ALL OVER AGAIN

[Paul says] One thing I do: Forgetting what is behind and straining toward what is ahead. (Philippians 3:13)

We all make mistakes. No one on earth has never had a problem of some kind or never made some mistake or another. Maybe you remember something you did that was a big mistake. The worst part is that sometimes you make the same mistake over and over again!

There are people who enjoy reminding you of this mistake that you made in the past. Then you hurt all over again. If you keep on thinking of past mistakes you can start feeling depressed.

But the Bible tells us if we have made a mistake and we are sorry about it, we must tell the Lord. The Bible calls it "to confess." And once we have confessed our sin, the Lord forgives us immediately. When the Lord forgives our sin, it means that he doesn't think about it again. It is over and done with.

Paul says that he will put everything that happened in the past behind him. He will look ahead and try to live the way he should. Tell the Lord that you are sorry about the mistakes you made in the past, thank him for forgiving you, and live to the full every moment of this new day.

Jesus would love and care for
people, faults and all.

 [Jesus] said ... "If any one of you is without sin, let him be the first to throw a stone at her." (John 8:7)

January 4

LAUGH AND CRY

Rejoice with those who rejoice; mourn with those who mourn. (Romans 12:15)

I'm sure you have sometimes had a good laugh about something that happened to you. But then again, you have also cried a lot about things that made you sad. All of us laugh sometimes and cry sometimes.

The Lord says we must laugh with those who laugh and cry with those who cry. We must not laugh when others cry. If you do that, then you are really being cruel. Sometimes when others are laughing, their friends get fed up with them because they are in a bad mood and don't feel like laughing. This is also wrong. When people are happy, we must also be happy because we love people and care for them. If someone hurts and cries, we must cry with them, because we don't like to see others hurting.

If the love of the Lord is in our hearts, we want to feel what others feel. Then we are happy when they are happy, and we are sad when they are sad.

If you know of a friend who is unhappy, go and tell him or her that you are sorry about it. If something good happens, tell him or her that you are happy for them.

Jesus would laugh and
cry with you and me.

When Jesus saw her weeping ... Jesus wept. (John 11:33, 35)

I'll Show You

Do not take revenge, my friends, but leave room for God's wrath. (Romans 12:19)

Has anyone ever hurt you or upset you? Often people do things that make us very angry and we want to pay them back. We feel like saying, "I'll show you!" Then some guys start fighting, using either their fists or their tongues. When they do that, it shows that they want to take revenge. They want to pay someone back because they hurt.

The Bible says this is not a wise thing to do. It is much better to forgive each other. And if we still feel in our hearts that the other person must be paid back, we should ask God to do it. The Bible tells us to let God decide. He is a fair Judge, and there is going to be a Judgment Day. At the end of our lives each one of us will stand before the great throne of God. Then God will pass judgment (Romans 2:3).

You must not judge. Leave that to God. Forgive any friend that hurt you. Do it right now, and then leave it in the hands of the Lord.

Jesus would forgive his wrongdoers.

Father, forgive them. (Luke 23:34)

IT'S ALL RIGHT TO GO

> Since we have confidence to enter the Most Holy Place by the blood of Jesus, let us draw near to God with a sincere heart in full assurance of faith. (Hebrews 10:19, 22)

Many people are afraid to go to God. Perhaps it is because they think the Lord will not understand how they feel. They think God is strict and just wants to judge them and punish them.

Surely this is not true! God loves us so much that he gave us his Son on the cross. Yes, he has proved his love for us, and that is exactly what today's scripture says. When Jesus died for us on the cross, the curtain of the temple tore from top to bottom. Since that time, everyone can enter into God's presence. We can talk to him every day and anywhere and be with him. He is there with you on the sports field, or wherever you may be today.

You must not be self-conscious about speaking to God about your whole life. Everything you do and say he knows about, and he is with you every moment of the day. You are in his presence. It's all right to take all your problems to him and to talk to him about everything that happens to you. He understands and he loves you.

Jesus would talk to his Father.

Jesus ... went off to a solitary place, where he prayed. (Mark. 1:35)

EVERY KNEE WILL BOW

> That in the name of Jesus every knee should bow ... and every tongue confess that Jesus Christ is Lord. (Philippians 2:10, 11)

The Bible says that everyone in heaven and on earth, and even under the earth, will kneel before Jesus Christ. This means that everybody will confess that he is the Savior, the only One who can free us from sin. Everyone will also confess that he is the Christ: that he has been anointed by the Holy Spirit to bring us salvation.

But they will also confess that he is the Lord. The word *lord* means king, master, or someone with the highest authority.

In biblical times, subjects of the king bowed before him. In this way they confessed that the king was greater and more powerful than they were. That is why each and every one of us will also bow to King Jesus.

If you accept Jesus as your Savior, then you bow before him in your heart and you confess that he has become your King. Then you want to live for him and do what he wants you to. Have you gone down on your knees before him yet? Those of us who do not bow down before Jesus now will have to do it one day, but then it will be too late.

Jesus would confess that
God is his Father.

[Jesus] looked toward heaven and prayed: "Father ... " (John 17:1)

January 8

WORK OUT THE COST

"Suppose one of you wants to build a tower. Will he not first sit down and estimate the cost to see if he has enough money to complete it?" (Luke 14:28)

Before you can buy something you want badly, you must first see if you have enough money. If you want to buy a football, a skateboard, a computer game, or anything else you would really like to have, you first have to figure out if you have the money to buy it. Most things we want, we have to pay for.

The Bible says there is also a price to pay if we want to follow Jesus. Yes, it is true that Jesus loved us so much that he died on the cross for us. But it will cost us something very precious to know that we will be with him in heaven forever: our hearts. We say to him, "Here is my heart, take it; I have decided to follow You." And if there are people who do not like it if I follow Jesus, or if some of my friends tease me because I say that I love Jesus, then that is the price I must pay for the joy of being his child.

But, you know, it is always a bargain to follow Jesus.

Jesus paid the price, so that we can be his children.

How great is the love the father has lavished on us, that we should be called children of God. (1 John 3:1)

CHARGE YOUR BATTERY

"[God] rested on the seventh day. Therefore the Lord blessed the Sabbath day and made it holy." (Exodus 20:11)

We all know that batteries are useful. New batteries make a flashlight shine brightly, and a car cannot go if the battery is dead. But batteries also go dead. Just as a battery goes dead, we humans also get tired. That is why we must rest. That is why it is important that we get enough sleep. If our batteries are dead, we cannot do our work properly, and we don't feel good.

Because God knows this, he set aside one day a week so that we can have a good rest. If we work hard every day of the week, do all our homework and go to sports practices, then we need to rest. Usually, we rest over weekends. But we must also rest spiritually. Our hearts must be tuned in to hear the voice of the Lord and to do what he asks. One can enjoy resting in God's presence. That is why we go to church, listen to his Word, and sing songs with some of his other children – because we are glad that he loves us. In this way we charge the batteries of our lives, all over again.

Jesus would be a regular churchgoer.

They found him in the temple ... (Luke 2:46)

January 10

THE SPECK AND THE PLANK

"First take the plank out of your own eye, and then you will see clearly to remove the speck from your brother's eye." (Matthew 7:5)

A plank is a long, flat piece of wood. It is quite thick and is used for making floors and framing houses. Planks must be strong because a floor carries a lot of weight.

A speck is very tiny, so tiny that you can hardly see it. If a speck of dust gets into your eye, you will feel it, but if someone wants to take it out, they may have a problem finding it.

We all have our faults, and sometimes these faults are so big that they are like a thick plank in our eye. But we pretend not to notice, as if we have no faults. The worst part is that we then blame others, just as if we were without faults. We like telling others how big their sins and faults are, but we are not honest about our own.

Jesus says we should not blame others. It is much better to first take care of our own faults and take the thick plank of sin out of our own eyes. Even better than that is not to find fault with others at all, just love them with their faults.

Jesus would be tender and loving
with those who have faults.

 Above all, love each other deeply, because love covers over a multitude of sins. (1 Peter 4:7)

January 11

TRAIN, TRAIN, TRAIN

Train yourself to be godly. (1 Timothy 4:7)

If you want to play the piano well, you have to practice a lot. Good athletes must also train hard and learn the rules of their sport so that they can be good at it.

It is not always easy to train or practice for something, but you do it anyway because you know that it will help you do better. It is the same with schoolwork: if you work hard, you get good grades in tests or exams.

The Bible says if we want to learn how to live successfully, we must also train ourselves in our relationship with the Lord. This means we have to read the Bible regularly, talk to the Lord, and do things that will help us in our relationship with him. But, just like an athlete, we must make time for God every day and be busy with him.

Will you do this today?

Jesus would make time
to speak to his Father.

Pray continually. (1 Thessalonians 5:17)

THE THIRSTY DEER

As the deer pants for streams of water, so my soul pants for you, O God. (Psalm 42:1)

If you visit a game reserve or state park, you will notice how far deer must walk to get to water. In Bible times, the deer in the desert also had to walk long distances to get to water. By the time they got there, they were desperately thirsty.

This is the image the Bible uses to explain that human beings are also thirsty for the water that only God can give us. Jesus said he is the Fountain of Living Water and that his water will quench a person's spiritual thirst. The Lord's love is like a cool stream of water where we can stand and drink to quench the thirst in our hearts.

We drink the Lord's water as we listen when he speaks to us through his Word, and we are filled with the Holy Spirit deep down. Why not tell the Lord right now that you are drinking his Living Water so that you may never be thirsty again?

Jesus would give you water
to quench your thirst.

"If anyone is thirsty, let him come to me and drink." (John 7:37)

January 13

LEAVE EVERYTHING AS IT IS

"Follow Me," he told him. (Matthew 9:9)

Matthew was most probably a very rich man. He had a tax collector's booth where people had to pay tax money. Often the tax collectors took more money than they were supposed to, and so they became very rich.

One day Jesus saw Matthew sitting at the tax collector's booth, and Jesus said to him, "Follow Me!" Maybe Matthew was surprised at this invitation, but what is even more surprising is that he immediately left everything and started following Jesus. Amazing!

Perhaps the love in Jesus' eyes made up Matthew's mind for him. Perhaps Matthew had a longing for peace deep in his heart that only Jesus could give. Perhaps Matthew realized that only Jesus could free him from sin.

Jesus has invited you to follow him. You would be foolish not to give him your whole life. Come!

Jesus calls you to follow him.

"Come, follow me." (Matthew 4:19)

Run Away!

She caught him by his cloak and said, "Come to bed with me!" But he ran out of the house. (Genesis 39:12)

Joseph loved the Lord very much, and the Lord had a wonderful plan for Joseph's life. Joseph's brothers were jealous of him because of the dreams that told him that the Lord had a plan for his life. They first threw him into a dry well and then sold him to some merchants who took him to Egypt and resold him as a slave. But the Lord was with him.

One day Joseph was in the home of his master, Potiphar, an important man in the palace of Pharaoh, the great leader of Egypt. Potiphar had an evil wife. She had her eye on Joseph and wanted him to go to bed with her. But Joseph knew it would be wrong.

When Potiphar's wife told him a second time that she wanted to sleep with him, he refused again. When he ran away from her and out of her house, she grabbed hold of his coat. Later on she told lies about Joseph, but the Lord helped him.

It is always better to run away from people who want you to do something sinful. If your friends try to get you to do something and you know it is wrong, say no, as Joseph did. If they don't want to listen, it is better to walk or run away. Even if they think you're a coward, the Lord will be on your side.

Jesus would not give
in to temptation.

"Away from Me, Satan!" (Matthew 4:10)

January 15

Seventy-Seven Times!

"Lord, how many times shall I forgive my brother when he sins against me? Up to seven times?" Jesus answered, "I tell you, not seven times, but seventy-seven times." (Matthew 18:21, 22)

Sometimes it is so difficult to forgive, especially if someone has hurt us or made us angry. We would much rather get back at them than forgive them.

But the Bible says that the best thing to do is to forgive someone for what he has done. Sometimes we say, "Yes, I'll forgive only this once, but not again." No, the Bible is quite clear about this. We must be prepared to forgive one another up to seventy-seven times. That's quite a lot! Actually, the issue here is not really how many times. The number seven is the perfect (complete or whole) number in the Bible, so what the Bible is really saying is that we must forgive perfectly or completely. Even if someone sins against me three thousand times, and the same sin every time, I must keep on forgiving.

Is there someone you need to forgive? Why not tell the Lord right now that you are sorry for wanting to pay the person back for what he or she did.

Tell Jesus now that you forgive that person.

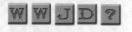

Jesus would forgive.

Who is a God like you, who pardons sin and forgives the transgression? You do not stay angry forever. (Micah 7:18)

WONDERFULLY MADE

> I praise You because I am fearfully and wonderfully made. (Psalm 139:14)

Just think how many people there are on this earth. Every person looks different and talks differently, and every person acts in a different way. Isn't it wonderful? Not even twins have exactly the same characteristics.

Some people have black hair, others are blond; some are tall, others are short; some are fat, others are skinny. Every person is unique and special. You too! You are wonderfully made. Maybe you don't think you're very pretty, or maybe you can't run as fast as somebody you know. Maybe you can't sing. But it doesn't matter, because you are special – you are you. The Lord gave you something that nobody else has.

Don't try to be like someone else. God made you unique. Just be yourself. Then the Lord will be able to use you, and you will also be happy. Won't you thank him right now for making you so special and unique?

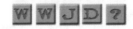

Jesus would share his
life with you and me.

 You ... crowned him [humanity] with glory and honor. (Psalm 8:5)

January 17

FEELING MISERABLE?

Hope deferred makes the heart sick. (Proverbs 13:12)

I remember it well: When I was still small, our family planned a wonderful holiday at a good resort. We talked it over and dreamed about it, and we were so excited when the holidays finally came. But then something happened and we couldn't go anymore. My father canceled the bookings, and we had to stay home. I felt miserable.

It often happens that things don't work out the way we plan them. Sometimes everything seems to go wrong at the same time and we can't help feeling depressed. Fortunately, the Lord knows everything, and if you are his child, you can trust him to help you. Through his Holy Spirit he helps and comforts us. Many times he assures us that there will be another opportunity to do what we would like to.

If you are feeling miserable about something, leave it in the hands of Jesus. He understands. Also, thank him for the things that you do have. It will make you feel better.

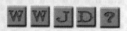

Jesus would cheer you up
in difficult times.

"Come to me ... and I will give you rest." (Matthew 11:28)

MRS. LOT LOSES EVERYTHING

But Lot's wife looked back, and she became a pillar of salt. (Genesis 19:26)

The Bible thinks so little of Lot's wife that her name is not even mentioned. Let's call her Mrs. Lot. She and Lot lived in Sodom. The people there would not do what God told them. So God decided to destroy Sodom. But because the Lord loved Abraham, and because Lot was a relative of Abraham's, the Lord warned Lot to flee. Mrs. Lot, however, did not want to leave all her nice things behind. She did not really believe that the Lord would look after her. When she turned around to look back at Sodom, she was changed into a pillar of salt, and she lost her life along with her possessions.

We must never love things more than God. He must be number one in our lives. He will look after us if we make him King in our lives. The Bible says when we give our lives to Jesus, we keep our lives.

Of course some things are very precious to us. But Jesus is much more precious than possessions. One day, when we go to him, we will have to leave everything behind anyway. Let's make Jesus number one in our lives right now.

Jesus would store up
treasures in heaven.

 "The Son of Man has no place to lay his head." (Matthew 8:20)

January 19

FOOD WITHOUT SALT

"You are the salt of the earth." (Matthew 5:13)

When we eat an egg, or any other food that needs salt, we sprinkle salt from the salt shaker onto the food. Salt gives food a better taste. When we are used to having salt on our food, it doesn't taste good without salt.

Jesus said we, his children, are the salt of the earth. Salt makes food taste better, and in the same way, we must flavor everything around us with our words and everything we do. People must enjoy having us around.

Today we use ointments and disinfectants to clean wounds. But in the old days they used salt to disinfect wounds – in other words, to get germs out. They rubbed salt into wounds to make them heal quickly. We, as children of the Lord, must sometimes be like salt in the wounds of others. With our words and our actions we must help heal people's wounds. If there is evil around us, we must overcome evil with good. For example, if someone swears, we should help him or her to see it is wrong.

Jesus would influence people with
his words and his deeds.

And he began to teach them. (Matthew 5:2)

January 20

ARE YOU A TREE?

They will be called oaks of righteousness. (Isaiah 61:3)

An oak tree grows tall and wide. It is a lovely tree with many branches and bright green leaves. In summer one can take a rest in the shade of an oak tree. Birds also like building their nests in oak trees.

Isaiah says that you and I are like these trees – oaks that stand tall and proud. When people look at us they must also be able to say that we are just as upright as oak trees. What the Bible actually says is that you and I, because we are saved and belong to Jesus, stand up straight like the oak: a tree of righteousness. As children of the Lord, we are like large, lush, beautiful oaks.

When people look at you today they must see an oak tree standing tall.

Jesus would show he is proud
to serve the Father.

 "I know him because I am from him and he sent me. " (John 7:29)

January 21

Light Is Stronger

The light shines in the darkness, but the darkness has not understood it. (John 1:5)

I'm sure you have walked in the dark before. As you know, it is very difficult to see where you are going. In the dark you can bump into chairs or other objects and hurt yourself. That is why we use a flashlight or switch on a light so that it can drive the darkness away. Light is stronger than darkness; we know that. The moment you switch on a light, the darkness disappears because the light is so bright.

The Bible says that Jesus is the light that came into this world. He who is the true light that gives light to every person was coming into the world (cf. John 1:9). Jesus himself said, "I am the light of the world." Jesus is like a bright light that drives out the darkness. And what is the darkness? It is the devil's influence. The devil is also called the prince of darkness. The work of the devil is just as dim as the darkest night. Jesus came to change the darkness of the devil into light.

Jesus will shine in you so that
you will be a light to the world.

"I am the light of the world. Whoever follows me ... will have the light of life." (John 8:12)

January 22

Love Builds

In humility consider others better than yourselves.
(Philippians 2:3)

When we really love someone, we do not want to hurt that person's feelings. When we love someone, we want to make that person happy. Paul writes in 1 Corinthians 13 that love is not self-seeking, which means it does not always want its own way. This means we want to build, or uplift, our loved ones and want what's best for them.

Uplifting someone is the opposite of criticizing that person. When we humiliate people, we make them feel small. All of us have, at some time or another, really felt like humiliating someone. But this is a very ugly characteristic. Let's try to uplift those around us with our actions and especially with our words and our love. This will mean that you and I must encourage friends and other people and say something like, "Well done; that was good." Or, "You tried your best. If you keep trying like this, you will be a winner."

Let's build one another in love.

Jesus would never turn a person
away but would help in love.

"I do not want to send them away hungry." (Matthew 15:32)

OUR FATHER

"Our Father in heaven ... " (Matthew 6:9)

Jesus taught us how to pray. When we pray, we talk to God. We open up our hearts to him and tell him everything that we think is important in our lives.

But before we can really pray, we need to have a personal relationship with the Lord. This means that we must not feel that God is far away, but that he is close to us, because Jesus introduced us to him. If we have worked out things between God and ourselves – because we accepted Jesus' offer on the cross – then the Almighty God becomes our Father.

The Bible also says he who has the Son has life; he who does not have the Son of God does not have life. If you have accepted Jesus, God is also your Father. Therefore you may call him Father. Then you can pray together with all Christians, *"Our Father in heaven ... "*

Jesus would help you
speak to God the Father.

In everything, by prayer ... present your requests to God. (Philippians 4:6)

DADDY - FATHER

"Our Father in heaven ... " (Matthew 6:9)

Every person on earth has a father. Most people know their fathers. Unfortunately, some children's dads have died or live somewhere far away, and some don't know who their dad is.

God is the Father of Jesus Christ. But he also becomes our Father, our Dad, if we accept him in faith. The Lord wants us to be his children. But not everybody on earth is God's child; only those who have accepted him. That is what we read in John 1:12, *"To all who received him, to those who believed in his name, he gave the right to become children of God."* Are you God's child yet?

If you become God's child, you soon find out that he is a wonderful Father. Because he loves us so much and wants only the best for us, we must feel free to speak to him and to hear him as he talks to us through his Word. He comforts and helps us through the Holy Spirit that he gave us. Yes, he is a wonderful Dad. Because he understands, and loves you, speak to him today.

Jesus would talk to
his Father regularly.

 Jesus ... went off to a solitary place, where he prayed. (Mark 1:35)

January 25

HEAVEN

"Our Father in heaven ... " (Matthew 6:9)

God lives in heaven. Heaven is a perfect, wonderful place. There are no tears or heartache or pain or hurt there. Everything in heaven is perfect and complete. God lives in heaven with his Son, Jesus, and also with millions of angels that praise and serve him all the time.

We don't really know where heaven is. We are also not sure what it looks like there. What we do know is that heaven is a wonderful place. God rules in heaven and there is no sin to hurt people. Also, there isn't room for the devil. He lives in hell. Heaven is a joyful place, and nothing will make us sad or upset there. We will be able to see God and live forever without illness or ever getting old.

When God has become our Father, then we know for sure that there will be a place for us in heaven. Jesus went there to prepare our place. Do you look forward to heaven? How about speaking to your Father in heaven right now?

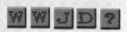

Jesus will be glad to see
us in heaven one day.

" ... that you also may be where I am." (John 14:3)

His Name

" ... hallowed [holy] be your name." (Matthew 6:9)

The Lord has many names. He is sometimes called Father or Almighty or Immanuel or Jesus or King. All these names are just to tell us more about him, who he is, and how he acts. Because the Lord can never sin, all his names are beautiful and show his holiness. To be holy is to be pure and without sin. God's name is holy. That is why it really is terrible when children or adults use his name carelessly, and even as a swear word. Do you know anyone who uses his name like this? You must never do it. If you hear one of your friends doing it, you must, in a nice way, tell this friend that you love Jesus and that his name is holy.

When we pray, we say, "Hallowed be your name." What we really mean is, "May your name be just as wonderful and lovely as you, Lord." And when his name comes from our lips, then we speak with respect.

Jesus would respect the
name of his Father.

"You shall not misuse the name of the LORD your God."
(Exodus 20:7)

January 27

THE KINGDOM
OF THE KING

"... your kingdom come." (Matthew 6:10)

In times past there were many more countries of the world ruled by a king or queen. The monarch ruled over the land, and that was his kingdom, or domain. Today there are many countries that have presidents or prime ministers. They also rule over a domain.

The most important kingdom of all is the kingdom of God. You might ask, "Where is the Lord's land?" Well, we could say it is in heaven, but it is also on earth. God does not have a piece of land like, say, America or Italy. His land or kingdom is everywhere that people accept his kingship. If you love the Lord and want to serve him, then he is your King. Then your heart becomes his kingdom. And wherever you might be, you take his kingdom with you: onto the sports field, into the classroom, or to any other place. Come, let's make him King in our country and also of the whole world.

We pray, "Your kingdom come; be King here on earth."

Jesus would build the
kingdom of God.

Jesus went throughout Galilee ... preaching the good news of the kingdom. (Matthew 4:23)

January 28

Your Will or His Will?

"... your will be done on earth." (Matthew 6:10)

God rules in heaven, and there his will is done. What he says is done. His will is always best. He is like a good government that only wants what's best for its citizens.

The devil also has a will, and he is so crooked that he always wants to get everybody to do his will. If we do what the devil wants, then we are asking for trouble. It is then that we get hurt and things start going wrong for us. On this earth there are many people that do the devil's will. Jesus teaches us to pray that the Lord's will be done on earth. You and I must choose to do the Lord's will, so that the earth can become a better place. I know I want to choose the Lord. What about you? Let's pray that the Lord's will be done in our homes and in our city.

Jesus would do his Father's will.

"My Father ... may your will be done." (Matthew 26:42)

BREAD

"Give us today our daily bread." (Matthew 6:11)

Many people have only bread to eat. They live on bread alone. We all need bread or food to stay alive.

Your mom and dad probably work every day. The money they earn is used to buy food for the family. There are, however, many poor people in countries all over the world. They are terribly hungry all the time, and they don't even know if they will live until the next day. We must pray for them and help them in whatever way we can.

Because God is our Father, we trust him to take care of us. We ask him to help us so that we will have bread to live on. The Lord promises in his Word that he will not allow his children to go hungry. He will look after us. If we really follow him and make him the King of our lives, he will take care of us. Let's thank him for everything he gives us, and let's give hungry people around us some of his bread.

Jesus would take care of people
who are having a difficult time.

Jesus then took the loaves ... and distributed to those who were seated as much as they wanted. (John 6:11)

HE FORGIVES ME

"Forgive us our debts [sins]. " (Matthew 6:12)

Jesus came to live on earth and to die on a cross so that God would forgive our sins. All of us are sinful. We are born with sin. Even when we are little, we do things that are wrong, and that is why we all need to be forgiven.

If our sins are not forgiven, we have not made our peace with the Lord. That is why God wants our sins to be forgiven. Actually, he is just waiting for us to say that we are sorry, and then he forgives us immediately. We must never be too proud or unwilling to tell the Lord that we are sorry about our sins.

That is why Jesus taught us to pray, "Forgive us our debts."

Jesus would forgive sins.

If we confess our sins, he ... will forgive us our sins. (1 John 1:9)

I FORGIVE YOU

" ... as we also have forgiven our debtors." (Matthew 6:12)

The Lord does not keep track of how often we have sinned against him; if we say we are sorry, he forgives us immediately. Sometimes we find it difficult to forgive others. But if the Lord forgives us so quickly, then we can also forgive a friend that has hurt us.

If a friend says, "I'm sorry," tell him or her right away, "I forgive you." Even if your friend does not say he's sorry, forgive him anyway in your heart. When you forgive someone, there is peace in your heart and your life is clean before the Lord. It is the same when the Lord forgives you.

When you have done something that hurt your friend, you must be prepared to say, "Please forgive me. I'm sorry I did this to you." If your friend forgives you then everything is forgotten. If your friend does not want to forgive you, you know that you have done the right thing and that God is proud of you. Children of the Lord are called peacemakers. Be a peacemaker for Christ.

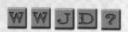

Jesus would forgive
someone who has hurt him.

Bear with each other ... Forgive as the Lord forgave you. (Colossians 3:13)

THE SPIDER'S WEB

"And lead us not into temptation ... " (Matthew 6:13)

A spider spins itself a web. This is its plan to catch insects so that it can eat them. The spider's web is shiny when the sun catches it and it looks very nice, but if you are an insect and fly into it, you're finished.

The Lord taught us to pray that we would not be led into temptation. That means not getting involved in things that can trap us like the insect in the spider web. The devil also spins a web for you and me. It looks very inviting, but once we are in his power, he destroys our lives. Sometimes we feel like taking part in things that seem like fun to do, but if doing these things is not the will of the Lord, it cannot be good for us.

When we do something we must always ask the Lord if it is his will for us. Sometimes we are tempted to take someone else's things, or to tell a lie, or to talk behind someone's back. It is not good to do that.

Let's ask the Lord to help us so that we can tell when we are being tempted. He must also help us to be strong enough to say no to the devil who wants to catch us.

Jesus would not give
in to the devil's demands.

"Away from me, Satan!" (Matthew 4:10)

February 2

The Nasty Old Spider

" ... but deliver us from the evil one." (Matthew 6:13)

The spider spins a web to catch insects so that it can kill them. The devil wants to catch you and me so that he can kill us. The Bible also calls him the "enormous fiery-red dragon" or the "snake" or the "evil one." He is the one who fights against the Lord and his children and makes war against us. He wants to destroy us.

Jesus taught us to pray that we may be delivered or saved from the evil one. There is only one way that we can be saved, and that is when the Great Savior protects us. His name is Jesus. Only he can save us from the evil one, and that is why we must be on his side. The devil wanted Jesus dead, but Jesus is much stronger than the devil. Jesus rose from the dead and in this way, he overcame the devil.

We must also take sides with Jesus against the devil so that he cannot catch us. We do not belong to the devil, we belong to Jesus. Say no to the devil and yes to Jesus today.

Jesus would say "no" to the devil.

Count yourselves dead to sin but alive to God. (Romans 6:11)

Amen

How can one ... say "Amen" to your thanksgiving? (1 Corinthians 14:16)

All our prayers usually end with the word *Amen*. The real meaning of this word is "let it be so." It is almost like wishing that what I have just prayed will come true.

But we can only say "Amen" if that which we have prayed is the will of the Lord. God cannot give you and me what is bad for us.

He loves us, and he wants only the best for us. That is why we must always ask if what we pray is his will. Many times we think we know what is good for us, but the Lord knows better. I have asked him for so many things that I did not get, and later on I saw that it was better that way. All the time God knew best. We can really trust him with our prayers.

By all means, pour your heart out to the Lord. It's all right to tell him what you would like to have. But then, make sure in your heart that what you are asking for is his will for you. Then you can safely end your prayer with "Amen."

Jesus would always ask
what the Father's will is.

"Father ... not my will, but yours be done." (Luke 22:42)

TAKE HIS HAND

"No one can snatch them out of my Father's hand." (John 10:29)

Little children like taking their father's or mother's hand. A child knows he is safe when his father takes his hand, especially if he has to cross a busy road or walk in the dark. He knows that he is safe when his father is holding his hand.

The Lord asks us to put our hands in his big, strong hand. It is the best thing any person can do. We don't always know what tomorrow will bring. We need help. Apart from that, we often do not know what road to take. We must be led. That is why a Christian puts his or her hand in the big, strong hand of the Father. He will show us the right way. He will not let go of us. He will keep us safe. The Bible says if we put our hand in his, no one can snatch us out of his hand. The devil may try, but he won't be able to do it. When we hold on to the Father's hand, we are really safe.

Put your hand in his now. Ask him to lead you through this day. He will hold you tight.

Jesus would take the
Father's hand every day.

Your hand will guide me, your right hand will hold me fast. (Psalm 139:10)

It Hurts!

I consider that our present sufferings are not worth comparing with the glory that will be revealed in us. (Romans 8:18)

At this moment, many children hurt. Some are in pain, some are very hungry, and some are dying of disease. Others have been in a bad car accident and have cuts and bruises.

At some time or another, you have been hurt. Perhaps you are ill even as you read these words. Because we are not in heaven yet, we will suffer pain.

Jesus knew pain and suffering. He was hurt very badly when he was nailed to the cross for you and me. But one day all the hurt in our lives will be over. There is no pain and suffering in heaven. This is because Jesus paid for our sins. Because of his pain and suffering, a day will come when you and I will not hurt in any way anymore.

Perhaps you are hurting now – in your body or your heart. Give the hurt to Jesus. Ask him to comfort you. He knows pain, and he understands how you feel.

Jesus would always take
my pain onto him.

Surely he ... carried our sorrows. (Isaiah 53:4)

GOOD WORDS

The tongue of the wise brings healing. (Proverbs 12:18)

Isn't it wonderful that we can talk to each other and understand each other? Words can heal or hurt. Words are very powerful.

The Bible says that the tongue is important because it can have a great influence on people. If you encourage someone with your words, it can mean a great deal to that person. But with your words you can also criticize people and hurt them.

The Bible says our tongues must be under God's control. We must ask the Lord to keep our tongues in check so that we don't hurt others. You get a nice feeling in your heart when you speak good words. Good, positive, uplifting words mean a lot to others. I hope you remember that when you speak to your friends.

Ask the Lord to help you speak only good, pleasant words to people today.

Jesus would be honest and
sincere and speak the truth.

 Let your conversation be always full of grace, seasoned with salt. (Colossians 4:6)

THE SULKY MINISTER

But Jonah was greatly displeased and became angry.
(Jonah 4:1)

God had a plan for Jonah's life. He wanted to use Jonah. The Lord decided to send Jonah to a big city called Nineveh. But Jonah didn't want to go. He tried to run away from God. He went aboard a ship that was going to Tarshish, which was in the opposite direction from Nineveh. He was disobeying the Lord.

The Lord then decided that a fish must swallow Jonah. In a wonderful way the Lord saw to it that Jonah changed his mind and decided to go to Nineveh. But when Jonah saw that the Lord was not going to punish the people there, as he had threatened to do, he became very angry. He went and sat outside the city, sulking. Can you believe it? Instead of being thankful that the Lord was kind to the people of Nineveh, Jonah wanted the Lord to punish them. And all because Jonah didn't like them!

You and I must not be like Jonah. We must be happy when the Lord's love changes people's lives, and we must also be willing to go if the Lord sends us to talk to someone.

Jesus would go wherever
God sent him, right away.

"As the Father has sent me, I am sending you." (John 20:21)

You Must Choose

"Choose for yourselves this day whom you will serve."
(Joshua 24:15)

Many people choose not to serve the Lord. They want to have nothing to do with him, or they are afraid of him. Some do not believe that he exists. Perhaps they hope that they won't have to stand before him one day and account for their lives.

The Bible says we must choose whom we want to serve. If we want to serve the devil or even ourselves, then we must choose to do so. But if we want to serve the Lord, then we must choose him.

You and I choose the Lord because we know he is the true God and because it is worth our while to serve him. We choose the Lord by saying yes to him: "Yes, Lord, here is my life, here is my heart, here is my everything. I want to follow You and I want to live for You." This is what Joshua and his family did. They decided to listen to the Lord and do what he said.

Have you made your choice for God yet? Do it now and tell him that you want to serve him.

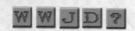

Jesus would always
choose a life with God.

Now choose life, so that you ... may live. (Deuteronomy 30:19)

THE REAL GOD

For there is one God. (1 Timothy 2:5)

There are many religions in the world. Every religion has its own so-called god. The people who believe in that god believe that theirs is the real god. Some people worship Hindu gods, some follow the Buddha, some pray to their ancestors, and some worship the devil.

The Bible tells us very clearly that there is only one real God. His name is God Almighty, the Father of our Lord Jesus. All the other gods will bow down before him one day. If we worship this God, we are safe and we are fortunate. He is a God of love. He loved us so much that he sent his Son so that we could be washed clean from sin.

Even in places like America or Europe there are many people who worship other gods. You and I must make it very clear that the only real God is the father of Jesus. He is our God and our Father.

Jesus would glorify
only his Father.

"... that your Son may glorify you." (John 17:1)

CONTROL YOURSELF!

The fruit of the Spirit is ... self-control. (Galatians 5:22, 23)

To control a horse most people put a metal bit into its mouth. This helps to control it and allows the rider to guide it. Without the bit and bridle, the horse would just run where it wants. Likewise, a train runs on two rails. When it is on these two rails, it cannot overturn. In the same way, a powerful truck has brakes. Brakes slow it down so that it does not get out of control and cause an accident.

People also need to be controlled. Some people are very silly and break things in a fit of temper. Others can't control their desires and take things that don't belong to them. Then there are those who get so angry that they hurt others. Yes, you and I also need to be under control.

The One that can really help us is the Holy Spirit. When he is in our lives, he helps us to control our behavior. This means that we won't fly off the handle; we will control ourselves. Actually, it's the Holy Spirit who takes control of our lives, and he helps us make the right decisions.

Open up your heart to the Holy Spirit. Ask him to fill you so that you can be under his control.

Jesus would be in control because
he is filled with the Holy Spirit.

He saw ... the Spirit descending on him like a dove. (Mark 1:10)

February 11

STICK TO THE RULES

Everyone must submit himself to the governing authorities. (Romans 13:1)

When you play football or basketball you have to play by the rules of the game. If you don't, the referee will blow the whistle. It is important to have rules, otherwise everyone would do just as he pleases.

Schools also have rules. If you don't obey them, you are in trouble. Countries have rules. The authorities or the government of a country make the rules. For example, we have speed limits in our country. We are not allowed to take another's belongings. If we break the rules, we can be found guilty and we must pay a fine, or even worse, go to jail.

Christians try to glorify the Lord in everything they do. They want to please the Lord. And the Lord tells us to obey the rules of a country. God likes to have order, and he likes us to do things the right way. Let's keep the rules of our country and obey what they tell us so that we can please the Lord. See that you stick to the rules today.

Jesus would obey authorities.

"Give to Caesar what is Caesar's." (Matthew 22:21)

February 12

FLAT OUT FOR JESUS

Do you not know that in a race all the runners run, but only one gets the prize? Run in such a way as to get the prize. (1 Corinthians 9:24)

Athletes taking part in a race give their best. They run flat out because they hope to win. But there is also another, much more important race than an earthly race. The race of life.

The Bible says it is almost as if every human being on earth is running a race of life. We know there is a finish line, same as for athletes, and a prize. There is a difference, though. The prize at the end of our lives is not just for winners, but for everyone who believes in Jesus. Still, we must do everything we can to finish the race, just like athletes. The Bible says that the one who doesn't give up will win the prize.

This means that we must keep the faith, even if we are having a hard time. We must believe the Lord is King and live for him. Read your Bible and talk to him. This will help you to not get spiritually tired. Give your everything today to follow Jesus.

Jesus would give everything
to finish the race.

"It is finished." (John 19:30)

WASHING FEET

After that, he poured water into a basin and began to wash his disciples' feet. (John 13:5)

In Jesus' time they didn't have paved roads, and people didn't have cars. Most of them walked on foot from one place to another. The streets were dusty and sandy, so their feet got very dirty. When they reached their destination, someone usually brought them water to wash their feet. Sometimes a servant washed their feet.

The Lord Jesus didn't think he was too important to wash the feet of his disciples. He went down on his knees and washed his friends' feet. He is our example. Today we don't need to wash a person's feet, because we don't have dirt roads. But we can follow Jesus' example and treat people well. We can make them feel at home when they visit us. We can be friendly. We can listen to them. We can give them food or money or love, and we can pay attention to them. All of this is just another way of washing their feet.

Think of ways how you can "wash someone's feet" today.

Jesus would serve
everybody in love.

Serve one another in love. (Galatians 5:13)

HE IS CALLING YOU

Then the LORD called Samuel. Samuel answered, "Here I am." (1 Samuel 3:4)

In the Garden of Eden, Adam and Eve were with God. The Lord talked to them every day, and they always knew he was there. But then they sinned and had to leave paradise. They hid from God, and the Bible says that he called them. Ever since that time God calls people to come to him. We read in the Old Testament that the Lord called Isaiah and Jeremiah.

Samuel was just a little boy when God called him. The Lord wanted Samuel to follow him. When Samuel heard the Lord calling him, he answered, "Speak, Lord, for your servant is listening."

Even today the Lord calls people to come to him. He wants to forgive them their sins and use them. He also calls you. And he calls me. I have answered yes. Have you said yes to him yet? Do it now.

When the Father calls, Jesus would answer him immediately.

"Here am I. Send me!" (Isaiah 6:8)

He Knows Everything

Everything is uncovered and laid bare before the eyes of him to whom we must give account. (Hebrews 4:13)

Have you ever done something that you kept quiet about? I think so. You didn't tell a soul anything about it. You thought nobody would ever find out. Sometimes we manage to hide things from people. But we can't hide anything from God.

God knows everything that happens on earth. He knows everything you and I do. He also knows what we think. Everything is laid bare before his eyes. That is why it is impossible to hide anything from him. The sooner we realize that, the sooner we can be honest about our sins.

Fortunately, God is not a God that just wants to punish us all the time; otherwise, we could never have peace in our hearts. He is a God of love. He wants to forgive us. When we have done something wrong, all we have to do is tell him we're sorry. He knows everything. He is just waiting for us to say we're sorry.

If we do not confess our sins, we will have to account for them one day before the throne of God. It is better to say you're sorry now. He will forgive you right away.

Jesus will know and see
everything you do.

O Lord ... you know me. (Psalm 139:1)

THE SAVIOR
OF THE WORLD

"We know that this man really is the Savior of the world." (John 4:42)

Have you and your friends ever played a game where you tie up someone? When somebody's hands and feet are tied up, he or she can hardly move. And that person cannot really untie himself. He needs someone else to free or save him.

The Bible says Jesus is called the Savior. He came to save us. From what? Sin, of course, and also from hell. Yes, and also from the devil. The name *Jesus* comes from the word *Yeshua*, which means "to loose or loosen." Jesus was sent to untie the shackles and cords of the devil. Only he can free us, for he is the Savior.

So many people are still bound tightly by their sins. We must tell them that Jesus is the Savior. I hope you have already asked the Lord to free you from sin and save you.

Jesus would tell everybody
that he is the only Savior.

"There is no other name ... by which we must be saved." (Acts 4:12)

NOT RULES, LOVE

Love does no harm to its neighbor. Therefore love is the fulfillment of the law. (Romans 13:10)

Some people think that to follow God means to keep a lot of rules and regulations. They say, "You may not do this and you may not do that." They think that God is like a strict teacher who watches them all the time, and the moment they break some rule, they are in trouble. This is not true. The Lord is not like that at all.

In the Old Testament, the children of God (the people of Israel) had to obey certain rules and laws. But they couldn't, because they were sinners. That's why God sent Jesus to help us. Jesus proved his love for us when he died for us to pay for our sins. Now we are so thankful that we want to show Jesus how much we love him, and that is why we do what he wants: Not because he orders us to, but because we would like to. We want to make him happy. We needn't worry about a lot of rules, but we must do what he would like us to do because we love him.

Jesus would do what God wants him to because he loves God very much.

"Love your neighbor as yourself." (Matthew 22:39)

I Am Afraid!

In God I trust; I will not be afraid. (Psalm 56:11)

Maybe you are afraid that something unpleasant will happen to you today. Maybe you didn't study for a test. Perhaps you are afraid of other things, like death. Many people are afraid of dying. Maybe you are afraid something terrible is going to happen to you. Everybody is afraid at some time or another.

When we are afraid we must give our fear to the Lord. This is what the writer of this psalm did. He called on the name of the Lord. Another psalm says the name of the Lord is like a strong tower, and if we go in there, we will be safe. Give your fear to the Lord today. Tell him what scares you. Ask him to help you. I am sure he will, because he promises to do just that in his Word. The Lord likes us to trust him. We must thank him and praise him for that.

Jesus will protect you,
so you needn't be afraid.

"Fear not, for I have redeemed you." (Isaiah 43:1)

I Am Sending You

"Therefore go and make disciples of all nations."
(Matthew 28:19)

The Lord decided to do his work here on earth using not only angels (that we can't see), but especially human beings. People like you and me – not just the pastor or some or other important person in the church.

We read in the Bible that the Lord called many men and women to do his work. He called Moses to lead his people. He called the Israelites out of Egypt. He called Jonah and told him to go to Nineveh. He called Gideon to fight against the enemy. He called Samuel to serve him in the temple. He called Esther to save the people of Israel from ruin. He called Mary to raise the child Jesus. The Lord also calls you and me, because he has work to do and he wants us to help him.

The Lord is calling you today. Go to the nations, or simply go to your classmates or your friends. All you have to do is to be willing. Tell him, "Yes, Lord, I am ready. Use me."

Jesus would work for God.

"Go into all the world and preach the good news to all creation." (John 20:21)

February 20

Just like an Eagle

Like an eagle that stirs up its nest, that spreads its wings to catch [its young] ... (Deuteronomy 32:11, 12)

Eagles are beautiful birds. They live high up in the mountains on rock ledges. There they build their nests and hatch their eggs. Baby eagles live in these nests. But the day comes when the mother eagle throws the baby out of the nest so that it falls down the steep cliff. Can you imagine how scared the baby eagle is? I suppose it thinks it is falling to its death.

But the next moment the mother eagle spreads her wings and catches the baby. Then she carries it back to the nest. The next moment she does everything all over again. The baby falls, flaps its wings, and she catches it again. This is the way it learns to fly.

The Lord does the same to us. All the bad times in our lives teach us to fly and to grow spiritually strong. Thank the Lord for the bad times in your life. These will make you spiritually mighty.

Jesus would carry you
through difficult times.

"The LORD your God carried you, as a father carries his son."
(Deuteronomy 1:31)

February 21

BITTER FRUIT

See to it that no bitter root grows up to cause trouble.
(Hebrews 12:15)

I'm sure you like delicious, sweet fruit. Some fruit trees give us the most tasty fruit. But there are also trees that give us bitter fruit. When you eat this fruit you feel like spitting it out, because it is certainly not nice to eat.

The Bible says you and I are also like a tree. We can bear good or bad fruit. We bear sweet fruit when we behave according to God's will. But there is something that makes our fruit taste really bad: bitterness.

Bitterness is when you are cross with someone and you are not prepared to forgive him. Then there is bitterness in your heart toward him, and this makes your whole life bitter. You become a grumpy, sour person, and others don't like being with you.

Are you perhaps not prepared to forgive someone today? Are you bitter? Tell the Lord now that you forgive that person, and your bitterness will go away.

Jesus would not be bitter.

"Father, forgive them." (Luke 23:34)

A Little Becomes a Lot

When they had all had enough to eat, they gathered [the leftovers] and filled twelve baskets. (John 6:12-13)

When Jesus was on earth, he performed many miracles. He wanted to show that he was the true Savior and Lord. One of the miracles was when he increased a little boy's fish and bread. Do you remember? There were thousands of people who became very hungry as they sat listening to Jesus. When he asked if anyone had food, a little boy brought him two small fish and five loaves of bread. How could thousands of people possibly eat this food? But Jesus turned it into much, much more!

When Jesus took the bread and fish and broke it, the disciples started handing the food out to the people, and right there in front of their eyes, it became more. There was even food left over! It was a miracle!

I think with this miracle Jesus wanted to show that even the little that we give him can become a lot in his hands. Don't you want to give what you have today – your talents, your beauty, your sport, whatever – to Jesus? He will use it and many people will be blessed by it. It's not how much you give that's important, but what you give him.

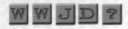

Jesus would give what he has to God.

Offer your bodies as living sacrifices ... to God. (Romans 12:1)

February 23

WONDERFUL !

He will be called Wonderful. (Isaiah 9:6)

The Holy Spirit prophesied through Isaiah that Jesus would be born for us and that his name would be "Wonderful." That means that no one is as fantastic as Jesus.

Everybody on earth has faults, and these faults make it so that we must forgive others. Sometimes we have to be patient with people. It's no fun having to deal with the weaknesses of others all the time. But Jesus had no faults, and he never sinned. It must have been wonderful to be with someone like him, to eat and drink and sleep and talk with him. No wonder thousands followed him just to be with him and listen to him.

Because Jesus is so wonderful, we praise and glorify him and tell others that it is worthwhile following him. Praise him, because you know he is wonderful and because you love him and follow him. The greatest miracle is that he loves us so much that he died on a cross for us.

Jesus would not sin.

God made him who had no sin to be sin for us. (2 Corinthians 5:21)

THE LION THAT ROARS

Be self-controlled and alert. The devil prowls around like a roaring lion. (1 Peter 5:8)

Lions are dangerous animals that prey on other animals and even gobble up humans sometimes. That's why we must stay as far away from them as possible.

The Bible tells us to be careful of the devil because he is just like a roaring lion. He wants to devour and destroy us. Many people's lives have been destroyed because they listened to the devil. Many things we see on television or read about seem so exciting. But everything that is not the Lord's will – no matter how much fun it seems to be – is not good for us. We must trust the Lord in this. His will is always best for us.

The best way to avoid the devil is to follow the Lord. Tell Jesus, now, that you love him and that you want to do what he says. That will upset the devil. Read the Bible and talk to God every day. The devil hates it. Also, tell the devil you want nothing to do with him because the Bible says you must resist him, then he will stay away from you.

Choose against the devil today. Choose the Lord.

Jesus would resist the devil.

Submit yourselves, then, to God. Resist the devil, and he will flee from you. (James 4:7)

Peace for the World

" ... and on earth peace." (Luke 2:14)

There is a lot of strife all over the world. There are men and women who fight with each other. There are families who fight a lot. There is also disagreement between friends and between countries and nations. There have been many wars in the world simply because nations could not live together in peace.

When Jesus was born, the angels sang that there was now a chance for peace on earth. Another name for Jesus is "Prince of Peace." Jesus wants so badly for us to have peace in our hearts. That is why he offers us peace when He forgives our sins. When our sins have been taken away by Jesus we also find peace with God the Father.

After that you must still make peace with your fellow humans. If you are in disagreement with someone, then you are not doing what the Lord wants. He says, "Blessed are the peacemakers, for they will be called children of God." Children of God don't want to make war. They want to make peace. Yes, we sometimes have arguments, but we want to say we're sorry afterward and make peace.

Are you in conflict with someone today? Make peace. Be God's instrument of peace in your class, your school, your home, your town, and even the whole world.

Jesus would live in
peace with everybody.

Live at peace with everyone. (Romans 12:18)

February 26

Erased!

He took it away, nailing it to the cross. (Colossians 2:14)

What a good feeling it is to erase a mistake you have made in your schoolwork. When I was in school, we always used an eraser, but these days you can use things like correction fluid and other modern stuff. Then you can remove all mistakes easily and start again.

We all make mistakes, and this makes things a bit difficult. But the best part is that a mistake can be corrected. The greatest problem in a person's life is sin. Sin makes us miss God's purpose in our lives and do the wrong thing. How can we be washed clean from sin? The Bible has good news: there is Someone who can erase our sins. His name is Jesus Christ.

When Jesus died on the cross, he paid for our sins with his blood. His death on the cross can erase our sins.

Give your life to the Lord today and ask him to erase all your sins. Then you can stand before him, clean.

Jesus will forgive your sins.

In him we have redemption through his blood, the forgiveness of sins. (Ephesians 1:7)

Hallelujah

Give thanks to the LORD, for he is good. (Psalm 118:1)

One of the best words in the Bible is *hallelujah.* In some modern translations of the Bible the words "praise the Lord" are used instead of "hallelujah." To me "praise the Lord" sounds more like an order than a suggestion. It's almost as if the Bible tells us that we must praise the Lord. Naturally! After all, he is the Great King of heaven and earth. There is nobody like him. Of course we must tell everybody that he is great and wonderful. We also want to praise Jesus. He is our Savior. He gave his life for us. How can we keep quiet about this? It is impossible. All Christians want to praise and exalt the Lord.

We praise the Lord when we say that he is great and good. We can also sing this with all our heart. Singing songs of praise is exactly the same as telling people that the Lord is wonderful. The original meaning of the word "hallelujah" is actually to be proud of the Lord. Are you proud of the Lord? Then tell others that he is great and wonderful.

Jesus would glorify God.

"God is glorified in him." (John 13:31)

THE VENDING-MACHINE GOD

"He gives [gifts] to each one, just as he determines.
(1 Corinthians 12:11)

I am sure every person who thinks that God exists has asked him for something at some time. Many people have in an emergency, when things have gone terribly wrong, quickly prayed to God and asked him to help. Often he does! But praying for something does not guarantee that they get what they ask for. God is not a vending machine.

Do you know how a vending machine works? You put a coin in the machine and you get something out of it. You put a coin into the machine and you get a drink or a snack. When you have put your money in, the machine spits out what you want. You ask, and the machine gives. But the Lord is not a vending machine! He loves you and me, and he wants to give us what's best for us; that is why he won't give us everything we ask for.

We must ask according to his will, and then he will give as he wants. And we can accept what he gives us. It will always be what's best for us.

Jesus would ask what the
will of the Father is.

"For I have come down from heaven not to do my will but to do the will of him who sent me." (John 6:38)

Thankfulness

... being watchful and thankful. (Colossians 4:2)

I'm sure you know people who are always moaning and groaning. It's as though they only see the dark side of life and complain about it all the time, just as if nothing is ever good enough for them.

Being unthankful is a very ugly characteristic. If you sit down and think, you will find many things to be thankful for. Think of the beauty of nature. Take a look at all the other things around us to be thankful for: friendly people, nourishing food, a home, a warm bed, a car to take us places. There are too many to mention.

But the best thing of all to be thankful for is that Jesus came and changed our lives with his love. When a heart is filled with his love, it overflows with thankfulness and spills over also onto others. Then we can find something to be thankful for even in the most difficult circumstances. Start right now and get into the habit of looking on the bright side, and say "thank you" for it. The Bible says we must be thankful for everything. What can you thank the Lord for today?

Jesus would be
thankful in everything.

Always giving thanks to God the Father for everything. (Ephesians 5:20)

March 1

LIKE FATHER, LIKE SON

... until Christ is formed in you. (Galatians 4:19)

You have probably heard the expression, "Like father, like son." We can add to that, "Like mother, like daughter." What does this mean? One says this when someone acts in the same way as his or her parent or looks like one of them. Some apple trees bear red apples. Others green apples. The kind of fruit they produce will depend on what type of trees they are. It is the same with children. They often act like their parents.

The Lord wants us to look like him. When God becomes our heavenly Father, when we understand what he wants from us and we hear him talk to us, then we will begin to think and act like him more and more. Paul wrote a letter to Christians and encouraged them to look more and more like Jesus. They must have his stature. This difficult word simply means that they should act and think like Jesus, so that people will know they belong to him.

Ask the Lord to help you become more and more like him. When people see how you live and hear what you say, they should know you are a Christian. Then they can say, "Like Father, like son."

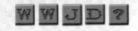

Jesus would help
people to be like him.

He must become greater; I must become less. (John 3:30)

March 2

BLESS YOUR ENEMY

> Bless those who persecute you; bless and do not curse.
> (Romans 12:14)

Enemies are people who do not like one another one bit. It can get so bad that they will even try to destroy one another. Perhaps there is someone that you don't like very much, and deep down you think that person is your enemy. Although we don't have to like everybody, it doesn't mean they must be our enemies. It's true, sometimes someone can hurt us. Maybe there's a bully in your school who makes you unhappy. He or she is nearly like an enemy. But Christians should not respond as others would.

The Bible says we must bless our enemies. It sounds nearly impossible to do. What does it mean? It means you must say, "I want the best for you in life. May the Lord pour his love out over you." But you must also say, "May the Lord work in your life so that you are also filled with love and goodness." Then you have blessed that person with only the best. Someone who comes closer to Jesus will have a change of heart. Then he doesn't want to be an enemy any more, but a friend, even a loved one. Ask the Lord now to bless your "enemy" and to draw him or her closer to Jesus. Then your enemy will become your friend.

Jesus would pray for his
enemies and bless them.

"Love your enemies and pray for those who persecute you."
(Matthew 5:44)

How Great Are You?

"Whoever wants to become great among you must be your servant." (Mark 10:43)

We all know important people. There are sports stars who are great football players or who run very fast. They are great in the eyes of people because they have achieved success. There are actors and actresses on television or in movies. They are also great in the eyes of some people.

Jesus said clearly that if you want to be great or important, you must be prepared to serve others. So we see that greatness is not about being famous, but about helping and supporting others by loving and serving them. Leaders who want to trample on others, who always want their own way, and who push others around as it suits them are not great in the eyes of the Lord. A true leader is someone who works hard, someone who supports others, someone who wants to help.

How can you serve someone today? What can you do to help others? Perhaps a friend needs your help. Go and serve him or her. Then you will be great in the eyes of the Lord, and people will respect you.

Jesus would serve others.

"Now that I ... have washed your feet, you also should wash one another's feet." (John 13:14)

March 4

THE HUMBLE

"God opposes the proud but gives grace to the humble."
(James 4:6)

Arrogant people are a real pain! They have this attitude that says, "I am much better than you." They think they are very important and want everybody to think so too. The Lord does not like this kind of pride. It is not good to have too much pride in your heart because it causes you to look down your nose at others and treat them without respect.

The Lord says in many places in the Bible that he will oppose the proud. One day every knee will bow before the King of kings and everyone will have to account for his or her life. Proud people should realize, while they are still on earth, that they are small in God's eyes, and they should treat others with respect.

A humble person admits his own shortcomings and faults. If you are humble you don't think you are wonderful. You accept your talents and good points, but you don't think you are better than others. You also thank God for everything you have received. The Bible says God will give grace to the humble.

Thank the Lord that you are who you are, but also tell him you know you have faults and that you need him. Ask him to help you build others up and enrich them.

Jesus would be humble.

"See, your king [Jesus] comes to you gentle, and riding on a donkey." (Matthew 21:5)

DRINK FROM A DIRTY CUP?

If a man cleanses himself [from wickedness], he will be an instrument for noble purposes. (2 Timothy 2:21)

In a large house there are utensils for everyday use, but there are also things for special occasions. Mom doesn't use her best cups every day. She uses the ordinary ones. But, when important guests visit, she brings out her best china. When we work in the garden we don't wear our best clothes. We wear just any old thing. Our best clothes we keep for special occasions.

The Bible says that we must be instruments that can be used for a specific purpose: *"there are articles not only of gold and silver, but also of wood and clay; some are for noble purposes and some for ignoble [everyday]"* (2 Timothy 2:20). You and I can be very special instruments for God if we keep ourselves pure. The Bible calls it sanctification. This means we must confess our sins and obey the Lord.

Do you want the Lord to use you for a specific purpose? Then you must be clean before God. Ask him to wash you clean of sin. Do what he wants. In this way you will also become a precious instrument of gold or silver.

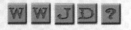

Jesus will help you to
be God's instrument.

 "If a man remains in me ... he will bear much fruit; apart from me you can do nothing." (John 15:5)

March 6

BELIEVE AND DO

What good is it if a man claims to have faith but has no deeds? (James 2:14)

Many people say they believe in the Lord. There are many people who go to church regularly and do all kinds of nice religious things, but one sometimes wonders if their faith is genuine. The Bible says quite clearly if we say we believe, then our deeds must show our faith.

This means that it is not enough to read the Bible and know it well; we must apply it to our lives. If the Lord tells us in his Word that we may not steal, we must say to ourselves, "I will not steal." If the Bible says we must not allow dirty words to come from our mouths, we must decide not to swear. If the Bible tells us to forgive others, we must not walk around with bitterness toward someone in our hearts. To follow Jesus is to believe in him, but also to do what he says. Faith without deeds means nothing.

I'm sure you want to do what the Lord asks you to do. I know it is not always easy. Let's try to follow the Lord properly. Let's ask him to help us today not only to believe in him, but also to do what he says.

Jesus will help you turn
your words into deeds.

Live by the Spirit. (Galatians 5:16)

March 7

DON'T KICK ME

If someone is caught in a sin, you ... should restore him gently. (Galatians 6:1)

Some people take pleasure in others' problems. If a person shows some kind of weakness, it is especially easy to point a finger at him. In this way, the one pointing the finger often feels good about himself. Some people enjoy gossiping about another's problems. Many don't stop at gossiping, they also pass judgment.

I'm sure you've heard the saying, "Don't kick a man when he's down." What we are really saying is, "Why keep on criticizing someone who has made a mistake?" Forget it so that he can put it behind him. This is also what the Bible says. The Bible admits that people sometimes sin, but it says that we must not keep criticizing them for it. Rather, we should be gentle and help them. We should not be hard on someone who has made a mistake. We must be prepared to forgive, to be friendly, to help him work things out. Gentle people are people that don't like hurting others. As Paul says in 1 Corinthians 13:5, *Love ... keeps no record of wrongs.*

Don't take pleasure in someone's wrongs today. It is much better to help.

Jesus would pick
you up if you fell.

"Blessed are the meek." (Matthew 5:5)

March 8

Holidays!

He said to them, "Come with me to a quiet place and get some rest." (Mark 6:31)

Holidays are fun. When the schools are closed, we can relax at home, or visit friends, or go away to a holiday resort.

Holidays are necessary because then we can do something other than just schoolwork. We can rest, because we don't have to get up so early in the morning. We can get together with family or friends. Everyone needs time to rest. Even Jesus realized that he and his disciples had to rest, and that is why he called them to one side and said, "Let's just get away from the crowds for a while to get some rest and relax in a peaceful, lonely place."

I hope you will take time to enjoy holidays or school breaks when you have them. See to it, however, that you also make time for the Lord, read your Bible every day, and take him with you wherever you go. Be his witness. Tell people about him. Fill your days with Jesus, and you will go back to school refreshed.

Jesus would also
make time to rest.

He withdrew privately to a solitary place. (Matthew 14:13)

SAMSON'S MISTAKE

> [Samson] fell in love with a woman in the Valley of Sorek whose name was Delilah. (Judges 16:4)

Samson was a very strong man. The Lord gave him great strength. This was because God had a plan for Samson. He wanted Samson to defeat the enemies of the Lord's people.

Samson was an Israelite. God told the Israelites that they were not to marry anyone from outside their nation. An Israelite was not allowed to marry a heathen man or a heathen woman. The Israelites believed in God, and that is why they were forbidden to marry someone who didn't believe in the Lord.

Samson fell in love with Delilah. She was a Philistine woman, and she did not believe in God. In spite of this, Samson decided to marry Delilah. It was against God's will; he had to pay for it. If we don't do what God wants, we are looking for trouble. In the end, Samson's love for Delilah cost him his life. She cut his hair, his strength left him, and he was overcome by the Philistines. Soon afterward Samson died.

It is not too soon for you to start praying that the Lord would help you marry the right man or woman someday. Don't do what Samson did. Don't just do what you feel like doing.

Jesus would help you
marry the right person.

Commit to the LORD whatever you do, and your plans will succeed. (Proverbs 16:3)

Too Young

"Ah, Sovereign LORD, I am only a child." (Jeremiah 1:6)

One of the most wonderful things is that the Lord uses people like you and me to do his work. He has a place and a task for each of us. Nobody is unimportant in his eyes. He uses some people when they are old, but he also uses young people, like Jeremiah.

Jeremiah was young when the Lord called him. The Lord told him to go and talk to the people of Israel about their sins and to bring the people to God. Jeremiah's first reaction was that he was far too young. He would never be able to do it. They would not listen to him. But God said he was not too young. The Lord wanted to use him and no one else, even if he was young.

The Lord does not just use older people. He also calls you, even if you are a child. There may just be something he wants you to do. Tell him yes. And see that you are willing to be used by him. Because Jeremiah was prepared to be used by God, he worked for the Lord for about fifty years as a minister. Not all of us need to become ministers, but this was the Lord's plan with Jeremiah. I don't know what the Lord's plan is with you; just tell him that you will be willing when he calls you.

Jesus would answer
when his Father calls.

At once they ... followed him. (Matthew 4:20)

March 11

GOD'S PLAN

> She got a papyrus basket. Then she placed the child in it and put it among the reeds along the bank of the Nile. (Exodus 2:3)

At the time Moses was born, the pharaoh was worried about the many Israelites in Egypt. He ordered that all the baby Israelite boys be killed. Moses' mother loved him very much. She didn't want him to be killed. So she put him in a basket and hid him on the bank of the Nile river.

But God always has a plan for our lives. His plan was to use Moses to take the Israelites out of Egypt. That is why God saw to it that the pharaoh's daughter found the baby Moses in the basket and took him to the palace with her. Here Moses grew up. He became a leader. And when he was older, the Lord told him to take the Israelites out of Egypt. God is truly wonderful! He has a plan for each of us. Even when Moses was in the basket the Lord already had a plan for his life. God also has a plan for your life. Follow him and trust him. Do what he asks you to. He can use you.

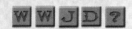

Jesus will show you
his plan for your life.

Trust in the LORD with all your heart. (Proverbs 3:5)

WHAT A SURPRISE!

At this, she turned around and saw Jesus standing there. (John 20:14)

A surprise is when something happens to you that you did not expect. This happened to Mary Magdalene.

Mary had been a very bad woman. Then she met Jesus. He taught her about peace and forgiveness and told her about his kingdom.

She believed him. This changed her life. She started loving Jesus as her Savior.

Then Jesus died on the cross. Mary's heart was broken. She loved Jesus so much and now he was dead. She must have cried a lot. Three days after Jesus' death she went to his grave. There a wonderful surprise was waiting for her. She saw Jesus himself standing there. Jesus was alive! She couldn't believe her eyes. This was the greatest surprise of her life. He was alive!

If we give our lives to Jesus, we find that he is just as wonderful toward us as he was to Mary. And he is alive in our hearts.

Jesus would keep on surprising
you with his love.

[May you] know this love that surpasses knowledge. (Ephesians 3:19)

March 13

TREASURE IN YOUR HEART

For where your treasure is, there your heart will be also. (Luke 12:34)

When you have been given something precious, you want to keep it close to you. If you have a shiny new bicycle, you won't leave it at school overnight. You want it near you because you are so happy about it. And you want to look after it. You are proud of it. Also, when you love someone, you want to be with that person. Loved ones say they "treasure" one another.

The Bible tells us to keep the right treasures in our hearts. We all have something that we treasure. There is always something that is important to us. But we must keep the most important things in our hearts. The Bible calls these the things of the Lord's kingdom. The Lord and our relationship with him are much more important than bicycles, cars, video games, clothes, or money. Of course it's nice to have these things, but they are not more important than our relationship with the Lord.

Make sure that Jesus is the most important one in your life. Your heart will be with your greatest treasure: the Lord of your life.

Jesus would store up
treasures in heaven.

 For where your treasure is, there your heart will be also. (Matthew 6:21)

March 14

RESIST THE DEVIL!

Resist the devil, and he will flee from you. (James 4:7)

By this time you know the devil is your enemy. He wants to destroy you. He does not love you. He comes with all kinds of lies, as he came to Eve, and tries to lure you away from the Lord. I hope this is not happening to you.

How will we know when it is the devil talking to us? We will only know it if we know the Bible. The Bible tells us what God's will is, and that is always what's best for us. When other thoughts come into our minds, and they are not from the Bible, we can know they are from the devil. He is trying to lead us astray. Then we must decide immediately not to do what is against the Lord's will. We must obey the Bible: we tell ourselves loud and clear not to be disobedient to God. In this way we resist the devil, and when we do that he has no power over us.

We can never resist the devil in our own strength. He is too strong for us. But if we resist him in the name of the Lord, we will win. Is there something in your life that you know is not the Lord's will? Decide now to do God's will and resist the devil, then he can do nothing to you.

Jesus would resist the
devil with the Word.

"I have given you authority ... to overcome all the power of the enemy." (Luke 10:18)

Be Honest

> He who conceals his sins does not prosper, but whoever confesses and renounces them finds mercy. (Proverbs 28:13)

Wanting to hide failure and sin is natural to all of humankind. If you spill something on your mom's new tablecloth, you quickly put a plate on the stain so that no one will notice it. If the teacher asks, "Who is using bad language?" you are quick to answer, "I didn't, Teacher." Actually, you are not telling the truth; you want to hide it.

When we sin, it always makes us feel a bit afraid and we want to hide, but this is not the way to handle it. The Bible says if we hide our sin, we cannot be forgiven: If we confess our sin, then God will forgive us (cf. 1 John 1:9). The secret is to be honest about our sins and to tell the Lord everything. I know it is very difficult, but truly, it's the best thing to do. The moment you know there is sin in your life, you must confess it to the Lord immediately. Tell him you are sorry; he will forgive you. You must also tell people you are sorry if you have treated them badly. We all appreciate a person who is honest about his or her sins and who asks for forgiveness.

Do not hide your sins. Apologize and let go, and God will give you his grace. Grace means the Lord will forgive you and put his loving arms around you.

Jesus would forgive you your sins.

... you forgave the guilt of my sin. (Psalm 32:5)

March 16

WHAT IS COOL?

I consider everything a loss compared to the surpassing greatness of knowing Christ. (Philippians 3:8)

A thing is "cool" when we like it a lot. Some things are obviously more cool than others. If you are really crazy about something, you tell all your friends about it. This is what Paul did.

Everybody knew how clever Paul was, and he liked certain things very much. But then something happened in his life. He was on the road one day when a bright light fell on him. It was the Lord Jesus who had a special plan for Paul. This changed his whole life. He got to know the Lord, and from that day on, everything he thought was cool before, was not cool any more.

Paul writes that the coolest thing on earth is to know the Lord, to love him, and to follow him.

I know there are many things in your life that you enjoy. The Lord wants you to enjoy yourself and to be excited about things that make you happy. Just make sure that the Lord is not pushed to one side in your life. I pray that you will think the Lord is so wonderful that the coolest thing on earth for you, as it was with Paul, will be to know and serve him.

Jesus would love God and people.

"There is no commandment greater than these [two]." (Mark 12:31)

March 17

THROW IT AWAY

Cast all your anxiety on him because he cares for you.
(1 Peter 5:7)

I'm sure you've seen someone who looks unhappy. If you should ask this person, "Why are you so unhappy?" the answer is often, "I have so many problems."

Problems are like a weight on our shoulders. They make us unhappy. And we worry.

If you are a Christian it is wonderful to know that the Lord knows about your problems. The Bible tells us to throw the weight of problems from our shoulders. Throw it away. "Cast all your anxiety ..." This means you should throw away this thing that is making your heart heavy. Throw it into the hands of Jesus. Let him handle it.

How do you do this? In the first place, you must realize that you are worried about something. Ask yourself, "Why am I so worried?" When you have found the answer, tell the Lord about it. Pass it into his hands. In this way you throw it away from you.

Do it now. Throw away your problems. Give them to Jesus. I am sure he will help.

Jesus would free you
from your problems.

"Therefore do not worry about tomorrow." (Matthew 6:34)

March 18

THE GIANT

A champion named Goliath was over nine feet tall.
(1 Samuel 17:4)

I am sure you know the story of the giant, Goliath. He was a Philistine warrior and an enormous man. The Philistines bet on him in the fight against Israel. Everybody was afraid of this big giant and no one had the heart to fight against him. This made him boastful. Every day he came out and asked, "Who will fight me?" Nobody wanted to because they were scared of him.

Only David was not scared. He was there because he had brought his brothers food so that they could be strong for the battle. He saw the giant challenging the Israelites. God then gave David courage. He was only a young boy, but he knew God was greater than Goliath, and he was not afraid. He said to Goliath, "You come against me with sword and spear and javelin, but I come against you in the name of the Lord Almighty."

God helped David. He was happy about David's faith. So he helped David to defeat the big giant, Goliath.

Even if you are still young, you can, like David, believe in God's great power and the Lord will be able to use you to win a victory.

Jesus will give you the
strength to be a winner.

It is God who arms me with strength. (Psalm 18:32)

March 19

The King's Sin

Then David said to Nathan, "I have sinned against the LORD." (2 Samuel 12:13)

David was the most important king Israel ever had. He was a good ruler and a brave soldier. What is more, David loved the Lord. Many of the psalms in the Bible are songs he sang to the Lord.

Then David made a big mistake. He saw another man's wife and thought she was very pretty. Her name was Bathsheba. In his heart David wished that she could be his wife. He sent for her and took her for himself. This was a sin in the eyes of the Lord, so the Lord sent a prophet to him to tell him that what he had done was wrong. David was sorry and confessed his sin to the Lord. He realized it was wrong to take something that did not belong to him. It was stealing. And it was wrong to use his position as king to get hold of Bathsheba.

There are things that we, just like David, would like to have. Have you ever taken something that did not belong to you because you wanted it so badly? That was wrong, wasn't it? I hope you told the Lord that you are sorry.

God forgave David, and he will also forgive you and me if we are sorry about our sins.

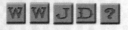

Jesus would forgive your sins.

... so far has he removed our [sins] from us. (Psalm 103:12)

March 20

RESPECT PEOPLE'S RIGHTS

> Therefore the law is paralyzed, and justice never prevails. The wicked hem in the righteous, so that justice is perverted. (Habakkuk 1:4)

In the book of Habakkuk we hear the writer pouring out his heart to the Lord. He wants to know why so much is wrong in the world. He looks around him and sees misery. He sees people fighting and arguing, and the laws of the country have no power any more. Human rights are violated because bad people have gained the upper hand over good ones.

We could almost believe that Habakkuk is living in our time. All over the world there is strife and fighting. The rights of many people are ignored. They are oppressed and hurt, and their property is stolen. They suffer because they work all day and get paid very little.

This situation grieves the Lord. We must treat everybody with respect because that is what the Lord wants us to do. If we really love others as the Lord tells us to, then we will not oppress them or hurt them. We will do right by them, just as the Lord would.

Make an effort today to treat all people with respect.

Jesus would respect all people.

Be devoted to one another in brotherly love. (Romans 12:10)

March 21

The Secret Is Out!

> The mystery that has been kept hidden for ages and generations, but is now disclosed. (Colossians 1:26)

When something is a secret, we know nothing about it. When somebody tells others a secret, then it is not a secret any more. Then the secret is out.

The wonderful message of Jesus was like a secret to some. No one in the Old Testament knew who Jesus was. Yes, the people of Israel did talk about the Messiah that would come, but they did not quite know who he was and what he would look like. But the secret came out!

Jesus was born in Bethlehem, and while he was growing up there, he started telling people about his kingdom. Then the big secret was out! Jesus wanted to tell everybody that he came to this earth as a Savior. He told the disciples to tell everybody this. They had to go to all the nations and tell them that only Jesus is the Way and the Truth and the Life.

The secret is out. We know that Jesus is the Savior. This message must be told to everyone. There are still many people all over the world that have never heard of Jesus. To them it is still a secret. What a shame! Let you and me tell everybody that Jesus is alive.

Jesus would preach
the message of heaven.

... that is, the mystery made known to me. (Ephesians 3:3)

A REAL PIG

Therefore, get rid of all moral filth. (James 1:21)

"You're as dirty as a pig!" This is what we say when someone is very, very dirty. A pig likes being dirty. A pig loves rolling around in the mud. It doesn't mind if the mud smells. A pig likes being dirty.

The Bible says sin is dirty. If you have not been washed clean of sin by Jesus, you are just as dirty as that pig rolling in the mud. The Bible invites us to have ourselves washed clean of sin. Only Jesus' sacrifice on the cross can wash you and me clean. I hope you have already asked the Lord to wash your dirty sins clean.

Because we are Christians it will bother us if we keep on sinning. We are not pigs anymore. No more mud for us; we are more like cats that cannot stand getting their feet dirty. You must have noticed how a cat hates stepping into water. It immediately starts licking itself clean. Even if a pig has been washed clean, it will take the first chance it gets to go and roll in the mud again. Christians should be like cats. If we have sinned, we must want to be washed clean as soon as possible. We tell the Lord we are sorry, and he forgives us.

Jesus will wash you
clean of all your sins.

"Though your sins are like scarlet, they shall be white as snow." (Isaiah 1:18)

March 23

THE SWEET BOOK

> So I ate it, and it tasted as sweet as honey in my mouth.
> (Ezekiel 3:3)

I'm sure you have tasted honey before. It is very sweet. You can spread it on bread, and some people even sweeten their tea or coffee with honey.

The Bible uses an image to tell us how good it is when you read the Word of God. Ezekiel saw the Lord coming to him with a scroll on which the words of God were written. The Lord told Ezekiel to eat this scroll, the Word of God. To his surprise, Ezekiel found that it was as sweet as honey. The message of this image is that the Word of God is always good for us. It is as healthy as honey.

If you and I love the Lord we want to listen to his words. And hearing his words – which come from the Bible – is just as good for us as eating honey. It gives us just as much energy and is just as tasty. Yes, the Word of God is good for us.

You must make sure that you "eat" the Word of God every day. It is good for you; even better than honey.

Jesus would read the
Bible regularly.

Your word is a light for my path. (Psalm 119:105)

JOSEPH BRINGS BLESSING

The LORD blessed the household of the Egyptian because of Joseph. (Genesis 39:5)

Joseph loved the Lord. And the Lord loved Joseph. The Lord had a plan for Joseph's life. That is why he allowed Joseph to be taken to a far away country and sold into slavery. But the Lord looked after Joseph and saw to it that he was taken into service in the house of an important officer named Potiphar.

Because the Lord had blessed Joseph, he also blessed the house of Potiphar. This just because Joseph brought the Lord with him to the house of Potiphar. It was good for Potiphar to have Joseph in his house because the Lord himself was with Joseph.

When you and I serve God, we are his blessed children. Then the Lord walks with us. Wherever we go, he goes with us. In this way you and I can also be a blessing for others wherever we are. Be a blessing today to your class, or in your church, or among your friends, or on the sports field.

Jesus would bless everybody.

Repay [evil] with blessing, because to this you were called. (1 Peter 3:9)

JESUS FORGIVES

And [Peter] went outside and wept bitterly. (Luke 22:62)

When Jesus was captured, his disciples were frightened and ran away. Peter ran too, because he was afraid of what could happen to him. Yet he followed Jesus at a distance and saw the soldiers taking Jesus away. Then Jesus got to the building where they were going to put him on trial. Peter stood in the courtyard while they were busy with Jesus. Three people said they had seen Peter with Jesus. But Peter denied it. He said they were making a mistake because he was scared of what they would do to him if they recognized him as Jesus' follower. And so Peter disowned Jesus. He was being false, and he denied that he had anything to do with Jesus. This means that Peter let Jesus down.

Jesus knew beforehand that Peter would disown him. He said a rooster would crow to remind Peter that he had let Jesus down. It happened just like that. When the rooster crowed, Peter went outside and started crying bitterly. He was so sorry that he had turned his back on Jesus.

Because Jesus loved Peter very much, he forgave Peter later after he had risen from the dead. He appointed Peter to look after the disciples. The Lord forgives easily because he knows you and I are weak. Still, he wants to use us in spite of our weaknesses.

Jesus would forgive people.

 [God] remembers your sins no more. (Isaiah 43:25)

WHY WORRY?

"Therefore do not worry about tomorrow." (Matthew 6:34)

Worried people do not laugh easily. When we are worried about tomorrow, we don't look forward to it, and we are a bit sad when the new day breaks.

In Proverbs 31:25, we read that a good woman who knows the Lord and loves him *"can laugh at the days to come."* Yes, if you belong to the Lord, you can learn to leave your worries in his hands and you can afford to laugh at tomorrow. This means being cheerful about what waits for us tomorrow. God is in control of my life, why should I fear tomorrow? I would rather laugh at tomorrow with joy in my heart because my Lord is in control.

A cheerful, laughing person can better handle all the problems of today and tomorrow. Give your worries to the Lord right now and be thankful that he is in control of your life. Then you will laugh at tomorrow. This is a good laugh, because you know the Lord will be with you.

Jesus would free you from worry.

Cast all your anxiety on him because he cares for you. (1 Peter 5:7)

WONDERFUL THINGS!

Lord, how majestic is your name in all the earth! (Psalm 8:9)

Even if many things are wrong on earth, even if there are bad things like pollution and endangered species, the earth is still a wonderful place. The Lord made heaven and earth. He made everything very good and beautiful. Just think of all the wonderful things. There are so many different kinds of animals in the wilderness, and there are so many kinds of plants in gardens all over the world. Just think of the variety of fish in the sea. If you studied birds, you would be amazed at the different kinds all over the world.

Yes, the Lord made the earth wonderful. The Bible also says you and I are crowned with glory and honor (cf. Psalm 8:6). Of everything the Lord made, we are the best. Just think of all the millions of people ... and every one is different. The Lord also gave us minds so that we can rule over the whole world.

Praise and glorify the Lord today for his wonderful creation. Praise him also for yourself. Let's tell everybody that the Lord's works are wonderful!

Jesus would care for creation.

"Look at the birds ... your heavenly Father feeds them." (Matthew 6:26)

March 28

Ask, Seek, and Find

"Ask, and it will be given to you; seek and you will find; knock and the door will be opened to you." (Luke 11:9)

We all want answers to our questions – we want to find what we are looking for and see doors open for us when we knock. Unfortunately, we often ask the wrong person or persons. We look in the wrong places. We knock at the wrong doors. That is why we do not really find what we are longing for deep in our hearts.

Jesus knows the plight of us humans, and that is why he invites us all to ask him. He would like to give us what we need. When we talk to him, we realize that we have a need in our hearts, not for earthly things, but for things that only he can give. Things like his redemption and his peace. Let's ask him, because he gives freely to those who ask.

He invites us to come to him for what we need. If we are looking for things with real meaning, Jesus will give them to us. Many people are looking for peace and quiet, but they do not find it because they are looking in the wrong places.

Jesus invites everyone to knock at his door. He will open for everyone, and he invites us to join him in a feast. Jesus opens the right doors for us so that we can live meaningful lives. By all means, knock at his door, and he will welcome you.

Jesus would give when you ask.

Then the Father will give you whatever you ask in my name. (John 15:16)

March 29

A Heavy or a Light Weight?

Let us throw off everything that hinders. (Hebrews 12:1)

There are many heavy loads that we can carry along with us. It can be anything, like a heavy suitcase with clothes, a friend that we give a ride on our back, or a bag of groceries that we carry in from the car. Whenever we carry a load, we need strength, and then we burn more energy.

A load can also be a weight that we carry in our spirit. This can be things like worries, or hurt deep inside. Sin is also a load that we carry around in our hearts.

The Lord wants us to travel light. This means that he wants us to feel free and not suffer unnecessary hardships. That is why Jesus came to free us from the heavy weight of sin in our hearts. Many people have so many other things that they have to attend to – like money or cars, or clothes or business problems – they are not free either.

Throw away the unnecessary baggage or load in your heart. Do it now. Give it to Jesus and see how free you feel.

Jesus would carry your load.

For he bore the sin of many. (Isaiah 53:12)

March 30

A Gentle Answer

A gentle answer turns away wrath. (Proverbs 15:1)

I'm sure at some time in your life someone has shouted at you or talked so loudly to you that it sounded as if that person was angry with you. Perhaps it was your brother that shouted at you because he was angry with you. The first thing we want to do is shout back. But it is not the best thing to do.

The Bible says it is much better to give a gentle answer. When someone lashes out at you and you are also furious, it can only mean war! It is much better to react to angry words in a soft and gentle manner. This makes the other person cool off.

Let us give a gentle answer when someone has been unkind to us. Let's try it out together. A gentle answer helps so that the devil doesn't win.

Jesus would always
give a gentle answer.

Do not be overcome by evil, but overcome evil with good.
(Romans 12:21)

WE ALL MAKE MISTAKES

If we claim to be without sin, we deceive ourselves and the truth is not in us. (1 John 1:8)

Some people pretend to have no faults. They always make excuses, even when they do make a mistake. The Bible says someone like this is misleading or cheating himself. Of course we all have faults! We all sometimes do something wrong.

If we realize that all of us make mistakes, we will be able to forgive more easily. Perhaps we won't be so impatient when someone makes a mistake with us. Because we also make mistakes!

But what should we do when someone has made a mistake? We must start praying for this person right away and forgive him in our hearts. We must say, "I forgive you." And if we have made a mistake, we must say as quickly as possible, "I am sorry! Please forgive me."

Jesus would forgive
you immediately.

... forgiving each other, just as in Christ God forgave you. (Ephesians 4:32)

April 1

Eyes on Him

As the eyes of slaves look to the hand of their master,
as the eyes of a maid look to the hand of her mistress,
so our eyes look to the LORD our God. (Psalm 123:2)

In the time of the Bible there were many slaves. These were boys and girls bought by rich people. Slaves were always ready to serve their masters. Anytime the master called them they had to be ready. They had to find out what the master wanted and carry out his orders. In exchange for their service, the master took care of them.

The slave girl or boy was close by when the master sat at the table having a meal. Throughout the meal the slave kept watch on the owner. If the owner wanted more salt, he lifted his hand and the slave would come immediately to serve him.

Psalm 123 says that in the same way, our eyes must be on the hand of the Lord. We must always be ready to serve him and please him. What he asks us to do, we must do. We must keep our eyes open and not leave his side. We must be available and notice it immediately when he indicates with his hand that we are needed. In this way we are of service to him and we please him.

Keep your eyes on the Lord today.

Jesus would do what the
Father tells him to.

"I have come ... not to do my will but to do the will of him who sent me." (John 6:38)

April 2

THE VIOLENT WIND

Suddenly a sound like the blowing of a violent wind came from heaven. All of them were filled with the Holy Spirit. (Acts 2:2, 4)

When the wind blows, you hear its sound through the trees, but you cannot see the wind itself. You hear its sound, and knowledgeable people can tell from which direction it is blowing, but the wind itself has no body or shape.

When the Holy Spirit came to fill the hearts of people on earth, he came in the form of a violent wind. While the disciples were together, waiting for the Holy Spirit to come, they heard something which sounded like a violent wind blowing. I'm sure you've heard the wind pulling and tugging at your house before. Earthly winds are very strong and can lift the roofs from buildings. Hurricanes have blown whole houses away in coastal areas.

The image of the wind tells you and me that the Holy Spirit is also very powerful. Just as the wind can blow into a room and blow things over, the Holy Spirit can come into you and me and change our lives. Don't be afraid of the Holy Spirit. He will never hurt us. Ask him to blow into your life and to fill your heart with his power.

Jesus will fill you
with the Holy Spirit.

 "But you will receive power when the Holy Spirit comes on you." (Acts 1:8)

April 3

THE HELPER

The Spirit helps us in our weakness. (Romans 8:26)

Another name for the Holy Spirit is the "helper." This name means that he has come to help us. Jesus sent him to earth for that purpose. He saw that we needed help urgently. The Holy Spirit likes helping us.

Sometimes we are really in need of help when we feel weak or are in some kind of trouble. This is when the Holy Spirit helps. He pleads for us with the Father the moment that he notices we are in trouble, and inside our spirit he gives us hope and strength. The Holy Spirit is a wonderful Person. He is our helper. No matter what difficult situation we get into, he is also in that situation, because he lives in us. If someone tries to hurt us, he feels it too. He shares everything with us, and he is the one who gives us strength when we are weak.

Thank the Holy Spirit, now, that he is also your helper – today and for the rest of your life.

Jesus will help you
through the Holy Spirit.

"The Holy Spirit, whom the Father will send ... will teach you all things." (John 14:26)

April 4

THE ADVOCATE

The Spirit himself intercedes for us with groans that
words cannot express. (Romans 8:26)

An advocate's job is to defend people's cases in court. If
you have to go to court there is usually a charge against you.
Then you must say if you have done something wrong or
not. An advocate helps prove that you are not guilty, or if
you are, helps that you perhaps get a lighter sentence.
Advocates are important to people who have been charged
with some or other offense. Advocates are attorneys or public defenders.

A charge is brought against each and every one of us. The
one who brings the charges against us is called the devil. In
Revelation 12:10 he is called "the accuser of our brothers."
These are the people who believe in God. He enjoys accusing us. He loves telling the Lord that you and I are not good
enough because we have sinned again! He is always busy
accusing us.

Fortunately the Holy Spirit is our Advocate. He speaks
for us and defends our case. He pleads for us with the
Father. He helps us in difficult times. The Holy Spirit is our
heavenly Advocate.

Jesus would speak to the
Father in our defense.

Even now my witness is in heaven; my advocate is on high.
(Job 16:19)

April 5

My Bosom Friend

Jonathan became one in spirit with David, and he loved him as himself. (1 Samuel 18:1)

I'm sure you have a friend you like very much. You like visiting your friend and being with him or her. One can say you are bosom friends. Your bosom is your chest – the area around your heart. Bosom friends can hold one another close to their hearts. It's like giving your mom or dad a hug. Bosom friends show that they love one another.

As a young man, David met Jonathan. Jonathan was king Saul's son. Soon David and Jonathan saw that they liked each other very much, and they became so close that they were bosom friends. They could tell each other their deepest secrets. When one was in trouble, the other stood by him.

I hope you have a very special friend. And even more so, I hope you are also a very special friend to someone. To have a bosom friend, you must also be a good friend. You must accept your friend just the way he or she is, be loving, and prove to that person that you can be trusted. Ask the Lord to help you be a good friend to someone.

Jesus would be your friend.

A friend loves at all times. (Proverbs 17:17)

ALL ALONE

"My God, my God, why have you forsaken me?" (Matthew 27:46)

No one has ever been as alone as Jesus. Sometimes you and I are also alone, and perhaps you are lonely. One does not always feel lonely when one is alone. Lonely is when you feel forsaken and very alone in your heart. This is how Jesus felt when he was hanging on the cross.

Jesus had to go through the worst of the worst, for our sakes. That is why there was a moment on the cross that the Father had to, in a sense, turn his back on his Son. At that moment Jesus knew that he was completely alone. There was not even an angel to make him feel better. The Father did not give him hope or strength. It felt to him as if he was the loneliest person on earth. He was also in pain, and he was suffering. The nails hurt his hands, and the wounds the soldiers gave him were bleeding and painful.

When Jesus asked why the Father had forsaken him, he felt lonely and deserted. He suffered this because of you and me. If we believe in him, we need never be lonely any more. Not even on the day that we die. He promised that he will always be with us.

Jesus will always be with you.

"Never will I leave you; never will I forsake you." (Hebrews 13:5)

April 7

MOCKED

The men who were guarding Jesus began mocking and beating him. (Luke 22:63)

While Jesus was on earth, people did not only praise him for the miracles he performed, they also mocked him. When he was captured, there were people who turned against him. Also, the soldiers that guarded him hit him and mocked him and said ugly things to him. Even when Jesus was nailed to the cross and suffering a lot of pain, they did not stop tormenting and mocking him. It was so bad that Jesus said, "Father, forgive them, for they do not know what they are doing."

Because the devil does not like Jesus at all, he will do everything he can to destroy the work and message of Jesus. One of his methods is to get people to make fun of Jesus and his kingdom, and also of Christians. Christians, as you know, are the followers of Jesus. The devil does not like us to follow Jesus. That is why he keeps on causing people to make fun of us – because we are Christians and follow Jesus.

Perhaps there is someone who teases you because you pray, or because you read your Bible. Don't let it get to you. Carry on. Even if people make fun of you, you know that they will stand before God's throne one day. In the meantime you must pray for those people and love them. Jesus loved people even if they made fun of him.

Jesus would bear the
scorn of people.

The arrogant mock me. (Psalm 119:51)

April 8

Good Friday

> Carrying his own cross...to the place of the skull....Here they crucified him. (John 19:17, 18)

Good Friday is one of the most important days in any Christian's life. It is even more important than Christmas. This is the day we remember Jesus' death on the cross at the place of the skull. Another name for it is Golgotha.

Jesus was completely innocent, yet the crowds captured him, beat him, and led him to this place for murderers, outside Jerusalem. This is where criminals were executed in a very cruel manner. Jesus was not a criminal; he was innocent when he was nailed to a cross. A crown made of thorns was pushed hard into his head, and he was bleeding. He had no strength left. He suffered terribly before he died. Why?

The heavenly Father knew that Someone had to die for our sins (yours and mine): Someone who was perfect, without sin. That is why Jesus died on the cross. He gave his life so that you and I wouldn't have to die because of our sins.

Tell the Lord Jesus how thankful you are that he was prepared to die on a cross for you. Also, decide now to give him your life as he gave his to you. Praise him, serve him, tell others that you have a wonderful Savior. Without him we would all have died in sin.

Jesus would lay down his life for you.

Greater love has no one than this, that he lay down his life for his friends. (John 15:13)

Soap and Blood

The blood of Jesus, his Son, purifies us from all sin.
(1 John 1:7)

One day a man explained why he did not believe in Jesus. He said Jesus died on the cross for us two thousand years ago and yet the world had not changed much. So many people around him were dirty with sin. Many crimes were still committed. Many people still did nasty things to others. If Jesus had really come to forgive people and to take the sins away, why was there so much sin still in the world?

Another man answered him. He said there must be millions of cakes of soap on shelves in shops all over the world. In spite of this there were still billions of dirty people. Why were they not all clean? Because they did not take the soap and wash themselves. Soap washes away dirt only if you use it.

It works exactly the same way with the blood of Jesus. Jesus' blood was shed for our sins. Yet there are many people who do not believe this and don't accept it. They reject his death on the cross, his blood, because they do not believe. That is why they are dirty.

Everyone who accepts, in faith, the death of Jesus on the cross is washed clean of sin.

Jesus will wash you clean.

"Though your sins are like scarlet, they shall be white as snow." (Isaiah 1:18)

ALREADY ROLLED AWAY

They were on their way to the tomb and they asked each other, "Who will roll the stone away from the entrance of the tomb?" (Mark 16:2, 3)

After the death of Jesus the women who knew him and followed him went to his grave because they wanted to embalm him. While they were on their way there, they wondered how they would roll the big stone away from the entrance to the grave. In those days people were buried in graves that looked like small rooms. Each "room" had a door, and a stone was placed in front of the door. The women were not strong enough to roll away the heavy stone. How would they get to the body of Jesus?

You can imagine how surprised they were when they got to the grave and saw that someone had already rolled the stone away. An angel did this, because by then Jesus had already risen from the dead.

You and I are often just like these women. We worry about how something can be done. The task ahead looks impossible. But when we get to the stage where we have to do something about it, we find that Jesus has already seen to it. Ask the Lord, in time, to help you. You needn't worry about what you must do later. He will see to it that you will be able to do the work.

Jesus would not
worry about tomorrow.

Do not be anxious about anything, but in everything, present your requests to God. (Philippians 4:6)

April 11

GOD IN YOUR HOUSE

He has remembered his faithfulness to the house of
Israel. (Psalm 98:3)

Homes are wonderful places. People live in homes. Inside
a house there are pictures, furniture, eating utensils, beds
to sleep on, and lots of other things. Some houses have
many of these things, others few.

More important in a house than things, are people. A
house can have beautiful furniture, but without people
there is no life. I trust your house has a nice atmosphere so
that you and your family can enjoy living in it together.

There are many houses with a bad atmosphere. There are
arguments and unhappiness, but no peace. There is no love.
A home like this needs the Lord.

The Lord wants to reconfirm his love and faithfulness to
every house in Israel (cf. Psalm 98). And to your house as
well. If you love the Lord, pray that his love and faithfulness
will reign in your house. Pray for your mom and dad and for
all the family members. Pray that the Holy Spirit will be in
your house. Pray for love that comes from God. Just keep on
praying, even if it doesn't seem to be working. Keep on
praying that the Lord will be king in your house.

Jesus would pray for
everyone in your house.

And this is my prayer: that your love may abound more and
more in knowledge and depth of insight. (Philippians 1:9)

April 12

LIGHT IN THE DARKNESS

"You are the light of the world." (Matthew 5:14)

Most towns and cities have streetlights that shine brightly so that people who travel at night can see where they are going. Maybe you also have a light at your front door or in the garden. Then you can see where to go.

The Bible says it is as if the world is dark with all the sin in people's lives. Even if the sun is shining, it is still spiritually dark in the hearts of many people and in their homes. They are just like people stumbling around in the dark. Their lives are without any purpose, empty and without direction. They are actually looking for light. Jesus said he is the light of the world. When one believes in him, it is like receiving the light, so that one can live a meaningful life.

But Jesus also said that you and I, his children, must be like a shining light. If he, who is light, lives in our hearts, then his light is inside us, and we shine brightly in a dark world. We must not hide this light of Jesus shining in us. We must be like lampposts that give light in the darkness around us. I hope you are like a lamppost with a light on top that shines in your street, or in your neighborhood, or in your town. Let's ask the Lord that his light will burn in us today, brightly and clearly.

Jesus would shine
like a bright light.

The light shines in the darkness, but the darkness has not understood it. (John 1:5)

April 13

SITTING OR MOVING?

He spoke with great fervor and taught about Jesus accurately. (Acts 18:25)

Some Christians seem to be sitting comfortably and relaxed in the armchair of their faith. They don't really seem excited about Jesus. They don't seem enthusiastic about the things of the Lord. Enthusiasm means that you are excited and glad about something and want to share it with others. The word comes from two Greek words that mean "God is in you." If the Lord really lives in us, we are enthusiastic. About what? About Jesus, of course, and about his kingdom.

I hope you are not someone who does nothing. I hope you want to move about and excitedly talk about Jesus and his kingdom. A Christian like this is on fire in his or her spirit. Someone even called it "boiling for the King."

Let's ask the Holy Spirit to fill us with enthusiasm for the kingdom of the Lord.

Jesus will fill you with the Spirit so that you can witness with enthusiasm.

Never be lacking in zeal, but keep your spiritual fervor, serving the Lord. (Romans 12:11)

April 14

TAKE OFF THE HANDCUFFS

... to proclaim freedom for the captives. (Isaiah 61:1)

Isaiah prophesied many years ago that Jesus would come to do important work. The Spirit of God would equip him for the task and anoint him. He would become the Savior of the world. He would proclaim freedom for everyone in captivity. This is an image the Bible uses to say that anyone who does not have the Lord in his life is like a prisoner. Humanity's prison is sin. Jesus came to free you from this prison.

A prison is a place where people are locked up and guarded by wardens. People cannot do what they want in prison. One day they can be set free. Then the prison gate is unlocked, and they can walk out because they are free again.

Jesus the Savior came so that we could be freed from prison.

When Jesus unlocks the door for us, the devil cannot keep us inside his prison any longer. Then we are really free.

When you accept Jesus as your Savior and Redeemer, the doors of your prison open for you. I hope you have already been freed.

Jesus will be your Redeemer.

... and free those who all their lives were held in slavery. (Hebrews 2:15)

April 15

Two are Better

Two are better than one. If one falls down, his friend can help him up. (Ecclesiastes 4:9, 10)

People were not made to be alone. People need people. There are billions of people on earth, and without one another there is not much purpose in our lives.

It's nice to know that when you are in trouble there is someone who will understand and who will not let you down. The Bible says in Ecclesiastes that two are better than one. If you struggle to pick up something heavy, it becomes lighter when you have someone to help you. Two people find it easier to carry something. There are many things you cannot do alone. If you don't understand your schoolwork, it helps if one of your friends can explain it to you. On the sports field you can encourage one another. If you take part in a team sport like football or basketball, it is important for teammates to support and help one another.

Do not isolate yourself from others. Make friends with everyone who crosses your path. Then you will have friends that can support you. You can also mean a lot to them. It makes our lives meaningful. Thank the Lord now for your friends and try to be a good friend to someone.

Jesus would be your Friend.

"You are my friends if you do what I command." (John 15:14)

Think the
Right Thoughts

Set your minds on things above. (Colossians 3:2)

Someone said that you are what you think. When you think nice thoughts, you become a nice person. You are beautiful, not only if you are good-looking on the outside, but if you are beautiful inside. On the other hand, if you think dirty and ugly thoughts, you become ugly in your actions also. Your thoughts are very important.

Every day thousands of thoughts come into our heads, even without our knowing about it. We must ask the Lord to help us think the right thoughts. Often bad thoughts just come up by themselves; we didn't want to think them. When the Holy Spirit lives in us he can help us. The Bible says we must think of things above. This means we must think about good and clean and noble things. This is what God thinks about. We must learn to have some of his thoughts.

If you catch yourself thinking something ugly, try to get a better thought immediately. Ask the Lord to help you. I'm sure he will. May you have beautiful thoughts today.

Jesus would think
the right thoughts.

 We take captive every thought to make it obedient to Christ. (2 Corinthians 10:5)

April 17

Pets

... which you formed to frolic there. (Psalm 104:26)

How God must have enjoyed making all the different animals on earth. When I see how cute and interesting some of the animals are that he made, I cannot help thinking that the Lord is wonderful. Perhaps the Lord also played with the animals. In Psalm 104 we read that the Lord created an animal called a Leviathan to frolic in the sea.

Do you have a pet? There are different kinds of pets like cats, dogs, parakeets, even mice and rats! People keep pets so that they can have a special animal to love and care for. In this way we learn that the animal kingdom is very important, and can also mean a lot to us humans.

When we have a pet we must thank the Lord for it. We must take care of it with the love Jesus taught us. The love that Jesus puts in our hearts for humans and animals will be seen in the way we treat our pets. Glorify God through your care for your pet.

Jesus would love animals.

"Look at the birds of the air ... your heavenly Father feeds them." (Matthew 6:26)

THE BEAUTIFUL GRAVE

"You are like whitewashed tombs, which look beautiful on the outside but on the inside are full of dead men's bones. (Matthew 23:27)

I don't know if you have ever been in a graveyard. Actually a graveyard is a nice place. There are usually beautiful flowers on the graves and also in gardens around the graves. Many graves are beautifully decorated in expensive marble. On the marble slabs all kinds of nice things are written along with the name of the person buried there. It is a good thing that our graveyards are made attractive, because then we think nice thoughts about our loved ones that have died. But we also know that a person's body decays in that grave under the ground. Later on only bones are left.

Jesus warned that our lives must not look like graves. Outside someone can look beautiful while he or she is stone dead inside. By this the Bible means that we must live for Christ and that our hearts must be alive in this relationship with him.

When you invite Jesus into your life, he lives inside you and then you are not like a grave. Live for Jesus!

In Jesus everyone would
have eternal life.

Count yourselves dead to sin but alive to God. (Romans 6:11)

April 19

WHO HURTS YOU?

The men came after me and surrounded the house, intending to kill me. (Judges 20:5)

One of the saddest things is when someone keeps on hurting you. Many children in the world are hurt by people who are very close to them. I'm not talking about an ordinary correction or discipline. No, I'm talking about someone who is hurting you very, very much, someone who does things that no one knows about.

There are children who are ill-treated and are beaten every day. Others have an uncle, or cousin, or brother, or even a father who touches them in a way that is not right and who does bad things with them. We call this child abuse. It is a very bad thing to do, and children who experience this are unhappy.

Perhaps someone is hurting you in this way, or maybe you know of a friend who is being molested. What can you do? Apart from telling the Lord about your hurt, you must also get help. Speak to your youth leader or teacher and they will give you a phone number you can phone where someone who understands will talk to you and help you.

Jesus would protect you from harm.

Put on the full armor of God. (Ephesians 6:11)

April 20

A Miracle in a Crisis

And he touched the man's ear and healed him. (Luke 22:51)

Jesus went to the Garden of Gethsemane to pray for strength on the night before he was crucified. He needed strength for the terrible time that lay ahead of him. His Father had sent him to die on the cross. That is why he prayed and asked God to help him. His disciples also had to pray, but they were so tired that they fell asleep. Jesus felt so alone. Fortunately, an angel came from heaven to be with him.

While Jesus was in Gethsemane with his disciples a lot of people arrived there to capture him. Judas, his disciple, had betrayed him. Another disciple, Peter, pulled out his sword to defend Jesus and cut off a man's ear.

Although Jesus was in a crisis situation, he stretched out his hand and, with love in his heart, touched the man's ear. There, in front of all the soldiers, a miracle was performed: the man's ear was healed. Isn't it wonderful that Jesus, in this moment of great crisis, still showed love and thought of others instead of just his own problems.

Jesus is never too busy with his own life, or with his kingdom, to touch you with his love. Allow him to show you his love today.

Jesus would help you in a crisis.

We know and rely on the love God has for us. (1 John 4:16)

April 21

THE BACK DOOR

[Sarai] said to Abram, "Go, sleep with my maid-servant; perhaps I can build a family through her." Abram agreed to what Sarai said. (Genesis 16:2)

One night the Lord made Abram look at the stars in the sky and told him to try and count them. The Lord then promised Abram that he would have just as many children as the stars in the sky. What God meant was that everybody who had a good relationship with him would be Abram's descendant. In a way, even you and I are children of Abram.

Abram and Sarai, his wife, were already old, and still they had no children. So Sarai made this plan. She told her husband to sleep with her maidservant, Hagar, and if she had a baby, then at least they would have a child. Sarai didn't think that she herself would ever have a child. After all those years they didn't believe God's promise anymore. They were making a big mistake!

When Abram and Sarai thought God's promise was not coming true, they kept a back door open (made their own plans). Our plans always make trouble if they are not God's will. Later on Abram and Sarai cried many tears about this plan of theirs.

We must learn from each other that making our own plans, without first talking to God, does not work.

Jesus would always
do the will of God.

"Father ... not my will, but yours be done." (Luke 22:42)

JOSEPH CHOOSES GOD

"How then could I do such a wicked thing and sin against God?" (Genesis 39:9)

When Joseph was in a difficult situation in Potiphar's house, he had to make a choice. Potiphar's wife wanted Joseph to sleep with her, but he knew if he did this, he would be sinning against God. So he had to make a choice. He did not choose Potiphar's wife, but God. That was the right choice.

You and I are often in situations where we must choose. You can choose to swear or not. You can choose to steal or not. You can choose if you want to gossip or not. Every day you and I can choose right or wrong, good or bad. We must ask the Lord to help us make the right choices. We cannot make the right choice if we do not know what God's will is. That is why it is important to read his Word. We must also listen to his voice in our hearts. The Holy Spirit will help us make the right choices.

Tell God today that you want to choose him. Ask his help to always make the right choices.

Jesus would choose to do
the will of his Father.

"Your will be done on earth ..." (Matthew 6:10)

THE ANGEL
NEXT TO YOU

For he will command his angels to guard you in all your ways. (Psalm 91:11)

Is there an angel next to you? You don't see him? Yes, of course you can't see him. But the Bible says that he is there.

God sends his angels to guard his children. I find this very exciting because I need God to be with me. Because Jesus is in heaven, he sent his Holy Spirit to be with me (cf. John 14:16). But God also uses angels to be with people. Angels are heavenly beings, created to praise and glorify the Lord and to carry out his instructions.

Because we can't see angels, we do not always realize how they help us. Some people think angels are babies with wings. This is not true! Angels are like strong winds or flames. Angels are big and strong and powerful. They can be with us in seconds, as they were with Daniel when they helped him in the lions' den.

You can be sure there is an angel guarding you today who will be with you on the road. Thank God for his angels.

Jesus will send his
angels to help you.

Are not all angels ministering spirits sent to serve! (Hebrews 1:14)

April 24

JESUS IS LIFE

"For the bread of God is he who comes down from heaven and gives life to the world." (John 6:33)

Many people have only bread to eat. But it keeps them alive. You probably like a sandwich with nice jam or cheese on it. You and I cannot survive without food.

The Bible says we cannot live on bread alone, however. We also need what comes from the hand of God, the life that he gives us. God sent us his Son. He is the bread from heaven. He came so that we could have life. The Bible tells us to eat this bread. This doesn't mean that we must eat Jesus! That is not possible. It means we must accept him as the one who came to give us real life. If we accept Jesus and believe in him, and if we follow and serve him, he is our bread that gives life.

You can eat delicious food and still be hungry in your heart. Only God can satisfy that hunger. Make sure that Jesus lives in you, and he will satisfy your hunger. He is the bread who gives life.

Jesus would satisfy your
hunger with the bread of life.

 "I am the bread of life ... [you] will never go hungry." (John 6:35)

Don't Keep a Record

Love keeps no record of wrongs. (1 Corinthians 13:5)

When we want to remember something, we often write it in a book, type it into a computer, or make a note of it on our calendars. If you want to remember how much money you have spent, you keep a record.

When we love someone, we should not write down all this person's faults and sins. We don't keep a record of faults. Love wants to forget wrongs as quickly as possible.

Love does not make a list of someone's sins to take out at a later stage and use against that person. Love forgives and forgets.

Maybe there is someone who wronged you. I hope you have forgotten about it. It is better to forgive and forget than to keep a record of everything others have done against you.

The best news is that Jesus does not keep a record of our sins. When we accepted him, he washed us clean from sin. He forgets about our sins and he doesn't want to think about them any more.

Jesus frees us. He forgives. He forgets. Let's forgive others just as Jesus forgave us.

Jesus wiped our sins
clean with his blood.

You will tread our sins underfoot. (Micah 7:19)

April 26

Under His Feet

> "Sit at my right hand until I put your enemies under your feet." (Mark 12:36)

The enemy of God's kingdom is evil. The devil fights against the Lord. The devil is the prince of darkness, and the Lord is the Prince of light. Jesus overcame the devil when he died on the cross and was raised from the dead. In this way he upset the work of the devil. Now people can believe in Jesus and break loose from the devil.

Unfortunately, the devil has not been defeated completely. He has not been finally destroyed. He still hurts many people. He still leads many people astray to follow him. Even though Jesus defeated him on the cross, he has not been finally bound.

A day will come when the Lord will have the devil under his control completely and will destroy him once and for all. He will have no more influence on the people on earth. The final judgment will take place. Each person will receive according to his or her works. Whoever did good things and followed Jesus will be rewarded. The others will go with the devil. Jesus will reign and rule forever and ever. The devil will be under his feet and have no more influence.

Until Jesus finally rules over the devil, we must just faithfully follow in Jesus' footsteps. He keeps us from evil.

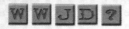

Jesus would keep us from evil.

 Take up the shield of faith, with which you can extinguish all the flaming arrows of the evil one. (Ephesians 6:16)

April 27

BEING FAITHFUL

But the fruit of the Spirit is ... faithfulness. (Galatians 5:22)

Faithfulness means that we can rely on something or someone. Faithfulness is very important in life. When you sit on a chair, you trust that it will not collapse under you. If the doctor gives you medicine when you are ill, you trust that it is the right medicine and not poison that will kill you. Without faith, life will not be easy on this earth. If you cannot trust someone, you will always be suspicious that he or she might do something you won't like.

Often people tell us they will do something and we trust that they will. But unfortunately they don't do it. Then they have not been worthy of our trust. This is not a nice thing to happen. The Holy Spirit wants to help us to be trustworthy in everything we do. He wants to help us keep promises we have made. Even when no one sees, we must still be faithful because the Holy Spirit encourages us to do the right thing.

Ask the Holy Spirit to fill you today and to make you faithful in everything you do.

Jesus would be faithful
to the truth.

You are a man of integrity in accordance with the truth. (Matthew 22:16)

April 28

IT HURTS TO BE SHARPENED

One man sharpens another. (Proverbs 27:17)

Have you ever seen someone sharpen a knife? Most people hold it against a grindstone. A grindstone is a hard stone used to sharpen knives (or other tools). I'm sure if a knife or a grindstone could talk, both would say, "Ouch!" It must be painful to be rubbed so hard. Luckily, a knife and a grindstone can't feel a thing.

Humans feel. We get hurt easily. Just like a knife rubs against a grindstone, people also sometimes rub against one another. I'm sure you've seen the smooth round stones one gets in a river. Those stones were not that shape to start off with. As the water rolled the stone around, it became rounder and rounder. It is the pushing and bumping of one stone against another that makes a stone take on a certain shape.

The Bible says you and I sharpen or polish one another in the same way. We shape one another. We don't always like it when people differ from us. When we humans clash, we shape one another. Another person's ideas can shape your ideas. What others say and think of you can sometimes hurt, but once the truth is out, we can just give it a better shape.

Don't be afraid to be shaped by friends or other people. Above all, allow the Lord to shape you the way he wants to.

Jesus would change your life.

"... unless you change and become like little children." (Matthew 18:3)

April 29

YOU ARE A TOE OR A PINKIE

Now you are the body of Christ, and each one of you is a part of it. (1 Corinthians 12:27)

When you belong to Jesus, you are part of his wonderful body. Not his body of flesh and blood, but the Christian body that has many members.

You and I have wonderful bodies. We have many body parts: a nose, eyes, ears, legs, arms, toes, and many, many more. Every body part has a function. With your hands you can take something. You use the muscles in your body when you walk or run. You see with your eyes, and you hear with your ears. Each body part has its own function, yet all the body parts need one another. The eye cannot say it doesn't need the ear, and the pinkie toe cannot say it doesn't need the kneecap. Together all the body parts form a lovely whole.

Every Christian has a place in the large body of Jesus. We need one another. Each of us also has a task. God has a plan for each and every one of us so that his whole body can work together wonderfully well. Never think you are not valuable. The Lord wants to use you; he needs you. Thank the Lord right now that you can be part of his body, and ask him to use you just as he pleases.

Jesus would use you,
no matter what you are like.

Now to each one the manifestation of the Spirit is given. (1 Corinthians 12:7)

April 30

Smoke in Your Eyes

As smoke to the eyes, so is a sluggard to those who send him. (Proverbs 10:26)

Have you ever sat at a fire somewhere in the open? It creates a cozy atmosphere. But if you sit on the wrong side of the fire, the smoke gets in your eyes. It burns your eyes. Soon your eyes water and you can't see much. It is very unpleasant when smoke gets in your eyes.

This is the image the Bible uses to tell us how it feels to work with a lazy person. Lazy is the opposite of diligent. A diligent person is hard working and zealous. A diligent child is not afraid of work. A diligent child enjoys helping others. When you give a diligent child something to do, he does it with a smile because it is no trouble to him. Lazy children and lazy grown-ups are irritating. They are like smoke in the eyes.

I hope you are diligent and that you enjoy doing something for someone.

Jesus would work diligently.

Always be zealous. (Proverbs 23:17)

CARRYING A CROSS?

"And anyone who does not carry his cross and follow me cannot be my disciple." (Luke 14:27)

There are people who think that to carry a cross means to have a hard time and to suffer. Jesus carried his cross. He had a very rough time and suffered a great deal because he loves us very much.

When Jesus tells us, his disciples, to take up our cross, it does not mean we must carry a cross in the way that he did. It simply means that we must be prepared to follow him. To follow Jesus is to do what he asks us and to obey what he says. If people tease us or humiliate us because we follow him, it is hard on us, but we do not suffer half as much as Jesus did.

In Jesus' time the cross was a sign of disgrace. Only bad people were nailed to a cross. But to you and me the cross is a wonderful symbol or sign, because it is on the cross that Jesus died for our sins. Let's tell him that we are very happy, and let's tell others that we are prepared to follow him. When we do this, we also take up our cross like he did, and we are his disciples.

Jesus would carry the
shame of the cross for us.

"Cursed is everyone who is hung on a tree." (Galatians 3:13)

CALL THE DOCTOR!

"It is not the healthy who need a doctor, but the sick."
(Mark 2:17)

When we are sick, our parents watch us closely, and if we don't seem to get better, they quickly phone the doctor or take us to his office. Doctors study a long time to help sick people get better. We can thank the Lord for doctors and pray for them.

Luke was a doctor. Jesus used the image of a doctor to tell people why he came to live on earth. Jesus came to heal sick people. Not only illnesses of the body, but especially of the soul. Everyone who lives far away from God is sick in his relationship with the Lord. Jesus was prepared to come down to earth for these lost, sinful people. The Bible says through his wounds we are healed. The wounds that he was given on the cross can be seen as medicine to make us spiritually well.

Some people think they do not need the Lord. The scribes in Jesus' time thought so. But Jesus says he came for the sick. Anyone who realizes that he needs the Lord to be spiritually healed experiences that the Word of God is true. Jesus really makes us well.

Be honest about your spiritual illness and ask the Lord to heal you now so that you can also be well.

Jesus will heal you from sin.

 Who will rescue me from this body of death! Thanks be to God – through Jesus Christ our Lord! (Romans 7:24-25)

May 3

THE MOST IMPORTANT

... so that you may be able to discern what is best.
(Philippians 1:10)

Something we have to learn in life is to know what is the most important. If you are taking a test tomorrow, then you know it is important that you study today. If you think it is more important to do other things today, like playing with friends, you may do very badly in the test.

To know what is important, more important, and even most important, requires the ability to discern. This means we must be able to tell one thing from another. The Lord helps us to sense things so that we are able to tell the important from the more important in our spiritual lives. There are many important things that can mean a lot to us, but there are more important things that we should do. It is more important to have a good relationship with Jesus Christ than to have a good relationship with people. Maybe the most important is to know that your sins have been forgiven.

May the Lord teach you through the Holy Spirit and through his Word which things are the most important.

Jesus would teach you
what is most important.

Be transformed ... Then you will be able to test and approve what God's will is. (Romans 12:2)

May 4

THE APPLE OF HIS EYE

For whoever touches you touches the apple of his eye.
(Zechariah 2:8)

Some people think they are not good enough for the Lord. They see their own faults, and they think the Lord will never be satisfied with them. And yet the Lord redeemed them and calls them his children. When we are the Lord's children, he loves us so much that we can say we are the apple of his eye.

The Lord also said this about the people of Israel, his people. He said he loved them so much that if anyone should touch them, it would be like touching the apple of the Lord's eye. One's eye is a very sensitive organ. When something gets into your eye, you feel it immediately and try to get it out as soon as possible. Also, one cannot touch a person's eye, because it is very, very sensitive. Our eyes are very precious because we see with them. That is why we take very good care of our eyes. If the Lord says that we are the apple of his eye, it means that we are very precious to him.

You must know that you are precious to the Lord. You are just like the apple of his eye. He wants to protect and keep you. When someone hurts you, it is like hurting the Lord. Remember today that you are very special and that you are the apple of the Lord's eye.

Jesus would shower you with love.

How great is the love the Father has lavished on us. (1 John 3:1)

May 5

OPEN ARMS!

"Let the little children come to me, and do not hinder them." (Matthew 19:14)

When Jesus was on earth, some people thought he was so important and so busy that he did not have time for children. Fortunately, this was not true. The Lord loves children very much. To tell the truth, he said if we don't become like children we will never enter the kingdom of heaven. The Lord's heart beats warmly for children. He wants to be with them. He understands how they feel. He wants to guide them, teach them, and show them how to become happy grown-ups – and how to be happy children!

When the disciples wanted to stop the mothers from bringing their children to Jesus, Jesus welcomed the children. Jesus worked very hard, but he was never too tired to have children around him. He put his arms around them. I imagine he hugged them and blessed them. This shows us that he wanted the best for them. I think that all the children who were with him knew right away that they were welcome and that he loved them and understood them.

The Lord also loves you, even if you are not a grown-up. He understands you and cares for you. You will always feel welcome with Jesus.

Jesus would always
make time for you.

Don't let anyone look down on you because you are young.
(1 Timothy 4:12)

May 6

Heart Transplant

"I will give you a new heart and put a new spirit in you ..."
(Ezekiel 36:26)

Some babies are born with bad hearts. They need medical help urgently. There are also grown-ups that develop heart problems at a later stage in their lives. Some develop such a bad heart that they must get a new one. We call this a heart transplant. This means that doctors put a healthy heart into a person with a sick heart. There is then new hope for the sick patient. The Lord is also like a doctor who does heart transplants.

You and I also have bad hearts. Our hearts are full of sin, and we need to get new ones. Only Jesus can give you a new heart. He wants to take the old one out of our lives and give us a completely new one. The new heart that he gives us will be clean and healthy, washed by his blood. We can live with this heart forever.

It is very important that we exchange our old heart for a new one. We don't have to lie on an operating table; the Lord does the operation quietly and without fuss when we tell him that we need a new heart. Have you asked him for a new heart? You can live with him, forever, with this new heart.

Jesus would give you a new heart.

"... and get a new heart and a new spirit." (Ezekiel 18:31)

May 7

STONE OR FLESH?

"I will remove from them their heart of stone and give them a heart of flesh." (Ezekiel 11:19)

The Bible says we must get a new heart because sin has made our hearts as hard as stone. Sin makes you look at things differently from what the Lord would like you to. This makes it so that we can't be happy people and causes us to hurt others very easily.

The Lord tells us to give our hearts of stone to him, and he will exchange them for hearts of flesh. Flesh can be cut with a knife, but a stone can't. The Lord asks you and me to give our hearts to him. He will make our hearts soft, so that we can live better lives, can act better, and just be nicer people. Before I gave my life to the Lord I was hard on others. But the longer I serve him and know him, the more he helps me to become softer. Of course I still, like you, make mistakes. But a heart of flesh that is flexible and can adapt is a heart that is prepared to learn.

Have you asked for a heart of flesh yet? Let's ask the Lord to help us even more to become soft-hearted.

Jesus would give you
a heart of love.

I will give you a new heart and put a new spirit in you. (Ezekiel 36:26)

May 8

Mother's Day

A woman who fears the Lord is to be praised. (Proverbs 31:30)

Mothers are wonderful. They look after us when we are not well, they help us when we don't understand things and they comfort us when we are unhappy. How often do you think about all the good things your mother does for you each day? Sometimes we take for granted all the things mothers do. Just imagine if your mother had to go away for a day or two. Who would do all the things she does for you? Whom would you go to if you were upset about something that happened at school? Who would prepare your lunch for school? These things wouldn't be the same without your mom, would they?

Sometimes you might moan and groan about the things your mother does, but you need to remind yourself always that she loves you and only wants the best for you in your life. In many ways she is like God's representative, letting you know about the things that please Him, and you can know something of the wonderful love God has for you by seeing the way your mother loves you.

Remember to pray a special prayer each day thanking God for you mother, and asking Him to help you appreciate her properly, and to help you to make it easy for your mom to look after you.

Jesus would obey and
love His mother.

Children's children are a crown to the aged, and parents are the pride of their children. (Proverbs 17:6)

May 9

Talk to the Lord

If you have anything to say speak up, for I want you to be cleared. (Job 33:32)

Sometimes we do not feel like speaking to anyone. Especially when we are feeling sad and we think no one will understand, we don't want to talk. Perhaps your mother sees that you are unhappy and then says to you, "Tell me what is wrong. Talk to me!" Yes, it is better to talk about it. It is better to say how you feel. When you have talked about it you will start feeling better. To bottle up all your feelings and say nothing is not a good thing at all.

Because the Lord knows this, he wants you to talk to him. It is better to open up your heart to Jesus and tell him everything. Don't tell yourself that he doesn't know about your problem, and then keep quiet about it. God already knows.

Is there something you want to tell the Lord? Are there things in your heart that no one knows about? Talk to God about it – now.

Jesus would talk to the
Father about his problems.

Cast your cares on the LORD and he will sustain you. (Psalm 55:20)

May 10

He Listens

His ear [is not] too dull to hear. (Isaiah 59:1b)

Some people can't hear because they are deaf. Something is wrong with their ears, and they can't process sounds. There are also those who do not want to hear. They can, but they choose not to. Sometimes when you speak to people they are thinking of other things, and they don't hear you. Or they pretend not to hear you, because they are ignoring you.

The Lord invites us to speak to him. He wants us to open up our hearts to him and tell him everything that is going on in our lives and what we are keeping ourselves busy with. He invites us to speak to him, and he will listen to us; he wants to. It is almost as if he pricks up his ears when we speak. He listens to everything we say or think. He is never too busy. He never ignores you. His thoughts are never someplace else. Isn't it wonderful! He is listening to you only.

If you want to speak to the Lord now, you can be sure that he will definitely listen.

Jesus would listen to
you when you speak.

While they are still speaking I will hear. (Isaiah 65:24)

May 11

THE SHORT ARM

Surely the arm of the LORD is not too short to save.
(Isaiah 59:1a)

People in time of the Old Testament thought that God was far away. He was there somewhere in the clouds of heaven. He was not yet Immanuel, God with us. Jesus had not come down to earth yet. That is why they always prayed that God must help them. Maybe they thought, "How can God help us if he is so far away? Maybe he has a long arm so that he can help us here on earth even if he lives in heaven."

Of course they were making a mistake. God is not in heaven only. He is everywhere. He can help anyone on earth in a second.

I know that the Lord can and will help us; we are his children when we believe in Christ. He has come very close to us, through Jesus and the Holy Spirit. His arm doesn't have to be long to be able to help. He is here, with us. His arms are powerful and strong enough to help us straight away.

If you need help, ask the Lord right now to help you.

Jesus would help you.

My help comes from the LORD. (Psalm 121:2)

May 12

Bad Spirits

For our struggle is not against flesh and blood, but ... against the spiritual forces of evil in the heavenly realms. (Ephesians 6:12)

The Holy Spirit is here with us. He is the helper and the Comforter. The Lord also has other spirits in his service; for example, angels that help us on earth. But there are also bad spirits.

The devil managed to get a lot of angels on his side, and he took them with him when he left heaven. They became bad. These evil spirits are the servants of the devil, and they attack people and want to destroy them. When Jesus was on earth he drove a lot of evil spirits out of people's hearts. Some of them screamed as they left a person, because they were afraid of Jesus. Jesus came to put an end to the work of the devil.

Evil spirits do the devil's work and they harass us. But if we belong to Jesus, the Holy Spirit lives in us and we do not have to be afraid of evil spirits. The best thing to do, really, is to ignore them. A heart that is full of the Holy Spirit and Jesus has nothing to be afraid of.

Give your heart and life over to the hands of the Lord and ask the Holy Spirit to fill you so that there won't be room for evil spirits, and they will leave you alone.

Jesus would destroy
the works of evil.

Do not tremble, do not be afraid. (Isaiah 44:8)

May 13

GOODBYE, JESUS!

After he said this, he was taken up before their very eyes, and a cloud hid him. (Acts 1:9)

Ascension Day is the day we celebrate Jesus' being taken into heaven.

When Jesus' work on earth was finished, he went to his Father in heaven. I would imagine that God was very pleased to see Jesus. It would be like your country's team returning home after winning the World Cup or Olympics. All over people would be cheering them. The angels and the Father may have also cheered Jesus when he got to heaven after suffering for us. He conquered death. He is the Winner, and that is why everyone in heaven must have received him with such joy. He then got a name above all other names.

Now Jesus is in heaven to plead with God for you and me. He prays for us when we are in trouble. He sends the angels to help us. He also went to prepare a place for us. When we get to heaven one day, we will have our own place where we can live with him. Jesus also promised that he would send the Holy Spirit as a helper so that he can be with us every day.

Thank Jesus that he went to prepare a place for us. Luckily, we know that he will come and get us, and then we will be with him.

Jesus will come back again.

"This same Jesus ... will come back in the same way you have seen him go to heaven." (Acts 1:11)

May 14

THE VOICE BEHIND YOU

> Whether you turn to the right or to the left, your ears will hear a voice behind you, saying, "This is the way; walk in it." (Isaiah 30:21)

Have you ever been in a situation where you didn't know which road to take? When you are on your way somewhere and you are not sure of the road, you sometimes make a wrong decision and lose your way. When people travel by car to places far away, there are sometimes forks in the road (one road turns left and the other to the right). How do they know which one to take? There are road maps to help, or someone will show them the way.

The Lord wants to direct us and show us the right way. The Bible says we will hear a voice behind us that will tell us if we should turn left or right. Of course it will not be the same as hearing one another's voices. The Lord's voice cannot be heard; he speaks through his Word and his Spirit. When we sometimes make the wrong decision and we go in a wrong and sinful direction, the Holy Spirit will guide us in our hearts. It is like a voice speaking inside us. That is why we must be quiet enough before the Lord so that we can hear him. When we focus our hearts on his voice, we will know which path to take. We will know to do something or not.

Listen to the voice of the Lord; he will direct you.

Jesus would be quiet
and listen to the Father.

Jesus got up ... and went off to a solitary place, where he prayed. (Mark 1:35)

May 15

Milk or Sausage?

I gave you milk, not solid food, for you were not yet ready for it. (1 Corinthians 3:2)

Three-day-old babies cannot eat a hamburger. I don't know any mom that would even think of giving a baby a burger, because it cannot digest it yet. Little babies can only drink milk because they have not developed enough to eat solids yet.

When you have given your life to Jesus you are like a little baby in faith. You must still be helped like a baby. You don't understand enough of what is written in the Bible. Someone must teach you about God's Word.

As a baby grows, he gets stronger. Quite soon this baby needs more than milk. Then his mom or dad gives him veggies and meat, and when he is older, he can eat grilled meat when the family has a cookout. The same goes for you and me. First we were babies in our faith, but we learned more and more about the Word of God. We have even become knowledgeable about the things of the Lord. It's not your age that makes you ready for the solid food of God's Word. There are young children who know a lot about these things. They know more about God's will than some grown-ups.

I hope you have finished with milk and are now eating the delicious, grilled meat of God's Word.

Jesus would help you grow.

Anyone who lives on milk ... is not acquainted with the teaching about righteousness. (Hebrews 5:13)

May 16

Ten Golden Rules

And God spoke all these words. (Exodus 20:1)

When the people of God were taken out of Egypt, the Lord gave them the Ten Commandments. He did this to help them so that they would know how he wanted them to live. If they kept these commandments, all would be well and they would be happy. God's Ten Commandments were like golden rules that helped them love one another and do things the right way.

Because we are sinners and make mistakes, the Lord must teach us how to live. We can read the Ten Commandments because they will help us do the right thing. If the Lord says we are not allowed to steal, then we must not steal. If the Lord tells us to rest, it is good that we rest on a Sunday so that we can work hard again on Monday. If the Lord says we are not allowed to kill, of course we must not kill. In this way the Lord helps us with his ten commandments.

Because Jesus came, we find it easier to do what he wants us to do. The Holy Spirit, who lives in our hearts, makes us willing to keep God's commandments. Let's do what the Lord wants. Only a fool would think that what God says is not important.

Jesus would help you
live the way you should.

Let us keep in step with the Spirit. (Galatians 5:25)

Enjoy Life!

Be happy, young man, while you are young, and let your heart give you joy in the days of your youth. (Ecclesiastes 11:9)

I am not a young man any more, but I can still remember many nice things that I enjoyed as a young boy. There were many things that I did alone or with my friends that were great fun. You're only young once, and when you are young, there are many things that are important to you.

The Lord wants you to enjoy your youth. I wonder what things you like best. We all have different interests. There are things that you enjoy more than someone else would. Maybe you like TV games, sports, or hobbies. Perhaps you like riding your skateboard, going to the movies, or visiting friends. Maybe you like going to parties. Perhaps you like nothing better than playing football or singing. Whatever you like, or whatever you want to do, the Bible says to enjoy it.

The Bible thinks that you and I can really enjoy our lives only if we do things the way Jesus would. That is why we ask in this book, "What would Jesus do?" Yes, we must try to keep sin out of everything we do. The Lord will help us, and his Holy Spirit will show us how. By all means, enjoy your life. I hope that this day will be a good one.

Jesus would enjoy life.

Follow the ways of your heart. (Ecclesiastes 11:9)

May 18

GOD WORKS WITH A FEW

"With the three hundred men, I will save you." (Judges 7:7)

God wanted to save his people from a very powerful enemy. The enemies were the Midianites. They had a strong army. The Bible says they were as many as a swarm of locusts.

The Lord told Gideon to get the Israelites together to fight against Midian. They got together twenty-two thousand very brave Israelite soldiers. But God said he did not want that many. Too many? Against the many soldiers of Midian they were just a handful. How could God say there were too many of them!

The reason for using so few men against Midian is that the Lord wanted to show very clearly that it was not the power of Israel that would bring them victory, but the power of God. The Lord knew that the Israelites would get swollen heads (feel proud) if they won the battle against the Midianites. That is why he made the impossible happen. When God wants to win, he can use anything. How much you and I can do is not important. It all depends on his great strength. This is how he made Israel win.

Maybe you have a big problem in your life. Perhaps you feel small and weak. But with God on your side, you come out on top. Ask him to help you.

Jesus would help you get
the better of your problems.

Blessed is the man who takes refuge in [the Lord]. (Psalm 34:8)

May 19

WHOM DO YOU TRUST?

He did not need man's testimony about man, for he knew what was in a man. (John 2:25)

People often disappoint us. We put our trust in someone, and then that person does not do what he said he would. It would be a pity if we feel we can never trust anyone ever again, because we all need one another in life. Jesus didn't trust just anybody. We read in the Bible that when Jesus was in Jerusalem for the Feast of the Passover, many people started believing in him when they saw the miracles he did. The Bible also says that he didn't put his trust in them, because he knew all about people (see v. 24). Yes, Jesus knew all about the weaknesses of humans. That is why he never put his trust in people, but in God.

You and I must learn from Jesus. People disappoint us because they have shortcomings and faults. We must never put our complete trust in people. We should rather trust God with all our hearts. We must ask him to help us and support us. Ask him to give you people that you can trust and who will comfort you.

Jesus would put his
trust in God alone.

Do not put trust in princes, in mortal men, who cannot save.
(Psalm 146:3)

The Small Man

He wanted to see who Jesus was, but being a short man he could not, because of the crowd. (Luke 19:3)

Some of us are tall and others are short. Short people have a problem seeing anything when they are surrounded by taller people in a crowd. Zacchaeus was a rich and important man in his town. But because he was short, he could not see Jesus passing by in the midst of the crowds. So he climbed a tree because he wanted to see this wonderful man who performed miracles.

Then there was another miracle! When Jesus passed underneath the tree that Zacchaeus was in, he looked up and said, *"Zacchaeus, come down immediately. I must stay at your house today"* (Luke 19:5). When he got over the shock, Zacchaeus invited Jesus to his house. Some of the religious people were upset. They thought it was wrong of Jesus to visit the house of a sinner. But Jesus had a plan for Zacchaeus's life.

That night Jesus told Zacchaeus all about his kingdom and how he wanted to bring salvation to the world. Zacchaeus promised to stop his sinful ways and to start treating people fairly from then on. This was another miracle!

You and I must also go to people's houses, visit with them there, and tell them about Jesus' love and forgiveness. Maybe it will work a miracle in their lives.

In Jesus no one will be lost.

Call on him while he is near. (Isaiah 55:6)

May 21

NEARLY, BUT NOT QUITE

"Do you think that in such a short time you can persuade me to be a Christian?" (Acts 26:28)

Paul was imprisoned by the Jews because he followed Jesus. They brought him before King Agrippa of the Roman Empire. He had heard about this Jesus and wanted to know more about him. So he asked Paul about Jesus and about why Paul followed him.

Paul thought it was wonderful that he was given an opportunity to speak to this important king about Jesus. He explained everything about Jesus' life on earth and how he came to set up his kingdom. Agrippa listened carefully. Paul tried to convince him that what Jesus said was the truth. Agrippa told Paul, "You are almost convincing me to become a Christian." Paul wanted Agrippa to accept Jesus as his Redeemer and become a Christian.

Many people are almost-Christians. They believe in Jesus and the Bible with half a heart. Still, they don't get around to accepting him. You and I should, like Paul, go on telling them it is worthwhile to acknowledge Jesus.

Jesus would tell everybody
about the kingdom.

Jesus went throughout Galilee, teaching [and] preaching the good news of the kingdom. (Matthew 4:23)

May 22

THE BAD WOMAN

He married Jezebel and began to serve Baal and worship him. (1 Kings 16:31)

King Ahab was a king of Israel. Unfortunately, he was not a very good king because he did what was wrong in the eyes of the Lord. One of the big mistakes he made was to marry a woman who did not love God. Her name was Jezebel. She was a heathen woman, and she worshiped a god named Baal.

Jezebel was a bad woman because she tried to kill the prophets of God. She took care of a few hundred false prophets that served Baal. She wanted to lure the people of Israel away from the Lord, and she also wanted to kill Elijah.

There are people today who do not want to do the will of God. Some of them are leaders. Like Jezebel, they are trying to sabotage the work of the Lord. We must be very careful of these people. The Lord says in his Word that those who serve him must be praised. We must pray for bad people like Jezebel and show them that it is better to serve the Lord.

Perhaps you know someone who does not love and serve the Lord. Be careful of his or her advice, and pray for this person.

Jesus would change
the lives of sinners.

Therefore, if anyone is in Christ, he is a new creation. (2 Corinthians 5:17)

May 23

THE COMFORTER

"He will give you another Counselor ... the Spirit of truth." (John 14:16,17)

A counselor is also a comforter. Has anyone ever comforted you? Of course! When we hurt ourselves, or something bad happens in our lives, it is wonderful to have someone who comforts us. A comforter is someone who says, "Never mind, things will get better."

The Lord knows that we, the people on earth, suffer. That is why he sent us a Counselor or Comforter. The Comforter's name is the Holy Spirit. He came to Jesus' followers on the day of Pentecost. Now he lives in the hearts of everyone who has accepted Jesus. The Holy Spirit is wonderful. He comforts us in difficult times. He encourages us. He inspires us and motivates us.

The more filled we are with the Holy Spirit, the easier it is for him to comfort us. Are you finding life hard to bear? Are you hurting because of someone or something? Ask the Holy Spirit to comfort you.

Jesus would comfort
you through the Spirit.

[The Holy Spirit] will teach you all things and will remind you of everything I have said to you. (John 14:26)

SHOES

... with your feet fitted with the readiness that comes from the gospel of peace. (Ephesians 6:15)

We know that soldiers who fight a battle must wear the right shoes. They cannot go to war barefoot. They would not be able to fight properly. The Bible uses the image to say that we also need the right "shoes" when we do battle with the devil.

The image of the shoes that the Bible mentions is the preparedness to talk about Jesus. As a soldier puts on the right shoes for the battle, you and I, as children of the Lord, must also wear the right shoes. We must be prepared to tell others about Jesus, and we must be prepared to live for him. If we want to, we can sing about him, or teach people about him, as long as we are prepared to tell them he is the King of our lives. When we do this we are like a soldier suitably dressed for battle.

Are you prepared to tell others about Jesus? If not, get prepared today. In this way, good soldiers win the war.

Jesus would not be ashamed
to spread the gospel.

I am not ashamed of the gospel. (Romans 1:16)

May 25

THE DOVE

Heaven was opened and the Holy Spirit descended on him in bodily form like a dove. (Luke 3:21-22)

The dove is a symbol of peace. Perhaps you have seen how doves are released at important gatherings. It is truly beautiful to see the doves fly in the blue sky. Maybe the dove is a symbol of peace because it is an easily tamed bird. It is not really frightened of people. And the soft cooing of a dove brings peace to the soul. Doves are not birds of prey. Doves are not aggressive. Doves are friendly birds.

When Jesus was baptized, the Holy Spirit descended upon him in the form of a dove. It must have been beautiful to see. The Holy Spirit enabled Jesus to do his work. The peace of the Holy Spirit also descended on Jesus at the same time. Jesus is called Prince of Peace. Yes, the Holy Spirit brings peace for you and me through the Prince of Peace, Jesus Christ. When the Holy Spirit lives in us, we also have peace in our hearts.

Ask the Lord to fill you with the peace of his Holy Spirit.

Through his Holy Spirit Jesus
will fill you with peace.

Peace I leave with you; my peace I give you. (John 14:27)

You Are a House

Do you not know that your body is a temple of the Holy Spirit, who is in you? (1 Corinthians 6:19)

In the Old Testament the people of Israel built the Lord a place where they could meet with him. They called it the house of God. Other words for it are temple, tabernacle, or place of assembly. But the Lord does not live in manmade buildings anymore. When Jesus came, he decided to live in a new home: our bodies. It sounds almost too good to be true. How can the mighty God of heaven and earth live in our bodies? When we accept the Lord, he comes to live inside us. When Jesus went back to heaven, he sent the Holy Spirit to come and live in us. That is why the Bible calls our bodies, yours and mine, the temple of the Holy Spirit.

Because the mighty, wonderful Lord lives inside you and me, we must care for our bodies well, look after them, and make sure our thoughts are clean and holy. You are not allowed to harm your body because it is the temple of God.

Jesus will live in you,
through the Holy Spirit.

The Spirit of God lives in you. (Romans 8:9)

Let Him Guide You

"But when he, the Spirit of truth, comes, he will guide you into all truth." (John 16:13)

Have you ever seen someone lead a blind person? A blind person cannot see. That is why someone takes his hand and leads him in the right direction. Some blind people make use of guide dogs to lead the way.

The Bible tells us in Romans 8:14 that the Spirit guides the children of God. This means that he shows us the right way. He shows us where to walk, what to do, how to act. He leads us in the truth. This is not just about church on Sunday or Sunday school. It is all about our thoughts, how we practice sports, how we relax, how we do our schoolwork. The Holy Spirit wants to teach us how to behave in every situation. He leads us in the truth of God's Word.

When we do not listen to the Holy Spirit, then all kinds of things go wrong in our lives. Then we make wrong decisions and take the wrong road. When the Holy Spirit is our Guide, we can be sure that we will always have the peace of the Lord in our hearts. Ask the Holy Spirit today to guide you in everything you do.

Jesus will guide you
through the Holy Spirit.

Since we live by the Spirit, let us keep in step with the Spirit. (Galatians 5:25)

A Stammered Prayer

He beat his breast and said, "God, have mercy on me, a sinner." (Luke 18:13)

Jesus told a parable about two men who went to the temple to pray. In Jesus' time the temple was like the church is today. This is where we go to listen to the Word of God and to pray and sing. When these two men got to the temple, they acted differently. One was a Pharisee. This meant he had a very important position in the church. The other was a tax collector. Tax collectors were not good people. They were not to be trusted. They did not have a good reputation.

When the Pharisee prayed, he thanked the Lord that he was good, and not bad, like the tax collector. This Pharisee was haughty and his heart was filled with pride. The Lord does not like this. The tax collector, on the other hand, felt very bad. He knew he was nothing but a sinner. He felt quite ashamed to be in the presence of the Lord. That is why he begged for forgiveness and asked the Lord to have mercy on him.

Jesus said that the prayer of the tax collector was the best one. He was humble and knew he needed God. He asked for forgiveness. That is why God answered his prayer and not that of the Pharisee. You and I must also be humble before the Lord.

Jesus would be humble.

[Jesus] ... gentle and riding on a donkey. (Matthew 21:5)

SOW THE SEED

"A farmer went out to sow his seed." (Matthew 13:3)

Farmers plow a piece of land and then sow seed in that land so that it can come up and bear fruit. In this way corn and wheat and all kinds of other plants that you and I eat are planted and grown. Some of the seed the farmer plants does not come up. Maybe that seed landed in the wrong place. It could also be that weeds choked this seed so that it could not grow.

The Lord said that his gospel is like seed that falls on the ground. Every Christian is like a farmer who sows seed. You and I must try to sow God's seed in the lives of people. Wherever we go, we can tell people about God and explain his Word to them. This is seed that can come up in people's hearts and bear fruit that will make God happy. Sometimes the seed falls on hard soil. This is like a person with a hard heart who doesn't want to accept God's Word. Sometimes there are weeds that choke the seed. This is the sin in a life that keeps the Word of God from coming up. Sow good seeds today, wherever you go.

Jesus would sow his
message like seed.

"The seed is the word of God." (Luke 8:11)

"STORM BE STILL!"

He got up and rebuked the wind and the raging waters.
(Luke 8:24)

One day Jesus and his disciples got into a boat, and Jesus told the disciples to go over to the other side of the lake. While they were sailing, Jesus fell asleep. He must have been very tired. A heavy storm broke over the lake, and water came into the boat. Soon they were in danger of sinking. They went to Jesus and woke him up. They asked him to help quickly; the boat was sinking.

Jesus got up and did an interesting thing: he spoke sternly to the wind. The waves died down and there was peace. It was a miracle. Just by talking, Jesus calmed the storm.

If you have problems, the Lord can also speak one word, and your life can change. Trust him with your problems. Ask him to help; the disciples did. He loves you very much and he takes care of you.

Jesus would take care of you.

"Will he not much more clothe [take care of] you!" (Matthew 6:30)

NOT LITTLE, BUT LOTS

> They all ate and were satisfied, and the disciples picked
> up twelve basketfuls of broken pieces. (Luke 9:17)

Once Jesus preached near the Sea of Galilee. The crowds were hanging on his every word. The day passed quickly, and perhaps the crowds could hardly believe their eyes when they realized that evening had already come. The people were hungry and there was not enough food for everybody.

In the book of John we read that a little boy brought Jesus two fish and five loaves of bread. Jesus looked up to heaven, said grace, and started passing the bread around. Thousands ate, and still there was food left over!

The gospel of Jesus does not just make good reading, but it is also strength from God. It can work a miracle in one's life. It is unlikely that a loaf of bread will become more in your house, but God can perform other miracles. The greatest miracle is that he forgives our sins so that we can live with God in his peace.

You and I must make sure that what we have is available to the Lord so that he can use it. The two fish and five loaves were good enough for the Lord to perform a miracle. Bring what you have to the Lord – your life, talents, time, money – and see him work a miracle with it.

Jesus will perform a
miracle in your life.

"... that I might display my power in you." (Romans 9:17)

June 1

On This Rock

"On this rock I will build my church." (Matthew 16:18)

One day Jesus gave Simon, son of Jonah, a new name. Jesus wanted to change his name to Peter, because he had a special plan for Peter's life. Peter means "rock."

There are many names that sound like Peter, and they have the same meaning: Pete, Petri, Pierre, Petra, Pedro, and many more. This shows us that Peter is an important name. Why did Jesus give this particular name to Peter?

Jesus gave Peter this name after asking what people were saying about him. People are forever talking behind one's back, and they talked about Jesus too. But was it the truth? That is why Jesus asked this question. The reply was that people said he was a great prophet like Elijah. When Jesus asked his disciples who they thought he was, Peter answered that he was the Redeemer and the Anointed One, that he was the Son of God. This answer pleased Jesus and he said, *on this rock I will build my church* (Matthew 16:18). What Peter said is true, and if we believe it, we are building the kingdom of Jesus.

When you confess that Jesus is Lord, the Redeemer and the Son of God, your words are also like a rock that the Lord can use to build his kingdom. Tell people that Jesus is alive!

Jesus will build his kingdom
with your testimony.

"Therefore go and make disciples of all nations ..." (Matthew 28:19)

June 2

YOUR LIFE IS PRECIOUS

"What good will it be for a man if he gains the whole world, yet forfeits his soul?" (Matthew 16:26)

Jesus taught his disciples something very important. He also teaches you and me. He says that our lives are very precious. That is why we protect ourselves. That is why we look after ourselves when we are ill. That is why we are afraid of criminals and murderers; they can destroy our lives.

Jesus teaches us that the best thing you can do to protect your life is to give it to him. You can be selfish and keep your life to yourself. This means that you want to be in control of your life. You want your heart to yourself. You don't want to give your heart and your life to Jesus. Jesus warns that if you think you are going to keep or protect your life in this way, you are definitely going to lose it. If we open up our hearts and give our lives to the Lord, then we will save our lives. We save our lives by doing what the Lord tells us to.

You might have everything in the whole world. You might have lots of money, a nice car, lots of toys, plenty of friends, and many other possessions, and yet, you can lose your life.

Decide today that you would rather follow Jesus – lose your life in him so that you can gain your life back.

Jesus will also protect your life.

Even though I walk through the valley of the shadow of death, I will fear no evil. (Psalm 23:4)

June 3

Sɪɴ Is Sɪɴ

For whoever keeps the whole law and yet stumbles at just one point is guilty of breaking all of it. (James 2:10)

There is no such thing as small sins and big sins. We think it is not such a big sin if we steal something small; we will be forgiven easily. But murder is a big thing, and maybe we won't be forgiven for that. It does not work this way in God's eyes.

Sinning means that we fail. If we fail in a big or a small way, we still fail. The Lord says stealing a pencil is just as bad as committing a murder. Sin is sin.

The Lord forgives both small and big sins. He is not like us. We will forgive something small quite readily, but whenever a big sin is committed toward us, it is very difficult to forgive. God forgives us if we confess our sins, whether it's a big or a small sin.

It is true that the result of one sin can be much more serious than that of another. If you have stolen something small, it won't affect others all that much. On the other hand, if you steal someone's credit card, the consequences could be widespread. In God's eyes both sins must be confessed and forgiven.

Let's thank the Lord that he is willing to forgive all sins. But let's try not to sin.

Jesus would forgive your sins.

"The Son of Man has authority on earth to forgive sins." (Matthew 9:6)

June 4

Build the Temple

"Not by might nor by power, but by my Spirit," says the LORD Almighty. (Zechariah 4:6)

When the people of Israel were taken away to Babylon, the temple in Jerusalem was destroyed. Years later, the Lord sent his people back to Jerusalem to rebuild the temple.

The people who had to rebuild the temple were not up to this task. They did not have the heart nor the money to start building. They couldn't get hold of building material. How were they to rebuild the temple? The Lord answered them in a vision. He showed Zechariah how they could build: not with might and power, but by the Spirit of the Lord. Zechariah told Zerubbabel, the man who had to build the temple, that all he had to do was get started with the guidance of the Holy Spirit. He must use whatever he can lay his hands on, and soon he would see the work running smoothly. The Holy Spirit would give him the courage to do the work. He also provide building material.

Zerubbabel got started, and, lo and behold, everything happened the way Zechariah said it would. The temple was completed and everybody said, "Wonderful, wonderful!" Although Zerubbabel began in a small way, the temple was completed. Maybe you also have a task that is getting you down. Ask the Holy Spirit to help you. If it is God's will, you will also be successful.

Jesus will be with
you and help you.

"Be strong ... For I am with you." (Haggai 2:4)

June 5

DEEP IN YOUR HEART

All a man's ways seem innocent to him, but motives are weighed by the LORD. (Proverbs 16:2)

We see the outside of people. We see someone laugh, being happy or friendly. It could be that this person is being friendly because he wants something from you. His motives are not quite honest, but you don't notice it at first. It can also happen that someone seems angry. For example, a teacher may be very strict with you or with your class. Deep in the heart of that teacher she may have a sincere wish to help you, and that is the reason for her behavior. Her motives are good.

The Lord does not look at the outside. He looks into the heart. He knows what our motives are. He knows why we do things. This is important to the Lord. He does not only see how we try to serve him on the outside. He sees many people going to church, or singing songs for him, or even praying to him. It could be that we do this for the wrong reasons. God looks into our hearts. Do we really want to serve him? Do we really want to be in his presence? Do we really want to love him? The Lord sees the answer deep in our hearts.

Why do you serve the Lord? I hope it is because you really love him. The Lord will know. Serve him for the right reasons.

Jesus would look at the motives in your heart.

 "Man looks at the outward appearance, but the Lord looks at the heart." (1 Samuel 16:7)

June 6

The Right Words

How good is a timely word! (Proverbs 15:23)

Words carry a message. What we say has a meaning. If you say there is a snake in the house, you are communicating a fact. Then everybody gets afraid. If you say a flower is pretty, you say it because you see a pretty flower and you want others to see it.

Words can also be used in the wrong way. Sometimes we say one thing and mean another. We must learn to use language correctly.

It can also happen that one uses the right words but at the wrong time. Perhaps you see someone who looks unhappy, and instead of saying something that cheers him up, you say something like, "Oh, come on, don't be silly." You have said the wrong thing. Perhaps you joked when you should have been serious. Or perhaps you were too serious when the time was not right for it.

We need wisdom to say the right words at the right time. Let's ask the Lord to help us. I have learned that the Holy Spirit helps me to say the right things. Still, I must also, same as you, ask the Lord to help me so that I don't say the wrong thing.

Jesus would know what
answer to give.

 Do not repay evil with evil ... but with blessing ... so that you may inherit a blessing. (1 Peter 3:9)

Work Hard

Diligent hands bring wealth. (Proverbs 10:4)

Being diligent means being hard-working. It is the opposite of being lazy. Diligent people know that there is work to do. They are not too lazy to do it. They don't sleep too late. When they are working, they do not allow their thoughts to be busy with other things. They are disciplined. They have realized that hard work is good for them.

The Bible says that one gets rich if one is diligent. If we work hard, the Lord will bless our work. Lazy people usually have a hard time being successful. A few people beg and don't want to work. They want to lie in the sun all day long, and then ask others for money.

I don't think this is right. Yes, it is true, many people are losing their jobs these days and they are suffering. But if they are diligent and ask the Lord to give them a new job – no matter how small, or what it is – I am sure the Lord will bless them. Someone who is not afraid to use his hands is someone who always has bread on the table. I hope you are diligent. Do your homework diligently. Help your mom in the house. Don't be lazy. Then you will also be one of those people who always have enough in life.

Jesus would be diligent.

 Diligent hands will rule, but laziness ends in slave labor. (Proverbs 12:24)

REFRESHING OTHERS

He who refreshes others will himself be refreshed.
(Proverbs 11:25)

There are so many needy people around us. There are hungry people. There are thirsty people. There are people who need clothes. There are people who need love. There are people who need friendship. Yes, and there are people with a "thirst" in their hearts.

We often think our own needs are so important that we cannot afford to help others. Sometimes we are stingy with what we have, and we don't want to share with others. The Bible teaches us an important lesson: you and I should be more eager to give than to receive. If you and I have learned this great lesson, all will be well in our lives.

I don't know a single person who gives freely to others and who doesn't receive much more in return. Someone once said that you can never give others more than what God can give back to you. The Lord knows what we give others. If we give others water to drink to quench their thirst, the Lord tells us he will also give us water to quench our thirst. Don't be stingy. Give to others, and you will also receive.

Jesus would quench your thirst.

A generous man will himself be blessed, for he shares his food with the poor. (Proverbs 22:9)

WORDS LIKE SILVER

The words of the LORD are flawless, like silver. (Psalm 12:6)

We often say things that we don't really mean. Often we say we will do something, but then we don't feel like doing it. We just talked; our words did not become deeds.

If you said you would do something and you didn't, your words were false. You lied. Your words meant nothing; they were just sounds. We must try to do what we promise. Sometimes something comes up and we can't keep our promises. But we must really try not to speak false words.

If we compliment someone on a pretty dress or a good voice, it must come from the heart. We must mean what we say. We must not be false. Flattery is when you say something just to make someone feel good, without meaning what you say.

There is someone whose words are never false: the Lord. What he says is true. He cannot lie. He will not bluff us with his words, because he is holy. His words are truth. His words are like genuine silver. It's good to know that, in a world full of false words, there are genuine, true words.

Jesus would speak only the truth.

God is not a man, that he should lie. (Numbers 23:19)

THE BEST!

He found none equal to Daniel, Hananiah, Mishael and Azariah; so they entered the king's service. (Daniel 1:19)

The Lord wants to be proud of his children. He wants to use them. They must be witnesses of his greatness. In everything, they must strive for the best. This does not mean that God's children are the smartest in the world, nor does it mean that they are the best at everything. They must give their best according to the talents that the Lord gave them.

In the time of King Nebuchadnezzar there were four men who knew the Lord and served him. The Bible says that God gave these men intelligence and also insight into everything they learned. They were full of the Lord's wisdom. They were better than the heathen young men, because they loved God. They lived the way the Lord prescribed. That is why they didn't eat the king's food and drink his wine. They ate only healthy food as they had been doing since childhood. That is why they looked healthier. They studied hard, they stood out from their friends, and they glorified God. The king appointed them to work in his palace.

When we serve the Lord, he uses us, just like Daniel and his friends. What the Lord prescribes is always best.

Jesus would live
according to the Word.

The commands of the LORD are radiant, giving light to the eyes. (Psalm 19:8)

June 11

ADVICE FOR THE KING

> Be pleased to accept my advice: Renounce your sins by doing what is right ... then your prosperity will continue. (Daniel 4:27)

God loved Daniel very much and wanted to use him, even in a heathen country. That is why God gave Daniel the ability to interpret or explain dreams. One night King Nebuchadnezzar had a dream that upset him. His advisers could not interpret the dream. Then the Lord helped Daniel to interpret the king's dream.

Daniel explained the dream and gave the king a message. Daniel was only a servant, but he gave the Lord's message to the king, loud and clear. The king had to stop sinning and doing things that were wrong. The king had to do what was right and help the needy. After Daniel had said all this, he must have held his breath. What if his message had annoyed the great king? He could have Daniel killed. Luckily he did not. But the king didn't listen to Daniel. He went on doing bad things. Later on he was not in his right mind any more, and he ate grass like cattle.

You and I must give people the Lord's messages faithfully and respectfully as Daniel did.

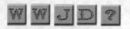

Jesus would give the
Lord's messages faithfully.

For I gave them the words you gave me. (John 17:8)

June 12

TAME LIONS

They brought Daniel and threw him into the lions' den.
(Daniel 6:16)

I'm sure you know the story of Daniel who was thrown into the lions' den. The enemies of the Lord tried everything to find something they could use against Daniel, but they could find nothing. So, they made a tricky plan. They knew that Daniel prayed to God three times a day. Then they went and asked the king to forbid the people to worship anybody but King Darius. Can you believe it? A person worshiping another person!

Because Daniel worshiped only God, they captured him and threw him into a lions' den so the lions could eat him. But God protected Daniel by sending his angel to shut the mouths of the lions so that they could not harm Daniel. The king was very glad that the lions hadn't eaten Daniel, because he loved Daniel very much.

King Darius realized that the people had been scheming against Daniel, and he ordered that the guilty ones be thrown into the lions' den. They had hardly even touched the ground in the lions' den before the lions tore them to pieces.

No matter who makes wicked plans against you, the Lord will help you out. Just trust him and be faithful like Daniel. Keep on praying to your God; he will be with you.

Jesus would keep on praying
in difficult times.

And being in anguish, he prayed more earnestly. (Luke 22:44)

June 13

WAIT FOR STRENGTH

Those who hope in the LORD will renew their strength.
(Isaiah 40:31)

When you walk far, your legs get tired and weak, and it feels as if you have no more strength left. Then you must take a rest to renew your strength. Only when your legs have new strength can you go on.

Your spirit can also get tired. We usually say a person who is tired in his or her spirit is depressed or despondent. There are many people around us who are so depressed they don't even want to live any more. They feel weak and have no strength. The Lord teaches us how we can get strength back into our spirit. It sounds almost too easy to work. But we must listen to what the Lord says, because if we do what he suggests, we will really have new strength. He says if we are despondent or feel weak, we must first be still. We must wait for him. We must quiet down our hearts, and by reading the Bible and speaking to the Lord, we will get new strength from him. In a wonderful way the Lord will give us new strength and courage. The secret is to wait for him and to trust him. You must tell the Lord that you trust him only. Be quiet before him, listen to his voice, and find new strength.

Jesus would become quiet.

In quietness and trust is your strength. (Isaiah 30:15)

I WANT IT!

An inheritance quickly gained ... will not be blessed at the end. (Proverbs 20:21)

There are things you want and don't always get. Yet you keep on thinking about them. You want them so badly that you nag your parents. You even ask the Lord to give you what you want.

It is not wrong to want certain things. Just make sure that things are not more important to you than people or God. If we want something badly, it is not wrong to ask the Lord. When I was a young boy there was something I wanted very badly. For quite a few months I wished I could have it; I even asked the Lord for it. When I gave up hope, the Lord gave it to me in a wonderful way, through an aunt and an uncle. The Lord sometimes gives us our heart's desire.

The Bible says we must not get something in a dishonest way. Some people want something so badly that they are prepared to be dishonest. They steal it. If you go on nagging your mother so much that she finally gives in and gets it for you, it is also dishonest. Grown-ups sometimes get possessions in a dishonest way. They tell lies. The Lord hates it.

Tell the Lord your wishes, and leave the matter in his hands.

Jesus would trust the
Father with his needs.

 In everything ... present your requests to God. (Philippians 4:6)

June 15

ADVICE FOR THE YOUNG

How can a young man keep his way pure? By living according to your word. (Psalm 119:9)

Young people are precious to the Lord. He wants to give them the best. His Word also speaks to young people. It is important to the Lord that young people keep their lives pure. If you are unclean in your youth, then you become a dirty grown-up. And you pass that dirt on to your children. When are you dirty in God's eyes? When sin has become a habit in your life.

Many young people in our country are caught up in the web of sin. They are destroying their own lives. Many young people are addicted to drugs, and some even have sexual relationships at a very early age. It hurts them, breaks them, and makes them dirty.

The Lord says a young person can keep his life pure in one way only: when he or she lives according to the Lord's Word. If we do what he wants, our lives will be pure. Hear the Word of God and live according to it.

Jesus would live
according to God's Word.

Your word is a lamp to my feet and a light to my path. (Psalm 119:105)

What Remains?

"The earth ... and the heavens ... will perish, but you remain." (Hebrews 1:10,11)

It's too bad that fun things don't last forever. A holiday is fun, but it passes so quickly. That delicious chocolate is finished before you know it. You wish you had more, but it is all gone. It is the same with life. Here on earth nothing lasts forever.

The Bible says God made heaven and earth. There are so many wonderful things on earth to enjoy. But these things pass. They will not be there forever. It is such a shame that some people live as if the earth will stay the same forever. They spend all their time and energy on their earthly possessions.

Yet only God will be there forever. That is why we should belong to him and he must be our Lord. We will never lose him. He is always there. He lives forever, and if we love him, we will live with him forever.

Make sure the Lord is important to you. Serve him and follow him. Love him. God and his kingdom, and that which he gives, will last forever. It will never pass away.

Jesus would store up his
treasures in heaven.

"Store up for yourselves treasures in heaven." (Matthew 6:20)

Bare Trees

They are ... autumn trees, without fruit and uprooted –
twice dead. (Jude 1:12)

Some people plant fruit trees in their gardens so that they
can enjoy the delicious fruit that the trees bear. They don't
just plant the tree, they water it and fertilize it so that the
fruit will be good. They wait the whole season for the fruit
to ripen so that they can enjoy it.

It sometimes happens that the fruit of a tree is disap-
pointing, in spite of the fact that it was cared for. Instead of
nice ripe fruit, there is sometimes no fruit at all, or the fruit
does not taste good. What a disappointment!

There are also people who don't bear good fruit. The
Bible says it is already late in the season, and some people
are still not bearing fruit. This means that they are already
getting old and still have no fruit in their lives. One would
expect people who have belonged to the church for a long
time and know about the things of the Lord to bear good
fruit so that everyone can enjoy the fruit on their tree of life.
But they are like dead trees that bear no fruit.

You must start bearing fruit when you are still young.
This is how you praise the name of the Lord.

Jesus would bear delicious fruit.

"For out of the overflow of his heart his mouth speaks." (Luke
6:45)

RICH AND POOR ARE EQUAL

Rich and poor have this in common: The LORD is the Maker of them all. (Proverbs 22:2)

It is typical of people to look down on those who are not as well off as they are. The rich sometimes have too much pride in their hearts and think a homeless person or someone who is very poor is not important. They think they are more important just because they have more money.

How fortunate we are that the Lord does not see us in that way. He doesn't mind if we are rich or poor. It does not matter to him how important we are in the eyes of people. It does not matter to him how much money we have in the bank. He doesn't even care if we are good-looking or ugly. He loves us just the way we are. He loves rich and poor – we're all equal in his eyes.

You and I must try to see people the way the Lord sees them. We must not treat some better just because they look better than others. You must not love that poor friend in your class less than the popular one who is rich. Ask the Lord to help you love all people equally, the same as he does.

Jesus would love
all people equally.

"For God so loved the world that he gave his one and only Son." (John 3:16)

June 19

Sun-Scorched and Dry

The LORD will guide you always; he will satisfy your needs in a sun-scorched land ... (Isaiah 58:11)

Israel is a very dry country. There are parts that are barren, just like a desert. In the time of the Bible there were no cars. People had to walk where they wanted to go. It was a slow way to travel, and they usually had some pack animal with them. This also made the journey difficult. In such a dry and barren place there is very little water. It is also usually very hot in a desert.

Our lives sometimes go through dry and barren patches. This means that things don't always go well for us. Sometimes you go through bad times, and you seem to be walking through a barren, sun-scorched desert. It could be that your mom and dad are getting divorced. You could be ill. Or you could be in some trouble at school. This makes you unhappy.

The Lord promises that he will help you and me and that he will guide us, his children, through the dry patches in our lives. He will take care of us. We need not be afraid. Even if you feel a bit down today, know that the Lord will take care of you and lead the way. Just trust him.

Jesus would ask for guidance
in difficult times.

"Father, if you are willing ... not my will, but yours be done."
(Luke 22:42)

June 20

I Give Back

"Whose ox have I taken?... Whom have I cheated? ... I will make it right." (1 Samuel 12:3)

Sometimes it's just not good enough to say you're sorry. You must also give back. If you have borrowed someone's pen and it broke, you must be willing to give that person a new one. If you have taken something from someone by accident, you must give it back. If you pick up something that someone has lost, you must try and find the owner so that you can give it back.

When Samuel came to the end of his life, he wanted to make sure that he did not have anything with him that belonged to another person. That is why he asked if he owed anyone anything. He wanted to set matters straight and give back. He wanted nobody to blame him for something he had not returned.

Maybe you have something that belongs to another person. You took it, or are still borrowing it. Give it back to its owner as soon as possible. Write a note or a card and say thank you for having it. Maybe you haven't thanked someone for something they did for you. Do it now. Don't be stingy with saying "thank you."

Jesus would never take
what does not belong to him.

"You shall not steal." (Exodus 20:15)

First Ask

He inquired of the LORD. Once again David inquired of the LORD. (1 Samuel 23:2, 4)

David was king of Israel and he had to fight the Philistines. The Philistines wanted to kill the Israelites. The Bible says that David inquired of the Lord. When you inquire about something, you ask about it. This means we must become quiet before the Lord. We must go to one side and speak to the Lord. We must pray, and we must also listen. We believe that he will give us wisdom. That is why we ask him. David asked.

Often something comes up in our thoughts and we decide that it is exactly what we want to do. We don't really ask anyone. Nor do we tell someone that we plan to do it. We just decide to do it. The safest way is to do what David did: first ask the Lord. Does the Lord want us to do it? Is it his will? First ask! Then we will not make so many mistakes.

Is there something important you have decided to do? Be quiet before the Lord, and ask him to help you. Ask him to open, or close, the door according to his will.

Jesus would ask the Lord
before he does anything.

"Father, if you are willing ... not my will, but yours be done." (Luke 22:42)

LIKE A FLEA

"The king of Israel has come out to look for a flea – as one hunts a partridge in the mountains." (1 Samuel 26:20)

Saul was the first king of Israel. He sinned against God, and the Lord renounced him. An evil, jealous spirit came into Saul's heart. One of the bad things he did was to try and kill David.

Saul and a few of his men went after David. David fled into the mountains and hid in caves. He knew Saul would kill him if he should get hold of him.

Yet, David was not bitter toward Saul. He trusted in the Lord. He still respected Saul because the Lord had made him king of Israel. There were times when David could have killed Saul, but he didn't. One day he was very close to Saul, and this is when he said he was like a flea, a tiny partridge that lives in the mountains. David's humility was so sincere that Saul felt sick at heart, *"I have sinned ... I will not try to harm you again."* (v. 21). Saul did not keep his promise, but the Lord kept David safe.

We must not think more highly of ourselves than we should. Be humble. The Lord will uplift you.

Jesus would be humble.

Do not think of yourself more highly than you ought. (Romans 12:3)

THE LORD LIVES!

The LORD lives! Praise be to my Rock! (Psalm 18:46)

Jesus died on the cross for our sins. When he breathed his last, his spirit passed into the hands of his Father. Then Jesus was taken down from the cross. He was dead. They wrapped his broken body in a clean linen cloth. Then they went and put him in a grave. Graves in those days were different from ours. They were like small rooms cut out of a rock. There they placed Jesus.

Jesus was in the grave for two days. On the third day, a miracle took place: Jesus woke up! The power of life in God overcame death in the body of Jesus. His heart began beating again. He was raised from the dead. The Lord was alive again. And he still lives!

If Jesus did not live today, we would not been able to talk to him. He would also not be in heaven to pray for us and to prepare a place for us. That Jesus lives is very important. Because he lives, he can talk to us through his Word and his Spirit. Because he lives, he is with us every moment of the day. You must allow him to live in your heart. Then you will also live with him forever.

Be still for a while. Tell the Lord you are very thankful that he is not dead. Praise him because he lives.

Jesus will always be with you.

 "And surely I am with you always, to the very end of the age." (Matthew 28:20)

June 24

THE STRANGE DONKEY

> Then the LORD opened the donkey's mouth, and she said to Balaam ... (Numbers 22:28)

Balaam was a messenger of the Lord. When the king of Moab wanted to use him to put a curse on the Israelites, God told Balaam that he must not do it. No one is allowed to put a curse on the people of the Lord. The king of Moab offered him a lot of money. But Balaam knew he should not go against God's will.

God said Balaam could go with the king's men, but Balaam was to say just what God wanted him to say. The Lord was a little angry with Balaam. Balaam had a donkey that was on the road with him. When the donkey refused to walk any farther, Balaam hit the donkey. Suddenly the donkey spoke to Balaam. Can you imagine how startled Balaam must have been? Surely donkeys cannot talk! After a while Balaam realized it was an angel talking to him. The angel told Balaam that his path was a dangerous one. Balaam then realized he had to do what the Lord said.

Because the Lord loves us and wants to use us, he gives us good advice. He can talk to us in many ways when we least expect it. Keep your ears open so that you can hear what the Lord wants to tell you. He even talked to Balaam through a donkey!

Jesus will talk to
you in many ways.

 One day ... he had a vision ... He distinctly saw an angel of God. (Acts 10:3)

June 25

THE PRIZE

Run in such a way as to get the prize. (1 Corinthians 9:24)

Athletes who run a race, run to win a prize. This prize is usually a cup or a trophy or a medal. Basketball, football, or hockey teams can also win a prize. In some sports, like tennis or golf, champions win big money.

We humans will also be rewarded or be given a prize at the end of our lives. There are both winners and losers in life, just like in a race or a match. The Bible says if you don't believe in Jesus and don't want to walk the road of life with him, you will be a loser one day. You won't get a prize. Only eternal damnation will be waiting for you. On the other hand, everyone who asks Jesus' forgiveness and has been led onto the right road by him, will get the prize of everlasting life.

Let's serve the Lord with all our hearts and with our whole lives. Then we will, one day at the end of our lives, get the prize from Jesus' hands.

Jesus will give you the best prize: everlasting life.

He who has the Son has life. (1 John 5:12)

June 26

THE RIGHT OINTMENT

The anointing you received from him remains in you.
(1 John 2:27)

In the time of the Bible, kings, priests or prophets were anointed with special oil. This oil had a lovely smell, almost like the nicest perfume today. This oil was usually poured onto someone's head as a sign that the person would be able to do his work. The ointment or oil was the sign of the Holy Spirit who would help that person.

When the Holy Spirit came down on Jesus, he was anointed for the work he had to do. The Bible says you and I have also been anointed. When we give our lives to Jesus, the Holy Spirit is like an ointment that gives us what is necessary to do the work of the Lord, just like in the Old Testament. The only difference is that every child of God is an anointed one, and not only special people. The Lord uses you and me, and he gives us the Holy Spirit so that we can be his instruments.

Thank the Lord that you have also received his Holy Spirit so that you can be used as his anointed one.

Jesus will anoint you
with the Holy Spirit.

Then the Spirit of the Lord came upon Gideon. (Judges 6:34)

June 27

GREET ONE ANOTHER!

Greet one another with a kiss of love. (1 Peter 5:14)

In some countries even men greet each other with a kiss. There are cultures where people don't kiss one another on the mouth, but they rub noses. Every country has its own customs, even with kissing.

In the time of the Bible, all people – not only those who were in love – kissed one another. When they greeted one another, they kissed. It was a sign that they loved and cared for one another. In our country, people who are close, like family or friends, also kiss when they greet each other.

We don't have to kiss everyone we see, but we must give one another a hearty greeting. A friendly person doesn't just walk past others; he or she greets them. It is always nice to be greeted with a smile by a friendly person. The Bible also says that Christians should always greet one another. They must do it heartily. They must show other Christians that they love them. They must not look the other way when they walk past someone.

Greet everybody you meet today, especially your Christian friends, and be friendly.

Jesus would greet everybody
in a friendly way.

Grace and peace to you from God our Father and from the Lord Jesus Christ. (Romans 1:7)

COME BACK

Return to the LORD your God, for he is gracious and compassionate, slow to anger and abounding in love. (Joel 2:13)

Sometimes people run away from God. Adam and Eve did. They lived close to God, but then decided to be disobedient. They ran away from God. It got so bad that they were chased out of the Garden of Eden. You and I can also run away from God. The Lord calls us to be close to him, but sometimes we go our own way.

Do you remember the story of the prodigal son? He decided to leave home, to go away from his father. He wanted to do his own thing and not what his father said. So he left home and thought he would have the time of his life in a country far away. But he made a mess of his life. He wasted all his money and started going hungry. He realized that he had made a mistake. He picked himself up and went back to his dad. There he was happy again. His father gave him the best. It was good to be back home.

The safest and best place to be is close to God. The Lord is full of love and very patient. If you are far away from him today, come back straight away. Tell him you are sorry that you strayed from him. He is waiting for you.

Jesus would not leave
his Father's home.

 "But while he was still a long way off, his father saw him ... He ran to his son, threw his arms around him and kissed him." (Luke 15:20)

June 29

Sow and Reap

Do not be deceived; God cannot be mocked. A man reaps what he sows. (Galatians 6:7)

Everything you and I do has consequences. If we put our hand on the hot stove, we will be burned. If we drive into a wall, we will get hurt. If we keep on watching ugly things on TV, we will become ugly in our hearts.

There are also positive consequences of what we do. If you have studied hard you will probably get good grades. If you sleep enough, you will be well rested. If you treat others well, they will do the same to you. When you serve the Lord, your love for him grows.

The Bible says what you sow, you will reap. A farmer sows wheat grain and expects to get wheat. If you plant corn, peach trees won't come up there. The fruit in our lives depends on the good or bad seed we sowed. If you think bad things, you will do bad things: *"The one who sows to please his sinful nature, from that nature will reap destruction; the one who sows to please the Spirit, from the Spirit will reap eternal life"* (Galatians 6:8).

See that you do what is good and right according to God's will.

Jesus would sow good seeds.

 Whoever sows sparingly, will reap sparingly, and whoever sows generously will also reap generously. (2 Corinthians 9:6)

June 30

WHOM ARE YOU INVITING?

Philip found Nathanael and told him ... "Come and see." (John 1:45, 46)

There once was a man called Philip. He had a friend named Nathanael. One day Philip met up with Nathanael. They stood talking, and then Philip told Nathanael about an exciting thing that had happened to him. It was something very important.

Philip met Jesus one day. He saw him and heard what he had to say. While he was listening to Jesus, he was sure that Jesus was the Redeemer that God had sent. The more he listened to Jesus, the more he realized the truth of this. When Philip saw Nathanael, he was very excited and told him about Jesus – that he was the one Moses wrote about in the Law and the one about whom the prophets had spoken. Nathanael was not impressed. His first reaction was to ask if anything good could possibly come from Nazareth. He could not believe that this Jesus could be so important. But Philip invited Nathanael to come and see for himself. A miracle took place. Jesus talked to Nathanael, and Nathanael realized that Jesus was the Son of God.

Nathanael believed in Jesus because his friend Philip told him about Jesus. Do you tell people about Jesus?

Jesus would tell everybody
he is the Redeemer.

So the other disciples told him [Thomas], "We have seen the Lord!" (John 20:25)

July 1

Two Roads

> "Wide is the gate and broad is the road that leads to destruction ... but small is the gate and narrow the road that leads to life." (Matthew 7:13, 14)

The Bible tells us there are only two roads to choose between. One road is a broad road. It looks like a good road. There are many people on this road. Unfortunately, this road leads to a very bad place. The Bible calls it the place of destruction. We also call it hell.

Fortunately, there is also another road. According to the Bible this is a narrow road. Not that many people take this road. Few people manage to find this road. This is the road that leads to life. Although few people walk on this road, they know they are on the right road if they do. They are very lucky, because the Lord walks this road with them. This is the road to life, or heaven.

You must choose which road you want to take. Some people travel on the broad road from birth and never decide to change to the narrow road. The Lord calls us to choose the narrow road. It is the Lord's road. On this road we ask what the Lord's will is and then we live according to it. On this road we follow Jesus. Which road are you on?

Jesus would take the narrow road.

"Make every effort to enter through the narrow door." (Luke 13:24)

ON THE ROAD WITH JESUS

"Were not our hearts burning within us while he talked with us on the road and opened the Scriptures to us?" (Luke 24:32)

After Jesus' resurrection, two of his disciples were on the road to Emmaus. As they talked, Jesus came up to them and started interpreting the Scriptures for them. This means he taught them about the things written in the Word of God. While they were on the way, they learned what the Lord's will was, especially about his own death and resurrection.

Later on he ate something with them, and only then did they realize it was Jesus. Then he suddenly disappeared. They were amazed and started talking to each other. They were excited about what had happened, and they told each other what a wonderful warm feeling came into their hearts when he talked to them about the things of his Father.

Something you cannot explain happens to you when the Lord speaks to your heart. You get a feeling of peace and joy. It is a warm feeling. Not hot like a boiling kettle, but nice and warm deep down inside you. You and I must make time regularly to listen to the Lord so that he can nourish our spirit and fill us with the warmth of his love.

Go on the road with Jesus today. Also talk to him while you are on your way. Allow him to explain his Word to you.

Jesus would teach you from his Word.

The unfolding of your words gives ... understanding to the simple. (Psalm 119:130)

July 3

FREEDOM DAY

"So if the Son sets you free, you will be free indeed."
(John 8:36)

Many countries have special days on which they celebrate the freedom which they enjoy. In South Africa, that day is 27 April, the French celebrate on 14 July and today is Independence Day in America. It is wonderful to live in a land of liberty where individual rights and choices are honored and protected.

The Bible, however, says that one is not free simply because one lives in a free country. Even if there is not war or a conflict in a country, there can be many bonds that bind people. It does not have to be political bonds; bonds of hatred and bad relationships between people are just as real. There are also all kinds of other ugly things that keep a person from being free. For example, people who are addicted to liquor can say they live in a free country, and yet they are the slaves of alcohol.

Jesus said very clearly that a person is never really free if he is not free from sin. Jesus is the great Liberator. He wants to free you and me from the burden of sin. He helps us rid ourselves of any addiction.

Spread this message of freedom: Jesus is the Person who brings true liberty and freedom. He frees us from sin, from the devil, and also from ourselves.

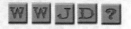

Jesus will free you.

Since we have now been justified by his blood. (Romans 5:9)

July 4

WHO ARE YOUR FRIENDS?

Blessed is the man who does not walk in the counsel of the wicked or stand in the way of sinners or sit in the seat of mockers. (Psalm 1:1)

Although we are children of this world, we are not to live like worldly children. We chose to follow Jesus, and that is why we try to do what the Lord tells us to.

The Word tells us that we will be blessed if we do certain things, and not blessed if we do others. Our scripture says we will be blessed if we choose our friends well. A Christian is friendly to all people, whether they know the Lord or not. But a Christian cannot become close friends with just anybody. Our best friends must be friends who also know the Lord and love him.

Although we need to be friends with all sorts of people, if we choose as our best friends people who don't have the Lord in their hearts (the wicked), or do not think the way they should (mockers), or have not yet given their sins to Jesus to be washed away (sinners), we might find it more difficult to serve the Lord. Bad friends can influence us in a bad way. It would be better to choose friends from those who follow the counsel of the Lord and want to think like him, those who have been washed clean of their sins. Who are your best friends?

Jesus would choose
friends who follow him.

So I stand aloof from the counsel of the wicked. (Job 21:16)

July 5

UNREST

Why do the nations conspire and the peoples plot in vain? (Psalm 2:1)

All over the world there is unrest and strife. Every day we see on TV or read in the papers about warring countries. People kill one another, and we hear of uprisings and dissatisfaction. Many children go hungry or get hurt and die because they are caught up in a war where they live. Why is there so much unrest and strife?

Psalm 2 tells us that the real reason for all the warring and strife is that the kings on earth are rising up against the Lord and against Jesus. They are saying, *"Let us break their chains ... and throw off their fetters."* (v. 3). There is unrest in the world because kings and presidents and the leaders of countries do not want to bow to God and accept his rule.

Jesus came to build a kingdom of peace. He promised that if we follow him we will live in peace. If countries and their leaders will accept the kingship of Jesus, there will be peace.

Let us pray for our country and our leaders. Ask that they will follow Jesus and do things according to his Word.

Jesus would pray
for the whole world.

We have one who speaks to the Father in our defense – Jesus Christ, the Righteous One. (1 John 2:1)

July 6

LIFT UP MY HEAD

You bestow glory on me and lift up my head. (Psalm 3:3)

What God thinks of you and me is most important. It is, however, also important what others think of us. Every one of us has an opinion of another human being. Opinions differ and are often wrong, but yet it is important what people think of us.

Sometimes we do something that makes people change their opinion of us. If we do something good, someone might think we are not as bad as he thought we were. If we do something wrong, someone's opinion of us can also change. Someone may have thought we were good inside, but now she's not sure any more.

It is important that the Lord's opinion of us must be correct. We all make mistakes and all of us sometimes do things that are not right. If we tell the Lord that we are sorry, he forgives us. His opinion doesn't change. He knows we are sinful, but he sees we are feeling bad about it, and that is enough for him. He can give us back our esteem and lift up our heads. If we, from now on, live our forgiveness as we should, the Lord will see to it that people's bad opinions of us will be corrected. You just serve the Lord faithfully. He will lift up your head.

Jesus would change
people's opinions of him.

"Repent and believe the good news!" (Mark 1:15)

July 7

My Heart Is Overflowing

> You have filled my heart with greater joy than when ... grain and new wine abound. (Psalm 4:7)

We all make the mistake of thinking if we have possessions we will be happy. Some think if they get a bigger house they will be happy. Others think if they can drive a better car they will be happy. Perhaps you think if you can get a new bicycle you will be happy. Or a nice watch, or a lovely dress, or that special something you so badly want.

David was a king and he had many possessions. Still he wrote these words to tell you and me that he has learned that many possessions do not really make one happy. It is not what you have that makes you happy, but what you have in you. You are not made happy by things that come from outside. It depends on what is in your heart. There are many happy people who have very few earthly possessions. There are also many unhappy people with lots of possessions.

The Lord gives us much more happiness in our lives than anything else can. This is what David says. His heart was overflowing with the joy of the Lord.

Jesus would choose life
above earthly possessions.

"What good will it be for a man if he gains the whole world, yet forfeits his soul?" (Matthew 16:26)

July 8

SCARED OF THE NIGHT

I will lie down and sleep in peace, for you alone, O LORD, make me dwell in safety. (Psalm 4:8)

We live in a very unsafe world. Every day we hear about people who are attacked and shot even in their own homes. This is enough to scare anyone. Bad people often use the dark of the night to commit their crimes. Maybe it is this that makes you scared of the dark.

David, as a king, had many worries. One day his son Absalom did something very bad. He rebelled against his dad. It was so bad that David had to flee for his life. Yet we hear him say that he will lie down and sleep in peace. This tells us that David had complete trust in the Lord. He believed that God alone could protect him. He slept peacefully.

You and I must tell the Lord every day and every night that he alone can protect us. Then we will be able to sleep peacefully. He is with us. He never slumbers or sleeps.

Jesus would not be afraid.

Even though I walk through the valley of the shadow of death, I will fear no evil, for you are with me. (Psalm 23:4)

THE NEW MORNING

In the morning, O Lord, you hear my voice; in the morning I lay my requests before you and wait in expectation. (Psalm 5:3)

In the morning when we get up, there is usually lots to do. Some of us must make our beds. We must rub the sleep from our eyes and quickly wash. We must eat breakfast and get ready for the day. We must brush our teeth and make sure that our hair is combed neatly.

An important thing we must not forget is that we must, as soon as possible after we have woken up, speak to the Lord. As soon as you are awake, say, "Good morning, Lord." Ask him to be with you all day long. If you have a moment later on, read a few verses of Scripture; see what he says and pray for specific things. The Lord listens to your voice in the morning.

If we pray, we will receive. Talk to the Lord now.

Jesus would get up early and speak to his Father.

He wakens me morning by morning, wakens my ear to listen like one being taught. (Isaiah 50:4)

HEAL ME

O LORD, heal me, for my bones are in agony. (Psalm 6:2)

There are many millions of people in the world who are sick today. Maybe you are also sick. It's not nice to be ill, because then you cannot play like other children.

There are many children of God who are in the hospital today or are suffering. When humans fell into sin, everything the Lord made was damaged. Our sick bodies are part of the brokenness, a consequence of the sin of Adam and Eve, and often not because you and I have sinned.

Fortunately, we as Christians can ask the Lord to help us when we are ill. David did. He asked the Lord to please make him well. The Lord helps us in all our troubles. He helps us when we are ill. He helps us in his way. Many people don't get well, but they can feel that the Lord is helping them. The way in which they can still joyfully praise the Lord, is a wonderful testimony.

Ask the Lord in faith to heal you. If you are not ill, think of someone you know who is ill. Pray for him or her now, or write a card and say you will pray for him and are thinking of him. Thank the Lord for your health.

Jesus would care for sick people.

People brought to him all who were ill ... and he healed them. (Matthew 4:24)

It's Not Fair!

God is a righteous judge. (Psalm 7:11)

People are often treated unfairly. It means that you get what you did not deserve. Someone else did something wrong and now you get blamed. You were not supposed to be punished, but you got in trouble anyway. Someone else was bad and now you are scolded! Surely that's not fair.

Sometimes you and I can say we didn't do it because we were not guilty. There are times we cannot even do that. We just hear that someone blamed us behind our backs for something we didn't do. It is impossible for us to defend ourselves. Then it is sometimes just better to let it go and to accept that there is nothing you can do. There will always be unfairness in life. It can happen that someone's electricity gets cut off because other residents in the neighborhood didn't pay their bills. That sounds most unfair!

Luckily there is a fair judge: the Lord. He knows what goes on in your heart. He can be trusted. Every one of us will stand before his throne one day. God will pass judgment. Every instance in which you and I were treated unfairly, or were accused of something we didn't do, will come out into the open. The Lord will clear us. He will also punish as he sees fit. If you are treated unfairly today, give the matter to God. Just make sure you live the way you should and do what he tells you.

Jesus would leave
everything to the Father.

You are always righteous, O LORD, when I bring a case before you. (Jeremiah 12:1)

July 12

Sing a New Song

Sing to the LORD a new song; sing to the LORD all the earth. (Psalm 96:1)

The Bible says in a few places that we must sing a new song to the Lord. Does this mean that we must look for songs that we have never heard? That we must sing only fresh, new songs?

When something is old, it is the opposite of something that is new. Thus the Bible says that old songs are songs sung in the hearts and thoughts of people still living with sin. Sin always makes things feel old. Sin often looks fresh and new, but very soon you find out that this is not true. Sin hurts. Sin gets moldy. Sin is dull. Sin brings unhappiness. Jesus, on the other hand, gives us new life. Together with new life, new songs come.

A broken guitar or a broken violin cannot play beautiful music. A broken instrument makes music that is off key, "old" music. Only when you fix the guitar or violin can you play fresh, new music. In the same way the Lord fixes us when we have sinned, and we can sing new songs to please him. Everything in our lives and in our hearts that praises the Lord – that is what the Bible calls a new song.

Let us praise the Lord with our new lives, and let's sing him a new song!

Jesus would sing a new song.

I will sing of your love and justice. (Psalm 101:1)

July 13

TIME IS IMPORTANT

Make the most of every opportunity. (Colossians 4:5)

Time is like a stream. The water flows past, and when each drop of water has flowed past, it will never come that way again. It is the same with our time. We have an opportunity to do things today. If we don't do them, we might never be able to do them again. Today's time we cannot have over again tomorrow.

It is important to the Lord that we use every opportunity to live for him. Every second is precious. Every minute is important. Every hour that we can live for him is valuable. We must know that every day could be our last. Every month gives us the opportunity to tell others about him and to live for him. Every year is a precious opportunity to learn more about the Lord.

We don't know how old we will get. We don't know if we will still be alive next year. That is why it is important to make the best of the time we have. Of course we must go to school, eat, play, rest, chat, and lots more. But while we are doing it, we must make sure we do it to the best of our ability and to the glory of God.

Thank the Lord now for this day. Make the best of it!

Jesus would make the
best use of every moment.

Making the most of every opportunity ... (Ephesians 5:16)

July 14

EMBRACE HIM!

Exalt the LORD our God. (Psalm 99:5)

To praise the Lord is wonderful. When we praise him, we sing merry, joyful songs that say the Lord is great and wonderful. Songs of praise are full of joy. We make sounds to say that we are excited because the Lord is wonderful.

Christians don't sing only songs of praise, but also songs to worship. Worshiping the Lord is a little different from praising him. The Bible uses a word for worship that means something like "to come closer, to embrace, or to kiss." What this word wants to say is that we must sometimes be quiet before the Lord and have the need in our hearts to embrace and to kiss him. When you love someone like your mom or dad, you enjoy holding them, giving them a hug, or kissing them.

We cannot embrace the Lord or kiss him like a human. He is not in a body here with us. But we can love the Lord with our hearts and in our thoughts, and we can show him this love. We can tell him of our love and feel it deep in our hearts. We can also sing him songs of worship. Come, let's worship him right now.

Jesus would worship the Father.

Worship him who lives for ever and ever. (Revelation 4:10)

July 15

LIKE GRASS

As for man, his days are like grass ... the wind blows over it and it is gone. (Psalm 103:15, 16)

Some people reach the age of ninety. Others forty. Then there are those who die very young. Our lives are transient. This means that nothing lasts forever, it comes to an end. I'm sure you have flowers in your garden. Today you see a beautiful flower, but tomorrow or the next day the flower has wilted and has died. You will never see that flower again. It is the same with the grass in the fields. One day the grass is green and luxuriant, but soon it wilts and dies. It is the same with a human life. We don't live on earth forever. People who may be fit and strong today, could be dead tomorrow.

Only people who accept the new life Jesus gives, will live forever. The Bible says only the Word of God will live forever. If we keep his Word in our hearts, this Word inside us means that you and I will not perish, but live forever. Yes, of course we will die, but we live forever in Jesus. God's Word is in you and me. Are you also pleased that you will live forever?

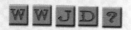

Jesus will let you live forever.

"He who believes in me will live, even though he dies." (John 11:25)

July 16

THE STONE

The stone the builders rejected has become the cap-stone. (Psalm 118:22)

One day some people wanted to erect a building. They built with stone. Among all the other stones was a very special stone. The builders were very fussy and they didn't want to use just any stone. This special stone looked quite ordinary to them, so they took this stone and threw it to one side. God, however, knew that this was a special stone. He used it as the most important stone in his building. He made it the cornerstone or foundation of the building.

This is just a story, but this is what happened to Jesus. When Jesus came to earth, the Pharisees and scribes thought that he was just an ordinary person. But Jesus was very special, even if they didn't think so. They renounced him and had him killed. But God used Jesus' life to become the most important stone in his kingdom. God used Jesus as a cornerstone to build the new Jerusalem, where all the children of God will live together happily.

Praise the Lord that he used Jesus as the cornerstone.

Jesus would choose God's plan.

Come to him, the living Stone. (1 Peter 2:4)

CALL OUT "LORD!"

I call on the LORD in my distress, and he answers me.
(Psalm 120:1)

Have you ever been in big trouble? Sometimes things happen to us that make us so anxious that we feel sick. It could be that you lost something very valuable. At that moment when you realized it, your heart missed a beat. Or you could have been somewhere on a cliff and your foot slipped. You could have been hurt very badly. You were really startled. It can also happen that you are walking across the street and suddenly you see a car coming right at you. You feel as if a cold hand is gripping your heart.

The Bible says a child of the Lord calls out to God in a moment of crisis. It is the right thing to do. You can even start praying out loud when you realize you are in trouble. Don't be ashamed to do it. Call out to God; he is there with you. It will be good for everyone, including the devil and his henchmen, to hear that you put your trust in the Lord. Calling on the name of the Lord, is like running to hide safely in a strong tower.

Remember that you can always call upon the Lord in your distress.

Jesus would call upon the Father.

"Call upon me ... I will deliver you." (Psalm 50:15)

July 18

THE TEARS WERE FLOWING

By the rivers of Babylon we sat and wept when we remembered Zion. (Psalm 137:1)

Israel did evil in the eyes of the Lord. Therefore God allowed them to be exiled to Babylon. The Babylonians were a heathen nation. They did not believe in God. The Israelites found it very difficult to live in a foreign country.

Someone then wrote a song that tells how they sat at the rivers of Babylon and cried because they missed Zion, the mountain on which the beautiful city of Jerusalem stood. Actually they didn't even want to sing any more: *"How can we sing the songs of the Lord while in a foreign land?"* (v. 4). Although the Israelites did sing, their songs sounded like songs of mourning, because they were sad.

If you are not prepared to do the will of the Lord, you cannot really be happy. If you drag your sins along with you, you will always reach a point where the happiness and joy in your heart disappear. Sin always brings unhappiness. You and I cannot sing in our hearts and be joyful if we sin. Then the tears flow in our hearts, and the joy of the Lord disappears.

Won't you make sure that you don't land up at the rivers of Babylon? It is a place of sin. There is no joy. There are no songs. There are only tears.

Jesus would wipe the tears from your eyes.

He will wipe every tear from their eyes. (Revelation 21:4)

July 19

A Parent's Advice

Listen, my sons, to a father's instruction; pay attention and gain understanding. (Proverbs 4:1)

Moms and dads must teach their children and advise them. When fathers and mothers don't really love their children, then it's not important to them what their children do. Parents who care about them, teach their children well. It is good when parents teach their children right from wrong.

Children, on the other hand, don't always take the advice of their parents to heart. This means they don't take notice of it. Or they are irritated by it. They don't want their parents' advice. The Bible says this is wrong. It is a foolish child who does not want to accept advice from his or her parents. We do not always like getting advice from older people because we often think what we want to do is better. Accept that grown-ups have more experience in life, and that is why their advice is good. Remember, they were children too; they know how a child feels.

My father and mother are not alive anymore, but I am very glad about the advice they gave me. It helped me to make the right decisions. Be thankful if you still have a father and a mother who can help you, talk to you, give you advice, and show you the right way. Thank the Lord for your parents right now.

Jesus would accept
his Father's advice.

Children, obey your parents. (Ephesians 6:1)

July 20

LIKE THE RISING SUN

"May they who love you be like the sun when it rises in its strength." (Judges 5:31)

Especially in winter, it is lovely when the sun shines brightly. Sun brings warmth. When you open the curtains in a cold house, the room quickly becomes nice and warm. When we sit in the winter sun, our bodies warm up. Do you also think sunrise is better than the cold, dark night?

The Bible says whoever loves the Lord can shine brightly like the rising sun. Their lives, the way they act, their friendliness and love, can be like bright sunshine on a cold winter's day. You and I can, as children of the Lord, bring light and warmth wherever we go. Jesus said we must be the light of the world. Jesus himself is called the light of the world. If he, the brightest light, lives in us, our lives are also lit up, and we will shine like bright sunbeams in the dark.

There is much darkness in life: the darkness of sin. There is pain, distress and heartache. Many people have no hope in their hearts. To them life is dark. You and I can make a difference in their lives. Let us shine with and for Jesus.

Bring sunshine today wherever you go.

Jesus would let his light
shine in the darkness.

The light shines in the darkness. (John 1:5)

ENOUGH

"Even if she gathers among the sheaves, don't embarrass her." (Ruth 2:15)

Ruth was Naomi's daughter-in-law. Naomi lived in a far country. After her husband's and sons' deaths, she wanted to go back to Bethlehem where she came from. Ruth decided to go with her mother-in-law, to be with her to support and help her. Ruth was a good woman.

In Bethlehem they had to find food to eat. Ruth went to the fields where they were harvesting the wheat. As the men were gathering the sheaves, some leftover grain remained in the fields. In those times poor people were allowed to gather behind the harvesters. This cornfield belonged to Boaz. Boaz was a good man. He saw how hard Ruth was working and he told his men to leave more grain behind so that she could gather more. It was the Lord working in Boaz's heart, causing him to take pity on Ruth. Later Boaz took Ruth as his wife.

The Lord looks after his children. Ruth didn't know where she would find food, but the Lord saw to it that she was noticed. Ruth worked hard, and the Lord blessed her. The Lord wants to take care of you too. He has a plan for your life, and he knows what you should have. He will see to it that you are noticed if it is his will. Just trust him, like Ruth, and the Lord will also bless your future.

Jesus would trust the Father.

"I am coming to you now." (John 17:13)

LEADERS

> In those days Israel had no king; everyone did as he saw fit. (Judges 21:25)

In Judges 21 we read how the young men from Benjamin (the Benjamites) hid in the vineyards, and when the young girls from the town of Shiloh came out to dance in the field, they rushed out from the vineyards, and each one grabbed himself a wife. What a way to get a wife! I don't know if the Lord was very happy with this because the chapter closes saying that at the time there was no king, and everyone did as they pleased. If all of us do what we please, life will be very confusing. Just think: if everyone drives a car as fast as he likes, there will be even more accidents on the roads. If all of us stole what we wanted to have, none of our things would ever be safe again.

That is why it is so important to have leaders. Leaders are people who are chosen or appointed to see that rules are obeyed. Rules or laws are necessary for order. Your school has rules. You can't do just as you please; you must keep the rules. There are principals or leaders who see to this. Obey them, pray for them, support them. It is your duty to keep to the rules and obey leaders.

Jesus would respect leaders.

The authorities ... have been established by God. (Romans 13:1)

SHE PLEADED

She named him Samuel, saying, "Because I asked the
LORD for him." (1 Samuel 1:20)

Long ago there was a woman called Hannah. Her husband's name was Elkanah. He loved Hannah very much.
Although Hannah lived a good life, she was deeply troubled. She could not have a baby. She wanted a baby badly,
but although they had been married a long time, she and her
husband had no children. Then Hannah went to the temple.

Hannah pleaded with God and begged that he would
work a miracle. She also made the Lord a promise. She said
if she had a child, she would give this child to the Lord. She
would bring this child to the temple, and he could work
there for the Lord and serve him. The Lord answered
Hannah's prayer. A miracle happened! Suddenly she was
expecting a baby. Later on the baby was born. His name was
Samuel. When Samuel was big enough, she took him to the
temple, and there he worked for the Lord. Samuel became
an important man in Israel. He was a prophet of the Lord.
He told people about the Lord.

Hannah kept her promise. She asked the Lord for
something and then did what she promised. Perhaps there
is something you want very badly. Ask the Lord for it. And
remember, if you make a promise to the Lord, you must
keep it.

Jesus would keep his promises.

"Simply let your 'Yes' be 'Yes,' and your 'No' 'No'."
(Matthew 5:37)

July 24

THE RIGHT FRIENDS

Accompanied by valiant men whose hearts God had touched. (1 Samuel 10:26)

The people of Israel wanted a king. Actually the Lord was their king, but because they did not have enough faith, they wanted an earthly king like all the other nations. So the Lord gave them a king, but he warned them that kings can make life difficult. The first king was Saul. Saul was just an ordinary young man and the son of a farmer. Suddenly he was a king. He must have felt a bit lonely and also unsure of how he should behave.

Then God made a plan. The Lord "touched" the hearts of a number of brave men. This means that the Lord put it into their hearts that they should support Saul. Deep in their hearts they got the feeling that they had to go with Saul and help him. We can also say the Lord called them to support the new king.

God knows that you and I can sometimes not do what we have to do when we are alone. Then he touches the hearts of friends so that they can love and support us. It is wonderful when the Lord gives us people to be with us and to help us. Of course, the devil also sends bad people to us because the devil wants to take us away from God. Pray that the Lord will send you the right friends.

Jesus would choose
the right friends.

"Is this the love you show your friend? Why didn't you go with your friend?" (2 Samuel 16:17)

July 25

God's Answers

But God did not answer him that day. (1 Samuel 14:37)

We know that we can't hear the voice of the Lord the way we can another person's. God's voice has no sound. God talks in different ways. He speaks to us through the Holy Spirit and through his Word. Sometimes he speaks through people, but what they say will never go against God's Word.

The Lord answers us. If you have prayed about a thing and have asked the Lord to give you wisdom, he will sometimes give you an answer deep inside your heart. You just know what his will is. Then there are times when you ask and ask and get no reply. It is as if the Lord is keeping quiet. That may be because you are asking things that go against his will. Sometimes you ask the Lord to give you things and you don't get them. You wonder why. The reason is perhaps that it would not be good for you to have those things. Then the Lord keeps quiet. He does not give an answer to your prayer. You must just trust that the Lord knows best. If what you have asked for is really meant for you, he will give it to you, at the right time.

Go on trusting Jesus, even if you sometimes wonder why he doesn't answer the way you want him to.

Jesus would be patient
when God keeps quiet.

O my God, I cry out by day, but you do not answer ... (Psalm 22:2)

GOD SEES INSIDE

"The LORD does not look at the things man looks at. Man looks at the outward appearance, but the LORD looks at the heart." (1 Samuel 16:7)

King Saul disappointed the Lord, and so the Lord decided to choose a new king. In Bible days the prophets anointed a new king. They poured oil onto his head, and that was the sign that he was the new king. Samuel was the prophet who had to anoint the new king. He didn't know whom he had to anoint. All he knew was that it would be one of the sons of a man named Jesse.

Jesse had eight sons. They were good-looking, big, and strong. Samuel thought the biggest and strongest and most attractive son would most probably become the king of Israel. But God wanted someone who was attractive in his heart. The Lord did not choose any of the elder brothers, and soon only one was left – the son named David. He was the youngest, and not the strongest or the best looking. When Samuel saw David, the Lord spoke in Samuel's heart and told him that this was the new king and that he had to anoint him.

The Lord does not always choose the strongest or the most attractive people. He chooses every one of us who is willing to do his will.

Jesus would look at your heart.

Motives are weighed by the LORD. (Proverbs 16:2)

July 27

Peace in Music

> Whenever the spirit ... came upon Saul, David would take his harp and play. Then relief would come to Saul, ... and the evil spirit would leave him. (1 Samuel 16:23)

Because Saul sinned, the Lord allowed an evil spirit to trouble him and make him unhappy. If we don't have the Holy Spirit in our hearts, evil spirits can come into our lives and make us unhappy.

David played the harp beautifully. The harp in those days was a stringed instrument, nearly like a guitar. David learned to play the harp when he looked after his father's sheep in the fields. That is where he sang many of the psalms that we can still read in the Bible today. Saul often asked David to play him some music. This happened especially when Saul's heart was troubled by the evil spirit in him. Whenever David began playing, the evil spirit would leave Saul, and he would have peace in his heart again.

Songs or music sung or played by Christians help to bring Christ's light and peace into the world.

Jesus would be there,
in your songs of praise.

Yet you are enthroned as the Holy One; you are the praise of Israel. (Psalm 22:3)

Someone Else

He is the one who will build a house for my Name.
(2 Samuel 7:13)

King David loved the Lord. He was a successful king and very famous. The Israelites prospered when he was king. David was happy and blessed.

Still, there was something David wanted to do very badly: he wanted to build a house for the Lord. In the Old Testament times the Lord did not live inside people like today. They had to go to a building or tent that was set aside for talking to the Lord or worshiping him. David wanted to build a big and beautiful temple for the Lord. He dreamed about it and he planned to build this place for God.

But the Lord had his own plan. The Lord wanted David's son to build this temple. The prophet Nathan came to tell David this.

Maybe David was very disappointed. But he accepted God's decision. Sometimes you and I also want to do something badly, but the Lord wants to use someone else. We may be disappointed, but the Lord knows best.

Jesus would always
obey the Lord's orders.

Then you will be prosperous and successful. (Joshua 1:8)

An Evil Plan

He got up and went down to take possession of Naboth's vineyard. (1 Kings 21:16)

King Ahab was a bad man who did not do what the Lord wanted. He even married a wicked woman, Jezebel.

Ahab had enough money and possessions. But he was not satisfied. He saw a very nice vineyard. It belonged to Naboth. He told Naboth that he wanted to buy the vineyard. Naboth did not want to sell it because he had inherited the ground. It was special to him. Then king Ahab started sulking and lay down on his bed with his face to the wall, and he didn't want to eat. His bad wife told him what to do; it was an evil plan.

Ahab arranged for two men to lie about Naboth. They accused him of doing things that he had not done. The men then came to the king and told him that Naboth had cursed both God and the king. Ahab ordered that Naboth had to be stoned to death. After Naboth's death the king took Naboth's vineyard for himself.

People will sometimes do terrible things for very wrong reasons. You should ask the Lord to give you what you want. Don't ever hurt someone just because you want something that belongs to him.

Jesus would be satisfied
with what God gives him.

"You shall not covet ... anything that belongs to your neighbor." (Exodus 20:17)

July 30

You Will Be Comforted

If you pick up a baby unexpectedly or put him in the arms of a stranger, he will usually start crying. This happens because the baby does not feel safe. You and I also have things that make us feel insecure and afraid.

The Lord does not want us to feel insecure. The devil likes it when we are scared at night and lie awake because we see all kinds of scary pictures in our heads of people killing or hurting one another. One of the weapons the devil uses is fear. The more he can scare us, the happier he is, for then he knows we can't give our best.

When a child feels insecure, he or she usually runs to Mommy, where there is safety. Mothers and fathers protect their children and take them in their arms so that they can feel there is no danger. *If there is any danger, Dad or Mom will make sure that I am not hurt*, the child reasons. As a mother comforts her child, the Lord will also comfort you and me. We must just trust him, run to him, and shelter with him. We can tell him all our fears. He will put his arms around us and we will feel safe.

Are you afraid of something? Allow the peace of the Lord into your heart. Put your trust in him. He will comfort you.

Jesus would put his
trust in the Father.

So do not fear, for I am with you. (Isaiah 41:10)

July 31

THREE IMPORTANT THINGS

"This is the one I esteem: he who is humble and contrite in spirit, and trembles at my word." (Isaiah 66:2)

When the Lord looks at a person, there are some things that are important to him. If he finds them in a person, he is like a father who looks at his child with satisfaction and love. The first thing of importance is that we must not be proud. We must realize our need and ask help. If we do, we can be helped. A proud person will not admit that he needs help. That is why the Lord cannot help a proud person.

The second thing is to repent of our sins. If you don't say you are sorry about your sins you cannot be forgiven. People who don't want to admit to their sins pretend they do not need God. If you confess your sins, God will forgive you.

The third important thing the Lord likes very much is when his words are important to us. He likes people who respect his words. In the Bible, God says that he honors the one who "trembles at my word." This means that we must have respect for what the Lord says, and we must know that it is important not only to hear what he says, but also to do it.

I hope that when the Lord looks at you today, he will feel satisfied because you tell him that you need him, you are sorry about your sins, and you listen to his words and then do what he says.

Jesus would do what the Word says.

With my lips I recount all the laws that come from your mouth. (Psalm 119:13)

August 1

BROKEN CISTERNS

... broken cisterns that cannot hold water. (Jeremiah 2:13)

In the time of the Bible, people didn't have taps in their homes that they could just turn on to get water. They had to go to a well, or another source of water, and there they had to draw water and carry it home in something like a stone jug or a pail.

A jug or a pail can hold water only if it does not have holes in it. Otherwise it will leak. Can you think how stupid it would be if you kept drawing water and the more you drew, the less you had in your jug? This would not work.

One day the Lord told Jeremiah that his followers were just like people trying to draw water with a jug that has a hole in it. The more water they drew, the less water they had, because they kept on losing the water. The Lord used this image to show that people did not put their trust in him, but in ordinary people with shortcomings. During that time, Israel had come to an agreement with Egypt that Egypt would help them. But God said they must not put their trust in Egypt, but in him. He would help them.

You and I also put our trust in things or people to help us. No, says the Bible, we must trust God. We must ask his help. He will never disappoint us like a broken jug.

Jesus would trust the Father.

Do not put your trust in princes, in mortal men, who cannot save. (Psalm 146:3)

August 2

GOD'S SAD HEART

My heart is faint within me. Listen to the cry of my people from a land far away. (Jeremiah 8:18, 19)

Have you ever wondered if God can be sad? After all, he is the great God of heaven and earth. Can he also feel as you and I do? Yes, the Bible talks about the Lord as if he can.

We read in the Bible that the Lord was very sad when he looked at the people of Israel. He wanted only the best for them, but they sinned. Then he looked at them and saw how they were suffering. A person who lives with sin always suffers. What the Lord saw made him sad and upset. He saw how troubled they were in their distress. Then he said, *"Since my people are crushed, I am crushed; I mourn, and horror grips me"* (v. 21).

The Lord so badly wants to comfort his people and heal them, to be like an ointment that will heal the wounds of their hurt. He wishes they will accept him and come back to him. He knows that will be the only solution. Only he can help them.

Sometimes the Lord is also worried about you and me. He is sad because we do the wrong things. He knows they won't make us happy. He wants so badly for us to come closer to him so that he can heal us. Come to the Lord today so that his heart can be filled with joy.

Jesus would make the Father happy.

... so that my joy may be in you and that your joy may be complete. (John 15:11)

August 3

Be Careful
of Boasting

But let him who boasts boast about this: that he understands and knows me. (Jeremiah 9:24)

When we can do something well, it is easy to boast. When we boast, we tell others how good we are at certain things. Of course may be very good. Some people sing beautifully, others run fast or are smart. Often our fathers and mothers or grandmothers and grandfathers boast about us.

The Lord said a wise man must not boast about his wisdom. The soldier must not boast about his great strength. A rich man must not boast about his great wealth. If we have to boast, there is only one thing to boast about, and that is the Lord himself. Someone who is wise never boasts about himself, but he says the Lord is good and wonderful. This person shows that he or she knows the Lord and understands who he is. God is so great and wonderful and without sin that we can really boast about him. He is without faults. The Lord is fantastic. If we really want to boast, we must look away from ourselves and praise his name. He is the one who gives us our talents. He must take credit for it.

Jesus would never
boast about himself.

I will boast about a man like that, but I will not boast about myself. (2 Corinthians 12:5)

August 4

WHEN ALL IS WELL ...

Give glory to the LORD your God before ... your feet stumble on the darkening hills. (Jeremiah 13:16)

Most people call out to God only when things go wrong. Every day they just go on living their lives, and when something goes wrong, then they call upon the Lord. Then they think he must help quickly. The Lord wants us to put our trust in him, and he wants to help people in need. But he does not like it if we ask his help just when we are in trouble. Christians follow and serve the Lord, not only when they are in trouble, but also when all is well in their lives.

The Lord says his people must glorify him before it gets dark in their lives. In the dark we can't see where we are going, and the Lord uses this image to say, "They will be like people who bump into the mountain in the dark." Once you have stumbled over a stone, it is too late to call upon God. You should have spoken to him long before you got to the hills. We must not wait until the moment of need. Speak to the Lord now, and glorify and praise him for everything he is and does. If trouble comes, then the Lord is with you already. Actually, he will warn you even before you get to the hills.

God wants to share our lives with us, not only our troubles.

Jesus would talk to
the Lord about everything.

You will fill me with joy in your presence. (Acts 2:28)

August 5

HE IS EVERYWHERE

"Do not I fill heaven and earth?" declares the LORD.
(Jeremiah 23:24)

There are really people who think they can hide from the Lord. The Lord says no one can *"hide in secret places so that I cannot see him"* (v. 24). God sees everything because he is everywhere. His eyes can see right through a wall or right through a person's body. He can see deep into our hearts. Yes, God knows everything and sees everything.

It scares some people to think that God knows everything about them and can see everything. If you are the Lord's child, it doesn't scare you; it makes you happy. It means that the Lord understands you. He knows what you are struggling with. He knows what your problems are. He also knows what your dreams are and what you want. He sees you when you are alone, and when you cry, and when you are afraid. Because God knows everything, he can help us the way we have to be helped, at the right time.

The Lord knows about all our sins. Because he sent Jesus to pay for our sins, this is not a problem. We can be honest with God about our sins. We don't have to hide from him. If we are honest about our sins, the Lord promises to forgive us.

Thank the Lord that he knows all about you and sees everything you do – and that he still loves you very much.

Jesus will be with
you wherever you are.

"And surely I am with you always, to the very end of the age."
(Matthew 28:20)

August 6

THE FIRE AND THE HAMMER

"Is not my word like fire," declares the LORD, "and like a hammer that breaks a rock in pieces?" (Jeremiah 23:29)

The Bible is very, very powerful. Many people have read the Bible just because they were inquisitive, and then their whole lives were changed. There are many people who have spent the night in a hotel room where a Bible was placed next to the bed, and when they started reading it, it was as if their attention was fixed on it, and they could not put it down. Suddenly they realized that God was talking to them, and they made their peace with God.

Small wonder that the Bible says that God's Word is like fire. Fire can burn down a whole town. The Bible is like fire because it has the power to change a person's life.

The Bible is also like a hammer sometimes. You can use it to drive nails in, but you can also use it to break down walls. With a big hammer one can even break a large stone or rock. Many people have hearts like stone, and when the Word of the Lord speaks to them, it is as if their hard hearts are broken. They become soft and open to the Lord.

The Word can change your life. We must share this Word with others so that the power of God can change their lives.

Jesus would share
the Word with others.

"Therefore go and make disciples of all nations." (Matthew 28:19)

August 7

The Past Is Past

"Do not dwell on the past. See I am doing a new thing!"
(Isaiah 43:18, 19)

We can all remember something that happened in the past. Perhaps it was something good, or perhaps something bad. What happened in the past can have an influence on our lives even now. If something terrible happened in your family, you don't forget it easily. We also remember the good things. Sometimes we take out our photo albums and think back to all the wonderful things that happened in the past.

One must not allow the ugly things of the past to spoil today's joy. The Lord prefers that we live each day to the full, one day at a time. We know that the Lord is the one who wants to make the good things in our lives even better. He wants to give us new experiences, new dreams. That is why he says we must not think too much about past things, because he is going to do something new, and it is about to happen. The Lord also makes another promise. Even if tomorrow is a desert, he will give us enough water.

The Lord tells you and me today that we must not look back too much and must not dwell too much on the past. Grab the opportunity the Lord offers today, and allow him to do something new for you. Leave all the hurt of the past in his hands, and trust him to give you a new, bright future.

Jesus would not look back.

"No one who ... looks back is fit for service in the kingdom of God." (Luke 9:62)

August 8

THE HOUSE COLLAPSED

"The winds blew and beat against that house, and it fell with a great crash." (Matthew 7:27)

The Lord told many parables. A parable is a story with a message. The parable that Jesus is telling here is about a man that built a house. But this house he built on sand. The storms and the rain came with lightning and thunder, and the house collapsed completely.

Another man also built a house. He made sure that his house was not built on sand, but on a firm foundation (a rock). When the storms came, his house was strong and safe. He could sit inside his nice, warm, and cozy house while it was cold and stormy outside. The lesson of this parable is that every person's life, yours too, is like a house. There are many storms in this world that can hurt us and destroy our lives. But if we build on the right Foundation, on the right Rock, that is Jesus Christ, then the house or our life will remain standing in the face of all the storms of life. His Word is like a foundation which helps us build our lives the right way.

Tell the Lord right now that you would like to build a house on a rock. Tell him that you believe his Word and that you want to build everything in your life on that Word.

Jesus will always be your Rock.

As you come to him, the living Stone ... (1 Peter 2:4)

MUSICIANS

Four thousand are to praise the LORD with the musical instruments I have provided for that purpose. (1 Chronicles 23:5)

Today there are many musicians and singers who are used by the Lord to glorify and praise him. Many congregations have members who sing beautifully, and they lead the congregation in praising the Lord. We often hear singers on Christian radio or television who make popular CDs. The message that they sing is the message of the wonderful gospel of Jesus.

This is nothing new. Although they did not have CDs or radios in the time of the Old Testament, singers and musicians were appointed, and it was their full-time job to help people praise and glorify the Lord. King David was a musician himself. In his time he appointed thousands of singers and paid them all a salary to praise the Lord. It was their job. They served in the house of the Lord.

Thank the Lord for singers and musicians who help us to praise and love the Lord better. Also pray that the Lord will bless them so that they can build his kingdom.

Jesus would thank the Father
for musicians and singers.

As they began to sing and praise, the LORD set ambushes. (2 Chronicles 20:22)

JOSHUA'S FILTHY CLOTHES

> Now Joshua [the high priest] was dressed in filthy clothes. (Zechariah 3:3)

Zechariah was one of the Lord's prophets. One day he saw a vision, which was like a dream. The Lord often talked to his prophets in dreams. In these dreams the Lord tried to tell them something he wanted them to know.

Zechariah's dream was about the priest called Joshua who did very important work. He was the high priest. Next to Joshua stood the devil. He was busy accusing Joshua. But the Lord scolded Satan because he still had a plan for Joshua. Joshua's clothes were filthy with sin. The Lord told an angel to take off his dirty clothes. Then the Lord said to Joshua, *"See, I have taken away your sin, and I will put rich garments [clean clothes] on you"* (v. 4).

Even a minister, or someone who is in the service of the Lord, sins. That is why we must pray often for our ministers and everybody in leadership positions. God forgave Joshua's sins and dressed him in clean, white clothes. Pray for your minister so that he can be clean when he stands before the Lord.

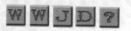

Jesus would pray for
ministers and leaders.

Pray also for me, that ... words may be given me. (Ephesians 6:19)

August 11

GOOD COMPANY

"Bad company corrupts good character." (1 Corinthians 15:33)

It is always interesting to see how people react when they are in the company of different people. When the minister or the pastor comes to visit, there are people who put on such a serious tone of voice. The same people talk differently when they are with friends they like visiting or when they are at a party. When they are in the company of noisy people who swear and argue, you will hear them behaving in the same way.

Our behavior is influenced by the company we keep. You can talk softly, but the minute someone starts shouting at you, it is not long before you shout right back at him. When someone is ticking you off and you speak softly, it is interesting that the noisy person quickly starts talking softly.

This is the way we influence one another. The company you keep is important. If you are always in the company of people who say and do ugly things, you eventually become just like them. That is why the Bible tells us we must be careful of the company we keep. If your friends are good, and they are good company, it is easier for you to live a good life.

Make sure you keep the right company today so that your behavior will be to the glory of God.

Being in Jesus' company will influence people's lives.

Large crowds ... followed him. (Matthew 4:25)

August 12

Good Gifts

There are different kinds of gifts, but the same Spirit.
(1 Corinthians 12:4)

It is always exciting to receive gifts. If you are a child of the Lord, you also receive gifts. The gifts the Lord gives you are handed out by the Holy Spirit who lives in a Christian. The Bible calls these gifts "gifts of grace." "Grace" means that these gifts are free; you and I just get them, not because we deserve them. "Gift" means just that – it is a present. So gifts of grace are gifts we haven't earned; we get them free from the hand of God.

The gifts handed out by the Holy Spirit are not given to you and me to make us happy, but to encourage and exhort the people around us. These are gifts to share with others. Every Christian has received a gift from God. This gift is something like wisdom, knowledge, special faith, or even the ability to bring God's healing to others. The Holy Spirit hands out these gifts to the children of God the way he chooses. You and I must just ask that the Lord will show us which gift he gave us.

As you grow closer to the Lord, he will show you which gifts he gave you so that you can use them to make others happy. Thank him for all the gifts he has given you.

Jesus would use his
gifts to benefit others.

Now to each one the manifestation of the Spirit is given for the common good. (1 Corinthians 12:7)

August 13

Pray for our Land

Righteousness exalts a nation, but sin is a disgrace to any people. (Proverbs 14:34)

We live in a beautiful country. It is a country of sunshine, lovely places where beautiful animals are found, and friendly people. Many people come from far and wide to visit our country. They like visiting here because it is such a beautiful country.

Unfortunately there are also things in our country that are not at all beautiful. Terrible things happen, and the people who do these evil things do not know the Lord and do not love him. They are people who sin. Sin always brings shame on a country and its people. We are ashamed when we think of people who are murdered in our country, or whose cars are stolen, or who are abused. We are ashamed of people who steal money as they please, even if they are leaders. That is why we need to pray a lot for our country.

The Lord says that when we pray he will answer our prayers and help us. Why don't you and I ask the Lord's forgiveness for all our sins, on behalf of our country. We must say, "Lord, we are sorry that not all of us want to serve you. Forgive us, help us, and heal our country. Grant that we can live here in safety, and in peace." Pray now for our country and its leaders.

Jesus would pray for our country and its leaders.

I urge ... that requests, prayers, intercession and thanksgiving be made ... for kings and all those in authority. (1 Timothy 2:1, 2)

August 14

Not Nice Anymore

> Better a meal of vegetables where there is love than a fattened calf with hatred. (Proverbs 15:17)

You can have the most delicious food at mealtime: fried potatoes and a big steak, with ice cream, or other sorts of goodies to follow. But if the atmosphere at table is not pleasant, then the food does not taste as good as it should.

Perhaps it has also happened to you that you were enjoying a good meal, when all of a sudden some argument started. When we argue we get angry with one another and start saying mean things to each other. I bet the food was suddenly not as nice anymore. You didn't even feel like finishing it. You just wanted the fighting to stop.

A wise man wrote in the Bible that he would rather eat plain vegetables served with love, than a delicious, exotic meal served with hatred. It is so important that we create the right atmosphere when we are having a meal. You also do not digest your food well if you are in a bad mood. Peace, love, and friendly talk create the best atmosphere at a table. Every day you when say grace before a meal, pray that the love and peace of the Lord be there with you all. Don't start an argument at the table.

Jesus would create a nice
atmosphere at mealtime.

Do it all in the name of the Lord Jesus. (Colossians 3:17)

BROTHERS AND SISTERS

He said, "Here are my mother and my brothers. For whoever does the will of my Father in heaven is my brother and sister and mother." (Matthew 12:49, 50)

Some people have very big families. My father had twelve brothers and sisters. To have family is wonderful. The members of a family can help, protect, and love one another. Normally, family members are supposed to give warmth and love to one another, like a harbor where boats can dock safely.

Christian families are not only brothers and sisters living in the same house. Jesus surprised people when he said he did not have only one mother and a few brothers. He said that everyone who does the will of his Father is a brother or a sister to him. We too, have more family than our blood brothers or sisters; we have millions of brothers and sisters all over the world. There are many people in many countries who decide to follow Jesus. We don't even know their names. If it were possible to meet them, wouldn't we have a lot to talk about? There is so much to say about our Father in heaven.

Christians must love one another like brothers and sisters. We must care for one another, support one another, and encourage one another to serve the Lord. Who are your brothers and sisters in Christ? Love them.

Jesus would accept you
as a brother or a sister.

So Jesus is not ashamed to call them brothers. (Hebrews 2:11)

August 16

Do It Now

Do not say to your neighbor, "Come back later; I'll give it tomorrow." (Proverbs 3:28)

It always feels good to help others. But when you are asked to help out, it isn't always easy to turn your attention to them immediately. Also, it might not be so easy or pleasant while you are busy helping them. But when you have helped them, you have a good feeling inside. It is good when people help one another.

Sometimes we are so busy that we do not think it will be possible to help the person asking for it now. Then we say, "I'll help you later." Perhaps it's your mother asking you to do something for her, and you reply, "I can't do it right now, Mom." The Bible says we shouldn't do that.

When someone asks us, we must do it immediately. If you tell them you will help tomorrow, it could happen that something can come up so that you just don't get round to helping him or her. No, if we are asked to help, do it now.

Jesus would help
people immediately.

 Do not merely listen to the Word ... Do what it says. (James 1:22)

Punishment is Painful

He who spares the rod hates his son, but he who loves him is careful to discipline him. (Proverbs 13:24)

When we are bad, we sometimes get a spanking. I'm sure you can remember a spanking you got when you were smaller. Perhaps your backside was stinging from the punishment your parents gave you because you were disobedient.

Parents punish their children because they want to teach them right from wrong. The government punishes people who break the law. The Lord punishes people who break his laws. Punishment is part of our lives.

Sometimes we think our parents don't love us when they discipline us. No parent or teacher or anyone else may punish someone without a good reason. Unnecessary punishment is unfair. If, however, we deserve to be punished, it will make us think twice the next time we want to do something wrong.

Because your parents love you, they punish you by spanking you, or taking something away from you, or making you stay in your room for a little while. If you have been punished, think about why you were punished. Apologize, and try not to do the same thing again.

Jesus would be obedient.

"But be sure to fear [obey] the Lord and serve him faithfully." (1 Samuel 12:24)

August 18

THE PRECIOUS PEARL

"When he found [a pearl] of great value, he went away and sold everything he had and bought it." (Matthew 13:46)

Jesus told stories to teach people important things. He told the story of a man who worked with jewels. He was a jeweler who knew a lot about pearls. He was always on the lookout for good pearls to string and sell, and he made a lot of money like this.

This jeweler came across a very wonderful pearl one day. It was the best pearl he had ever seen. He knew immediately that it was very valuable. He knew that he could sell this pearl again at a profit, so he immediately went and sold all his goods so that he could buy this most important, most valuable pearl. He knew that nothing he had ever had was as important to him as this pearl.

Jesus told this story to tell us that his kingdom is just as important as the most valuable pearl. There is nothing more important than to know the Lord, to serve him as your king, and be his follower in this kingdom. That is why people will do anything and give everything, yes even their own lives and their hearts, to know Jesus and to follow him. Nothing is more important than this.

Jesus would give everything
up for the kingdom.

You were bought at a price. (1 Corinthians 7:23)

August 19

Seed Becomes a Tree

"Though it is the smallest of your seeds, yet when it grows, it is the largest of garden plants and becomes a tree." (Matthew 13:32)

The seed of the mustard plant is so small that you can hardly see it. But this little seed can become a big tree.

One can hardly believe that some big trees grow from a small seed. A small mustard seed also grows into a tall tree, and many birds build their nests in the branches of that tree. This is the image the Lord used to say that his kingdom will be like that. Just think of this: Jesus began, as one Person on earth, to tell people about his kingdom, and today millions of people are part of this kingdom. From one person to millions! Yes, the seed of the kingdom falls into a person's heart and then it comes up just like a real seed, and very soon a tree is growing. This tree bears fruit, and from it we get more seeds to plant so that there can be more trees. This is how Christians build the kingdom. We carry the seed of the Word, and it grows in our hearts; we give some to others so that the seed can also come up in their hearts. Before we know it, the kingdom is like a big garden with many trees. All of this started with only one seed.

Pray and ask the Lord that the seed of his kingdom will keep on coming up so that many people will believe in him.

Jesus would preach the Word.

 Jesus went throughout Galilee ... teaching ... preaching the good news of the kingdom. (Matthew 4:23)

On the Water

> But when [Peter] saw the wind, he was afraid and, beginning to sink, cried out, "Lord, save me!" (Matthew 14:30)

Jesus did the most wonderful things to show how mighty his Father was so that people could believe in him and follow him.

One day the disciples were all in a boat a few miles from the shore. Jesus had stayed behind on the mountain to pray. Suddenly the wind started blowing, and it whipped up great waves on the Sea of Galilee. The disciples were on this stormy sea all night. At daybreak, Jesus came walking toward them on the sea. The disciples were afraid because they thought it was a ghost. Jesus said to them, "Don't be afraid, it is I." Peter could not believe it was Jesus. He said, "Jesus, if this is really you, tell me to walk on the water to you." Jesus told him to do that.

Peter began walking on the water, but when he saw how big the waves were, he was afraid and started sinking. He had to call out to Jesus to save him from sinking.

We must trust in the Lord completely. If he tells us something, we can be sure he won't make a mistake. The minute we start thinking about the position we are in or the waves, we sink.

Jesus would trust in God alone.

Let us throw off everything that hinders ... Let us fix our eyes on Jesus. (Hebrews 12:1, 2)

August 21

THE LONE SHEEP

"Will he not leave the ninety-nine ... and go to look for the one that wandered off?" (Matthew 18:12)

Jesus told the parable of a man who had one hundred sheep. Every day he left them to graze in the fields so that they could eat enough and be satisfied.

One sheep wanted more green grass and went after it. This sheep strayed from the others. All of a sudden he was alone and couldn't see the other sheep anywhere. What if a beast of prey should come along and eat him, or what if it got dark and he was all alone?

Because the shepherd knew all his sheep, he soon noticed that one sheep was missing. He left the ninety-nine others together and went looking for the lost sheep. When he found him, he was so happy that he held him close. At that moment he was happier about that one sheep than about the ninety-nine waiting for him where he had left them.

People are like sheep. The Lord is the Shepherd. He knows which sheep have strayed. He loves each and every one so much that he wants to go and find any lost sheep. There are people who are very far away from the Lord. He will take trouble to find them. And when he does, he is very pleased.

You and I must also be like this. We must go and find all the lost people for Jesus. They are very important to him.

Jesus will lay down
his life for his sheep.

"The good shepherd lays down his life for the sheep." (John 10:11)

August 22

COMMANDMENTS

"Love the Lord your God with all your heart ... Love your neighbor as yourself." (Matthew 22:37, 39)

If we should ask what the Lord really expects from you and me, we would be able to give two answers. The Bible says there are two things the Lord wants from us.

The first important thing is that we must love the Lord our God with all our heart and all our soul and all our mind. This means only that we must love the Lord with all our life. We must choose God. We must tell him that we love him. We must also tell him that we are thankful that he forgives our sins and makes us new. We must want to live for him. This is the first and greatest commandment.

The second thing the Lords wants from us is that we must love not only him but also all people around us. We must love our neighbor. Our neighbor is every person near us. Not only family and friends, but all people we come into contact with every day. We must show them the love of the Lord. We must care for them. We must help them. We must show them the way to heaven.

Love for the Lord and love for people – this is what the Lord wants to see. Love God today and also everyone you meet.

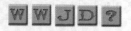

Jesus would love his
Father and also people.

Whoever loves God must also love his brother. (1 John 4:21)

August 23

PREPARING THE WAY

"A voice ... calling in the desert, 'Prepare the way for the Lord, make straight paths for him ... And all mankind will see God's salvation.'" (Luke 3:4, 6)

Already in Isaiah it was prophesied that someone would do the work to prepare the way for the Lord. Was it a real road that they built that Jesus could walk on? No, this was the work of a man called John the Baptist.

Before Jesus started telling people about his kingdom, John the Baptist (who was a relative of his) was already preaching in the desert near the river Jordan. He told people to repent. He also told them that someone was coming who would bring salvation. In this way he prepared the way for Jesus; that is, he told people that Jesus would come with a plan for salvation.

John the Baptist realized he was an instrument who had to explain God's salvation plan to people. He only prepared people for the great and wonderful work that Jesus would do himself.

You and I must also try to make it easier for Jesus to reach people with the gospel of salvation. You and I must, like John, "make straight paths for him" so that people can be prepared for him.

Jesus would help you to witness.

"But you will receive power when the Holy Spirit comes on you; and you will be my witnesses." (Acts 1:8)

August 24

USELESS LAMPS

"Give us some of your oil." (Matthew 25:8)

Jesus told the parable of ten girls who took their lamps to meet a bridegroom. In Jesus' time wedding celebrations lasted much longer than they do today. They celebrated for a week. Because it was getting dark they needed lamps. Five of the girls didn't take extra oil with them. The bridegroom was late, and their lamps started going out. They asked the other girls for oil, but there was not enough for everyone and they had to go and buy oil. While they were gone, the bridegroom arrived, and everyone who was there went with him. When the girls whose lamps had gone out came back, the bridegroom and his guests had already left. The other five girls had taken enough oil with them and so they were ready to go with the bridegroom.

This parable means that you and I must always be prepared so that when Jesus comes back again as he promised, we will be ready to go with him. We must not be like the foolish girls, but like the sensible ones. We must not let things slip. We must not think that Jesus' return is still far off. Jesus can come back tonight or tomorrow. We must be ready.

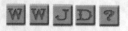

Jesus would be prepared.

The day of the Lord will come like a thief. (2 Peter 3:10)

August 25

PERFUME FOR JESUS

A woman came to him with an alabaster jar of very expensive perfume, which she poured on his head. (Matthew 26:7)

In the days when Jesus was on earth, people liked sweet-smelling stuff. After all, they could not shower as frequently as we can. Instead, they used perfumed oil. This oil was made of all kinds of scented things and was very expensive. It was usually kept in an alabaster jar.

One day when Jesus was in Bethany, in the home of Simon, a woman came to him where he was sitting at the table and poured a very expensive jar of oil on his head. It was a wonderful thing to do. These days we don't put perfume on our hair, but in those days it was an honor if someone put such expensive oil on your head. Jesus was very thankful and pleased with what the woman had done. One of Jesus' disciples was angry because so much money was wasted on Jesus' hair, but Jesus knew that this woman was glorifying him. That is why he was thankful.

You and I cannot honor Jesus with scented oil, but we honor him when we praise him, give our lives to him, follow him, and just tell him that we love him. This is just as precious to him as scented oil.

Jesus would be thankful for love.

The poor you will always have with you, but you will not always have me. (Matthew 26:11)

Are You Hospitable?

Practice hospitality. (Romans 12:13)

It is always nice to visit hospitable people. Hospitable people have open hearts for visitors. Anyone who walks through his or her door instantly feels welcome. There is an atmosphere of warmth and friendliness. It almost feels as if you are at home.

Hospitality is a very good characteristic. If you open up your heart and home to others, they enjoy being with you. The Lord likes us to be hospitable. He likes it when we show others that we love them. We show our love when we make others feel at home. We make them a nice cup of tea or coffee, and we offer them food if they are hungry. If they want to sleep over, we give them a warm bed.

Think of ways you can be hospitable today. Although we must be careful not to let just anybody into our homes, we can offer hospitality and love to those we know.

Jesus would be hospitable.

Offer hospitality to one another without grumbling. (1 Peter 4:9)

Your Good Favor

> The king had granted him everything he asked, for the
> hand of the LORD his God was on him. (Ezra 7:6)

The people of Israel were exiled to Persia because they did not do the will of the Lord. Ezra was one of the Israelites who lived in Babylon, in Persia. God had a plan for Ezra.

The Lord decided that his people had lived in a foreign country long enough. It was time for them to go back to Israel. He wanted the temple to be rebuilt. Ezra was one of the important people he wanted to use for this purpose. The Lord kept his hand on Ezra in a special way, and he found favor with the king of Persia, Artaxerxes. When you find favor in somebody's eyes, it means that this person will go out of his way to help you. Not only did the king order that Ezra go back to Jerusalem, but he also gave him silver and gold to rebuild the temple. And just listen what the king said, *"And anything else needed for the temple of your God ... you may provide from the royal treasury"* (v. 20). Small wonder that we read in Ezra 7 how happy Ezra was: *"Praise be to the LORD ... who has put it into the king's heart to bring honor to the house of the LORD ... and who has extended his good favor to me ..."* (v. 27, 28).

If you serve the Lord, he will even use non-Christians to favor you so that you can finish your work.

Jesus will keep his hand over you.

The LORD ... blesses his people with peace. (Psalm 29:11)

August 28

Three Things

For Ezra had devoted himself to the study ... of the Law of the LORD, and to teaching its decrees and laws in Israel. (Ezra 7:10)

Often people ask us what we are going to do during the holidays or what we want to do when we have finished school. We all have a dream or an ideal. What is your ideal? Ezra had a specific task. The Bible says he devoted himself to do certain things. "Devoted" means we do something with enthusiasm and faith. If you want to see or do something very badly, you will go to a lot of trouble to make it happen.

Ezra'a first dream was to know the law of the Lord. (The law of the Lord is the Word of God.) He decided that he would study the law of the Lord. You and I must also learn the Lord's Word with devotion.

The second thing he wanted to do was to learn the Word of God so that he could live it. It is one thing to learn it and another to do it. You and I should also live the Word of God.

It was not enough for Ezra that he knew and lived the Word; he wanted all his friends to know and do the same. You also have friends that need to know and live the Word of the Lord.

Follow Ezra's example.

Jesus would learn the Word of God.

 Let me understand the teaching of your precepts [laws]. (Psalm 119:27)

THE LORD ALWAYS WINS

They hired counselors to work against them and frustrate their plans. (Ezra 4:5)

When Ezra came from Persia to rebuild the temple, the devil tried everything to put a stop to it. He knew that if the temple was rebuilt, the Israelites would praise and serve the Lord. That is why he tried to prevent the rebuilding of the temple.

The people who were not satisfied with the building of the temple first told Ezra that they would help build. But Ezra knew that they were actually enemies, and he did not want to allow them to help with the work. They would not do good work. Then the enemies tried to frighten the builders and discourage them from going on with the building operations (cf. v. 4). They told the king he would lose money if they finished this project.

Fortunately, the Lord saw to it that the devil's plan to stop building altogether did not work. Unfortunately, though, the work was stopped for fifteen years.

If you serve the Lord you will notice that people will try to discourage you. They will also try to frighten you. You will be blamed for all sorts of things, and people will tell lies about you. Don't worry. The Lord always wins.

Jesus would carry on,
no matter what.

He who stands firm to the end will be saved. (Matthew 10:22)

August 30

BE STRONG, BE BRAVE

> Be strong and courageous. Do not be afraid ... for there is a greater power with us than with him. (2 Chronicles 32:7)

Hezekiah was a king of Israel. He reigned in Jerusalem almost thirty years. He was a good king and really wanted to serve the Lord. One of the wonderful things he did was to clean up the house of the Lord. He had everything unclean taken out of the temple so that it could be holy again.

Then a king of another foreign country came on the scene. He invaded Israel and he wanted to put and end to Hezekiah's rule. Hezekiah had faith in God, and so he spoke to his army, *"Be strong and courageous. Do not be afraid or discouraged because of the king of Assyria and the vast army with him, for there is a greater power with us than with him. With him is only the arm of flesh, but with us is the LORD our God to help us and to fight our battles"* (v. 7, 8). These are beautiful words. They tell us that Hezekiah had faith in the Lord. No wonder the Lord worked a miracle. He sent an angel, and every soldier and leader and official in the enemy camp was killed. This is how the Lord saved Hezekiah and the people of Jerusalem from a bad king.

If you are on God's side, you will ultimately win. Put your trust in him today.

Jesus would put his trust in God.

 Do not be terrified ... for ... God will be with you wherever you go. (Joshua 1:9)

August 31

The Test

God left him to test him and to know everything that
was in his heart. (2 Chronicles 32:31)

All of us have to do tests so that we can see if we know
things. King Hezekiah of Judah was also tested.

Hezekiah was a rich and respected man. He had treasu-
ries built for his valuables. He also built cities and had many
possessions. He was prosperous in everything he did. It
was because God blessed him. However, Hezekiah became seriously ill, and he prayed to God. The Lord made a
miracle happen. Hezekiah got well again. But the Bible says
that Hezekiah was not thankful that the Lord had mercy on
him. He started feeling self-satisfied. He started boasting.

One day the Lord decided to test Hezekiah. The Bible
says God left Hezekiah or withdrew from him. When God
withdraws from you and me, things get very bad for us. God
did this so that Hezekiah could know his own heart – not his
physical heart, but his attitude and his feelings toward the
Lord. This is what the Lord tests. And Hezekiah's heart was
not altogether what it should be. God tested him so that he
could know his own heart.

Test your heart today. Is your attitude toward the Lord
what it should be? Is there pride in your heart? Or sin?
Confess it!

Jesus would have
the right attitude.

"Blessed are the pure in heart." (Matthew 5:8)

September 1

OFFICIALS AND JUDGES

... officials and judges over Israel. (1 Chronicles 26:29)

If there is no law and order and justice in a country, there is confusion. We need order and justice. Order means everything is arranged and run properly.

In every country there are people who maintain or keep order. It is usually done by the police and traffic officers. All people who have to maintain order are important. We must never look down on them. It is God's will that there must be order in a country, or in a town, or in a school. That is why we have to obey police officers and pray for them. It is not easy to maintain order in our country. Even in the time of the Bible, Kenaniah and his sons were instructed to maintain order in Israel.

When two people have a disagreement, a judge must decide who is in the wrong and who is right. This is decided in a court of law. This is where people are tried. We must pray for those whose job is to pass judgment. We must pray that they will be fair and decide according to God's will.

Thank the Lord now for those who help with law and order and justice in our country.

Jesus would obey authority.

Thanksgiving [must] be made for everyone ... for kings and those in authority. (1 Timothy 2:1, 2)

September 2

We Want to Be Like Them

"Then we will be like all the other nations." (1 Samuel 8:20)

We often see things others have and then wish we could have the same. Perhaps your friends have certain toys that you wish you could also have. You feel out of place because you don't have what they do.

The Israelites were not happy. Yes, the Lord was their king, and he did bring them out of Egypt. He also gave them the Ten Commandments and showed them how to live. Furthermore, he sent them priests and prophets to speak to them and show them the right way. But they were not happy. They wanted more. What did they want?

They saw that all the heathen nations around them, and all the other nations on earth had a king. Having a human king was unnecessary because they had the best King, the Lord himself. He ruled over them and he wanted to keep it that way, but they did not want to. Samuel warned them that it would not be the best thing for them to have a man for a king. Later on because of the disobedience of the kings, the people of Israel often suffered.

Don't want something just because someone else has it. Ask the Lord what his will is, and trust that he knows best.

Jesus would do the
will of the Father.

"Father, if you are willing ... not my will, but yours be done." (Luke 22:42)

September 3

THE ARK

"Have them make a chest of acacia wood." (Exodus 25:10)

T he Lord instructed the Israelites to make an interesting thing. It is called the Ark of the Covenant. It was about three feet long, two feet wide, and two feet high. It was covered with pure gold and made of acacia wood.

This almost square wooden chest had an important function. It was carried all over when the Israelites were busy moving. It was as if the Lord wanted to tell them he was with them, just as the Ark was with them. It was as if he wanted to tell them he was with the Ark and that they could talk to him there. He would also meet them there. The Ark was usually placed in a tent, the tabernacle, and there the spiritual leaders and the people worshiped the Lord. When the people moved on, the tent was taken down, and they picked up the Ark and carried it along with them. In this way they knew God went with them.

You and I don't need an Ark anymore to carry around with us. Neither do we need to pitch a tent or go to a particular building to meet God. We serve him right inside of us if we open the doors of our lives for him. He goes wherever we go. Serve the Lord today with your life.

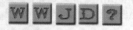

Jesus will always be with us.

"So you will be my people, and I will be your God." (Jeremiah 30:22)

September 4

Is He Going with You?

But if the cloud did not lift, they did not set out – until the day it lifted. (Exodus 40:37)

When the Israelites moved out of Egypt, the Lord was with them on the road during the whole journey. No one should be on the road without him. We need the Lord to bless us and to be with us. This the Israelites knew very well.

Whenever they reached a place where they were to spend the night, they pitched camp. They also put up the tabernacle (the Tent of Meeting), and put the Ark inside. Something wonderful happened: a cloud covered the tabernacle, and the mighty presence of the Lord filled the tent. The cloud stayed there until the Lord wanted them to go on. When the cloud lifted from the tabernacle, the people knew they had to move on. If the cloud did not lift, they stayed there until it did. If they were to move without the cloud, the Lord would not be with them. Then they would be in trouble.

Learn today that you shouldn't just do things without first making sure the Lord will go with you.

Jesus would walk with God.

"If your Presence does not go with us, do not send us up from here." (Exodus 33:15)

September 5

Offerings

"When any of you brings an offering to the LORD ... "
(Leviticus 1:2)

In the time of the Bible, and especially the Old Testament, many offerings were brought to the Lord. We read of many different kinds of offerings: burnt offerings, grain offerings, animal offerings, fragrant offerings, guilt offerings, and a few others. An offering was brought because people felt they had to give God something. Because we are human and are sinful, we need to answer to God for our sins. The offerings of the Old Testament did this. Offerings were also brought to God because it was a way of thanking him.

The Old Testament offering is not in use any more. Does this mean that we no longer have to give the Lord anything? Does it mean that we no longer have sins that need to be taken away?

Jesus brought an offering in our place. His offering pays for our sins. We need just accept it. The thanks offering that you and I can bring now is the offering of our hearts and our lives.

Jesus would give
thanks to the Father.

Enter his gates with thanksgiving and ... give thanks to him.
(Psalm 100:4)

"CHRISTIANS"

The disciples were called Christians first at Antioch.
(Acts 11:26)

Many people in our country call themselves Christians. Some people talk about "Christian nations" and even say we live in a "Christian country." Where does the word "Christian" come from?

The name "Christian" comes from "Christ." Christ means "the anointed one," and that is one of Jesus' names. Remember he was anointed by the Holy Spirit so that he could do his work. Christians are people who follow Christ, and because we are his followers, we also take his name. It was in Antioch that people were called Christians for the first time, because they told and showed everybody that they belonged to Christ.

Actually it is wrong to call someone a Christian if that person does not know and follow Christ. Many people are only Christians in name. If we want to call ourselves Christians, we must follow Christ.

If Christ means " the anointed one," then Christians are also "anointed ones." That is why the Holy Spirit anointed us. Like the fragrant anointing oil of the olden days, you and I must spread the fragrance of the gospel to everybody around us. Live like a true Christian today.

In Jesus you will be a Christian.

Through us spreads everywhere the fragrance of the knowledge of him. (2 Corinthians 2:14)

September 7

GOD'S THOUGHTS

"For my thoughts are not your thoughts." (Isaiah 55:8)

We think with our brain, and what a wonderful instrument it is. It gives us all kinds of thoughts. Each one of us has many thoughts. Our thoughts make us behave in a certain way. God also has thoughts. He thinks in the same way that you and I do, but his thoughts are not like our thoughts.

You and I often think wrong thoughts. Sometimes we think we are right, but then we have made a mistake. Because we don't know everything, we often think just as far as we know. Because we don't have more facts, our thoughts are limited. The Lord is not limited. He knows everything and he sees everything and what he thinks is perfect.

Often we ask the Lord for certain things, and we expect him to give them to us. If he doesn't, we wonder why. It is then that we must trust him. His thoughts are not like our thoughts. He looks differently at what we want. He sees the whole picture. He knows if it will be good for us to have them. He knows if it will be good for our lives to have them. And if he decides we are not to have them, it is because he knows best. He says, *"As the heavens are higher than the earth, so are my ways higher than your ways and my thoughts than your thoughts"* (v. 9).

Jesus would trust the
Father in everything.

Commit to the LORD whatever you do, and your plans will succeed. (Proverbs 16:3)

September 8

CHICKENS OR EAGLES?

They will soar on wings like eagles. (Isaiah 40:31)

Chickens are quite different from eagles. Chickens stay on the ground. They make their nests on the ground. Chickens cannot really fly. A chicken will try to fly only when it is frightened. That doesn't really mean a thing, though, because chickens don't fly high at all. By the time it gets airborne, it's on its way down again.

An eagle is a majestic bird. An eagle is not like a chicken! An eagle does not build its nest on the ground, but high up in the mountains. He can fly magnificently and ride the wind for hours on end. An eagle is very strong and fast. Oh yes, there is a big difference between a chicken and an eagle.

I don't think the Lord wants us to be like chickens. He wants us to be like eagles. He wants us to be as strong and as majestic as an eagle. That is why he says in his Word that if we put our trust in him, or wait upon him, we will be given new strength, and we will take off like eagles. He wants us to reach heights because he gives us the strength to do so. He does not want us to move awkwardly, like chickens. God's strength helps you and me to be winners.

Listen to the voice of the Lord today, allow his Spirit to fill you and soar with the eagle wings of faith.

Jesus would live like a winner.

He is the God who ... puts the nations under me. (2 Samuel 22:48)

September 9

NEVER UNDERSTANDING

[These people are] ever hearing, but never understanding.
(Isaiah 6:9)

Sometimes people know what they should do, but they do exactly the opposite. They just ignore what is right and carry on doing their own silly things. This is foolish.

The Lord looked at his people, Israel, and he thought they were foolish. He says they heard, but did not understand. He taught them certain things, and although they heard what he said and seemed to understand, they didn't do what he said. This is being foolish: when you hear things and even understand, but still you don't want to do whatever you are told to do, especially if it will be good for you. It is almost like someone who doesn't eat and goes hungry even though there is plenty of food. Israel was like this. They were "never understanding." They did not want to do the right things.

You and I must ask the Lord to help us so that we will not be foolish when it comes to his things. Ask him to make you diligent and willing and also smart, so that you can know his will and do it.

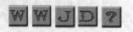

Jesus would ask his
Father for wisdom.

 If any of you lacks wisdom, he should ask God, who gives generously. (James 1:5)

Fearless

> The wolf will live with the lamb ... The infant will play near the [nest] of the cobra. (Isaiah 11:6, 8)

You may have seen on a nature show how careful antelope are when they drink water or walk in the plains of Africa. They are afraid of lions and leopards that can catch and eat them. Then again, leopards hunt antelope to stay alive.

Snakes are poisonous reptiles. Not all snakes are poisonous, but if a poisonous snake should bite you, you have to get to a doctor very quickly, or you will die. That is why we avoid snakes or kill them if we should find them near our homes. If a baby were to put his hand out as if to touch a snake, you would try to get the child away from the snake immediately. People are afraid of snakes, often for good reason.

Isaiah prophesies that a time will come when people will not fear snakes any more. Babies will be allowed to play near the nest of a cobra. Antelope will no longer be afraid of leopards; they will live together. Of course he is talking about heaven. You and I can look forward to living together with everything we were afraid of, because there will not be any fear or danger in heaven.

Thank the Lord that he makes it possible for us to look forward to a place where there will be no more evil or fear.

Jesus will take all
fear away one day.

But perfect love drives out fear. (1 John 4:18)

September 11

To Love

Love the LORD your God and keep his requirements.
(Deuteronomy 11:1)

When we love someone, we want to do what makes that person happy. True love is taking someone else into consideration and not doing just what we want to do. If you love your mom and you know she expects you to behave in a certain manner, you show your love for her by being obedient and doing what she would like you to. The Bible says if we love the Lord, we will also do what he asks us to. John writes, *"This is love for God: to obey his commands"* (1 John 5:3).

How can one love God? We can't see him. We can't touch him. He doesn't talk to us in a way that we can hear him. Is it really possible to love God? Yes, of course! The best reason for loving God is because he sent us his Son Jesus, and Jesus was prepared to give his whole life for us. He was tortured and hurt, but he died on the cross for you and me. God loves us so much that he gave us his Son. Because he loved us first, we love him back.

Show your love by doing today what he wants you to.

Jesus would obey
the Lord's commands.

This is love for God: to obey his commands. (1 John 5:3)

September 12

SHE GAVE EVERYTHING

"This poor widow has put more into the treasury than all the others." (Mark 12:43)

One day Jesus sat at the temple near the place where the offerings were brought. He saw people putting their money into the temple treasury. Rich people came past and put a lot of money into the box. Then Jesus saw a poor widow. She opened her purse and put two small coins in the box. They were not worth much. But Jesus knew that she was very poor. Calling his disciples to him, Jesus said, *"I tell you the truth, this poor widow has put more into the treasury than all the others"* (v. 43).

Jesus said this because he knew the rich people had so much money that they would hardly miss what they put into the box. The poor widow, on the other hand, was so poor that she couldn't even really afford to put those two coins in the box; she needed the money for food. But because she loved God, she gave everything she had.

God likes us to give because we love him – not because we have a lot, but because we want to give, even if it is all we have. Give God everything today. Remember also, whenever you get a little money, give a little something for the Lord's work.

Jesus would give
us his everything.

 Offer your bodies as living sacrifices, holy and pleasing to God. (Romans 12:1)

September 13

JUDAS'S WEAKNESS

With the reward he got for his wickedness, Judas bought a field. (Acts 1:18)

Jesus chose Judas to follow him, and he taught Judas about the things of the kingdom. Judas loved Jesus. He had the very important job to look after the money matters of the disciples. But Judas had a weakness.

Every one of us has a weak spot. Some people get angry very quickly, and this makes trouble for them. Others are greedy, and they will do something wrong to get hold of what they want. Some people are too proud. They think they are better than others. Judas liked money; he was greedy. He always wanted more and more. He was never satisfied with the money he had (See John 12:4-6).

The devil knew about Judas's weakness, and that is why he saw to it that the Pharisees bribed Judas with money to hand Jesus over to them. He pointed Jesus out to the Pharisees so that they could capture him. Later on Judas felt very bad about this. He bought himself a piece of property, but there he hanged himself.

Ask the Lord what your weakness is. Ask him to make you strong so that your weakness will not tempt you to do the wrong thing.

Jesus would resist temptation.

"Away from me, Satan!" (Matthew 4:10)

STOP DOUBTING

"Stop doubting and believe." (John 20:27)

Thomas was one of the disciples Jesus chose to follow him. After his death and resurrection, Jesus appeared to his disciples. On the day Jesus rose from the dead, he went to his disciples and said to them, *"Peace be with you!"* (v. 19). The disciples were very happy to see Jesus. Thomas was not with the other disciples at the time. The first thing the disciples told him when they saw him again was that they had seen Jesus. He did not believe them.

Thomas could not believe that Jesus had risen from the dead. He said that if he didn't see the nail marks in Jesus' hands, he would never believe it. Eight days later Jesus appeared to his disciples again, and this time Thomas was with them. Jesus said to Thomas, *"Put your finger here; see my hands ... Stop doubting and believe"* (v. 27). Right then Thomas went down on his knees and worshiped Jesus.

You and I must not doubt like Thomas. Jesus said he would rise from the grave, but Thomas did not believe it. We can believe everything that Jesus says in his Word.

Jesus would motivate us to
believe with all our hearts.

"God is not a man, that he should lie." (Numbers 23:19)

September 15

ALL THAT IMPORTANT?

"How hard it is for the rich to enter the kingdom of God!" (Luke 18:24)

There was a rich young man. He had a lot of money and many possessions. His money and possessions were more important to him than anything else. Yet, deep inside his heart he had a need because he came to Jesus and asked him how he could get everlasting life. Jesus knew that this young man had a problem: he was not prepared to let go of his obsession with money. When you are obsessed with something, it is all you think about, and it becomes your master. Money was this young man's master. That is why Jesus said a strange thing. Jesus told him to sell all his belongings and follow him. This was difficult for the young man to accept, because he was not prepared to do what Jesus said. Money was too important to him.

You and I do need money. We need certain things to stay alive. Money is important, and possessions are also important. But they should never be the most important things in our lives. Money is not as important as knowing the Lord, following him, and being rich inside. We are rich if we do the Lord's will and experience what he gives so plentifully. Make sure that money doesn't become the most important thing in your life.

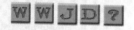

Jesus would store
up riches in heaven.

"For where your treasure is, there your heart will be also."
(Matthew 6:21)

September 16

I'M STRESSED

"Who of you by worrying can add a single hour to his life?" (Matthew 6:27)

Some people are worriers. They worry about anything and everything. They complain and see problems and more problems. They are afraid of all sorts of things. They lie awake nights about the things they fear. They are worried people.

We all have our worries at times. Yes, we do worry about things that can go wrong. Yet the Bible tells us that we should not get into the bad habit of worrying about everything. To tell the truth, Jesus did not allow his disciples to worry about their lives. He said, *do not worry about your life* (v. 25). He also questioned them, asking if it was possible that a person's worries could make him live even one hour longer. As a matter of fact, all the knowledgeable people tell us that worry makes our lives shorter. Worry makes us stressed, and that makes us unhappy. Stress can also make our bodies ill.

Learn to put your trust in the Lord and thank him for everything. Don't get stressed out!

Jesus would talk to the
Father about his worries.

Do not be anxious about anything. (Philippians 4:6)

THEY FORGOT

But they did not understand what he was saying to them.
(Luke 2:50)

Before Jesus was born, the angel told Mary and Joseph that they would be his father and mother on earth. They also knew that he was the Son of God, and that this made him different from other children. He would be the great Redeemer who would pay for the sins of the world, even though he had a human form.

One day Mary and Joseph journeyed to Jerusalem for the Feast of the Passover. Jesus was twelve years old at the time. Mary and Joseph started the journey home in a group with many grown-ups and children. After a day on the road, they noticed that Jesus was not with them. They went back to Jerusalem to look for him. Three days later they found him at the temple where he was listening to the learned people and asking them questions. His parents asked him why he had made them worry about him like that. Jesus answered, *"Didn't you know I had to be in my Father's house?"* (v. 49). Mary and Joseph did not quite understand what he meant by this. For a moment they forgot that he was the Son of God and that his life was not like that of other children.

Don't forget that the Lord does not think like us. Even if there are things you don't understand, just trust him. He knows best.

Jesus would do the
will of his Father.

"For my thoughts are not your thoughts, neither are your ways my ways." (Isaiah 55:8)

September 18

ASHAMED?

I am not ashamed of the gospel, because it is the power of God for the salvation of everyone who believes. (Romans 1:16)

*A*shamed can mean that one doesn't want to be seen or heard. When Saul was anointed as king, he hid because he didn't want people to see him. That is more like being embarrassed, which is similar to being ashamed. You and I are also sometimes embarrassed – like if we have torn our clothes in front of strangers.

One can also be ashamed to identify with Jesus. "Identify" means we openly agree with who Jesus is and what he teaches; we want to be like him. Christians identify with Christ. They have accepted him as their Savior and Lord. When you are still a young Christian, you are sometimes embarrassed to show others and to tell them that you belong to Jesus.

As you get stronger and grow in Jesus, it becomes easier to admit openly that you are his follower. You know, as Paul did, that it is nothing to be ashamed of. We should rather be very happy and talk about it, because then it can also help others confess their sins. Jesus' message is a happy message. It is a gospel. Share it with others without being ashamed so that they can find out for themselves how wonderful it is to know him.

Jesus would preach the
gospel unashamedly.

Jesus went throughout Galilee, teaching [and] ... preaching the good news of the kingdom. (Matthew 4:23)

September 19

THEY LAUGHED

But they laughed at him. (Mark 5:40)

One of the worst things we can do is to tease others or to make fun of them. When you make fun of others, you make them feel small; you humiliate them. It's okay to laugh because we are happy – no one should feel bad about that.

One day Jesus was busy healing people, and a ruler of the synagogue saw everything Jesus did. While he was watching Jesus' healings, someone came from his house and told him that his little girl had died. Jesus heard this sad message and he told the synagogue ruler, *"Don't be afraid; just believe"* (v. 36).

Jesus went to the house of the ruler and saw the people there weeping bitterly. Jesus told them the little girl had not died but was just sleeping. They laughed at him, mocked him, and scorned him. They had seen for themselves the child was dead. Then Jesus took the child by the hand. When he told her to get up, she did just that. Everybody was speechless with surprise.

Today there are still many people who scorn the message of Jesus. They laugh and say the Bible is just stories. But we know the truth. Pray that people will not laugh at the Lord, but will praise him.

Jesus would keep on
believing, no matter what.

"Do not let your hearts be troubled. Trust in God; trust also in me." (John 14:1)

September 20

Go for It

"Well done! ... You have been faithful with a few things;
I will put you in charge of many things." (Matthew 25:21)

Jesus told the story of a man who wanted to go on a journey. He asked the people who worked for him to look after his property while he was away. He gave one worker five gold coins, another one two, and the third received one coin. The master told them to use what he had entrusted to them in the best way.

The worker who received five coins put his money to work and made a profit of five coins. The worker who received two coins doubled the money to four. But the worker who got one was worried that he would lose it, and so he buried the coin.

When the master came back from his journey, he praised the first two workers, but he was fed up with the last worker who had not put his money to good use. With this story, Jesus wants to give us a message: We must work with what he gives us in such a way that we build his kingdom. We must develop the talents he has given us, as well as all our spiritual gifts, and use them well. Go for it! As we use what he has given us to his glory, he will give us even more so that his name will be glorified.

Thank the Lord for everything he has given you. Don't bury your talents.

Jesus would use his talents.

Now to each one the manifestation of the Spirit is given for the common good. (1 Corinthians 12:7)

September 21

No Favorites

"You pay no attention to who they are." (Matthew 22:16)

Sometimes we treat people as if some are more important than others. Yes, I know that there are people who are important because of their rank or position. Think of the president. He is an important person because he has an important position. This, however, does not mean that as a person he is worth more to God than you or me. God has no favorites. All people are equal before God. The president will not be treated better than you and me one day before the throne of God. To God we are all equal.

The Pharisees saw that Jesus did not favor certain people and ignore others. *"We know you are a man of integrity and that you teach ... in accordance with the truth. You aren't swayed by men, because you pay no attention to who they are"* (v. 16). Jesus did not try to gain favor with people. Jesus also didn't like it when people tried to win his favor just for show. He was always honest.

Remember that you are just as important to the Lord as any other person. If Jesus likes you it is not because you are pretty or good. He loves you and cares for you. You don't need to impress him. Just be yourself. Decide to serve him with all your heart. He will always be honest with you.

Jesus would be honest.

"We know you are a man of integrity ... " (Mark 12:14)

September 22

KING ON A DONKEY

"See, your king comes to you, gentle and riding on a donkey, on a colt, the foal of a donkey." (Matthew 21:5)

Donkeys are very humble animals. In ancient times donkeys were used more often than today. Nowadays we see a donkey cart only on farms or in museums.

In the time of Jesus, a donkey was a very common pack animal. People put their goods on a donkey's back and then walked alongside the donkey or rode on another donkey. In this way they transported their goods and traveled from one place to another.

Jesus decided to ride into Jerusalem on a donkey. Many years ago a man called Zechariah prophesied that Jesus would enter Jerusalem in this way (see Zechariah 9:9). Zechariah said that Jesus was the king, but not a proud king who would look down on people. No, he was a king who showed us how humble he was by riding into Jerusalem on the back of a donkey. The king of our lives, Jesus Christ, was not haughty or boastful. He was humble. Doesn't the fact that he came down from heaven to live on earth prove that he was humble? He, the Son of God, was prepared to become human, a human like you and me.

As the children of a humble king like Jesus, we must also behave humbly. We must not think too much of ourselves.

Jesus would be humble.

"For I am gentle and humble in heart ... " (Matthew 11:29)

A GREAT HERITAGE

Surely I have a delightful inheritance. (Psalm 16:6)

Every day new babies are born. Their lives start new. As they grow older, they will start noticing the world around them, and they will start living life. Everything will be new and fresh to them. And yet the earth has existed millions of years. As Ecclesiastes says, there is actually nothing new under the sun.

There are many things around us that you and I can enjoy. Just think of the beauty of nature. Every day we can still discover something new – that is, new to us – for we are given these things. The Lord made everything for us to enjoy.

Today we should think about things that have been, things that we have inherited and that have been passed down to us. There are people in this country whose families have lived here for ages. Your grandfather and grandmother and their grandfathers and grandmothers before them most probably lived here, and they passed certain things down to you, like your language, your religion, and all kinds of everyday things.

You and I can thank the Lord today for all the good things we have received. Everything comes from the hand of the Lord, but there are also people who worked hard to keep what the Lord gave them in a good condition for you and me.

Jesus would be
thankful in everything.

And be thankful. (Colossians 3:15)

September 24

Tomorrow

Do not boast about tomorrow. (Proverbs 27:1)

You can live out tomorrow and the day after in your thoughts so much that you let today pass you by. It is good to have plans for the future, but we must not be so excited about tomorrow that we don't live today.

The Bible says you must not boast about what you expect tomorrow. Whoever boasts about tomorrow pretends that he or she has already received what must still come tomorrow. That is dangerous. How can we know what is waiting for us tomorrow? We don't even know what is going to happen to us in the next hour. That is why Christians say, "God willing ..." This saying means that it all depends on the Lord if we will have a tomorrow. Perhaps you have heard of "DV." This is short for the Latin *Deo Volente*, which means "if God is willing."

Are you looking forward to something? Then remind yourself, *if God is willing.*

Jesus would not
worry about tomorrow.

"Why, you do not even know what will happen tomorrow."
(James 4:14)

GOOD FOR EVIL

If your enemy is hungry, give him food to eat. (Proverbs 25:21)

The Lord's way of doing things is so very different from our way. If someone doesn't like us, it is very easy not to like that person. If someone is cross with us, it is just as easy to be cross with that person. The Lord's way is different. He says we must love our enemies; we must not hate them. If someone who hates us is hungry, we must give him something to eat, and if he is thirsty, we must give him something to drink.

Only God can help us to love people like this. It is also a very good way to show that we love Jesus and belong to him. We must not return evil for evil. Ask the Lord to help you show love to that person. Perhaps the love you show him or her will make that person stop hating you, and it will please the Lord if the heart of such a person is changed.

Is there someone who goes out of his way to hurt you and hate you? Be nice to that person. Give him or her something. Give it with love. In this way you are the Lord's instrument of love.

Jesus would be nice
to his enemies.

"Love your enemies." (Matthew 5:44)

September 26

AT PEACE

A heart at peace gives life to the body. (Proverbs 14:30)

Our heart is the place deep down where we feel. Sometimes we feel good, sometimes not so good. Sometimes we feel excited, and sometimes we are calm and relaxed. When we are scared, our hearts are filled with fear. If we are glad, our hearts are full of joy. If we are anxious, our hearts are stormy, almost like the waves of the sea that can't stop breaking.

Doctors and the Bible tell us that it is not good for us if we are anxious all the time. Restlessness, worry, and fear are all things that upset us, and they are not good for our bodies. It is much better to be calm and restful.

The Lord helps you to have peace in your heart. Give him all your worries, pray to him, and trust him. He will fill you with his peace. This will also help make your body healthier.

Jesus will give you peace.

"Peace I leave with you; my peace I give you." (John 14:27)

Stand Up for Them

Moses ... stood in the breach before him. (Psalm 106:23)

We read in Psalm 106 how the people of Israel forgot God, their Savior. He did great things in Egypt and brought them out of this country. Still they did not go on believing in him, but kept on doing bad things. The Lord was very angry with them and decided to destroy them. He wanted them all to die. The Lord will not decide to do such a thing unless a person has sinned very, very badly. (If you are a child of the Lord, you don't have to worry that he will destroy you, because Jesus paid the price of your guilt and took your sins upon himself.)

Fortunately, Moses was prepared to speak to God on behalf of these people. The Bible says he "stood in the breach" for Israel. This means that he asked God very nicely to forgive them, and the Lord decided to spare their lives. Just because one man prayed, the lives of thousands and thousands of people were spared.

Moses stood in the breach for others. You and I can also do it. There are many people who live under the judgment of God because they renounced Jesus, but you and I can pray for them, plead for them, and ask the Lord to change their hearts and spare their lives. If you see someone who is careless about living for the Lord, you must plead with the Lord for him or her.

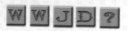

Jesus would stand in the breach
before the Father for us.

Far be it from me that I should sin against the Lord by failing to pray for you. (1 Samuel 12:19)

September 28

Satisfied

If we have food and clothing, we will be content with that. (1 Timothy 6:8)

It is so easy to complain about the things we don't have. So many things are advertised, and everything looks so attractive that we think we cannot go without it. We can want something so badly that we become dissatisfied with what we have.

To be satisfied with what you have is a wonderful characteristic. Some people have so much, and yet they are never satisfied. Others have very little, yet they are content and satisfied. The Bible says if we have food and clothes we have nothing to complain about. Food keeps us alive, and clothes keep us warm and protected. It is as if the Bible is saying that if we have the basic things in life, we can be happy. We are satisfied because we are thankful for what we have received. The Lord promised that he would give us food and clothing if we put our trust in him. Children of the Lord should never be dissatisfied.

Don't you want to thank the Lord for everything you have? If there is something you want very badly, tell the Lord, but don't be dissatisfied with your life.

Jesus would be satisfied
with what he has.

Let us be thankful. (Hebrews 12:28)

September 29

THE NURSE

"Let us look for a young [girl] to attend the king and take care of him." (1 Kings 1:2)

When King David was old, he suffered a lot. Like many old people even today, he was sickly and needed care. His servants suggested that they must look for a nurse who could be with him every minute of the day and night to serve him and take care of him. From all the girls, they chose Abishag. The Bible says she was very young and also very pretty. One can just think how much she meant to David. She saw to all his needs and looked after him well.

Today nurses still care for sick people. It is a wonderful job because nurses care for those in need. They work in hospitals and also in private homes. They make sure that the sick are well taken care of. They also help the doctors who treat their patients.

Thank the Lord for nurses. Many of them are also Christians, and they care not only for the bodies of the sick, but also talk to them, encourage them, and tell them about Jesus. Pray for nurses today.

Jesus would pray for nurses.

"Come, you who are blessed by my Father ... You looked after me." (Matthew 25:34, 36)

ROAD SIGNS

"Set up road signs; put up guideposts." (Jeremiah 31:21)

We find road signs on all major roads. Large signs are placed along the roads to give information as to where we should go. There are road signs that tell us speeding is dangerous or warn us of a sharp curve ahead. Other road signs give us information about a rest stop along the road or a gas station where we can fill up. Then there are signposts that indicate direction. They point out in which direction a specific town lies.

The Lord told his people to erect road signs and guideposts. This is the Lord's way of telling them that they must keep to the road that has been indicated and make sure they reach the right destination. You and I also need road signs and signposts that show us the way. What road signs are these?

Examples of road signs or guideposts for you and me are ministers, pastors, and teachers. They could also be good advice from friends, counseling from our parents, and, of course, the Word of God and the Holy Spirit. Take note of all these road signs and obey them. Erect your guideposts today, keep your eyes on the main road, and don't wander off in your own direction.

Jesus would show you
the way to the Father.

"I am the way and the truth and the life." (John 14:6)

October 1

WHO DOES HE THINK HE IS?

And they took offense at him. (Mark 6:3)

Jesus did many wonderful things. In his own hometown, Nazareth, he started teaching in the synagogue. Many people came to listen to him, and they were amazed and touched by his message. Yet, they asked one another, *"Isn't this the carpenter? Isn't this Mary's son and the brother of James ... Aren't his sisters here with us?"* (v. 3). They didn't want to have anything more to do with him.

It was because they had known Jesus since childhood that they didn't take him seriously. They thought of him as an ordinary person because he grew up before their eyes. That is why Jesus said a prophet is respected everywhere, except where he grew up. Jesus even said his own family would not accept him as others did.

Often we find it more difficult to live for Jesus and to be a witness for him in our own surroundings. People don't readily accept that you can give them a message from the Lord because they know you so well. Perhaps you are finding it difficult to follow Jesus in your own home, but just keep at it, even if your own family is negative and discourages you. The same thing happened to Jesus. You just go on praying for your family and friends.

Jesus would preach the
gospel everywhere.

He was teaching the people in the temple. (Luke 20:1)

October 2

CHEERED UP

For they refreshed my spirit ... (1 Corinthians 16:18)

Paul did wonderful work for the Lord. He worked very hard. Paul was a tentmaker, but in between he preached and helped people to find the Lord and to grow in faith and in knowledge. Sometimes he worked so hard that he became very, very tired in both body and soul.

Paul wrote in a letter to his friends in Corinth how pleased he was when three men visited him. They had very interesting names: Stephanas, Fortunatus, and Achaicus. Paul then tells them why he was so glad to see these men: They refreshed his spirit; in other words, they cheered him up. I'm sure they talked and laughed a lot, and they praised the Lord and prayed together. After this visit, Paul was filled with new courage and strength for all the work he had to do for the Lord.

You and I also need friends who can be with us when we need encouragement and cheering up. Good friends are like a cool glass of water when you are thirsty. They refresh you and make you feel much better. Thank the Lord for your friends who are there for you and cheer you up when you need it. Be a friend like this to others.

Jesus would cheer others up.

[The LORD] has sent me to bind up the brokenhearted. (Isaiah 61:1)

THE THORN

There was given me a thorn in my flesh. (2 Corinthians 12:7)

Have you ever had a thorn in your foot? It makes your foot very sensitive, and after a while you can't really walk on it any more. One of the reasons we wear shoes is so that we don't get thorns in our feet.

Paul also talks about a thorn in his flesh. This was not a real thorn, and it was also not in his foot. He had some hurt or difficulty in his life. We don't really know what it was. Some say it was a weakness he had. Others think it was some kind of illness or deformity, or weak eyes. We don't really know what was wrong. Three times he asked the Lord to take this away. The Lord's answer was short and sweet: *"My grace is sufficient for you"* (v. 9). Later on Paul writes that he knows he has this problem to keep him humble. It made him realize that he needed God.

Is there something that makes your life difficult? Perhaps you also want the Lord to take it away. Perhaps this difficulty is there for the same reason as Paul's. One thing we know: the Lord's grace is enough for us. Yes, he carries us through and supports us.

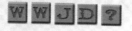

Jesus will be with us
even in our hurt.

There you saw how the LORD your God carried you, as a father carries his son. (Deuteronomy 1:31)

October 4

WHERE IS DEMAS?

Demas, because he loved this world, has deserted me.
(2 Timothy 4:10)

Demas was a Christian, and at first he served the Lord with all his heart. We don't know much about his life, but what the Bible tells us of Demas is not very positive.

Paul writes that Demas was with him at first. Most probably he worked with Paul, helped him, and prayed with him. The two of them told people about Jesus. Then something went wrong, because Paul writes that Demas decided to leave him. Paul says the reason was that Demas loved the world.

When the Bible talks about "the world," it means everything that is not the will of the Lord. Everything that does not belong to the kingdom of Jesus is "the world." There are many good and wonderful things in life, and also many wonderful people. But if they do not accept Jesus as King and Lord, they are part of "the world." Often it is all the glitz and glamour of a world without Christ that seems so inviting to us. To Demas it was so attractive that he decided not to serve the Lord any more. He loved things better than the Lord and his kingdom. What a shame!

Jesus would focus on
the things of heaven.

Set your minds on things above, not earthly things.
(Colossians 3:2)

October 5

JUST YOU

No one came to my support, but everyone deserted me.
(2 Timothy 4:16)

Has anybody ever let you down? Have you ever ended up alone with a problem because everybody disappeared when the work had to be done? It happened to Paul.

Paul served the Lord with his whole being. He was not ashamed to be a witness for him and to tell people that Jesus Christ is the only Savior. The devil did not like this at all. So he got some people together to go after Paul and make his life very difficult. This got so bad that Paul was even taken prisoner at a later stage for preaching the gospel. Many of his friends left him. Perhaps they were afraid, or some may have been embarrassed. Paul says when he had to appear in court the first time no one was there to support him. Can you think how unhappy that must have made him?

Yet, just listen what Paul adds: *"But the Lord stood at my side and gave me strength ... I was delivered from the lion's mouth"* (v. 17). Remember, even if people let you down and disappoint you, the Lord stays at your side. He will support you.

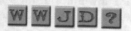

Jesus would support
you in everything.

The Lord stood at my side and gave me strength. (2 Timothy 4:17)

Do Love?

"A new command I give you: Love one another." (John 13:34)

Many people think love is a feeling. If you feel good about someone, or you feel that you love someone very much, you think it is true love. It a fact that we often have a special feeling for someone we love. But this does not mean we must first feel loving before we can love.

The Bible sees true love as a command from the Lord. Because the Lord tells us to love one another, we must love one another; it's as simple as that. Love is not a feeling. It is a choice. This means that you and I must say, "We will love because God tells us to."

Love is one of God's commandments, and it means that I must do deeds of love for all people, whether I like them or not. The question is not how we feel about people; the question is whether we are prepared to love them as Jesus loves them. Even if we don't like them, we are friendly to them, and we help them, support them, and want what's best for them.

Decide that you will love all people that you meet today, even if you don't like them.

Jesus would love his enemies.

"Love your enemies." (Matthew 5:44)

Ham Makes a Mistake

"The lowest of slaves will he be to his brothers."
(Genesis 9:25)

Noah had faith in God. God told him to build an ark, and it did not bother Noah at all that everybody made fun of him for doing it. Noah just went on doing what the Lord had told him to do.

Noah had three sons: Shem, Ham, and Japheth. After the flood, Noah planted a vineyard. Noah made wine with the fruit of the vine, and one day he drank too much and got drunk. He did not even realize that he had taken off all his clothes. Just then Ham came into his father's tent. It seems that Ham laughed at his father scornfully when he found him naked and drunk. He went and told his two brothers about this. His brothers were ashamed and took some clothing and covered their father without looking at him. They did not scorn their father. Instead they wanted to give him back his dignity.

When Noah woke up, he realized that he was naked, and when he heard what Ham had done to him, he cursed Ham. Noah said Ham would be a good-for-nothing slave in his brothers' service.

The lesson is that we must respect our parents and honor them even if we don't like what they do. Even if they get drunk and do things that embarrass us, we must still love them and respect them, because love always protects (see 1 Corinthians 13:7).

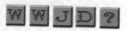

Jesus would respect his parents.

"Honor your father and your mother." (Exodus 20:12)

October 8

Abraham's Big Test

The Lord Will Provide (Genesis 22:14)

Abraham was already very old when the Lord gave him a son. Abraham loved Isaac very much. When Isaac was a young boy, the Lord told Abraham to sacrifice his son.

In the Old Testament animals were sacrificed. They were placed on an altar and killed. How could God tell Abraham to do this to his son? The reason was that God wanted to test Abraham's love. God knew how much Abraham loved Isaac, and God had a very specific plan for Abraham's life.

Abraham did what God had told him to do. He saddled his donkey and chopped wood for the burnt offering. Then he set off for the place the Lord had shown him. On the third day they saw the place in the distance. Isaac asked his father what animal they were going to sacrifice. Abraham answered that the Lord would provide. When they reached the place of sacrifice, he tied up his son and placed him on the altar. Just as Abraham took the knife to slaughter his son, an angel of the Lord called down from heaven and told him to stop. Then the Lord said, *"Now I know that you fear God, because you have not withheld from me your son, your only son"* (v. 12). How much do you love God?

Jesus would love God.

 He ... became obedient to death – even death on a cross! (Philippians 2:8)

THE GRACE OF JESUS

May the grace of the Lord Jesus Christ ... be with you all. (Galatians 13:14)

I'm sure you've heard a minister use these words as a blessing at the end of a church service. This blessing is the same prayer that Paul often wrote in his letters to Christians living in different cities. Many times he ended his letters with words similar to these: "May the grace of the Lord Jesus Christ, and the love of God, and the fellowship of the Holy Spirit be with you all."

What does this mean? The word *grace* comes from the Greek word *charis*, and in its simplest form it means simply "gifts." When the minister, or Paul, says that the grace of Jesus will be with us, he is praying that all the gifts that Jesus wants to hand out to us with his death and resurrection will become real in our lives. Which gifts?

Jesus saw to it that you and I are saved through his life and death and everything he came to do for us, that we are forgiven and made new, and that we receive the fruit of the Holy Spirit and much more. All these are spiritual gifts or "mercy" that the Lord gives us.

My prayer is that you will receive the grace-gift of Jesus in your life.

Jesus will bless you
with gifts from heaven.

Jesus Christ ... has blessed us in the heavenly realms with every spiritual blessing in Christ. (Ephesians 1:3)

THE GIFT OF LOVE

May ... the love of God ... be with you all. (2 Corinthians 13:14)

Yesterday we saw that Paul's blessing was something he wished for his Christian friends. He did not pray that they would receive Jesus' grace-gift only, but also the love of God.

Without God's love you and I cannot live meaningful lives. We need God's love. His love makes us strong. His love changes our lives. God proved his love for us when he gave us his Son. He loved us too much to allow us to perish, and that is why he sent Jesus. Yes, he proves his love through Jesus on the cross. It is this love that he also wants to give to you and me today.

He wants you to know now that he loves you very much, that he cares about you, and that he will be with you in everything you do.

All of us need love. We cannot live without love. We need the love of people, but above all, we need the love of God. Jesus forgave us our sins so that we could have a loving relationship with him, our Father. The love of God will be with you.

Jesus would always love others.

Love never fails. (1 Corinthians 13:8)

WHAT IS FELLOWSHIP?

May ... the fellowship of the Holy Spirit be with you all.
(2 Corinthians 13:14)

The last part of the blessing with which Paul ended his letters mentions the fellowship of the Holy Spirit. He prays that people will experience the fellowship of the Holy Spirit. What does this mean?

The word *fellowship* means two or more different people sharing a common interest or aim, and this unites them. When people have something in common it means they are the same in one or more ways. They may have the same color eyes, or speak the same language, or have the same father.

When someone is a child of God and has accepted Jesus Christ as Savior, that person has the Holy Spirit. All Christians have this in common: they have the Holy Spirit in their hearts and lives. This unites them, leads them in truth, fulfills them, and gives them the fruit and gifts they need. The Holy Spirit is like an invisible person in our hearts, and this makes it so that we look at things in the same way. This is how Christians can live together in harmony: They have the same Spirit who encourages them to love one another.

I pray that you will share the fellowship of the Holy Spirit with other Christians today.

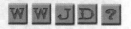

Jesus will send the Holy
Spirit to you as well.

I will pour out my Spirit on all people. (Joel 2:28)

October 12

JESUS AND THE WHIP

So he made a whip out of chords, and drove all from the temple. (John 2:15)

One can hardly imagine that Jesus was ever angry. But he was. The question is this: If Jesus never sinned, why did he get angry?

Getting angry is not a sin. It is a sin to do something out of selfishness and go against the will of God. But God himself was also disappointed and angry about all the wicked things the people of Israel did.

Jesus was angry because the temple, where people were supposed to worship, was beginning to look like a supermarket. The main reason people were coming to the temple was not to pray anymore, but to make a lot of money. Jesus was angry and disappointed. He made a whip and chased out of the temple all those people who were buying and selling, along with their sheep and cattle. I think the merchants must have been very upset with Jesus. The news probably spread that Jesus was whipping people. Jesus did not care what the people thought of him. He wanted what was right.

We must also take a firm stand on things that are not right. It doesn't mean we have to whip people, but we need to be very firm out of respect for God.

Jesus would be firm
when necessary.

 Jesus turned and said to Peter ... "You are a stumbling block to me." (Matthew 16:23)

October 13

WHAT'S DONE IS DONE

But one thing I do: Forgetting what is behind and straining toward what is ahead. (Philippians 3:13)

Life is wonderful. Every day we have opportunities to do things. When tomorrow comes, today's opportunities will be over and done with. Yesterday was unique. Yesterday is behind us.

When I think of certain things that happened in the past, I'm very glad they are over. We all know about things that happened in our past that we don't like thinking about. The good news is that it's over.

Paul was very sorry about his past. He had people killed because he thought it was wrong to follow Jesus. That was a big mistake, but he could not make it go away. He was a murderer. Then the Lord changed his heart, and Paul became a Christian. He asked the Lord to forgive him, and when he had been forgiven, he decided, "I am forgetting what is behind and looking toward what is ahead."

Do the same. Don't keep thinking about past failures and sins. Free yourself from things that happened yesterday. If you have confessed your sins, you are forgiven. Look ahead. Like an athlete, you must focus on what lies ahead.

Jesus would look ahead.

Let us throw off everything that hinders and ... let us fix our eyes on Jesus. (Hebrews 12:1, 2)

October 14

Before You Were Born

Your eyes saw my unformed body. (Psalm 139:16)

Medical technology is so wonderful nowadays that we can see a baby with ultrasound even before it is born. In the time of the Bible, none of these discoveries had been made yet. However, the Lord saw us before we were born.

It is wonderful to know that the Lord had a plan for your life and mine long before we are born. Even before your birth the Lord had already decided what your name would be, what you would look like, which talents he would give you, and what his plan for your life would be. King David realized that he was not simply one man among many, but that the Lord knew him personally, long before his birth.

Who you are and what you look like are all part of God's plan for your life. Thank him for all your talents and for what you are, even if you are not all that happy with yourself. Praise and thank the Lord that he knew all about you even before you were born. Decide today to live for him and his kingdom.

Jesus would accept God's
plan for his life.

"For I know the plans I have for you ... plans to prosper you and not to harm you." (Jeremiah 29:11)

WE'RE GETTING MARRIED

For the wedding of the Lamb has come, and his bride has made herself ready. (Revelation 19:7)

Have you ever been to a wedding? A wedding is an exciting and festive occasion. The bride spends a lot of time on herself, doing her hair and makeup and then putting on a stunning wedding dress. The groom himself looks sharp, because this wedding day is a very important day. Usually many friends and family come to the wedding to share the happiness and excitement of the bridal couple.

In Revelation 19 we read about a very special wedding. It is called the "wedding of the Lamb." The Lamb is Jesus Christ. The Bible says Jesus is like a groom. And who is the bride? You and me! Every one of us who belongs to Jesus is Jesus' bride. One day he will come and get us and we will be "married" to him in heaven. Yes, we will be with him forever and ever. There we will celebrate and be joyful. Are you ready for the heavenly wedding?

Jesus will come again to get us.

I will come back and take you to be with me that you also may be where I am. (John 14:3)

October 16

THE OPEN DOOR

See, I have placed before you an open door that no one can shut. (Revelation 3:8)

Nowadays there are so many thieves and criminals that one has to keep the doors locked. Luckily we can buy strong locks. When you turn the key in a strong deadbolt, the door is locked so securely that it is very difficult to open it without the key. This is a wonderful message for every Christian. It is as if the Lord is telling us that he alone can open or shut a door for us. Often we want to open a "door" ourselves. Say, you want to play the lead in the school play and you try just about everything to get that role. Or you so badly want to play in the team for your school that you try everything to make that team. You try opening the "door" to that team.

Rather, you should ask God to open and shut doors for you. If he opens a door for you, no one on earth will ever close it again.

Jesus would accept
his Father's will.

"Father, if you are willing ... not my will, but yours be done."
(Luke 22:42)

October 17

READY FOR HARVESTING

"The harvest is plentiful, but the workers are few."
(Luke 10:2)

One of the best things to see is a field ready for harvesting. Farmers work very hard to prepare their land before they sow seeds or plant trees. All the preparation must be done before the plants can produce a crop. Jesus also talks about a harvest field, a cornfield. A cornfield is green at first while the corn grows, and later the grain growing on the ears becomes yellow. Then it is ready for harvesting.

The Lord sees billions of people on earth, and he sees their needs. They are like uncountable ears of corn. There are millions of people in countries like India, China, Russia, France, and Kenya. The Lord says, "See, they are ripe in the fields." We must tell them about the kingdom of Christ. We must tell them they can be saved and go to heaven – that they can be given a new life.

We must not only pray for the billions of people who have not even heard about Jesus; we must be prepared to tell them about Jesus. We must be like workers, willing to harvest.

Jesus would preach the
gospel all over the world.

 Jesus went throughout Galilee, teaching ... preaching the good news of the kingdom. (Matthew 4:23)

October 18

WORKERS

" ... to send out workers into his harvest field."
(Matthew 9:38)

Farmers who have big farms and many cornfields need a lot of workers to help with the harvest. Although we have large and wonderful machinery to harvest the crops, the help of people is still necessary. In the time of the Bible many workers were needed because then, of course, they did not have the machinery we have now.

Every worker on a farm has his or her own specific task. Some drive tractors. Others must bag up the grain. Others fasten the bags, or load and unload the bags. If one decides not to do his part, the whole harvest is slowed down. Every one must do his or her part.

You and I are workers in the Lord's service, and we also have a task. Some are ministers or pastors, others have a specific duty to perform in the church, and some are singers. Others take part in prayer meetings or talk to people about Jesus. Then there are those whose calling is to be witnesses for the Lord as doctors, nurses, or business people. We all have a task to carry out. In this way God's bumper crop is harvested because each of us is a worker in God's huge field. We must also pull our weight. We are workers, and we have to help harvest the Lord's crop.

Jesus would be a fellow
worker in God's field.

For we are God's fellow workers ... (1 Corinthians 3:9)

October 19

JUST A CUP OF COLD WATER

> "And if anyone gives even a cup of cold water to one of these little ones because he is my disciple ... he will certainly not lose his reward." (Matthew 10:42)

Jesus said that our hearts, our homes, and our hands should be open to receive those who preach the message of his kingdom. He said, *"he who receives you receives me, and he who receives me receives the one who sent me. Anyone who receives a prophet because he is a prophet will receive a prophet's reward, and anyone who receives a righteous man because he is a righteous man will receive a righteous man's reward"* (v. 40, 41).

We must help people who work full-time for the Lord and try to make their task easier. We must give them our support, give them money when necessary, and see that they get what they need to do the Lord's work. Even if we give them a cup of cold water when they are thirsty, the Lord sees it, and he will reward us. He promised.

Think of ways to help those who work for the Lord. Perhaps you can pray for them. Perhaps you can give them a hand and encourage them. Or you can contribute money. You can invite them to join you for a meal at your house. If we support people in this way, it is as if we are doing it for Jesus himself.

Jesus would help others
and support them.

So he went to her, took her hand and helped her up. (Mark 1:31)

October 20

WORTHLESS?

A bruised reed he will not break, and a smoldering wick
he will not snuff out. (Matthew 12:20)

Sometimes we think we are not good enough for the Lord.
We feel that we have failed and because of that we have been
disqualified. God does not think so. He can use anything,
even the greatest failure.

Reeds were used in the days before bridges were built.
When people had to go through a river, they used a reed to
show them how deep the water was. But a bent or bruised
reed was no good. It could not be used anymore. The Bible
says that even if you and I are sometimes like bruised reeds
we can still be of use to the Lord.

There was no electricity in the time of the Bible. They
used lamps that were filled with oil. Inside the lamp was a
wick, and it was the wick that burned and made the light.
Sometimes the wick started smoldering and smoking. Then
it was better to put it out, otherwise the whole house would
be full of unpleasant smoke. A smoldering wick was use-
less. Even if you and I sometimes feel as worthless as a
smoldering wick, with our smoke getting into the eyes of the
Lord, he will not put us out. He will still be able to use us.

Thank the Lord that he uses you in spite of all your
shortcomings.

Jesus would regard you
as an important person.

"You are worth more than many sparrows." (Matthew 10:31)

October 21

DON'T PULL THEM UP!

> "The servants asked him, 'Do you want us to go and pull them up?'" (Matthew 13:28)

Jesus told the parable of seed and weeds. A farmer sows seed to produce a good crop. Unfortunately, farmers must have their lands weeded regularly, otherwise weeds will kill the seed. A weed is a worthless plant that can really harm the crops.

Jesus tells the story of a man who sowed good seed. One night when everyone was asleep, his enemy came and sowed weeds among the wheat. The weeds started becoming a danger to the new wheat. The farmer's servants asked him if they should pull up the weeds. He answered, *"No ... because while you are pulling the weeds, you may root up the wheat with them. Let both grow together until the harvest. At that time I will tell the harvesters: First collect the weeds and tie them in bundles to be burned; then gather the wheat and bring it into my barn"* (v. 29, 30). What did Jesus mean?

Jesus is saying that you and I must not judge people. If it seems as if someone doesn't love and serve the Lord, we must not shun or reject him. Don't pull him up like a weed. The Lord knows who the weeds are – and who is wheat. We can trust him to judge the weeds eventually.

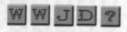

Jesus would be the good seed.

"The good seed stands for the sons of the kingdom." (Matthew 13:38)

October 22

NO MORE QUESTIONS

"In that day you will no longer ask me anything." (John 16:23)

Because we wonder about so many things, we ask a lot of questions. There are also many spiritual things we do not understand. Sometimes we ask our pastor to explain something that we don't understand.

We ask questions especially when things happen that hurt us and we don't understand why they happened. The poet Totius was a minister, but when two of his daughters died very young, he asked many questions. Job also questioned God, because he could not understand why everything was suddenly going so horribly wrong for him. Some questions have clear and definite answers. Other questions, however, are more difficult to answer. Even learned people sometimes disagree about answers to certain questions. Likewise, pastors differ about the answers to certain spiritual questions. Only God knows all the answers.

Luckily Jesus says a day will come when you and I will not need to ask any more questions. In that day we will know all the answers. Everything that we couldn't understand before will be crystal clear to us. This is the day that we will be in heaven with the Lord. We will know everything and understand everything. Until then we must just believe and trust the Lord.

Jesus will answer all
your questions one day.

Now I know in part; then I shall know fully." (1 Corinthians 13:12)

October 23

I HAVE TO!

I am compelled to preach. Woe to me if I do not preach the gospel! (1 Corinthians 9:16)

The word *gospel* means "good news." Paul said he couldn't help preaching the good news of Jesus Christ. He told it and explained it to all who would listen, if they understand it or not. He could not help himself; he simply had to do it.

Paul tried to put a stop to the gospel of Jesus Christ at first. Those who preached the gospel were persecuted by him. Then the Lord touched Paul's life, and he repented and his whole life changed. Suddenly he had a longing in his heart to preach the gospel. Do you remember that the Lord called him to do it? God gave him the specific task to preach the gospel to the gentile nations in particular. The Holy Spirit encouraged him.

Every one of the Lord's children should, like Paul, have a longing to preach the gospel. Jesus wants the whole world to know about him. We must preach the gospel. Woe to us if we do not do it! Tell God today that you will preach the gospel.

Jesus would preach the gospel.

"I must preach the good news of the kingdom of God." (Luke 4:43)

October 24

WILD PEOPLE

Where there is no revelation, the people cast off restraint. (Proverbs 29:18)

Today's scripture means that when the will of God is not made known to people they are uncontrolled and become wild. Wild horses are dangerous. If you try to ride one, it is very likely that it will throw you because it will buck and go wild. Your life can even be in danger. It is the same with a wild bull. Many farmers and farmhands have been trampled by wild bulls. Wild people are just as bad. I'm sure you've heard people talk about a wild party. When people go wild (often because they have had too much to drink), they do all kinds of very stupid things. They hit each another, break furniture, and do a lot of irresponsible things.

Civilized people are not wild, but "tame." They have peace in their hearts and are well-mannered. Wouldn't it be wonderful if all the people of our country could behave like this?

The Bible tells us that if the will of the Lord and the Word of God are not brought to the people, they become wild (they have no restraint). It is the Word of God that changes our hearts and our will, so that we become better people.

Pray that God's Word and his will may be preached loud and clear in our country.

Jesus would preach God's
Word to all people.

Now the tax collectors and "sinners" were all gathering around to hear him. (Luke 15:1)

October 25

DON'T YOU KNOW ME?

"Don't you know me, Philip, even after I have been among you such a long time?" (John 14:9)

I think we often surprise the Lord, like Philip, one of his disciples, did. Philip lived with the Lord and shared everything with him. Philip heard him talk about his kingdom. And then Philip made a strange request, "Lord, show us the Father ..."

This was when Jesus said that it seemed as if Philip didn't know him even though he had been with him such a long time.

The Lord speaks to us in many ways and in many places. Often we hear, but we don't really hear. Will the Lord not perhaps say to you or me, "You've known me so long; how can you ask such questions?" I don't think the Lord minds that we ask him questions, but I do think that he sometimes expects us to know more answers, seeing that we have his Word and we are his children.

Make an effort to get to know the Lord even better.

Jesus would teach
you about the Lord.

"He who loves me will be loved by my Father, and I too will love him and show myself to him." (John 14:21)

October 26

GO THE EXTRA MILE

"If someone forces you to go one mile, go with him two miles." (Matthew 5:41)

This really does not seem fair. Why must I carry someone's things a longer distance, especially if he is forcing me in the first place? Most of us would refuse. The issue here is the attitude in our hearts. If God does not work in our hearts, it is impossible to do what Jesus says in this scripture. But if he has changed our hearts, then we can do things we would never have done before.

It is precisely when we must do things that we don't enjoy that we reveal Jesus' love and attitude. It is when we love our enemies that we glow with a wonderful testimony for all to see. It is when we serve others that people will ask why we are so different. Then we can tell them it is Jesus who taught us to be like him. He served. He gave people his best. He came to save us and give us life, although we did not deserve it. This is what our attitude should be.

We must amaze others with our loving ways – especially those that least expect it. Our enemies will be so surprised at a deed of love from the heart of the Lord himself. Come, let's walk that extra mile without being asked. Then we will please the Lord, and we will be a bright light in the dark world.

Jesus would serve others
without asking questions.

"I, your Lord and Teacher, have washed your feet." (John 13:14)

October 27

Come a Little Closer

Come near to God and he will come near to you. (James 4:8)

I'm sure you have tried to get closer to someone. Perhaps you were the odd one out in a group of friends. Often when you try to draw near to someone they won't allow you to. It is as if they keep us at arm's length. You can feel very lonely if people won't allow you to come close.

Fortunately, the Lord is not like that at all. He wants us near him. He came nearer to us. That is why Jesus' other name is *Immanuel*, meaning "God with us." Because God saw that we were far away from him, he decided to send us his Son. In this way he came near us. James tells you and me that we must draw nearer to God: Draw near to him and he will draw near to you. This is a promise from God's Word. I do not know of a single person who tried to draw near to the Lord and was pushed away by him. The arms of the Lord are always ready to receive us. He wants us to be very near to him. When he is near to us, our hearts are full of peace, love, and true happiness.

Decide that you want to draw even closer to the Lord today. Tell him this, and tell yourself. Don't allow anything to keep you away from the Lord. He is waiting for you with outstretched arms if you want to come near to him.

Jesus would not turn you
away if you draw near to him.

 Let us then approach the throne of grace with confidence. (Hebrews 4:16)

October 28

FOR THE SAKE OF THE GOSPEL

I have become all things to all men so that by all possible means I might save some. (1 Corinthians 9:22)

Paul had such a burning desire to share the gospel that he was prepared to make allowances. This means to act differently in order to get something to work.

For the sake of the gospel Paul was prepared to become a Jew to a Jew and a Greek to a Greek. He knew that if he wanted to preach the gospel, he couldn't expect people to become like him. He had to become like them. This doesn't mean that he was prepared to sin; rather, it means that Paul saw to it that he was on the same level with his hearers. He talked to the Jews in their language, and to the Greeks in theirs. With children, he talked on a child's level. With clever people he used suitable language for them. It's no good to try and tell people things if they don't understand you.

Jesus was also prepared to mingle with bad people so that he could speak to them. Because Jesus loved people and didn't mind being on their level, he could preach the gospel to them.

You and I must also be like this. We must be able to speak to anybody about his or her interests, and when we get the opportunity, we must tell him or her about Jesus.

Jesus would tell
everybody the good news.

Now the tax collectors and "sinners" were all gathering around to hear him. (Luke 15:1)

October 29

Afraid, but Obedient

Samuel ... was afraid to tell Eli the vision. (1 Samuel 3:15)

Do you remember how Samuel's mother prayed for a child? When Samuel was born, she dedicated him to the Lord. From the time he was a small boy, Samuel lived in the temple where he was raised to serve the Lord.

One night as Samuel was sleeping, the Lord called him. When Samuel woke up, he thought at first that Eli had called him. Eli was the priest who worked in the temple. Later on Eli realized it was the Lord who had called Samuel, and he told Samuel to say, "Speak, Lord, for your servant is listening."

Then the Lord spoke to Samuel and gave him a message for Eli. Unfortunately, it was not good news.

It couldn't have been easy for Samuel to give Eli this message. But he had to be obedient. Often we find it very difficult to tell someone the truth. Even if the truth hurts, we must tell it. But we must do it in love and obedience to the Lord. If Samuel had not obeyed the Lord, Eli would not have been prepared for what was going to happen. Then Samuel would not have had peace with God. When the Lord asks us to do something, we must do it.

Jesus would tell the truth.

"Then you will know the truth, and the truth will set you free." (John 8:32)

YOU MUST MOVE

Abraham ... obeyed and went, even though he did not know where he was going. (Hebrews 11:8)

The Lord called Abraham from a far land, Ur. Because the Lord had a plan for his life, and for the people of Israel who would later descend from him, the Lord told Abraham to move away from Ur. There was just one problem. Abraham had no idea where to go.

The Lord calls many people to follow him, even today. He calls you too. He also wants you to "move away" in the direction that he thinks is best for you. It's difficult if you don't really know where you're going. The Lord doesn't tell us exactly where we're headed either. What he does tell us is that he will be with us. What he is asking is that we trust him. That is faith. Abraham believed that the Lord knew what he was doing, and so he moved away from Ur. Because Abraham believed, the Lord did wonderful things through him.

Every day must be a step along the road with Jesus. We don't know what will happen this day, but let's trust him to show us the way. What an adventure! Following Jesus with your whole life is not being sure about what tomorrow will bring, but we know that if we are moving with God, we will be contented and happy.

Jesus will be with
you wherever you go.

"And surely I am with you always, to the very end of the age." (Matthew 28:20)

October 31

LOOK TO THE HEAVENS

Lift your eyes and look to the heavens: Who created all these? (Isaiah 40:26)

In the time when Isaiah lived, the people of God had become spiritually dull. They were sinful, and their sin made the Lord seem vague and far away. They put their trust in heathen gods and not in God. Then Isaiah made them look at the heavens. He told them to see the stars again.

When you see the wonders of the galaxy, you cannot help but realize that a great and mighty Creator made it all. We see so much of God's greatness in nature. We see him in the mountains, in the flowers, and even in modern technology. If we allow our minds to open our eyes, we will see God in everything around us. When Israel really looked at the stars again, they realized again who God was. They started worshiping him once more.

At school you learn about wonderful things. You take in new knowledge. If you read books and encyclopedias, you will get to know about the most interesting things. If you are a child of the Lord, you cannot help but see the hand of God in everything. You must thank and praise the Lord for all the wonderful things. He is the Creator and Lord of your life.

Jesus would be happy
with creation.

You have set your glory above the heavens. (Psalm 8:2)

ALL DAY LONG

Pray continually. (1 Thessalonians 5:17)

One of the best habits you can get into is to speak to the Lord all the time. The Lord wants us to speak to him; he is always with his children. By his Holy Spirit he lives inside us. That is why he is never away from us, and we can be in contact with him every moment of the day.

Paul writes a letter to a Christian church and tells them to pray continually. Continually means without stopping. So what he is actually saying is this: Pray without stopping. How do we do it? We pray continually when we talk to the Lord in our thoughts all the time. We share everything with him: what we see, what we hear, and what we experience.

As the day goes on, we can talk to the Lord all the time about everything that is happening to us. We can talk about our feelings. We can talk about things we want to see or have. We can say thank you for things we enjoy. We can pray for someone else. We can speak to the Lord if we feel we are in danger. Yes, we can really speak to the Lord about everything.

Let's make it a way of life to talk to the Lord continually. Share everything you do today with him by talking to him in your thoughts or even out loud.

Jesus would talk to
the Lord all the time.

In everything, by prayer and petition, with thanksgiving present your requests to God. (Philippians 4:6)

JEALOUSY AND QUARRELING

For since there is jealousy and quarreling among you, are you not worldly? (1 Corinthians 3:3)

Paul wrote a letter to the Corinthians. They had accepted the Lord Jesus and followed him. Yet they sometimes still acted like non-Christians. This is a problem with all Christians. We still sometimes do things that are not proper and that God does not want us to do.

Paul writes that the Corinthians were sometimes jealous and quarreled with others. When you are jealous you don't want anyone else to have anything good unless you can have it too. You don't want someone else to be successful. You are jealous of a friend if you want him or her for yourself only. You don't want your friend to have any others friends but you.

To quarrel is to be angry and to have an argument. You lose your temper if something happens that you don't like. You are angry with others, and you behave in a very ugly way.

Paul says that when we are jealous or fighting with others, we are not acting like Christians, but like worldly people. Worldly people don't have the Holy Spirit in their hearts. They don't live according to the Word of God. So, we would expect them to fight and be jealous. We do not expect this behavior from Christians. Try to live in peace with all people, and don't begrudge them the good things in their lives.

Jesus would live in peace with all people.

"Blessed are the peacemakers." (Matthew 5:9)

November 3

WAKE UP!

"Wake up, O sleeper, rise from the dead, and Christ will shine on you." (Ephesians 5:14)

Sleep is good for you. It gives you new strength. But if you are spiritually asleep, then it's not a good thing. The Bible says you must not be asleep spiritually; you must be spiritually awake.

This means that we must be on fire for the Lord. One singer says, "Boil for the King." This means we must be diligent, wide awake, and serving the Lord with energy and enthusiasm.

Spiritual sleep is almost like spiritual death. When you sleep you can't do anything. A person who is asleep is not active. There is no sign of real life as there is when someone runs or plays or sings or talks. The Lord does not want us to be spiritually dead. He wants us to be alive and lively; others must see that we know the Lord, that we love him and follow him, because our behavior shows it.

If we are awake and not spiritually asleep, the light of Jesus will be seen clearly in our lives. We usually sleep when it is dark. People who are awake are awake in the daytime. This is the time we usually work. Let us then live and work in Jesus' light, and serve him zealously.

Jesus would help you serve
him with enthusiasm.

  Always be zealous for ... the LORD. (Proverbs 23:17)

November 4

Even More Fruitful

"Every branch that does bear fruit he prunes so that it will be even more fruitful." (John 15:2)

The Lord wants to see fruit in our lives so that he can be glorified. You and I are like a tree. If one cannot see fruit on a tree, then it is not a fruitful tree. A tree that bears good fruit is the owner's pride and joy. He picks the fruit and enjoys giving some of it to others. Our heavenly Father wants to see fruit on the tree of our lives so that he can be glorified.

The Lord often uses suffering, pain, and heartache to teach us, his children, important lessons. In this way he makes us strong in spirit and helps us to grow spiritually. The Lord is a great gardener, and he prunes you and me so that we can bear more fruit in our lives. A tree is pruned so that it can produce more fruit.

Pruning may not be pleasant for us, but God does it so that we can bear more fruit. The Lord wants to prune all bad things out of our lives, like bad habits and sinful thoughts. Because of God's pruning, we can bear better fruit.

Jesus would prune you
to bear better fruit.

He [Jesus] must become greater; I must become less. (John 3:30)

He Will Receive Me

Though my father and mother forsake me, the LORD will receive me. (Psalm 27:10)

There are many children who are in foster homes. While the parents of some of these children have died, there are also children whose parents are alive but cannot take care of them. They must feel very alone, not being with their parents. These children are taken care of in foster homes.

Grown-ups sometimes also miss their parents. Their parents might have passed away, or they might live elsewhere. Sometimes when grown-ups feel a little lonely, they long to see their parents again and to sit and talk to them. Loneliness is part of life. We are sometimes lonely because we cannot have our parents with us all the time. But the Bible has comfort for us. The Lord promises to take us in his care and says that he will be with us always. After all, his name is also Father. He is not an earthly father, that is true, but he is the heavenly Father who, in Jesus, is with us all the time. He wants to take us in his Father's arms, and he assures us that he will take care of us. Thank the Lord that he, like your father and mother, will take you into his care and will be with you always.

Jesus will take care of you also.

"If that is how God clothes the grass of the field ... will he not much more clothe you!" (Matthew 6:30)

HE GIVES BACK!

"I will repay you for the years the locusts have eaten."
(Joel 2:25)

In the time of the prophet Joel, the Lord sent a swarm of locusts to eat the Israelites' crops. A very difficult time lay ahead of them. God wanted to teach them a lesson. Yet he promised that he would give them his blessings again.

The Lord is like that. Often things happen in our lives that we find very difficult to accept. A family member dies, or our family goes through a difficult financial crisis. It could be that your mom or dad has lost a job. The Lord helps his children in times of hardship. One day in heaven, we will be given the perfect reward, when everything will be perfect and there will be no more tears and hurt. The Lord also sometimes rewards us on earth. He knows what happens in our lives, and gives us wonderful times of happiness and peace and joy, even if we have our bad times. The Lord is the great God of heaven and earth, and he will help us when things go wrong. You just put your trust in the Lord. Leave your life in his hands and know that he will take care of you.

Jesus would take your hurt away.

For the past troubles will be forgotten ... (Isaiah 65:16)

TEARS

Record my lament; list my tears on your scroll. (Psalm 56:8)

There is certainly not one person on earth who has not cried. You cry with joy when you are so happy about something that it makes you very emotional. Heartache can make you cry. Or you can cry because you have been hurt. Pain also makes you cry. And you can cry if someone has treated you badly or unfairly.

They say it is good to cry. It is never good to bottle up our feelings. It is better to cry about things and get them out of our system than to keep them inside and pretend that nothing is wrong. Tears help to lighten our load. We must never be ashamed or afraid to cry. Of course we must not cry about every little thing. But if we really hurt it is all right to cry.

Do you remember that Jesus also cried? Jesus cried when he realized that Lazarus was dead. He saw how sad Lazarus's sisters, Mary and Martha, were. He was deeply moved. Because he also loved Lazarus, he cried.

The Bible says that God keeps a record of all his children's tears. One day he will wipe the tears from our eyes, and there will be no more tears (see Revelation 21:4).

Jesus would cry when he is sad.

He [Jesus] was deeply moved. (John 11:33)

November 8

BE CARING

> "Where is your brother Abel?" "I don't know," he [Cain] replied. "Am I my brother's keeper?" (Genesis 4:9)

We read the story of Cain and Abel in the Bible. Cain was a crop farmer, and Abel was a sheep farmer. The Lord accepted Abel's offering, but not Cain's. Cain was very angry and jealous. He killed his brother in a field. When God asked Cain where his brother was he gave the Lord a rude answer and said he was not supposed to look after his brother. What he was, in fact, saying was that he didn't care about his brother.

People need people, and we must care for others. We cannot pretend that we can get on without each other. We must take care of each other. If we have brothers or sisters in the same family, we are responsible for them in a special way. It is as if the Lord gives one to the other so that they can care for each other. We must encourage each other and be loving and caring, and we should also show each other in a nice way where we each go wrong.

Cain felt nothing for his brother. Actually, he wanted him dead. He committed a terrible murder. This is not the way to behave. We must not walk around with mean thoughts toward our brothers and sisters. We must pray for them and love them.

Jesus would care for others.

Each of you should not look not only to your own interests, but also to the interests of others. (Philippians 2:4)

November 9

CROUCHING AT YOUR DOOR

"Sin is crouching at your door; it desires to have you, but you must master it." (Genesis 4:7)

As long as we are living on earth sin will be a problem. Every day brings its share of sin possibilities. It is as if sin is crouching out there, just waiting to pounce. The minute we are disobedient, sin grabs us.

The Lord told Cain that joy waits for everyone who does what is right. But if you don't, sin is there, waiting to get you into its power. The Lord said that you must master sin. Although the possibility of sin is always there, so is the possibility of saying no. That is often the most difficult thing to do. We must ask the Lord to help us. To master sin is to say no to it. Often sin comes in the form of something so inviting that you find it very difficult to say no. Ask the Lord to help you and to give you the wisdom to recognize sin when it uses sly ways of getting to you. If we are willing, the Lord will help us to master sin.

Jesus would master sin.

"Away from Me, Satan!" (Matthew 4:10)

ONE BAD APPLE

He who walks with the wise grows wise, but a companion of fools suffers harm. (Proverbs 13:20)

Isn't it interesting that if there is one bad apple in a box, all the others go bad more quickly, and before you know it there is not one good apple left in the box.

There is a saying, "He who sleeps with dogs gets up with fleas." We are all influenced by one another, and that is why it is important whom you talk to, who your friends are, where you visit and spend time. You are the way your friends are. If your friends have bad habits, it will be easy for you to pick up these habits. It is almost like the apples in the box. The Bible tells us that if we keep company with wise people and listen to them, we also become wise. If, however, we are with fools all the time, we become just as foolish. You and I want to be wise and do what is right. Choose Christians for friends so that they can have a good influence on you.

A Christian should have Christian friends. You can be friendly with all people, but remember, those who are close to you are the ones who will influence you. If they love Jesus and know him, they will help you serve him even better.

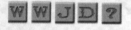

Jesus would choose
the right friends.

Blessed is the man who does not walk in the counsel of the wicked. (Psalm 1:1)

Happy to Go

I rejoiced with those who said to me, "Let us go to the house of the Lord." (Psalm 122:1)

David is called "a man after God's heart." The Lord loved him very much. Although David made mistakes, he loved the Lord and showed it. When he made a mistake, he confessed it, and he really tried to do the will of the Lord.

In the Old Testament the Lord's presence was in the tabernacle (the portable temple). It was called the house of the Lord. David was very pleased when his friends said, "Let's go to the house of the Lord." David knew that in the house of the Lord God would talk to him. Today the church is not the only house of the Lord. The Lord now lives in our hearts. God's house is in our bodies. Our bodies are the temple of the Holy Spirit. Wherever we go, God goes with us. Still, we go to church to listen to the Word of God together with other Christians; we encourage and uplift one another. There we pray and sing together to the glory of God.

If you love the Lord, you want to be where he is praised and where his Word is preached. Pray for your congregation and pastor and give them your support. Then you will also be happy when someone says to you, "Let's go to church!"

Jesus would go
to church regularly.

They found him in the temple. (Luke 2:46)

November 12

EVER BRIGHTER

> The path of the righteous is like the first gleam of dawn, shining ever brighter till the full light of day. (Proverbs 4:18)

The life of someone that loves and knows the Lord is different from that of one who does not know him. One way of describing the life of a Christian is to say it is a light-life. A person who knows the Lord, lives in his light and also has this light in her or his heart.

One of the wonderful things about being a Christian is that we are lit up by the light of Christ shining ever brighter as we go along. When we accept Jesus, his light is in our heart. The further we walk the road of life with him, the brighter his light in our hearts and life. At first our life is like the first gleam of dawn in the morning, before sunrise. Later on the sun rises and soon it is bright daylight. Such is the life of a person who lives with the Lord. The longer we live with him, the brighter his light shines in our life.

Let the Lord's sunshine light up your life today.

Jesus would let his light shine.

"In the same way, let your light shine before men." (Matthew 5:16)

ARE YOU DRESSED SUITABLY?

Before me was a great multitude that no one could count ...
They were wearing white robes. (Revelation 7:9)

Y ou dress to suit where you are going and what you are doing. You might have to wear a uniform to school. When you play sports, you wear sports clothes. When you go to a wedding, you wear dressy clothes.

Jesus told the parable of a man who held a wedding. Someone arrived who was not suitably dressed and he was thrown out. This is just a story, but Jesus tells it to us so that we know we must be dressed correctly if we want to be with him one day.

What must we wear for the Lord? Not ordinary clothes, like a suit or a pretty dress. No, the Bible talks about clean, white clothes. This is an image to say we must be washed clean of sin. In Revelation we read that people standing before the Lord were dressed in white clothes. These are redemption clothes. Only people washed clean from sin can enter into the presence of the Lord.

When the Lord washes you clean from sin, you will be given clean, white redemption clothes. Then you are dressed correctly. No one will throw you out of heaven. You can enter into the presence of the Lord joyfully.

Jesus will dress you
correctly to enter heaven.

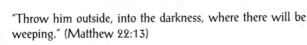

"Throw him outside, into the darkness, where there will be weeping." (Matthew 22:13)

November 14

BEAUTIFUL LOVE

For love is as strong as death. (Song of Songs 8:6)

Song of Songs is a beautiful book in the Bible. It is a song written about the love between a man and a woman. In this book we read how much the man loves the woman of his dreams, and the woman tells how wonderful the man is that she loves.

Nowadays there are so many love stories on television or in books that make true love between a man and a woman sound cheap. Couples fall in love, and the next thing you know, they are sleeping together even though they are not married. This is not the way the Lord meant it to be. It is a wonderful experience when a man and a woman fall in love. Perhaps you have felt in love with someone of the opposite sex, even though you are still very young. The beginning of love between a boy and a girl is beautiful. The Lord made it this way.

Because love is such a strong feeling, the devil can make use of it as well. That is a pity. Often people fall in love, but then they become very jealous. People have even committed murder because of jealousy. Love is a gift from the hand of God. He gives the love between a man and a woman, and he can help you to love in the right way – without jealousy and without giving into sexual temptation. Ask the Lord now to help you love someone in the right way.

Jesus would love in the right way.

Love ... is not self-seeking. (1 Corinthians 13:4, 5)

November 15

Fishing for Jesus

"Come, follow Me," Jesus said, "and I will make you fishers of men." (Mark 1:17)

Jesus grew up near the Sea of Galilee. It is a large inland lake. There are a lot of fish in that lake. Even today people still fish in the Sea of Galilee. Jesus often watched fishermen fishing from their boats. Some of the fishermen became his friends and disciples. Simon Peter was a fisherman who decided to follow Jesus.

Jesus uses the image of fishing to tell us how important it is that we catch "people." A fisherman puts bait on a fish hook, or he lets a net down the side of the boat and pulls the fish in like that. What he catches belongs to him. Jesus taught his disciples to catch "people" so that they can belong to him. How do we catch people for Jesus? We tell them about him. We also tell them how wonderful it is to know him and to follow him, because he is the one who forgives our sins and will let us live in heaven with him. When people hear this, many of them will come to him.

The Lord uses people like you and me to bring others to him so that they can belong to him. Be a fisher of people today.

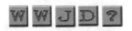

Jesus would invite
people to follow him.

 "Follow Me," he told him, and Matthew got up and followed him. (Matthew 9:9)

NOT EMPTY RELIGION

Even though you bring me burnt offerings ... I will not accept them. (Amos 5:22)

The Lord does not like it when someone pretends to worship him, but is not sincere. The Lord does not like religion that is nothing but show. Many people seem to be children of God. They listen to sermons; they sing and look God-fearing. Yet they don't mean it. Israel was like this.

The Lord spoke through a prophet named Amos and told his people that he did not think much of their religion. He said he hated their religious feasts. He told them to stop singing him songs, because they were just making a noise (see v. 23). Why did the Lord feel so strongly about this? The reason is that they sinned so much and didn't really love him in the least. It is as if the Lord was saying, "What good is your religion if you are not in a proper relationship with Me?" The Lord does not really care what we do on the outside. He looks into our hearts. He knows if we confess our sins. He knows if we are forgiven. If we serve him thankfully and go to church and sing him songs, he is pleased with us. But he does not like an empty religion.

Work on with the Lord, and see that in your religion you serve him wholeheartedly.

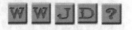

Jesus would serve the
Lord with his whole life.

Always be zealous for ... the LORD. (Proverbs 23:17)

November 17

A FATHER FOREVER

And he will be called ... Everlasting Father. (Isaiah 9:6)

Although we all have fathers, many of us no longer have a mother and father that we can see or visit. Then there are children whose dads are still alive, yet they never see them. Their dads have disappeared, or have decided not to have any contact with their children.

Whether we know our earthly father or not, we have a Father who will always be there. He is the Father of Jesus, and he also becomes our Father when we accept Jesus. Jesus shows us the way to the Father. He introduces us to his Father. His Father becomes your Father and mine. He is a Father that will never disappoint us, who never makes mistakes, who will never turn his back on us, who will never leave us. Jesus saw to it that we have an everlasting Father. He is with you today.

In Jesus you will be
a child of God the Father.

Everyone who believes that Jesus is the Christ is born of God.
(1 John 5:1)

November 18

CLOUDS

> Like clouds and wind without rain is a man who boasts of gifts he does not give. (Proverbs 25:14)

Farmers depend on rain. If it does not rain, the seed they sow will never sprout. Without rain there is no grass in the fields for sheep and cattle to graze. If it doesn't rain, the world becomes very dry.

Rain comes in the form of clouds. If the wind blows in the right direction, the clouds gather, and when the clouds have enough moisture, rain starts falling from them. Not all clouds give rain, however.

The Bible says we are sometimes like clouds without rain. We are full of promise, but nothing happens. It is easy to make promises. People say they will do this or that, and then nothing comes of it. People even boast about things they will achieve and how they will do things for you. Perhaps you have had friends like this: full of promises about what they want to do for you, but it ended there – with the promise. They are like empty clouds without any rain.

We must not be like empty clouds. What we say, we must do. People must be able to rely on us. Don't be quick to boast about what you are going to do. It is better to keep quiet and first do it.

Jesus would do what he promises.

"Simply let your 'Yes' be 'Yes,' and your 'No,' 'No.'" (Matthew 5:37)

November 19

A Cooking Pot or Pen

On that day HOLY TO THE LORD will be inscribed on the bells of the horses, and the cooking pots in the LORD's house will be like the sacred bowls in front of the altar. (Zechariah 14:20)

Sometimes we think some things are holier than others. To be holy is to be devoted to the Lord. Perhaps you think the church is holier than your bedroom. But this is not necessarily the case. Wherever the Lord is, there it is holy: in your bedroom, or in the kitchen, or in church, or at school.

Zechariah saw a vision in the Old Testament. He saw the words "Holy to the Lord" written on the bells of the horses. Also the cooking pots in the house of the Lord were to be sacred or holy. With this vision the Lord was saying that the time has come where all things are equally holy to the Lord. Actually he was saying that all things we use can be instruments to glorify the Lord. The pen or pencil that you write with, the clothes you wear, your soccer ball, or the CD player in your home can be "holy to the Lord."

Let us make everything we work with every day, holy. Because everything belongs to the Lord.

Jesus would use everything
to the glory of God.

"See to it that you complete the work you have received in the Lord." (Colossians 4:17)

November 20

THE ELDERLY

Gray hair is a crown of splendor; it is attained by a righteous life. (Proverbs 16:31)

Many children are impatient with old people. Some even make fun of old people because they can't move fast, or because they do things differently.

Do you realize that today's old people were once just as young as you are? As the years went by, they got older, and later they started getting weaker. The Bible says the gray hair of old people is like a splendid crown they wear on their heads. Make time to speak to old people. If you still have a grandpa and a grandma, make sure you call them regularly, or write them a letter or email just to say you love them. Let's pray for all old people who live in homes for the elderly.

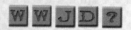

Jesus would treat old
people with respect.

Do not rebuke an older man harshly, but exhort him as if he were your father. (1 Timothy 5:1)

His Promises

They will never be silent day or night. You who call on the LORD, give yourselves no rest. (Isaiah 62:6)

In the Bible the Lord makes a lot of promises to his children. There are many, many promises, so many that there is a promise from the mouth of God for every day of the year. We can claim these promises for ourselves.

The Lord promises to be with us, that he will always love us, that he will give us strength, that his Holy Spirit will guide us, and much more. Isaiah tells us in this verse that we must remind the Lord of the promises he made. It's not because the Lord forgets that we have to remind him. It is because you and I sometimes forget about the Lord's promises that we must remember them again and must say them out loud to ourselves and to the Lord. If we do that, we show that we really put our trust in him and that we need him. The Lord is pleased when we do that. He doesn't like boastful people who think they can help themselves. You and I must show that the Lord's promises are important to us by claiming them for ourselves.

Every time you are in a difficult situation, think about one of the Lord's promises. Make it your own, in faith. Thank God that his promises are also meant for you.

Jesus would trust the
Father's promises.

You will receive an inheritance from the Lord as a reward.
(Colossians 3:24)

November 22

FILTHY LANGUAGE

But now you must rid yourselves of ... filthy language from your lips. (Colossians 3:8)

It is never necessary for a father to teach his child bad language. The child manages to learn it all by himself. Most moms and dads have quite a struggle with children who use dirty words they heard somewhere. So many people around us use bad language all the time – dirty words, words one does not like hearing.

Whatever is in your heart comes out of your mouth. If your heart is not clean, it is much easier to speak dirty words. Swearing is a sign of a heart that has not yet been cleaned well enough. The Lord wants to help us so that our words can be good and clean.

When we give our hearts to the Lord, his Holy Spirit comes to live in our hearts, and he can help us to get our language nice and clean. I know many people who once used very bad language, but when they gave their hearts to the Lord, they felt they did not want to do it any more. I think many Christians have the problem of a bad word slipping out every now and again. But we can say we're sorry right away and ask the Lord to help us so that we do not use that word again.

Jesus would speak
only good words.

Do not let any unwholesome talk come out of your mouths, but only what is helpful for building others up. (Ephesians 4:29)

November 23

WHO IS RIGHT?

> All the nations may walk in the name of their gods; we
> will walk in the name of the LORD our God forever and
> ever. (Micah 4:5)

Many gods are worshiped all over the world. This was
true in Bible times, and it is true also today. There are many
different religions, and everyone believes his god is the real
one. As Christians we believe in the God of the Bible. He is
the Father of Jesus Christ, and he gave us his Holy Spirit to
stay with us and teach us all about his will.

The question is this: Whose god is the real one? As
Christians we know the Bible is correct. Micah said all nations may live in the name of their gods here on earth, but we
will always live in the name of the Lord our God. Christians
say it is not only in this life that we must have a God and bow
down before him, but above all, it is in eternity that we will
live with him. It is the Lord God who lives in our hearts.

Jesus would serve
only the Father.

"Worship the Lord your God and serve him only." (Luke 4:8)

WHEN PARENTS DIVORCE

"Is it lawful for a man to divorce his wife for any and every reason?" ... "What God has joined together, let man not separate." (Matthew 19:3, 6)

Nowadays many parents are divorcing. Maybe you know someone whose parents are divorced. It could even be that your own mom and dad felt they could no longer stay together and decided to get divorced. It is very sad when this happens. Divorce makes it so that families no longer live together in love and harmony. Often children do not know where they fit in – with Dad or with Mom. The Lord does not want people to get divorced.

Often something happens between moms and dads and their marriage breaks down and just gets worse and worse. Where there was love at first, there is now growing disagreement. It is sad.

Even if people divorce, however, the Lord will heal the hurt. He can also forgive all the sins that have been committed. In Jesus we can always start again, make a new beginning. Let's pray for marriages and families and ask for the Lord's blessing on these.

Jesus would pray for
every marriage.

Submit to one another out of reverence for Christ. (Ephesians 5:21)

November 25

Stone Throwing

"If any one of you is without sin, let him be the first to throw a stone at her." (John 8:7)

In this scripture we read about a married woman who cheated on her husband and had a relationship with another man. The Bible calls her an adulteress. This woman was caught, and the religious people brought her to Jesus. They wanted to see what Jesus would do. The Old Testament said if anyone committed this sin, then that person must be stoned. This means that the people would pick up stones, or even bricks, and throw them at the adulterer. In this way that person was stoned to death.

Jesus knew that the woman was guilty, but he wanted to forgive her. The Lord wants to forgive us because he loves us. Jesus said that the person who was without sin could pick up the first stone and throw it at her. No one could do that, because all of them had known sin in their lives. Perhaps they didn't think their sins were as serious as hers, but they knew they had their faults. Jesus looked at the woman tenderly and told her that he didn't condemn her, but that she should not sin any more.

You and I cannot throw stones at others, or accuse them, because of all the sin in our own lives. Let's not judge others, but rather pray for them.

Jesus would forgive others.

Forgive as the Lord forgave you. (Colossians 3:13)

November 26

Protect His Name

"You shall not misuse the name of the LORD your God."
(Exodus 20:7)

I'm sure you've heard people use the name of the Lord in a disrespectful way. They are actually swearing with the name of the Lord. The Bible calls this using the name of God in vain.

The name of the Lord is holy. The Jews in the Old Testament felt so strongly about the name of the Lord that they did not say it, not even when they prayed. They were afraid to do it because to them God was too great and holy. Jesus taught us in the New Testament that we can pray in his name. With the Lord's Prayer he taught us that it's all right to talk to the Father.

As a Christian you may cringe when you hear how people use the name of Jesus, or God the Father, carelessly. It's as if they are putting the name of the Lord on the same level as any ordinary name like Jack or William or Alice. God's name is noble and wonderful, and it must be used only when we speak of him respectfully. If we hear someone misusing the name of the Lord, we must pray for that person. We must say in a nice way that we think that name is very special, and that we love that God because he is the Lord we worship. Ask the Lord to help you so that you will also not misuse his name.

Jesus would respect
the name of the Father.

Yet he ... gave glory to God. (Romans 4:20)

November 27

NURSE THE HURT

"But a Samaritan, as he traveled, came where the man was; and when he saw him, he took pity on him. He went to him and bandaged his wounds, pouring on oil and wine." (Luke 10:33-34)

Jesus told the story of the good Samaritan. A man went on a journey. On the road robbers attacked him. They took off all his clothes and beat him up until he was lying there, half dead. Then they fled. A few people passed by and saw that he had been hurt, but they pretended not to notice. When the Samaritan saw him, he took pity on him and started taking care of his wounds.

It is so easy to look the other way if there is hurt around you. There are many people in hospitals, or at home, who are in pain. There are also many unhappy people with problems in their families, or who have experienced great disappointment. These are all people in need. The Bible says we must not look the other way, but must try to help them as the Samaritan did. The Samaritan not only bandaged the man's wounds, he also helped him onto his own donkey and took him to an inn, where he paid so that the man could stay there until he was well. This is real love. You and I must do the same with people around us who need help.

Jesus would help people in need.

"Blessed are the merciful." (Matthew 5:7)

November 28

THE CHURCH
IN THE HOUSE

*Greet also the church that meets at their house.
(Romans 16:5)*

In the time just after Jesus ascended to heaven, Christian groups were formed, and they often met in people's houses. Of course there were not as many Christians then as there are today. The children of the Lord had their meals together, prayed together, and talked about the Lord. They also read the letters Paul and others wrote them. In this way they encouraged one another, and their faith was strengthened.

Today people are once again meeting in homes. People are getting together in smaller groups in people's homes. These small groups are connected to large congregations, and they get together regularly to study the Bible, pray, and worship the Lord. The members of these small groups get to know one another well, they know about one another's problems, dreams, and plans. In this way they can care for each other better and support one another.

What a privilege to get together openly in one another's homes to worship the Lord and to praise him. Pray for these groups all over the world. Fortunately, we don't have only the church where we can praise God. He is with us in our own homes.

Jesus would pray for
all Christians.

 Holy Father, protect them by the power of your name. (John 17:11)

November 29

WONDERFUL FRIENDS

Greet Priscilla and Aquila, my fellow workers in Christ Jesus. (Romans 16:3)

The Lord gave Paul wonderful Christian friends. Just like you and me, Paul needed close friends to support him and help him. In the letter to the Romans we read about quite a few of these friends. Shall we name a few?

Priscilla and Aquila were two of Paul's coworkers. They not only made tents with him, they also preached the gospel with him. He says they *"risked their lives for me"* (v. 4).

Andronicus and Junias were two friends who became Christians before Paul did, and they were in prison with him. There they supported him (cf. v. 7).

Apelles was another good friend of Paul's. Paul says of him that he was *"tested and approved by Christ"* (v. 10). He was a reliable Christian friend.

Tryphena and Tryphosa were two Christian lady friends. He calls them *"women who work hard in the Lord"* (v. 12).

There are many other names we could list, but it is clear that Paul was very thankful for all these friends that were at his side and helped him to serve the Lord and follow him. You and I should have friends like these.

Jesus would choose friends
who also serve the Lord.

"You are my friends if you do what I command." (John 15:14)

November 30

TWO EARS, ONE MOUTH

When words are many, sin is not absent, but he who holds his tongue is wise. (Proverbs 10:19)

Someone pointed out, "A person has two ears and only one mouth." This means we must listen twice as much as we speak. Unfortunately, the opposite is often true; we talk much more than we listen. If we listen more and speak less, it is quite possible that there will be fewer problems in the world.

Proverbs 10 says if we speak a lot, sin very easily comes to into our speech. It is with all this talking that we sometimes say the wrong thing, or get the wrong idea, and it is then that we hurt others or start spreading rumors so that things eventually get out of control. This is where sin comes in. No, says Proverbs, you and I must keep count of our words, which means we must speak less and be careful of what we say. Then we are wise, and we leave less room for sin in our speech. Remember that your tongue is the single most important instrument that can cause you to sin. Be careful with it. Ask the Lord to help you speak less and listen more. Ask the Lord to help you so that when you do talk it will be wise words.

Jesus would help you to listen.

He ... wakens my ear to listen. (Isaiah 50:4)

GOOD ADVICE

And he will be called Wonderful Counselor. (Isaiah 9:5)

All of us need advice because we don't know everything. There are many things we don't understand, and sometimes we need to have things explained to us. This is one reason for going to school. Although it is not always fun to be at school, we get good counseling there. Knowledge is good counsel, and it teaches us to do what is right in our lives. It is good to know about all kinds of things so that we can make the right decisions.

We can have all the knowledge in the world and still not know the right way to live. We need more than book learning; we need good advice. Although we can get good counsel from people, the best counsel comes from the Lord. That is why the Bible calls Jesus "Counselor." He is a wonderful Counselor who can advise you and me about all things in life. The most important counsel he wants to give us is how to live successfully. To choose Jesus and to follow him is to have a wonderful Counselor. He talks to us in his Word and counsels us in many things. His Holy Spirit also leads us in truth. If we follow the Lord's advice, we should be happy.

Jesus would give you
the best counsel.

 If any of you lacks wisdom, he should ask God, who gives generously to all. (James 1:5)

December 2

Nicknames

> James ... and his brother John (to them he gave the name ... Sons of Thunder). (Mark 3:17)

James and John were two disciples that Jesus chose to follow him. We don't know much about them; the Bible says Jesus gave them a nickname. Jesus called them *Boanerges*, which means "Sons of Thunder."

It seems that James and John came from a family with quick tempers. They sounded almost like thunder. Thunder is heard when a storm is brewing and it builds up until the storm breaks. Many people are like thunder. They get angry and angrier still, and later they explode like a peal of thunder. Everybody witnesses and experiences their temper. James and John must have acted like this.

John is later mentioned as the disciple whom Jesus loved very much, and John also loved Jesus. It is John who writes at a later stage that we must love one another. He mentions it, not once only, but many times in 1, 2, and 3 John. When you give your life to Jesus, a miracle takes place: he changes your negative characteristics to positive ones. The Sons of Thunder later on became the Sons of Love. Allow the Lord to change you as he wants to.

Jesus will make you new.

"I am making everything new!" (Revelation 21:5)

YOUR NAME
IS IMPORTANT

A good name is more desirable than great riches.
(Proverbs 22:1)

People know you by your name. Your name is like a picture of you in someone's mind. A name is important, and that is why we must see to it that we do not lose our good name.

You get a good name when you do good things. If you have a lovable nature, or you like helping others, people know you as a lovable and helpful person. If you are humble, people know you as a person who does not think too much of himself or herself. If you are trustworthy, people know that when your name is mentioned they can rely on you.

The same goes for a bad name. If you have become known as a person who does mean things, or if you always behave in a flirtatious manner, people link these things you do to your name.

We all make mistakes, that is true, but if we don't say we are sorry and try to put things right, then people know us only as someone who does unkind things. Then we have a bad name.

The Bible says a good name is worth more than riches. Once you have lost your good name, it is very difficult to get it back again. How lucky you are that the Lord helps you to live in such a way that, even if you do make mistakes, people know you mean well.

Jesus would always keep his good name.

A good name is better than fine perfume. (Ecclesiastes 7:1)

December 4

DO NOT LOSE HEART

Each helps the other and says to his brother, "Be strong!" (Isaiah 41:6)

It is easy to give up hope. If things do not work out the way we planned them, we easily just give up, especially if we have tried something a few times and it still won't work out. Each one of us has, at some stage, given up.

Certain people are wonderful at giving others hope. They motivate people. They tell us about the good qualities we have. They talk to us and build us up and show us they believe in us. These people bring out the best in us. When we are downhearted, they notice our sadness and do something to lift us out of it.

Perhaps you have seen on television when athletes run in a Marathon. It is a long distance to run, and many runners get tired and feel like giving up. But along the road there are thousands of people who encourage them and tell them they're doing well and that they will make it to the end if they just keep going.

Then, of course, in our lives there is God who helps and encourages us through his Holy Spirit. He fills our hearts with hope and courage. He is there to support us many times when there is no one else to give us hope.

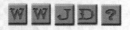

Jesus would not let you down.

 The Sovereign LORD has given me an instructed tongue, to know the word that sustains the weary. (Isaiah 50:4)

December 5

Streams of Water

"Whoever believes in me, as the Scripture has said, streams of living water will flow from within him." (John 7:38)

No plant, animal, or human can live without water. Water is absolutely necessary for you and me. If you have ever really been thirsty, you will know how good it feels to drink a glass of cold water. Just think how you enjoy jumping into the cool water of a pool or the ocean on a hot summer's day.

Jesus once talked to a sinful woman. She was busy getting water from a well just outside the town where she lived. Jesus said to her, *"If you knew the gift of God ... you would have asked him and he would have given you living water"* (John 4:10).

Jesus also told her that if she drank ordinary, earthly water, she would get thirsty again, but if she drank the water that he would give, she would never get thirsty again. What does Jesus mean?

The water the Lord gives becomes like a fountain inside of us. Jesus himself is like water to you and me. If we believe in him, we are filled. Our thirst for sense and meaning in our lives is satisfied. He fills our hearts with his living water. Then we don't want all sorts of other things anymore; he has given us fulfillment. Thank the Lord, right now, for his living water. If you are still thirsty, drink from the fountain that is Jesus himself.

Jesus will give you living water.

"Indeed, the water I give him will become in him a spring of water ... to eternal life." (John 4:14)

December 6

FROM LAMBS TO THE LAMB

"Look, the Lamb of God, who takes away the sin of the world!" (John 1:29)

In the Old Testament people brought offerings to receive forgiveness for their sins and to thank the Lord for what he had done for them. They usually sacrificed a perfect lamb.

The Father sent Jesus to earth to be sacrificed for our sins. In the same way that the lambs in the Old Testament took away sin, Jesus as the Lamb of God had to take away our sins. Long before Jesus died on the cross, John the Baptist knew in his heart that Jesus would die for our sins. When he saw Jesus coming toward him one day, he said, "There is the Lamb of God who will take away the sins of the world." And he was right, because that is exactly what happened. Later on when Jesus was captured and tortured and nailed to a cross, he suffered like a lamb for you and me. When his blood flowed and he died, he was the sacrifice for your sins and mine.

Today we do not sacrifice lambs any more because the Lamb of God, Jesus Christ, was the last and perfect offering. You just need to accept it, and you will also be free of the guilt of sin.

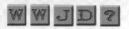

Jesus will take also
your sin away.

 Christ was sacrificed once to take away the sins of many people. (Hebrews 9:28)

December 7

EAT, DRINK, WATCH TV

So whether you eat or drink or whatever you do, do it all for the glory of God. (1 Corinthians 10:31)

The Bible tells us that we serve the Lord all the time, not just when we go to church, read our Bibles, or pray. True religion is when we do things to the glory of God, even if no one sees us. We serve him as the King of our lives if we praise him in everything we do.

Paul says whenever we eat, drink, or whatever, it all must be to the glory of God. When is something to the glory of God? When we do it the way Jesus will do it. When we do it in love. When we serve others by doing it. When we do it in such a way that it does not go against the Word and the will of God. Anything we do that is not God's will is wrong and not to his glory.

The question we must ask ourselves when we watch TV, or eat, or drink, or chat, or visit someone is this: "Would Jesus do it this way?" We must remember that the Lord is always with us. Will he always want to be with us wherever we are? Will he like watching what we do, and what will he think of the way we talk? Come, let's make the Lord feel at home with us! Let's do everything to his glory.

Jesus would do everything
to the glory of God.

Do it all in the name of the Lord Jesus. (Colossians 3:17)

December 8

JESUS WITH A PLUS

For this very reason, make every effort to add to your faith. (2 Peter 1:5)

Just believing is not good enough. This may sound a bit strange to you. Can't we just believe in the Lord, and all will be fine? Yes, it is true that faith is the most important thing. We must believe in Jesus as our Redeemer. But the Bible tells us to do something more than just believe.

Faith is the beginning of our spiritual life. If we believe in Jesus, we start a new life with him, and he leads us on a new road. As we walk this road with him, he teaches us through his Word, and the Holy Spirit speaks with us deep in our hearts. As we learn new things, our faith grows and becomes richer. Faith is like the foundations of a house. A house cannot stand strong and firm if the foundations have not been made very strong. Faith is a strong foundation for you and me. Only when our faith is strong can we start building our faith-home: our lives.

That is why Peter says we must add certain things to our faith. We must work hard to add good qualities: knowledge, self-control, perseverance, love for one another, and love for all people. We must work hard at building our faith through good habits and by adding these qualities.

I hope you will do just that today!

Jesus would help you
live your faith.

Faith without deeds is dead. (James 2:26)

December 9

Dry Bones
Come to Life

> "I will put my spirit in you and you will live, and I will settle you in your own land." (Ezekiel 37:14)

Ezekiel was a prophet in the Old Testament. One day the Holy Spirit showed him a vision like a dream. The Lord used visions to carry important messages to his servants so that they could teach people the right way.

At first this vision was not very nice. He saw a valley full of dry skeletons; the bones were so dry they were white. The Lord asked Ezekiel if these bones could ever live again. Ezekiel replied that only God could tell. So the Lord told him the meaning of the vision.

The Lord said his people, the people of Israel, were like dry bones. God would put flesh and muscles on the bones and cover them with skin, and then he would give them a spirit so that they could live again.

Often people are like skeletons. Although they are breathing, they have no real life, no spiritual life. If you do not believe in Jesus and have not been saved, you are spiritually dead, just like a skeleton. Even Christians can be half-dead spiritually, like the people of Israel. Then we need revival: the Holy Spirit must refill our lives so that we can do God's will.

Jesus will send his spirit
so that you can live again.

> "And I will put my Spirit in you and move you to ... be careful to keep my laws." (Ezekiel 36:27)

December 10

I WILL, BUT FIRST . . .

> "I will follow you, Lord; but first let me go back and say goodbye to my family." (Luke 9:61)

The Lord calls people to follow him. Many say they want to follow him. They do so with their whole hearts, and that is the right way to do it. Unfortunately, there are also those who follow him half-heartedly. They are touched by his words, and they say they are willing to follow him, but other things are still more important to them.

One day when Jesus was on his way, someone said to him, *"I will follow you wherever you go"* (v. 57). Jesus answered him that it is not always easy to follow the Lord. When Jesus told someone else that he should also follow him, his answer was, *"Lord, first let me ..."* (v. 59). He had an excuse: I will follow you but first I must do something else. Yet another person said he had to go and say goodbye to his family.

The lesson is that we must not follow the Lord if we're not going to do it wholeheartedly. Of course we can go and say goodbye to our families, but Jesus knew this man was just making a poor excuse for not wanting to follow him. Do you perhaps also make excuses for not following the Lord with all your heart? I hope there aren't a lot of "buts" in your life.

Jesus would do his Father's
will, without making excuses.

 "I have brought you glory on earth by completing the work you gave me to do." (John 17:4)

December 11

WHAT MAKES YOU HAPPY?

"However, do not rejoice that the spirits submit to you,
but rejoice that your names are written in heaven."
(Luke 10:20)

Jesus sent out seventy-two of his followers to every town
and place he planned to go. They had to go and preach his
peace, heal people, and tell people about the kingdom of
God.

When they got back, they said to Jesus, *"Lord, even the
demons submit to us in your name"* (v. 17). They thought it was
wonderful that the name of Jesus was so strong that even the
devils listened to them. In those days there were many
people who had evil spirits. These demons left the people
when they were told to in the name of Jesus.

Jesus' answer to his followers is a bit surprising. He was
glad that they saw how wonderful his name and his power
was, but they should rather have been happy to know that
their names were written in heaven. To witness miracles
and the power of the Lord is important, but it is more
important to know that your relationship with God is good,
and that your name is written in the book of life.

Jesus will write your
name in the book of life.

[No one] will ever enter it ... but only those whose names are
written in the Lamb's book of life. (Revelation 21:27)

December 12

LIKE THE DEAD

When I saw him, I fell at his feet as though dead.
(Revelation 1:17)

John was one of Jesus' followers. After the resurrection of Jesus, John preached the gospel of Jesus to many people. He was exiled to the island of Patmos because he preached the Word of God and of Jesus.

One Sunday, through the Holy Spirit, John heard a voice speaking to him. Then the Lord appeared to him. It was a miracle! Jesus, in all his glory, was standing in front of John. He wore a long robe with a golden sash around his chest. His hair was as white as snow. His face was like the sun shining in all its brilliance.

Although John loved the Lord and was on earth with him, he said, *"When I saw him, I fell at his feet as though dead"* (v. 17). He was completely overwhelmed by the appearance of Jesus. But Jesus touched him with his right hand, and said, *"Do not be afraid. I am the First and the Last. I am the Living One"* (v. 17, 18).

One day you will also see Jesus in all his glory. You don't have to be afraid. He will be loving toward us.

Jesus would say,
"Do not be afraid."

I will dwell in the house of the LORD forever. (Psalm 23:6)

December 13

HIS GREATEST WISH

So we make it our goal to please him. (2 Corinthians 5:9)

I wonder what your answer would be if I should ask you what your greatest wish is. Maybe your dream is to have something special – something so expensive that you can barely afford it.

We all have our dreams and goals for our lives. Paul was an ordinary person like us, but when the Lord changed his life, his dreams and goals became new. Yes, he also had his wishes and things he wanted to have or wanted to do. He writes that he wanted very much to visit his friends, but then he mentions his most important wish: that his life would please the Lord.

Perhaps it sounds like rather a boring wish, but actually it is a beautiful goal. If you live to please the Lord, you will be happy and will always have peace in your heart. Then there is also the Lord's promise: if we do his will and seek his kingdom, he will give us everything we need. In Psalm 37:4 we read, *"Delight yourself in the LORD and he will give you the desires of your heart."* So, we see that Paul is not stupid with this wish to please the Lord. Is it also your wish to do the Lord's will?

Jesus will help you
make this wish come true.

I want to know Christ. (Philippians 3:10)

December 14

It Was Night!

As the sun was setting, Abram fell into a deep sleep, and a thick and dreadful darkness came over him. (Genesis 15:12)

I'm sure you remember that the Lord called Abram from a far-away country called Ur. Abram was obedient and did what the Lord wanted. The Bible says the Lord was pleased with Abram for doing his will (see v. 6). But we must not think that if we follow the Lord nothing will ever go wrong for us.

One night it became dark for Abram; not only outside, but also in his heart. The Bible says fear like a thick and dreadful darkness came over him. Yes, Abram was afraid. He must have wondered about his life and his future. What was going to happen to him in years to come? Often it is also in the dark of night that we start worrying about things that can happen to us.

Just when Abram's fear was becoming too much for him to bear, the Lord started talking to him. The Lord promised that he would be with him and would help him in everything he did. Sometimes when things are at their darkest in our lives, the Lord wants to comfort us and tell us that he is with us and that he will keep his promises for our lives. Trust him. As he cared for Abram, he will care for you and me, his children.

Jesus will always be with you.

I will fear no evil, for you are with me. (Psalm 23:4)

December 15

First Make Peace

"Leave your gift there in front of the altar. First go and be reconciled to your brothers; then come and offer your gift." (Matthew 5:24)

In Jesus' time people brought gift offerings to the altar to thank the Lord for his goodness and mercy. The Bible calls these thank offerings. They also brought other kinds of offerings to ask for forgiveness of sins. With these offerings people wanted to make sure that they would always have a good relationship with God.

You and I also bring the Lord offerings. We go to church to worship him. We give money to thank him for taking care of us.

But Jesus tells us, *"If you are offering your gift at the altar and there remember that your brother has something against you, leave your gift ... First go and be reconciled to your brother."* (vv. 23, 24). Jesus tells us that we must first sort out all bad feelings between us and someone else before our relationship with him can work. Often when we are in God's presence, he reminds us of something in our hearts that we have against another person. Then we must stop what we are doing, the Bible says, and go and make our peace with that person. Is there someone you need to make peace with? Why not call him or her right now and say you're sorry? Then you can bring the Lord an offering.

Jesus would help you
do the right thing.

 The effect of righteousness will be quietness and confidence forever. (Isaiah 32:17)

December 16

THE BABY MOVED

> When Elizabeth heard Mary's greeting, the baby leaped in her womb, and Elizabeth was filled with the Holy Spirit. (Luke 1:41)

Mary was Jesus' mother. After the miracle of Jesus being formed in her body, she decided to visit her family. She came to the town where her cousin Elizabeth lived. Elizabeth was also expecting a baby. That baby would later be known as John the Baptist. When Mary moved closer to Elizabeth to greet her, another miracle took place: as Mary greeted Elizabeth, the baby moved inside Elizabeth for the first time. The actual words are that the baby leaped inside her. It was a joyful movement, almost as if the baby inside Elizabeth was pleased that Jesus had come with Mary. At that moment, Elizabeth was filled with the Holy Spirit, and she started praising the Lord for the miracle of Jesus' coming birth.

If an unborn baby could react so wonderfully to the Savior, you and I should also be filled with great joy. We must glorify and praise the Lord with our mouths and with everything we do.

Jesus would be thankful
in everything.

Give thanks in all circumstances. (1 Thessalonians 5:18)

He Brings Peace

And he will be called ... Prince of Peace. (Isaiah 9:5)

When Isaiah prophesied that Jesus would be born, he said that one of his names would be "Prince of Peace." A prince is the son of a king, and he often becomes king himself. But Jesus would not be a king who rules with power and strength. No, he would be a prince that brings peace.

Peace is the opposite of war. When people make peace, they are not angry with one another anymore, and they no longer fight. It is good to live in peace. God wants us to live in peace with him, and this is only possible if Jesus makes us free from sin.

Jesus is our Prince of Peace because he makes peace with God on our behalf, through the Holy Spirit.

The Lord helps us to live in peace with others. That is why the Bible calls the children of the Lord "peacemakers."

Another important kind of peace is the peace we must have with ourselves. If God accepts us the way we are, we must also accept ourselves.

Thank the Lord that he came to bring peace in our hearts: peace with God, peace with others, and peace with ourselves.

Jesus would give you peace.

"Peace I leave with you; my peace I give you." (John 14:27)

December 18

A Wicked King

He gave orders to kill all the boys ... who were two years old and under. (Matthew 2:16)

The devil knew that Jesus would be born. He could not stand it because he knew that if Jesus grew up, he would be the Savior of humankind.

One of the things the devil did to try and put a stop to Jesus' plan of redemption was to work in the heart of King Herod. When Herod heard that someone had been born who would become a king, he decided immediately that this child had to be killed. But he did not know where to find him except that the wise men told him that the boy would be found in Bethlehem. So he gave orders to kill every baby boy born in and around Bethlehem within two years. Fortunately, an angel warned Joseph so that they could flee with Baby Jesus.

Can you imagine how sad all the mothers and fathers were who lost their baby boys? Herod was very cruel. The devil put him up to this wicked plan. Herod did not, however, manage to kill Jesus, and Jesus grew up to be our Redeemer.

The devil will also try to ruin God's plans for your life, but God is stronger than the devil, and he will protect you. Just put your trust in him.

Jesus would feel safe in the hands of his Father.

I will fear no evil, for you are with me. (Psalm 23:4)

December 19

A Small Town

> "But you, Bethlehem Ephrathah, though you are small ... out of you will come for me one who will be ruler over Israel." (Micah 5:2)

Long before Jesus was born, it was already prophesied in which town it would happen. The Holy Spirit prophesied through Micah that Jesus would be born in Bethlehem. Bethlehem was a small town and not at all important in the eyes of the people of that region.

Two things about this fact are important. The first is that Jesus was not born in an important place. One would expect that a person as important as Jesus would be born in a palace. He is, after all, the King of the whole world. But Jesus was born in a manger. He was laid down in a hay crib. Jesus was born in a plain and simple town. He was prepared to come to the humblest place on earth so that even the humblest person could know Jesus is not too good or too important to follow.

The second meaning of Jesus' birth in Bethlehem is that it did not happen by chance. It was predicted long before by Micah. God never makes a mistake. His prophecies always come true.

Praise the Lord because he was prepared to be an ordinary baby for your sake and mine, to be born in an ordinary place as God had prophesied.

Jesus would never think
he is better than others.

Whoever exalts himself will be humbled. (Matthew 23:12)

December 20

OUR STRONG GOD

And he will be called ... Mighty God. (Isaiah 9:5)

Nobody is as strong and powerful as God, the Father of Jesus Christ. He made the whole world. And he makes sure that everything is kept up. He is the great, strong, mighty God.

Isaiah prophesied that Jesus would also show the might of his Father. One of Jesus' names is "Mighty God." Jesus came to show God's power when he not only lived on earth and performed many miracles, but also when he died on the cross and afterward powerfully rose from the dead. When you and I are afraid, we are comforted by the thought that we have someone with us who is strong and who can help us. God is always prepared to be with us. Trust in him. He is also your mighty God. Ask him to help you today.

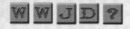

Jesus will be with
you as the mighty God.

"I am with you always, to the very end of the age." (Matthew 28:20)

December 21

THE GREATEST GIFT

"For God so loved the world that he gave his one and only son." (John 3:16)

What is the best present you have ever been given? I'm sure that gift made you very happy. It is always wonderful to receive a gift from someone.

A gift is something we are given. We don't work for it or earn it. A gift is free because someone else pays for it. The best gifts are those we don't expect; someone loves us so much that he or she wants to give us a present. God also gave you and me a gift: his Son, Jesus.

Christmas is that time of year when we give one another presents because we want to remember that God loved us so much that he gave us the best gift of all gifts. The Lord looked at us and saw that we needed him very much. Someone had to come and help us so that we would not perish in our sins. That is why the Father sent his Son. Everyone who believes in him will have everlasting life, and there is no gift in heaven or on earth as great as this one.

Thank the Lord right now for the wonderful gift of Jesus. Does it make you happy?

Jesus will give you everlasting life.

 The gift of God is eternal life in Christ Jesus our Lord. (Romans 6:23)

December 22

GOD LIKES US

"On earth peace to men on whom his favor rests." (Luke 2:14)

When Jesus was born, an angel appeared to the shepherds near Bethlehem. And the angel said to them, *"Do not be afraid. I bring you good news of great joy that will be for all the people. Today ... a Savior has been born to you ... This will be a sign to you: You will find a baby wrapped in cloths."* (vv. 10-12). Suddenly millions of angels appeared, praising God and singing, *"Glory to God in the highest, and on earth peace to men on whom his favor rests"* (v. 14).

The angels praised the Lord because Jesus would bring peace on earth. Anyone who accepts Jesus as Lord finds peace because his sins have been forgiven. Peace is the Lord's Christmas gift to us. Why does the Lord do it? Because his favor rests on us. This means that God likes us very much.

God likes people because he made them. He also knows we are unhappy because the devil tempts us. But because he loves us, he gives us his Son to save us and to make us new. Yes, the Lord loves you and me. That is the Christmas message: God loved us so much that he was prepared to give us his Son.

Jesus would give his
life for others.

"For God so loved the world that he gave his one and only Son.
(John 3:16)

December 23

AVAILABLE

"I am the Lord's servant," Mary answered. "May it be to me as you have said." (Luke 1:38)

The Lord sent the angel Gabriel to a young girl who lived in Nazareth. This girl was engaged to Joseph. Her name was Mary. Even today many people are named Mary because she was such an important person. Mary was the mother of Jesus.

The angel came up to Mary and he greeted her. She was startled, but the angel told her not to be afraid. He told her that she would become pregnant and would have a baby boy and that she had to name him Jesus. He went on to say that he will be called the Son of the Most High and that he will reign as King forever. Mary was very surprised. She wanted to know how that was possible. He answered that the Holy Spirit would perform a miracle so that Jesus' life would start inside her body. God can do anything; nothing is impossible to him. Then Mary said she was available to God and that he could do with her as he pleased.

How wonderful it is if you can say to the Lord that you are available, that he can do with you anything he wants to. You can be a wonderful instrument for him to use, like Mary. Are you available?

Jesus would be available.

"Whom shall I send?" ... "Here am I. Send me!" (Isaiah 6:8)

December 24

CHRISTMAS

"Today in the town of David a Savior has been born to you; he is Christ the Lord." (Luke 2:11)

Today is Christmas Day! It is one of the most wonderful and most important days of the year. This is the day we are happy to get together as families and tell everybody that we love them. We give each other presents and remind each other that Jesus was born on this day.

Today we remember that Jesus was born a little baby in a manger in Bethlehem. He did not stay a baby. Jesus grew up and said he was the Redeemer. He also proved it by dying on a cross for you and me. There he paid the price for our sins. He is also the Lord, because he rose from the dead: "Lord" means he reigns as king over all the powers of darkness.

I hope you will have a very blessed Christmas and that it will be a wonderful day for you. Praise Jesus for being willing to come to this world as our Savior.

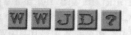

Jesus will save you.

In him we have redemption through his blood. (Ephesians 1:7)

Goodwill

Let your gentleness be evident to all. (Philippians 4:5)

The word *gentle* means kind, careful, not rough or violent, merciful, sweet-tempered, willing. The Amplified Bible uses the word "unselfishness" in this verse and explains it as being considerate. All of this means that we are open to others, willing to meet them halfway. Another word that is used in this text is *friendliness*. Friendly people are easy-going, open, loving, and considerate. How our country needs people like this!

There are many people in our country who don't like each other one bit. They make fun of each other, and they say bad things about each other. We have so many different cultures in our country yet we sometimes don't know members of another group. This means that we are not open to them. We are sometimes unfriendly toward others and sometimes even afraid of each other. We need goodwill.

Decide that wherever you go you will be friendly toward everybody, even if you don't know them. Show friendliness and goodwill to all people.

Jesus would be considerate
toward all people.

Be devoted to one another in brotherly love. (Romans 12:10)

December 26

MARANATHA

Come, Lord Jesus. (Revelation 22:20)

I'm sure you have been in the situation where you missed someone. Perhaps it was a grandpa or a grandma, or a very good friend. Maybe you haven't seen this person for quite a while, and now you wish you could be with them again. Perhaps you call them now and then and say to them, "Please, won't you come and visit?" When we love someone, we like being with him or her. When they go away, we long to see them again.

Christians are people who belong to Jesus, and they love the Lord. They would like to see him and be with him. I don't know about you, but I would love being with Jesus one day – not only in faith, but really with him, in his presence. I would like to talk to him and even touch him if I may. The first disciples were very sad when he went up to heaven. They were sad because they didn't want him to go away from them. In the very last verses of the Bible we find the words, spoken longingly, *"Come, Lord Jesus!"* (This is what "Maranatha" means.)

Jesus said that he will definitely come. Perhaps it will be soon. Let us be ready when he comes to get us. Until then, our hearts are longing for that day. Tell him now that you are longing to see him and that it will be wonderful to be with him.

Jesus will come again to get you.

"I will not leave you as orphans; I will come to you." (John 14:18)

December 27

In Heaven . . .

The rich man ... died and ... he looked up and saw Abraham. (Luke 16:22, 23)

Have you ever wondered what it looks like in heaven and what we will do there? Heaven feels so far away to us, but maybe it is much nearer than we think.

One of the things that we wonder about is if we will recognize the people we loved on earth when we get to heaven. The Bible says yes. When the rich man died, he recognized Abraham. You and I will also recognize our loved ones in heaven. If there is someone in your family who has died and is with Jesus, you will see each other again. Perhaps you will sit and talk under the same tree for ages, because there is no such thing as time in heaven. It is wonderful to know that one day we will be with our loved ones again in heaven. It seems to me that people will also see one another in hell, but there won't be time for anything good because of all the pain and suffering. The people in hell will have a very bad time. I hope you belong to the Lord and that you are on your way to heaven.

Jesus will be pleased
to see us again.

 "Blessed are those who are invited to the wedding supper of the Lamb!" (Revelation 19:9)

December 28

THE COURT WILL SIT

"The court was seated, and the books were opened."
(Daniel 7:10)

The Bible tells us about a very important court that will sit at the end of the world. Everybody will appear before the great white throne of God. There we will all have to account for our lives. This means that we will have to explain why we did all those things that we knew were wrong. God will decide if we are to be punished or not. He will acquit some of us. This means that we will be found not guilty.

All those who do not believe in Jesus Christ will be judged. They will be found guilty of sin. Things people thought no one would ever know about will then be made known to everyone. What was done in secret will then be seen by all.

But Jesus is our great Advocate. His blood will cover our sins. Jesus will speak for each one of us who believes in him. We will not be punished – not because we did not sin, but because Jesus paid for our sins. It is so wonderful to know that you and I will walk out, free, because of Jesus. That is why our relationship with Jesus is so important. Have you asked him yet to forgive your sins? Have you accepted his death on the cross as payment for your sins. He will pronounce you not guilty on Judgment Day. Thank the Lord now because he is good.

Jesus will free you
at the Second Coming.

[All] are justified freely by his grace through the redemption that came by Christ Jesus. (Romans 3:24)

December 29

THE TRUMPET CALL

"And he will send his angels with a loud trumpet call, and they will gather his elect." (Matthew 24:31)

A trumpet is an instrument that makes a very clear sound. It is a difficult instrument to play, but it plays beautiful notes, and its sound is really something. In former times a trumpet call was the sign for a war to start. Also, when important announcements were made, someone blew on a trumpet so that people knew something important was about to be said.

The Lord says there will be a loud trumpet call on the day Jesus comes back to earth. We know he will come back as he promised. The Bible tells us that when the trumpet sounds, Jesus will appear in the sky, and all the nations of the earth will be dismayed. Everybody will see him come with power and great glory. Then he will send his angels out to gather everyone who loves him and knows him, from all over the world. They will then live with him forever.

Won't it be absolutely wonderful to see the Lord coming on the clouds? I think people who don't know him will be very scared. You and I must be ready for him when he comes again.

Jesus will come again to fetch us.

"I will come back and take you to be with me." (John 14:3)

December 30

EBENEZER

He named it Ebenezer, saying, "Thus far has the LORD helped us." (1 Samuel 7:12)

The Israelites were in trouble because the Philistines were making war against them. The Philistines were very strong and powerful. Then Israel decided to get rid of all the heathen gods and serve only the Lord. They got together at Mizpah and confessed their sins. Samuel also pleaded with the Lord for Israel, and the Lord answered his prayers.

The battle against the Philistines was won by a miracle. The Lord sent loud thunder, which threw the Philistines into such a panic that they could do nothing against Israel. Then Samuel set up a stone like a monument. He admitted that the Lord helped them.

At the end of this year, we can look back and say the Lord has helped us. He helped us against an enemy that tried to destroy us. He helped and encouraged us with our schoolwork and in everything we did. There are so many things to thank the Lord for. Set up a monument for him in your thoughts and in your hearts. Tell your family and your friends, "Up until now, the Lord has helped also me." If we know the Lord was with us during this past year, we can look ahead and know that this same Lord will also be willing to be with me in the new year.

Jesus will always be with us.

"And surely I am with you always, to the very end of the age." (Matthew 28:20)

December 31